THE FIXER -
THE GOOD CRIMINAL -
PART ONE

JILL AMY ROSENBLATT

THE FIXER -
THE GOOD CRIMINAL -
PART ONE

Cover Concept Art: Alan Gaites/Graphic Design
Cover Design: Mark Lawrence/Lawrence Studio

Chapter 12 and Chapter 44: Professor Talbot's direct quotes, information on *People v. Deitsch* and *People v. Warner-Lambert* come from *Criminal Law and Its Processes: Cases and Materials,* Kadish, Sanford H.; Schulhofer, Stephen J.; Steiker, Carol Publisher: Wolters Kluwer Law & Business, Publication Date: 2007

Chapter 25: Quotes from Shakespeare's *Macbeth*, Act 1, Scene 1 and Act 1, Scene 7, and Mary Shelley's *Frankenstein.*

First Printing, 2025

ISBN: 979-8-9916883-2-1

ACKNOWLEDGEMENTS

This series would not exist if not for the kind and gracious people giving their time and expertise to keep me on track. They all have my utmost thanks. Any errors or poetic license in this manuscript are mine, not theirs.

Former NYPD Detective Glenn Cunningham, thank you for always being there throughout this entire journey. You stuck with me from the beginning, and I can't thank you enough for your time and expertise, and correcting inaccuracies or mistakes. The John Reynolds storyline would never have happened without you.

Fellow thriller writer Eric J. Gates, for his kind assistance with technical information related to computers and passwords. His help was invaluable in writing Rebel One's activities.

Alan Gaites, who started this journey with me, creating his amazing book covers. Thank you for being a part of this journey.

Mark Lawrence, Lawrence Studios, for taking on this project and taking the concept of the cover art and making it his own. Thank you for the incredible book cover. It's everything I hoped for.

Mirea Gibilaro, thank you for checking the Italian, and for the corrections. You are a wonderful teacher! You can visit Mirea at her Instagram page, https://www.instagram.com/learnandloveitalian

Raquel, the amazing aerialist. Thank you for being so kind to read the scene for the aerial silks lesson and make suggestions and corrections. And thank you for trying out the routines to

check my work! You can visit Raquel and see her amazing routines at her Instagram page, https://www.instagram.com/
raquel_minisangre/#

And to my mother, who never steers me wrong with her cri-
tiques. Her constructive comments were critical to the story and
revisions for the book. I can never thank you enough.

For Mrs. Danvers

PACTA SUNT SERVANDA

Agreements must be kept

"There's no such thing as a good criminal, Katerina."
Detective Ryan Kellan

20 YEARS EARLIER

"**W**hat have you to say about this, Master Tom?"

Thomas Gallagher met the chuckles of the all-male executive circle with a good-natured smile, even as he smarted at the slight. The owners of MFG Oil and Gas delighted in putting on the Cockney accent of Gallagher's home country, treating him like their own Oliver Twist, an orphan unworthy to be in the company of kings.

"Come now, an honest answer," Jonah McKittrick said. "Do you believe that all men are equal under the law or are there rules that don't apply to everyone."

McKittrick, tall, robust, with a ready smile and an easy-going nature, made up one half of MFG Oil and Gas. His partner, Alan Fogerty, presented himself as the opposite in appearance and personality, medium height, with a taciturn demeanor and a dour expression to match. The partners ran the company like a roulette wheel, betting big on everything they did, spending millions on mineral rights, pursuing fracking when few others would; if it was in the ground, they would get it out. MFG's projected profits for the year stood at over a billion dollars.

"There are those who are beyond the reach of God and man," Gallagher said, parroting McKittrick's favorite expression. The executives, puffing on after-dinner cigars and sipping cognac, chuckled at the familiar saying.

"That's not an answer," Fogerty said.

Gallagher felt the electric charge of panic within. For over a year, he had been chasing after this golden ticket, an invitation to the East End mansion hidden by acres of reserve. Standing in the Great Room among Greek-inspired architectural columns, a Steinway grand piano, and Modigliani's painted nudes gracing the walls, he had breached the castle. He could not fail now. *I will never go back.*

"He knows that, Alan," McKittrick said, putting down his glass. He draped an arm around Thomas Gallagher's shoulder. "Come with me," he said. "I want to show you something."

***

They entered the wood-paneled library, a staid room filled with the scent of cigar smoke and immeasurable wealth. Chippendale cherrywood furniture, an executive desk and a Persian area rug. Two, comfortable wingback armchairs sat on either side of the cold fireplace, mirroring each other. Gallagher imagined the men seated in those chairs, discussing global issues, making decisions that would affect millions, no, billions of lives. McKittrick went to the drinks trolley; he fixed two drinks and came to Thomas, holding out one as an offering. Gallagher's hand shook as he took the glass and brought it to his lips. In his head, he swore. *Steady. Steady.*

Fogerty entered the room with a nod toward McKittrick.

"Thomas, we've been very impressed with you. You've shown ingenuity, creativity, the willingness to take risks–"

"You've got balls," Fogerty interrupted.

McKittrick laughed. "You have all the qualities needed to achieve success beyond your wildest dreams."

Gallagher smiled even as his heart pounded.

"Governments come and go, but natural resources, oil and gas, go on forever. Those who control those resources, control their destiny, and the destiny of everyone else."

"We control the world," Fogerty said. "The people out there," he said, nodding toward an unknown distance, "everything they have comes from us. They'd be lost without us. They wouldn't survive."

McKittrick nodded. "We give them a comfortable home, a vacation every year, a little extra spending money, and they're happy. In return, they watch and listen to what we feed them on the radio and television. We tell them what to think—"

"Who to vote for," Fogerty cut in.

"... and they submit, willingly," McKittrick said. "Think about that. Actually, you've had your moment to think. What's your answer to my question?"

Thomas Gallagher squared his shoulders. *So close. Almost there.* "Yes, I believe some are chosen to take their place out in front while the rest follow. That responsibility requires risk, necessary decisions to achieve the end, by whatever means necessary. Yes, not all laws are for all men."

McKittrick and Fogerty exchanged a glance between them.

McKittrick pressed a button on the desk. "There is a book—"

"Jesus Christ," Fogerty interrupted.

McKittrick ignored him. "This book is fiction, written many years ago. It's about a young woman brought to a chateau where she is – trained – for a group of wealthy men."

"Trained for what?" Gallagher asked.

McKittrick gave a soft smile. "Submission. The premise being the more the young woman, her body, her life, is completely given to men, for whatever they want, the happier she is."

"I don't imagine any woman would agree to that," Gallagher said.

Fogerty gave a snide laugh. "A woman wrote it," he said.

"And she wrote it to please a man, her married lover," McKittrick went on. "This made us curious. We control the world, but we decided to explore this control in a more personal way."

At the sound of footsteps, Gallagher turned. A young woman entered the library. A beautiful girl, doe-eyed, with long bangs, and loose, shoulder-length hair framing her face. Her slender figure peeked through a short, untied silk robe.

McKittrick maneuvered the girl to stand before Gallagher. "What if I were to say that I'm giving her to you."

Thomas Gallagher, dumbstruck, shifted from McKittrick to the doe-eyed young woman and back again, like a spectator at a tennis match.

"I – uh – I –"

"Francine, come here to me," Fogerty said.

The girl obeyed.

A sliver of fear rippled up Gallagher's spine as Fogerty slipped his hands inside the girl's robe, moving over her bare skin, exploring her as she stood in quiet compliance. She looked at Gallagher, her docile, empty eyes staring through him. Gallagher glanced away, the heat of embarrassment rushing to his cheeks.

"Frannie is our first," McKittrick said. "She has been with us for a while; it took time to get the kinks out. As I always say, sometimes, to get a desired result, you have to be creative. You have to drill horizontally."

Fogerty released the girl and went to the drinks trolley.

McKittrick took the young woman by the hand and drew her to himself. Lifting her chin with one finger, he kissed her lips. "I love you," he said, soft and low. "Do you love me?"

"Yes," she whispered.

The sound of shouting jolted Gallagher, the glass wobbling in his hand, the liquid spilling over.

"Of course, there's always someone who doesn't understand progress," McKittrick said.

Fogerty made a noise of disgust and took a swallow of his drink.

McKittrick went to the desk, extracting something out of the drawer.

Two men burst into the library. Gallagher recognized them as private security. They had a captive in tow, his hands and feet shackled. Positioning him on the rug, they forced him to his knees.

"Francine, Francine!" the man shouted. "You sick bastards. You're going to pay for what you did to her. When the police find your little torture chamber down there, you'll rot in prison for the rest of your lives."

The young woman's eyes clouded with confusion.

Gallagher's heart pounded in his chest. He looked toward the entrance to the library, the hallway, expecting someone would come running at the commotion. When he turned back, he found Fogerty's eyes on him, cool and calm, as if the older man knew his every thought.

McKittrick stood behind the young woman. "Do you hear this?" he whispered in her ear. "He's going to take you away from me. He won't take care of you like I do. What will become of you? What will happen to me? Are you going to let him hurt me?"

She turned, gazing up at him, her eyes wide with fear. "I love you," she said.

"Don't tell me," McKittrick said, pressing the object into the young woman's palm. "*Show* me."

The young woman turned to the man on his knees. She held out her arm, her hand gripping the gun, pointing, aiming.

Gallagher, dazed, opened his mouth, but no words came out.

"Francine," the man cried out. "Francine, please – my God, I'm your husband–"

At the cracking sound, Gallagher's glass fell from his hand, hitting the floor and shattering.

Jonah McKittrick slipped the gun out of Francine's hand and kissed her lips. "That's a good girl."

Gallagher gaped at the inert body, the bile rising in his throat as blood spread across the fabric of the rumpled shirt and seeped out underneath onto the rug. The private security wrapped the rug around the body and carried it away.

"We'll have to buy another rug," Fogerty said, knocking back another swallow of his drink.

Gallagher struggled to find his voice. "I'm sorry?"

McKittrick gave a chuckle. "Thomas, this never happened. You said yourself, not all laws are for all men. They're not for *us*. The world, and everything in it, is ours." McKittrick placed Francine in front of Gallagher. "Now, it could be yours."

The young woman offered her hand.

"Unless we were wrong," Fogerty said. "It'd be a damn shame to come this far and lose everything."

Thomas Gallagher, the son of a shopkeeper, scraping and scrapping all those years to shed that life of struggle and poverty . . . *And now I made it. I'm here. Why should I give it all up? For what? She agreed. She . . . submitted.*

Gallagher took her hand.

"Our dear Frannie has graduated," McKittrick said. "She's ready. And so are you."

***

Gallagher led the young woman out of the library and down the hall into the Great Room. Outside the glass wall, beyond the bluff, pale moonlight threw shadows across the bays until they disappeared at the curve of the earth. *Beyond the reach of God and man.*

He saw each executive take in the young woman, the raw hunger of anticipation on each face as the men removed jackets and loosened ties. Gallagher stopped at McKittrick and Fogerty.

McKittrick motioned with his hand for the men to gather in a circle around Gallagher and Francine.

"Welcome to the team, Thomas. Start us off, won't you?"

Gallagher turned to Francine. With a swipe of his hands, he brushed the robe off her shoulders, and it fell to the floor.

Staring into those wide, docile eyes, Thomas Gallagher saw a woman conquered and content to be so. A woman who didn't want to be free.

PRESENT DAY

Where the hell is the hit man? The familiar, silent monologue raged until Katerina Mills swore the other office workers heard the screaming in her head.

The morning's inner tirade had kicked off from something small, as it always did. The stapler had jammed.

I shouldn't be here.

I should be in Paris.

I should be with Alexander Winter.

The struggle continued until she heard, "Give it here, girl."

Katerina released her enemy to Luella, the office manager. A tall, regal woman, Luella had a no-nonsense attitude wrapped in polite efficiency. Katerina did her best not to be a burden. After all, someone had pulled strings to get her the job. *And I'm supposed to be grateful.*

"Take it easy, baby," Luella said, handing it back.

The office décor screamed nineteen-eighties with its drab, brown-patterned carpet. The zig-zagged desks with peeling laminate forced human proximity. Technicolor Coatings, a paint manufacturer, would have made a perfect setting for Sartre's masterpiece about Hell: *No Exit* – in Brooklyn.

Katerina resumed her rote tasks: open the envelopes, remove the checks, make the photocopies, staple the check copy to the backup of the bill and receiver. She had done accounts payable before. As a teenager, she worked after school for her father, William Mills, the manager of a plush toy factory. In reality, Kat had been an unwitting cog in his real business, heroin distribution, paying the fake invoices, helping to launder the money.

Next, Katerina separated out the thick, stapled packets of Safety Data Sheets. She knew the pictures in their little red diamonds by heart, the flame, the exploding bomb, the skull and crossbones, and more. She updated a spreadsheet, a mind-numbing exercise of typing in each product's name and chemical ingredients, xylene, toluene, ethyl benzene, and the hazard and precautionary statement codes she knew by heart. *Ground/bond container. Extremely flammable liquid and vapor. Contains gas under pressure; may explode if heated. Keep away from heat, hot surface, sparks, open flames, and other ignition sources. No smoking.*

The work had piled up while she had been out. This time, it had been bronchitis. You have to be careful, the doctor had warned. The pneumonia could return. *So? Let it come. Better for me.*

Trapped behind the desk, Kat's mind created havoc, the fear and guilt running wild and unchecked.

I'm sitting here doing paperwork and three people are dead. Murdered.

Today could be the day it's four.

If the hit man had done his job . . . John Reynolds would be dead. John Reynolds, her first client as a professional "fixer," introduced through the shadowy MJM agency. A loving husband who just wanted someone to follow his young, beautiful wife, Felicia, and recommend a birthday gift. *How could I have been so stupid? How could I not have seen he only wanted a dupe to follow his wife and discover her lover . . . so he could take his revenge.*

Like a disaster movie stuck in a loop, the replay button in Kat's head flipped on. Following the young socialite, tracking her every move, even arranging to bump into her at Saks. The lover, Will

Temple, showing up at Kat's apartment looking for a film company and an audition. And then seeing it all on video, seeing herself with both victims, falling into Reynolds' spider web trap of blackmail, forced to do his bidding.

Five months, gone. Five months of waiting every day to hear if the killer had trapped and caught his next victim. *Alex.*

The hysteria in Kat's head reached its zenith and then, like the pop of a balloon, spent itself. Exhaustion washed over her, leaving her hollow and empty.

The door between the factory and the office opened, letting in the sharp, stinging scents of the chemicals. Kat's nose congested and her eyes burned. A brief thought occurred to her: a stuffed nose might linger. It could buy her some time. Another night on the couch. Maybe.

Sensing someone standing nearby, Kat's head snapped up. A Hispanic man in his late fifties peered around the hallway corner, a tentative look on his face. Immigrants made up the factory workforce. Katerina had surmised that management asked no questions about the validity of work authorization documents. "We're not detectives," was the official line.

"Hello, miss," he said.

Katerina hoped she had shed any sign of her anger. She hoped the smile on her face looked real. "Hola Juan," she said. "Como ésta?"

"Bien, bien," he said. "Tu madre?"

"Mi madre ésta bien," she said, enjoying their ritual conversation. She asked after his family.

"Bien, gracias a Dios," he said, raising a hand to indicate the heavens.

Once, he had shown her a picture of his daughter, a beautiful girl with two children of her own. He sent her money so she could live well with his grandchildren.

And I bet you didn't use your daughter as bait for a corrupt DEA agent so you could flee after your drug trafficking operation was stolen by the competition. Nope. I'll bet you didn't.

"En que puedo servirle, Juan," Kat asked, the familiar, "How may I help you?"

"Please, I have one problem," he said, and held out his pay stub. Together, between his poor English and her poor Spanish, they tried to understand each other.

Luella appeared at the desk and spoke flawless Spanish to Juan. "That's okay baby, I got this," she said to Katerina.

Katerina gave him a kind smile and Juan said, "Thank you, miss," as Luella whisked him away.

***

At the end of her shift, Katerina exited the building, stepping into the still, warm air. Glancing to her left, she noted the usual gathering of factory employees by one of the doors, clustered together, some smoking. A few waved, others stared, their thoughts unknown. Kat walked away toward the subway. She had a moment's trepidation she was being followed; giving a half-turn, she relaxed. Juan, heading to the same subway station, always followed a short distance behind.

Kat took the steps down into the subway and came out onto the platform just as the train screeched into the station, bringing a rush of tepid, sodden air until it came to a nails-on-a-chalkboard stop.

As the doors opened, Kat gave a wistful thought that she should speak Spanish better. Moose could help her. But of course, she couldn't go near Moose. She couldn't go near anyone.

It's too dangerous.

I could get someone killed.

I already did.

When Katerina came up out of the subway, she meandered along Third Avenue and Seventy-sixth Street. The Bay Ridge neighborhood had a quiet, sleepy quality, more so than usual due to Ramadan. The sound of music and prayers from the mosque PA system reached her ears as she resumed her daily ritual, stopping in at a candy store. She bought a handful of individually wrapped Turkish Delight, the only things that calmed her constant sick stomach.

Behind the counter, the young girl with dark hair and dark eyes nodded at Kat in recognition, eyeing her with curiosity as she tallied up the total. Kat peeled off the few dollars she had been allowed to have and placed them on the counter, snatching up the sweets and depositing them in her pocket.

"You feeling okay?" the girl asked.

"Yes, okay," Kat answered. She didn't want to talk about the past five months, the sicknesses that came and went, the endless rounds of antibiotics. *What should I say? I worked at it until it finally happened, thanks.* The ear infections, colds, flus, bronchitis, and pneumonia . . . all gone now, like a last line of defense, broken. She would have to sleep in the bedroom.

The girl nodded in a way that said, *I don't believe you.*

Katerina left the change behind and went on her way.

She continued her walk in the unusual quiet of an ordinary spring day. As if a switch had been flipped, one of the worst winters on record had disappeared and May had come on pleasant and bright. With her latest recovery, her return to Manhattan and her classes meant everyone waiting to get at her would be out of hibernation as well: the Italians, the Russians, a dirty DEA agent, drug dealers . . .

She could hide no longer. They would be coming.

But none of it mattered. Somewhere, right now, Alexander Winter, "Bob," and "Professor" to Katerina, a good man, an expert thief, a lover denied, was on the run. *How many times did I vow I would never see you running for your life because of me.* If Reynolds' killer caught him . . . *what if he's already been caught?* Kat turned her face as if turning away from the thought.

Approaching the end of the block, she saw the familiar utilitarian brick building on the corner of Fifth Avenue and Eightieth Street looming closer with every step. Her gait slowed. She couldn't think about any of it anymore.

She had to get ready.

Twisting the key in the deadbolt lock, Kat let herself into the apartment. The simple setup of bulky furniture in shades of brown and black, coffee table, a small dining table for four, a flat screen television bolted to the wall and an overstuffed couch, had not changed since that day in late January. The day Kat had appeared at the door as ordered. The first "assignment" from John Reynolds.

Kat tidied up the coffee table and cleared away the rumpled, spare blanket from the couch. She grabbed a bible off a side table, a gift from her "Uncle" Sergei, an old friend of her parents.

Sergei had given her the book in January, his advice more earthbound than heavenly. *This is not book about only God, but book about men. Read it. You will know what men have in their hearts, what they will do. And you will find how to defeat men.*

Throughout the winter, cooped up in the apartment, sick and alone, Kat had read the book. She memorized the stories, hoping they would bring her an answer; an answer that Alexander Winter would have provided, after he asked his familiar question.

Did you go to Sunday School?

***

Kat changed into a spaghetti strap, flimsy blouse and a pencil skirt that clung to her non-existent waist. She stopped in front of the mirror. She kept her long, chestnut hair tied back in a simple ponytail; she refused to cut it. If she didn't cut her hair, Winter would come back. They would escape, disappear together. He would lay her down and run his hands through her hair...

She shook her head to clear away the thought. Turning around and looking over her shoulder, Kat examined her back; only vague, discolored shadows remained.

This girl, with the pale complexion, dull hair, and dark circles under her eyes, looked nothing like the girl in an LA hotel room in January. The girl who had held out her hand while Alexander Winter placed the delicate engagement ring on her finger.

The ring.

She had left it in her luggage at the safe house apartment in January – before going to her apartment. When she had returned ...

Gone.

***

Katerina stood at the kitchen counter, making dinner. *Making a mess.* The clicking of the key in the lock jolted her from her thoughts. Her heart jumped, the familiar fight or flight response kicking in as the apartment door opened. She knew the routine without turning around: the backpack set on the floor, the jacket slipped off and draped over the back of the kitchen chair, the tug at the tie. The service weapon shoulder holster came off next, draped over the jacket by the strap. The gun dangled in the holster.

Kat closed her eyes as he came up behind her. The acid churned in her stomach as the powerful arms snaked around and squeezed. *The wrong arms.* The hands explored her belly, making their way toward her breasts, insistent. *The wrong hands.*

She plastered the smile on her lips, turning on the obligatory sounds of pleasure and waited for the first words of Detective Ryan Kellan, assigned to the murder investigation of Felicia Reynolds.

"What's cooking, good-looking?" he whispered, nuzzling her ear with his nose.

"A surprise," she answered. "You'll like it."

He laughed. "I'm not sure about that," he said, his hands moving toward her lower abdomen. "You sound all better," he whispered.

Katerina's heart sank. *No more excuses.*

Be careful. If you hesitate ...

"I am," she said.

His hands shifted, running down the length of her arms until his hands smothered hers. She felt the iron grip, manipulating her fingers to release the knife and the pepper.

"Let's test that out," he said. "Right now."

He turned her around.

Kat's smile stayed glued in place, the eyes lit with practiced excitement. She gazed at his face, running her hands through the dark mane of his hair, then caressing his neck.

And the screaming in her head raged on, unheard.

Ryan Kellan reached over and turned off the stove. Gripping one of her hands, he led her to the bedroom.

***

Katerina stared up at the ceiling, listening to Ryan's rhythmic snore, the space deep inside her pulsing with a heartbeat pain of its own. She imagined she had been outside herself, watching the performance of a young woman pretending to enjoy making love, making noises alien and strange to her, noises she would not normally make in the heat of passion. Slipping out of bed, she stole out of the bedroom, closing the door with a snick of a noise.

Crossing the tiny living room, she stood with her back to the kitchen sink and watched the bedroom door, waiting. After a few moments, she retrieved his backpack, placing it on the kitchen table and conducted her ritual investigation of the contents. Her stomach turned at the crime scene photos of Felicia Reynolds,

Will Temple, and Cheryl Penn, another socialite murdered to muddy the water of the investigation; the hideous mosaic of damage to each victim's body served as a testament to their torment and suffering.

Katerina clamped her eyes shut, unable to escape the memory of that fateful night in January, the terrible choice John Reynolds had demanded. He would unleash his murderous disciple once again.

Who is your choice, the lover, or your dear mother?

She had pleaded. She had begged.

Choose, or I choose for you.

Katerina swiped her arm across her cheeks to take the tears away, inhaling a silent, shaky breath at the thought of the promise she had made to Alexander Winter only days before she broke it.

I will always protect you.

***

Pulling out the notebook, she flipped through the pages, deciphering his chicken scratch with ease.

Her head shot up. She froze. After a second, she returned to the notebook. Her eyes locked on a late entry.

Morse

O'Connoll

5/12

112 W. 52

Reynolds office.

Kat's heart thumped in a spasm of panic.

Day after tomorrow.

One more day, I would have been too late.

Completing the first task, she moved on to the next step, looking for copies of amended DD-5 reports with new details. Her eidetic memory held every word. When she finished, she returned everything in its order. Each time she performed the ritual, she remembered the first robbery she had committed with Winter, a retrieval of a client's damning VCR tape, forgotten in a recently sold cabinet. Winter had walked her through the robbery, guiding her, correcting her for ripping items out of the cabinet with no rhyme or reason as she searched for the hidden compartment and the tape. *I've learned, Alex. I remember what you taught me.*

Kat returned the backpack to its spot and went into the bathroom for her cover story. She washed her hands and face and flushed the toilet. When she crawled back into bed, Ryan stirred and rolled over, his arm draping over her, heavy and confining.

Katerina stared at the ceiling. Tomorrow, she returned to her classes in Manhattan. She would give her report to John Reynolds on the state of the investigation, and she would warn him to prepare; the police were coming to see him.

Where the hell is the hit man?

CHAPTER

5

Staring out the window, Katerina watched the throngs of people crowding the sidewalks, hustling to their destinations. She wished she could be one of them, any of them. Even in the cacophony of human voices, accelerating engines, and blaring horns, they had more peace. They weren't trapped in a car, listening to Ryan's voice drone like a local train on the Long Island Rail Road, slow, endless, and making every stop, all the way from Brooklyn to Manhattan.

"Thank Christ you'll be done with this shit in a couple of weeks," he said.

"I'd finish my degree quicker if I took classes five days a week next semester," she said.

"What about the job?" he asked.

She held still, the bird trapped in the cage. *Shit. Here it comes.*

"You want to throw away another job, Kate? I had a nice job for you, remember? You didn't want it, so it was gone. Wheelan went out of his way to make a spot for you and give you that job, as a favor to my father. You want to shit on that now?"

"No — no, of course not," Kat stumbled, shifting to face forward, her head down. "I really appreciate it. It's a really good job — and I really appreciate it."

"Uh-hunh," Ryan said, shifting in his seat, adjusting his hand on the wheel, squeezing.

Kat turned back to the passenger window. She would pay for this. It was just a matter of when.

Her anxiety ramped up as the familiar Washington Square Arch loomed larger. Ryan eased the car over to the curb, putting it in park.

"Thank you," she said, "I really appreciate everything, I do."

Kat gathered her backpack off the floor, feeling his eyes on her. She kept her face blank and vacuous, as she had practiced, as if she had no presence, no personality. When she sat up, she turned to him.

He considered her for a moment. "Be good," he said.

"Promise," she said, and waited for the kiss she could not avoid. Ambling out of the car, Kat stood at the curb, watching him maneuver the car back into traffic, waving to him as he went. Crossing the street, she headed onto the campus, her stomach churning. Reaching the building, she pulled open the door and slipped inside.

***

The narrow staircase had a landing at each level with its own door. Katerina took the stairs to the bottom, as she had countless times during the semester, her heart pounding as if it were the first time. Grabbing the handle, she hesitated, then pulled open the door and forced herself to walk inside.

Entering the auditorium, the stage sat on her left, the seating stretched out to her right. In the middle section of the first row sat John Reynolds. He sported a head of wavy salt and pepper hair and had the appearance of a kindly uncle. The grieving widower appeared fit and healthy, having busied himself with good works over the long winter; his signature achievement had been the creation of a foundation in the memory of the dearly departed wife he had murdered. Standing a few feet away from his employer, Garrett, the driver, stood silent, watching.

"Now is the winter of our discontent made glorious summer," Reynolds said, a wide, "Joker" smile on his lips.

A violent tremble broke out within Katerina.

"We have a standing appointment Miss Katerina – do we not? Yet, this is the fourth, or is it the fifth time that you disappear for weeks –"

"I was sick again."

"And you don't call?"

Katerina found her voice. "I'm sorry, I should have asked my boyfriend, the police detective, if I could borrow his phone," and her cheeks flushed at the insolence. *The problem is your temper. That's what Winter always said. Watch your temper.*

Reynolds glossed over the comment. "Well, you're here now. You owe me a performance," he said with a wave of his hand, indicating she should take the stairs to the stage.

Katerina didn't move.

Reynolds shook his head with a chuckle. "I am on the board of this fine institution. This affords me special privileges, including visits to the grounds and facilities anytime I wish, and special performances. You wouldn't be thinking of doing something foolish like refusing me, would you?"

Katerina went to the stairs and took them up to the stage.

"Come, come, you know the procedure," he said, nodding at her purse.

Kat let the purse fall to the stage, the thud reverberating in the space.

"And ...?"

Kat dropped the backpack.

"In the center, please," he said, a tick of annoyance in his voice.

Katerina obeyed.

"Do tell, how is life with the policeman? I want a complete update."

Katerina remained silent, stubborn in spite of her better judgment.

"Oh, my apologies. A director must be clear. I should have asked, how are your *evenings* with the policeman? What *sportive tricks* do you have to report? You are certainly made for them, not like our *poor* Richard."

Katerina glared at Reynolds, as if she could stare daggers into his chest.

Reynolds clapped his hands together. "It has been recent! How delicious. Was it yesterday? No mind, no matter. A command performance today. I want every detail. A pity my wife is not here. She could offer her expertise on the subject. Come, my little Desdemona, what did you say, hmmm? 'Will you come to bed, my lord?'" he parroted.

"Yes," Katerina said.

"No, no, that will not do. Louder. And with every detail."

Kat pursed her lips until she trusted herself to speak. "I laid him down. I straddled his hips. I took him inside me," she said through gritted teeth. She consoled herself with her small victory of lying to him. *I didn't do what you wanted at all. He took me to bed. He took me. But I never said yes. Never.*

"Excellent," Reynolds said, his eyes bright with glee. "It's what you all do. You "lie" in the marriage bed. And when questioned if there is any crime you have not confessed, you look with eyes of innocence and say, 'Alack, my lord, what do you mean by that?'" he said, his voice a high-pitched falsetto.

Reynolds rose from his seat and stood at the foot of the stage. "Your class completed *Othello*," he said, his eyes darkening now. "You know every word by heart. Say the rest."

Katerina didn't answer.

"Say it!"

"'Since guiltiness, I know not,'" she said.

"Very good, Miss Katerina," he said. "Not true, of course. But you "lie" beautifully. Where does the investigation stand now?"

"The detectives, all of them, from all the connected cases, are coming to see you."

"When?"

"Tomorrow," she said.

"Why?"

"I don't know. There's nothing else in the notepad."

"And you tell me today," Reynolds said, shaking his head.

"I was sick," she protested. "He wouldn't let me go to school."

Reynolds gave a heavy sigh of disappointment. "Always lying and deception. It would have been better if my Felicia had been a Cordelia, unwilling to give lip service to affection."

He had moved on to *King Lear.*

It wouldn't have made a difference if your wife had been Joan of Arc. She would have ended up like Cordelia all the same. Dead. Because you would have killed her.

"No, she was my Goneril, my Regan, declaring her love to her king with a false tongue. And after I gave her life, as if I had begot and bred her. I made her what she was – and she betrayed me," he said as he gazed up at Katerina. "So young and so *untender.*"

Reynolds turned his back on Katerina and gave Garrett a flick of his finger toward the door. Garrett fell in step to leave. "I will be sure your beloved knows you couldn't be bothered to save him, because you had a sniffle," he called over his shoulder.

The terror struck like a knife. Kat rushed to the edge of the stage. "When? Where?"

"He is – situated."

Katerina sucked in a breath as the nausea swirled in her stomach. She rushed down the steps, skidding to a stop as John Reynolds turned to her.

"How many times have I been caught off guard by the antics of the police. Because of you. I have endured months of nonsense.

Newly discovered soils and fibers on one of the bodies, household staff as suspects, and on and on. One too many mines I almost stepped on because you kept me waiting. Disobedience requires punishment. My Bruce does enjoy the hunt, but I felt it was time. He has your beloved now. He's quite secure. Of course, when I say secure, I mean–"

"Don't," Kat blurted, and she felt her body weaving, giving out within her.

"No details?" Reynolds shrugged his shoulders. "As you wish. What happens to your beloved next depends on whether you carry out my instructions, exactly as I give them, when I give them. Is that understood?"

Katerina nodded.

"Upset the policeman, my little Desdemona. Ensure his mind is preoccupied with you, understand? Be creative. You have options. What about the classmate in your law class? Mark something or other. He would do nicely."

Katerina nodded, the pain from her clenched teeth traveling the length of her jaw.

Reynolds and his driver left the auditorium, the slam of the door echoing in the space and vibrating in her chest.

Katerina sank down onto a step, rocking back and forth, hearing Winter's voice in her head. *If you can walk out the door, you're not caught. If there's even one move left to make, it's not over.*

Now you're caught, Bob.

With shaking hands, Katerina rooted in her purse, ripping out items and tossing them aside. Digging under a false bottom, she pulled out a finger-sized cell phone. Her body trembled as she struggled to punch in the correct numbers, blinking hard, trying to see. She brought the phone to her ear, listening to the endless ringing. She hit the stop button.

Last year, two half-brothers, private operators, Carter and Keyes, had been hired by Alexander Winter to watch over her, protect her. Carter remained in Vermont to watch over her mother, but Katerina had hired Keyes in January to go after Winter, come to his aid, and bring him home. She tried again, the phone ringing until it disconnected.

Katerina moved on to the next number, mumbling her mother's name as the ringing continued. Pulling the phone from her ear, she jabbed at the button to stop the call. With tears clouding her eyes, she jabbed at the keypad again, and then again, until she had the last phone number right. As the ringing droned on, she rocked back and forth until she gave up and hit the stop button.

Where is Keyes?

Where is my mother?

Where the hell is the hit man?

Dazed, Katerina buried the tiny cell phone back in its hiding place, collected all the detritus and returned it to her purse. She pulled the strap onto her shoulder and gathered her backpack. As if in slow motion, Katerina left the auditorium.

Alex.

Oh, God.

"*B*uongiorno studenti."

"*Buongiorno,*" the class repeated.

Katerina repeated the words while her twenty questions quiz to Alexander Winter in January blared in her head.

Have you ever been to a foreign country?

Yes.

Can you speak the language of that country?

Yes.

Say something.

Voglio fare l'amore con te ora.

I want to make love to you right now.

If I spoke the language, we could talk to each other when you returned.

If I spoke the language, it meant you were coming back.

A late addition to her course load, Katerina had counted on the Italian I class to calm and soothe her nerves. But it could not quell the hysteria that rolled over her now like a tidal wave. The noise of the student's voices swirled around her, while the crime scene photos looped in her head like a horror movie. Then the photos changed; instead of Felicia Reynolds, Will Temple, and Cheryl Penn, now she saw Alexander Winter suffering, screaming . . . and the screaming she heard in her head was her own.

Professor Rinaldi continued walking around the room, asking everyone what they did over the weekend.

"E signorina Katerina, che cosa hai fatto?"

"What have you done?"

What have I done?

I waited. Ho aspettato.

I hoped. Ho sperato.

Sei viva? Are you alive?

Not for long.

I've killed you.

Katerina's eyes welled with tears. She realized Professor Rinaldi was waiting.

"Ho studiato l'italiano," she said.

The class chuckled.

"Va bene, bene, essato. Brava, signorina, brava."

Professor Rinaldo walked back up to the front of the classroom. *"Pronti, abbiamo l'esame finale. Quindi, studiamo, facciamo pratica, ripetiamo."*

Study, practice, repeat.

Katerina gave up concentrating on the drills, her mind tormented with imaginings until she heard Rinaldi ask her the question, *"Posso aiutarla?"*

Tomorrow, four NYPD detectives will pay a visit to a man who had his wife, her lover, and an innocent woman, murdered. And that man will be prepared to avoid capture and punishment for his crimes.

Because of me.

I wish you could help me.

"Si, grazie, mi dica . . ."

The detectives crowded the waiting area. Tom Morse, early forties, sporting a short, neat haircut, the detective who caught the Will Temple case when the young actor had first disappeared. Denis O'Connoll, the veteran detective with a world-weary look, the lead detective investigating Will Temple's death. They made a mismatched pair as they milled around the small space, keeping to themselves.

Ryan's partner, Detective Walter Lashiver, another seasoned veteran, planted himself near the desk of Elizabeth, John Reynolds' secretary.

Using the desk like a moat around a castle, Elizabeth's hands fluttered from one task to another. Lashiver waited for her nerves to get the better of her and make eye contact. When she did, he smiled. She ignored the olive branch, choosing to concentrate on her paperwork.

Lashiver edged closer, hovering near a cell phone box sitting on the edge of the desk, watching Elizabeth's hands flutter faster until she swept paperwork off her desk.

She came around to the front of the desk, crouching down to pick up the sheets of paper. Her head darted up, staring at Walter Lashiver kneeling down in front of her, gathering up a few papers. "Got yourself a new phone?"

Elizabeth didn't answer as she snatched up the truant items.

Lashiver understood people's discomfort being on the receiving end of questions, even innocuous questions, from a police officer. Questions didn't bother criminals; they lied all the time. But your average law-abiding citizen panicked, the natural inclination being they *had* to answer, as if under interrogation.

"I can't get used to the new technology," he went on. "I'm an old school kind of guy. Four G, Five G, Nine G, who knows what it all means?" he said with a laugh. "You don't like the phone you have?"

"Mr. Reynolds got a new phone," she said, snapping the papers from his outstretched hand as she rose to her feet.

Lashiver nodded, standing up with her. "Oh. How come?"

"He lost his phone," Elizabeth said.

Lashiver nodded. "When did that happen?"

"Yesterday."

Lashiver nodded again.

Morse and O'Connoll remained off to the side, silent as a grave.

"That happened before, didn't it?" Lashiver remarked. "We checked the call log on his phone, last year. Standard procedure. There was nothing unusual. Actually, there was nothing. Because he lost his phone last year, isn't that right? That's what you told my partner and me in the interview. It happened just a few days before Mrs. Reynolds' murder. He lost his phone. That's what you said, Elizabeth."

"Yes," Elizabeth said.

The door to the executive office opened and John Reynolds emerged, lips curled into a smile. "Detectives, apologies for keeping you waiting. Please," he said, opening the door wide, "come in."

As Lashiver passed, Reynolds said, "You are without your partner today?"

"He'll be along in a minute," Lashiver said and leaned in, his voice low. "I know you feel more comfortable with him handling the investigation."

"Oh, absolutely," Reynolds said.

***

"We've retraced your wife's schedule for the last year, again," Ryan went on, keeping his eyes on the open notepad. "We've identified at least three individuals, at a minimum, that your wife was potentially intimate –"

"My wife had several lovers," Reynolds interrupted. "And I believe the report provided by my private investigator, retired Detective Green, outlined that information, as he has been sharing the efforts of his work with you. So once again, detective, that which you have 'discovered' is no discovery at all. I certainly hope the people of this city were not overcharged for you to recover this ground."

"Mr. Green's list was not complete. Once we catch who did this – things like this can come out at the trial. The suspect's lawyer could try to discredit your wife's reputation."

"But you don't have a suspect, detective," Reynolds said. "That you haven't been able to accomplish. But finding every lowlife my wife exposed herself to, that you seem to be managing."

"From Mr. Green's list, those men have been ruled out as suspects. We will have to determine if these other men are suspects."

"And we've retraced Will Temple's movements," O'Connoll cut in, gesturing toward Detective Morse. "They don't match up with your wife's time of death."

"Where does that leave us, detectives?"

"I'm afraid we may still not have the complete list of your wife's lovers," Ryan said. "There may be one or more still out there, closer than we first suspected."

Reynolds leaned against the desk. "And how do you suppose to discover this?"

"We're going to need a list of *all* of your employees," Lashiver announced. "Current and former."

Reynolds gave a short chuckle. "You think one of the employees, executive or otherwise, was sleeping with my wife and then proceeded to murder her? Was that before or after the weekly budget meeting?"

"Clearly your wife was determined to humiliate you," Ryan said. "What better way to do that than sleep with one of your employees, right under your nose."

Reynolds gave a small laugh of wonder. "Over these last months, I have worked to come to a place of peace about my wife's many betrayals," he said. "I have learned that you can never truly know the person sleeping next to you. You have no idea what they're doing when they're not with you."

Reynolds smiled. Detective Ryan Kellan broke eye contact and looked down at his notepad, the muscles in his jaw working.

"You didn't have any suspicions at all? You didn't ask Mr. Green to keep an eye on your wife, see what she was up to?" Detective Morse asked.

"Detective, you know the answer to that question. You have spoken to Mr. Green. You know very well I didn't engage Mr. Green for any investigative services into my wife, prior to her death. Mr. Green was not following my wife," John Reynolds said with a chuckle. He looked at Ryan. "Do you think I should have known, detective? Would you? Do you have a wife?"

"Girlfriend," Ryan answered.

"I think we should come back to the subject," Lashiver said.

"Tell me, do you know what your girlfriend does all day while you're at work? Would you have any idea if she were unfaithful?"

"Maybe you weren't paying attention," Ryan snapped.

"Detective, we both know the answer is no. Your companion can look you in the eye, full of innocence. I can't imagine how many times my wife did that. And yet she could have just come from seeing a lover. Perhaps I should have paid closer attention to the physical distance she kept between us so I wouldn't pick up the scent of another man." He shook his head and pushed himself off the desk. "You won't mind if I have Mr. Manning coordinate this with you. I would like my attorney to ensure everything is done in the proper order."

"As long as no one impedes the investigation," Lashiver said.

"I hope you won't be chasing my executives away. I take a dim view of my employees being harassed at home."

"No problem. We'll conduct the interviews on premises," O'Connoll said.

Reynolds gave a thin-lipped smile.

"We'll need to speak to each of them privately," Morse added.

While Reynolds picked up the telephone receiver and gave Elizabeth instructions, O'Connoll turned his attention to the oversized poster displayed on a stand in the corner of the room. He wandered over to the stand, the words "Felicia Reynolds Foundation for Justice," and "First Annual Scholarship for the Arts," emblazoned across the poster.

John Reynolds hung up the phone.

"Who's getting a scholarship?" O'Connoll asked.

"The fund is for young women striving for a career in the performing arts, drama, dance, the theater. The dinner to announce the scholarship winner will be in six weeks. One lucky young lady will be chosen, and I will be her patron for the next year."

"Lucky," Tom Morse said.

"As I have said," Reynolds continued as if he had not heard the comment, "I have come to a place of peace. And I think it's appropriate to honor my wife as I knew her, perhaps not as she was. I hope I will have good news to report during my speech at the dinner. It would be a shame if I had to say that after six months of a hopelessly bungled investigation, there has been no arrest and no justice for my wife, and the other victims, of course."

Reynolds came around his desk and moved across the room to stand by the poster. "At least one young lady won't have to worry. She will be under my personal protection. I will make sure this tragedy doesn't happen again."

***

Ryan dug into his pocket and pulled out a few bills, handing them over to the pushcart vendor. He took the hotdogs and caught up with Lashiver, walking with O'Connoll and Morse.

"He didn't seem annoyed at all," O'Connoll said.

"It's all part of the dance," Lashiver said. "The foundation is a cute touch."

"He's lining up his next victim," Ryan said. "We have to move."

"We can only go as fast as we can go," Lashiver cautioned his partner.

"You got under his skin," Morse said to Ryan.

"From where I stood it went both ways," O'Connoll said.

Ryan shook his head to blow off the comment. "No chance. He can think that if he wants."

"There's still no connection to Cheryl Penn," Lashiver said, "but digging into the employees will annoy him."

"Did you hear what he said?" Morse asked.

The detectives stopped.

"He said he wasn't having Green follow his wife."

"So?" O'Connoll asked.

"This guy likes to go out on the ledge," Morse said. "He's getting his kicks from it. He knows exactly what he's saying. I re-canvassed Will Temple's block half a dozen times. Nobody saw anything out of the ordinary. Not the deli, the pizza parlor, or the nail salon — excuse me, the prostitution ring. Not the mama-san who runs the prostitution ring, wandering back and forth all day, looking out the window while clutching her purse at her side."

"What did you expect?" Lashiver said with a laugh. "What she's got in that purse is probably more than my yearly salary."

"What I'm saying is, I was looking for Felicia Reynolds' killer. Maybe, what I should have been looking for is the person *following* her. Because there is no way he wasn't having her followed."

"Aren't they one and the same?" Ryan asked.

"Maybe not," Morse said.

The detectives fell into silence. Of all of them, Morse had taken Will Temple's death the hardest. He had been assigned to the young man's disappearance and had treated it as a feckless actor taking off for a film role or a weekend getaway. He felt responsible for the lost time and opportunity.

"A re-canvass never hurts," O'Connoll said.

"Hey, I've done them a year later," Lashiver added.

"If Reynolds isn't concerned, that tells us whoever the doer is, he's convinced we'll never find that person. So, let him shoot off his mouth. The more the better. He's arrogant. He'll screw up," Ryan said.

"Just make sure it's not running both ways," O'Connoll said, turning to Ryan. "He wants to be clever, kid, you gotta let him be so clever he cuts his own throat. But *you* keep cool."

"I am, and he will," Ryan said.

Tom Morse's cell phone buzzed, and he took the call, moving a few steps away.

Lashiver watched Morse on his cell phone, lost in his own thoughts.

Kat gripped the steering wheel as she drove on the upper level of the GW bridge. *He's in John Reynolds' office right about now.* In sharp contrast to the harsh, unforgiving sun glare of the picture-perfect day, Kat remembered the same drive on a frigid December night last year. She drove for the Canadian border during a snowstorm, a gun pointed at her side by the passenger, her client, Simon Marcus. A stop on the side of the road. A forced march into the woods. *I was never supposed to live to see the morning. If it hadn't been for Winter . . . he saved me. I have to save him. What do I do? I don't know what to do. I don't know what to do.*

Her current passenger, her first and former boss, her first and former lover, her first and forever mistake, Philip Castle, put out his hand, bracing against the glove box.

"Jesus, Kat," he said, "slow down."

He reached to push the radio knob, and she smacked his hand away.

"Jesus, Kat," he whined. "What do you want from me?"

Katerina gave him a side-eye; his frat boy good looks had been worn away by stress. He was a lawyer with a lower-cased "l," and he took his oath as more of a suggestion than a requirement. Philip's roster of clients consisted of criminals and con men. He never encountered a conflict of interest he didn't like or an angle he couldn't find. The blackmail scheme had been the Big Kahuna, the one that would push him into the big leagues. She wondered yet again what spell had been cast over her that she had ever found Philip Castle handsome or desirable.

"What was up with your Houdini act?"

"I was in Boston for three months, stuck like everyone else. Freakin' blizzards, every freakin' day. Just like here. You think I would leave you hanging out to dry? You know I wouldn't do that."

Kat's silence of disbelief hovered between them.

"So, uh, have you seen Federov?"

Kat shook her head. "Not in a while."

"When you last saw him, did he say anything about me?"

"Yeah, he asked about your other nine fingers," Kat said.

"That's not funny, Kat," Philip said, massaging his bent pinky on instinct.

"I'm surprised the poor widow is letting you visit after you never bothered to call."

Philip shifted in his seat.

"I thought so. Bet you didn't tell her we were coming, either."

"No, I did," Philip said.

"What did you say to her?" Katerina said, annunciating each syllable. "I'd like to know why we're going."

"We're recanvassing to see if anything new comes up. You live with a *cop*. You don't know this?"

Kat's knuckles turned white as she squeezed the wheel harder.

"What's the play?" she asked. Working for Philip, Katerina had learned multiple roles for his schemes: the straight man, the shill, the lookout. Either distract the mark, delay the mark, or dangle the carrot they can't refuse, leaving Philip to collect whatever he came for.

"Just keep her occupied. I'll handle the rest."

"Great. Are you going to mention you hired her husband to take blackmail pictures of the Governor, so you could *lease* them to organized crime? Don't forget to add that you got her husband killed and then you lost the negatives.'"

"I didn't *lose* them, they were stolen," he said, crossing his arms.

***

The quaint saltbox house, white with a blue roof, stood on a postage stamp-sized lot. The outside of the neat house boasted a row of flowerpots and a garden decoration of a man on a bicycle, its wheels still in the unforgiving heat of the midday sun.

While the twenty-first century raged out of doors, it couldn't penetrate the Unghar home. Time had stopped, right down to the wood paneling and the crocheted arm rest covers on either side of the mustard-colored couch. Bunny Unghar sported a pleasant, non-threatening demeanor and an easy smile revealing slightly crooked teeth. She wore a buttoned-down shirt with polyester pants that didn't hide her thickening middle as well as a dress might. She wore her short hair in soft waves, and she smelled of inexpensive gardenia-scented perfume.

The cramped kitchen couldn't accommodate a dining table, so they settled on the couch, a fisherman afghan draped across the back, a makeshift tea service set out on the coffee table. Kat ran her hand over the afghan and before she could say, "This is so beautiful," Bunny was off and running. Kat smiled as Bunny gave a soup to nuts review of her many craft projects, pointing out each doily and cross stitch sampler. As she recited the particulars of each item, she said, "I make them with ribbons, you see," fingering the spools of ribbons, from small to large, lined at attention in an open case. "Abe never liked clutter in the house, so I tried to keep everything neat. And these larger spools are so handy," she said. "I didn't want to bother him. Now that he's – well, it just spreads out and grows on its own."

As Bunny chattered on, Kat sensed a feeling, a kind of madness creeping up on her. An urge to run screaming into the street, to scream until her voice gave out and no sound would come out again. *She's a grieving widow. Don't be a bitch. Do not be a bitch. Can't you be nice? Just this one time? Can't you be good?*

"Did Abe take those pictures?" Kat interrupted, gesturing at the photographs traveling up the wall by the staircase. The black and white photos featured trees and flowers, stark, sparse, lovely in their lonely simplicity. A long way from a man who made his living documenting men and women *in flagrante delicto,* Kat thought.

Bunny nodded. "He always wanted to be a fine-arts photographer," she said, as she fussed over pouring more tea in the cups and handing them to Kat and Philip, one at a time. "But it was hard, and money was tight. You know how it is. He gave that up years ago. He had put them away, but I thought it would be fitting to show them, even though I don't get many visitors. I had no idea he was feeling bad about anything. I never would have dreamed he would hurt himself."

He didn't, Kat thought. *The person who killed him made it look like a suicide.*

Katerina pushed her thoughts away for fear they might do an end-run around her and come out of her mouth. "I'm very sorry for your loss," she said.

Bunny's emotions welled again, and she grasped Kat's hand. Leaning over, she caught Philip's hand with her other hand and they stayed like that, trapped, tied to each other.

"He appreciated you so much. You were a good man to work for."

Kat glanced over at Philip. *Yes, you are an exceptionally good man, getting good old Abe killed.*

Philip patted Bunny's hand and turned on the charm. "Abe was the best, he really was one of a kind. He was meticulous, a real pro. Whatever I needed, he delivered, exactly as I asked for it, no more, no less."

"He'd been talking about retiring," Bunny said. "Late last year. All of a sudden. He said we would sell the house and pack it in and just travel around."

Katerina shot Philip a look and found his posture had stiffened.

"Listen, Bunny, I was reviewing a few open cases Abe was working for me. I'm missing some information. Abe was obviously in distress. Did he have any other clients late last year? I think, because of his condition, he accidentally gave the wrong stuff, notes, pictures, things like that, to the wrong client."

"I didn't know anything about his clients. Abe never talked about his work."

"What about his files? Did he have any files? It's okay to let me look at them. Abe used to ask me for advice. I never charged him, though."

"Advice about what?"

"What I'm saying is, I was like his lawyer, was his lawyer. So, it's okay to share information with me. It's all confidential. Do you have anything from his office?"

"There's some stuff in the basement, but we don't have anything in storage. Everything was cleaned out."

"What do you mean cleaned out?" Philip asked.

Who's we? Katerina thought.

***

They bustled down to the basement, Bunny still chattering. When she reached the bottom stair, Bunny pulled on a hanging string and a bare bulb snapped on. Kat surveyed the hodgepodge of equipment; one table held a development tank, reels, graduates for measuring while the other had a printer, desktop computer, and an ancient Selectric typewriter, a piece of plain paper still wound around the roller. In a corner by itself, a Beseler enlarger.

"See that," Bunny said, pointing at the corner. "He had that for his darkroom."

Katerina wandered around the tables, taking a mental inventory of the equipment.

"Abe loved shooting thirty-five millimeter. He hated digital. He said you should only have to snap once–"

"Bunny," Philip interrupted, "what did you do with all his files from his cases?"

Bunny opened her mouth to answer, but the heavy clomping of footsteps stopped the conversation. They all turned in unison.

Kat tensed at the sight of the short, squat man with a square, thick neck and a deep widow's peak in his hair. He wore a white T-shirt, black pants, and a gold chain around the neck. He had a five o'clock shadow at eleven in the morning, and his beady eyes landed on Kat and Philip. The sharp, pungent scent of his acrid aftershave attacked her nose.

I guess that's the other half of the "we."

"Ronnie, these are friends of Abe's. Abe used to do some work for Philip."

Philip came forward and extended his hand. The heat of instant dislike warmed Kat's face as Ronnie smirked at the gesture, a twinkle of amusement in his eyes.

"I don't remember seeing you when my brother-in-law dropped dead," Ronnie said, staring at Philip's outstretched hand.

"I was out of town," Philip said. "Your brother-in-law was first-rate, really. Great guy. Turns out he and I had some leftover business."

"I'll get some more tea," Bunny said.

"They gotta go now, Sis," Ronnie said. "They can't stay for tea. I'll see youse out."

They trooped upstairs. Katerina accepted a crushing embrace from Bunny Unghar. Trapped in the woman's grasp, Katerina stared into the eyes of Ronnie. He watched her with that same amused twinkle, a cruel smile twisting one end of his mouth.

***

Outside, Ronnie walked on ahead of Katerina and Philip; every few steps he did a half-turn, glancing back to see if Bunny had retreated into the house and closed the front door.

Turning back, he said, "You're the lawyer my brother-in-law took the peekaboo snaps for." He turned to Kat. "You're not in the snaps, are you? If you are, I'd like to see that."

"That one's gonna die on your bucket list," Kat said.

"This is my assistant – was my assistant. Abe did some domestic case work for me," Philip said.

"Peekaboo snaps," Ronnie said.

"Look, we're sorry about Abe," Philip said. "He was a good guy, and I appreciated him."

"He was a lowlife and so are you," Ronnie said mildly and without malice.

"Whoa," Philip protested. "Is that really necessary?"

Ronnie appeared thoughtful as he considered the question.

The heat beating down on the top of Kat's head made her feel unsteady on her feet. She wanted to be back in the car and driving back to the city.

He's caught.

He's trapped. In chains.

He's suffering. Right now.

He's suffering.

"My sister's a fish," Ronnie said. "You know what that is?"

Philip wore a stupid grin; Kat knew the expression all too well. It meant he'd been caught in shit and thought turning on the charm would get him out of it.

"Your sister is a nice lady," Philip said.

"I didn't say she wasn't nice. I said she was a fish," Ronnie said and directed his attention to Kat. "You know what it is about a fish?" he asked.

Katerina felt a pang of commiseration for Bunny, playing Adrian to this oaf in front of her. She thought of the adage "you can't choose your family." She wished she could have that needle-pointed on a pillow and then she thought it would be ironic if Bunny made it for her. Kat thought of her own brother, Kevin. She wondered if he was back at base camp as he lived the high life on the down-low in Costa Rica; she wondered if she should try again to reach him.

"No, I don't," Kat said, the heat searing the skin on her bare arms.

"A fish swallows everything," Ronnie said. "My sister's a fish. She swallowed everything my brother-in-law said. But he was just a two-bit loser, taking jobs for other two-bit losers, making his living taking peekaboo snaps."

"And what are you, Paulie, a captain of industry?" Kat shot back.

"Kat," Philip said.

Ronnie laughed. "Oh, look who's got a smart mouth. You should put a muzzle on your bitch. She needs to be fixed."

"Said the bulldog with a tiny dick," Kat said as she lunged forward. She snapped back as Philip's arm clamped around her waist and yanked her away.

Ronnie laughed.

"Let's all calm down," Philip said. "Look, I need to look at a few of his case files. I used to give him advice, so really, I was his attorney, so I can look at the files. It's all confidential."

Katerina, still struggling against Philip's grasp, winced at his desperation.

"You think I'm stupid?"

Philip vacillated, unsure of the trick question. When he didn't answer, Ronnie leaned in.

"I asked you if you think I'm stupid?"

"No, of course not," Philip said.

"Good, because for a minute, I thought you were sayin' I'm stupid. The files are gone. All of them."

Philip's eyes widened and he let out, "Oh," and then added, "I see."

"My sister tell you about the burglaries?"

"No," he said.

"Funny thing, a month or so after Abe died, the house was broken into. They made a real mess, but they didn't take nothing. Then, two months after that, there's another burglary. Funny, hunh?"

Ronnie stepped forward; Philip planted himself in front of Katerina.

"What do you think they was looking for?"

"No idea," Philip said.

Ronnie laughed. "I can see you got some kind of problem. Why don't you loan out your tootsie here, and me and her can talk privately. Maybe if we do that, I'll suddenly remember something I saw in the files. Maybe we could work something out for you."

"Work something out yourself," Kat said. "It won't take you long. You don't have enough for two hands."

Philip pushed Katerina away as Ronnie pointed his finger. "Take your bitch and get lost. Whatever you was looking for, it's gone, and it ain't coming back."

***

"That was a great idea," Kat said, staring out the window.

"I had the situation under control."

Kat scoffed.

"Oh, what? I'm stupid now?"

"No, you're a Rhodes scholar."

"C'mon, Kat, that's not nice," Philip said as he eased the car over and pulled into a diner parking lot.

"What are you doing?" Kat demanded.

"What? I thought you'd be hungry," he said.

"I have to get back into the city," she said.

"We can stop for a bite to eat."

"I don't want a fucking bite to eat," Kat said, and she lunged for the car key.

Philip put out a hand, keeping her at bay while holding the keys in the other.

Kat struck out, landing blows against his arms and face while letting loose a string of obscenities.

Philip drove her further back into the passenger seat. "Kat. Stop. Stop. What the hell is wrong with you?"

The words enraged her; she struck out with a fresh set of blows.

"Katerina, *stop*. Take it easy." Dropping the key on the driver's floormat, Philip grabbed her wrists with both hands, pushing his body weight against her, pinning her against the seat.

Kat let out a cry, shrinking back against the door.

Philip released her. Heavy gasps of air between them intruded on the sudden stillness.

He examined her as she held her arms tight against herself. "Kid, *I* would never hurt you."

Katerina glanced away, staring out the window.

"And we shouldn't be fighting each other, you know? We should be in this together. We are in this together."

"You gave everything away."

Philip made a face. "Look, I'll go back to the widow. I'll talk to her again, alone."

"Why? Why did we go in the first place? She doesn't know any-thing."

"All right, okay," he said throwing up his hands. "It was a worth a shot."

"Another fuck-up. Perfect."

"It's not my fault."

"Right, none of this is your fault. You didn't come up with this brilliant plan for Rent-A-Blackmail to organized crime, you schmuck!"

"I'm as good as any one of those high-powered, overpriced windbags. I wanted something bigger."

"Right. 'You coulda been a contender.'"

"Hey, I do good work for my clients. Yeah, I wanted a seat at the table. I was almost there. I had it all worked out. I had it! I said I was sorry!"

Katerina shook her head, tears escaping. "I don't give a shit about your apology. A set of negatives we have no idea how to find and every moron within fifty miles of the five boroughs is in the way – but none of this is your fault."

Philip shrugged in defeat, the towel thrown in on the conversation. He gave Katerina a pointed stare as she massaged her wrists.

"It's not unusual for them, Kat. Some of them do it, not all. Some of them, they can't take the stress of The Job."

Katerina listened, but it didn't matter. Nothing mattered. Every thought was Winter. Since that day in January, he had stayed with her every minute, every second. Now, he had been caught. And there wasn't a damn thing she could do about it. Because Reynolds had no intention of letting Winter go. Not today, not tomorrow, not if the murder investigation of Felicia Reynolds blew up or shut down. Reynolds would never let Winter go. His death would be slow and painful. And John Reynolds would make sure she saw it.

Lost in her thoughts, Katerina heard Philip's voice. "Katerina, are you listening to me?"

She nodded to acknowledge him.

"If you want to get out, I'll help you," he said. "You know me. I care about you. I wouldn't leave you hanging."

"I've got it covered," she said.

Philip shook his head, fished the car key off the floormat and started the car.

CHAPTER

9

As Katerina stepped off the subway, she had the tiny cell phone at her ear, waiting for Ivan, the hitman, to answer the call. With every ring, a new string of obscenities came to mind as the blood pounded in her ears. She killed the call and tried her mother again. She stopped short at the click of the connection.

"Mom?" Kat said, and her breath caught in her throat. "Why haven't you been answering your phone? Is everything okay?"

"Fine, my girl," Linda Mills soothed.

Katerina scanned her surroundings. Coming upon the ice cream shop, she ducked inside. The black-and-white floor tiles screamed nineteen-fifties. Booths lined one side of the shop, a small vase with a flower or two on each table.

"Tell me what's happening."

"Mommy, I heard – I was told –" and she stopped.

"Katie, tell me," Linda Mills said.

The woman behind the counter wore her familiar stern, impatient expression. Kat motioned toward the large cup and pointed at one of the tubs. "Have you heard anything about my professor, the one who went on sabbatical?"

Linda Mills had no trouble deciphering Kat's code; they had been speaking their own private language since January. "No, why?"

| 51 |

"I saw the head of the department yesterday," Kat stammered. The shop's doorbell tinkled behind her. She lowered her voice as she said, "He said the professor was stuck, and wouldn't be coming back anytime soon. Can you check this, please? If there's an update, why didn't someone tell me?"

Katerina heard silence from the other end of the line. Carter never left his post outside the farm. Why didn't his half-brother call with an update?

"Where are you now?" Linda Mills asked. "You're not home, are you?"

"No, I'm at the ice cream shop."

"Stay there, can you do that? Stay there for a few minutes. I'll call you back."

As Kat clicked off the call, the woman placed the overstuffed cup of ice cream on the counter, a spoon jutting out of the top. Still holding the tiny cell phone in one hand, Katerina dug into her purse with the other to pull out a few bills.

"You like coconut, hunh? It's my favorite, too."

Kat froze, her hand still in her purse. Vincent, Anthony Desucci's bodyguard, maneuvered around her and held out several bills. The woman snatched the money, ignoring Kat.

Kat turned to see Carlo the enforcer, an immoveable object of a man, flipping the sign on the shop door from Open to Closed.

"How you doin', miss?" Vincent said, his amiable style on full display. "Haven't seen you in a while. You look a little under the weather, if you don't mind me saying."

"I don't mind," Kat said.

Vincent slipped the tiny cell phone out of Kat's hand and tucked it into a dark pouch. "I'll just hold this for you. You got any other cell phones? Better let me have them, too."

Katerina handed over her regular cell phone and watched Vincent place it inside the pouch and then hand it off to Carlo.

Vincent took Kat's cup of ice cream. "I got this too, don't worry. We're in the back."

Katerina steeled herself, preparing to see Anthony Desucci, or worse, Vito Massone. She didn't expect a man in his mid-thirties with a handsome face and full head of black hair, dressed in a white shirt and dark pants.

Kat felt Vincent's hand on her upper back, gentle but firm. "C'mon now, miss."

Katerina allowed herself to be brought in tow to the last booth where the man sat, relaxed, waiting.

"I thought it was time we met," he said. "Anthony Desucci – Junior."

***

Katerina slid into the booth and sat across from him. She knew him from newspapers and television, from the cop shoptalk at the Kellan house weekend barbecues. He had a dapper style with a model-ready face, lean body, and a megawatt smile. College educated, he carried himself more like an accomplished businessman than the first-born son of a reputed mob boss. For the past ten years he had been learning the ropes of the family business. He was billed as a more sophisticated, twenty-first century criminal. Still, the rumors said the son could outdo the father: people who got in his way disappeared, no body, no crime.

Vincent placed the ice cream on the table, in front of her, and then receded with Carlo to hover behind Anthony Junior.

He gave her a smile. "I had wanted us to meet months ago, but I was out of town, schedules, weather . . ." and he let the thought die out. "How are you feeling?"

"Better," she said, deciding not to bother asking how he knew she had been ill. "Do they call you Junior?" she asked.

The smile widened. "Tony is fine. How did it go in Jersey?"

"It didn't."

He nodded but the smile had disappeared. "What's the story with the widow?"

Kat shook her head. "There is no story," she said. "Just a widow and her craft projects."

"You think the lawyer took you on a fool's errand."

Katerina shrugged. "Yeah. But he doesn't have the negatives, and he's not faking his panic. He doesn't believe the photographer killed himself and he doesn't want the same thing happening to him."

Tony grimaced and leaned forward, his hands folded together.

"This situation has gotten out of control. We can't have this excitement anymore. We can't have any more people dying over this."

Kat surmised Tony Junior had substituted "dying" for "killed." He didn't believe Abe's suicide story either.

"It brings too much attention," Tony continued. "This has to be taken care of now with calm and quiet. That's where you and I come in. It's you and me." He gave her a sharp look. "But I have to know you're not gonna pull a switch on me."

That damn business in December. Simon Marcus had hired Kat to retrieve his car from his soon-to-be ex-wife. Back then, Kat would never have imagined why Marcus wanted it back so badly or why Desucci wanted the car at all. Without thinking, Katerina rolled her eyes in annoyance. "I didn't know there was a trap in the car with a stashed Van Gogh. I thought your father wanted the Porsche to prove a point."

Tony viewed her with a cynical eye.

"If it makes him feel any better, the Van Gogh was a fake."

"Who told you?"

"The widow. Betsy Marcus had stolen the painting months before and replaced it with a forgery."

"Why did she tell you?"

"She wanted someone to know she won."

Tony shook his head. "You and I will be working together to fix this little problem."

"Did you mention that to Vito Massone?" Kat asked.

"Vito Massone understands what he can and can't do. He stays in his place." Tony leaned back. "My father built this family. I intend to protect him and his legacy, but times have changed. I have my own way of doing things. It's not my father's way."

"Like having Philip set up offshore shell companies for you."

Tony smiled. "Offshore shell companies aren't illegal, Katerina."

"Great. I'm happy to hear the Desucci family will be completely legitimate in ten years," Kat said without thinking.

Tony Junior laughed and shifted forward, reaching his hand toward Kat.

Like a boomerang, Katerina recoiled. When she made eye contact, she saw the shock on Tony's face, and then the realization. She averted her eyes, the shame burning in her cheeks.

"Hey," he said softly, holding up his hand and then laying it over hers, patting it with a soft touch. "That's never gonna come from me. You understand?"

Kat nodded.

"I was going to say, I see why my father likes you," he said. "You're quick, like my sister, Angelica. She doesn't let anyone get away with anything, including my father." He nodded at Vincent. "Doesn't she remind you of Angelica?"

"Absolutely," Vincent chimed in. Carlo nodded, the extent of his participation.

Tony leaned forward. "You want to see the end of this, don't you?"

"Yes," she said.

"So do I. We can do this, if we work together. We can make sure it works out for both of us."

Katerina nodded. "Pareto efficient."

His eyebrows quirked.

"You talked to your father about what you studied in school."

"I did," Tony said.

"He was paying attention. He and I discussed pareto efficiency last year, in an empty warehouse, after he had me drugged and kidnapped. It didn't seem to bother him if his situation improved, but mine didn't."

"He didn't feel that way, Katerina. Trust me. Does this look like an empty warehouse to you?"

Kat shook her head.

"If I tell you, it's you and me, then that's what it is."

Katerina nodded. "I will get *you* the negatives."

Tony considered the statement. "Good. The lawyer *is* holding out on you. That trip was smoke and mirrors. And I'm not convinced the negatives were stolen from him."

Katerina nodded; and then a thought came to her, a light that dawned. "How would you feel about Pareto optimality."

Tony smirked. "You want to be better off without hurting me. Okay, what'd you have in mind?"

"I'm looking for a friend of your father. I know I don't have any right to ask, but if you could pass a message, I would appreciate it."

Tony's eyes narrowed. "What friend?"

"He calls himself Ivan." *He calls himself a cleaner. The hit man.*

Tony exchanged a glance with Vincent. "He's not my father's friend. What do you want with him?"

"We had an agreement. He was supposed to – take care of something – something personal. He hasn't done it."

"Listen, if you want to take care of your domestic problem – that can be done."

The word "yes" sat on the tip of her tongue. One word, that's all it would take, and Ryan would disappear . . .

"No, that would cause more problems, for both of us," she said. "Ivan was supposed to take care of something, something else that would make it possible for me to leave my domestic problem, and get out of Brooklyn."

Tony considered her. "You work on the negatives. I'll work on Ivan. Deal?"

The anvil of anxiety laying heavy on her chest lightened for a brief second. "Thank you," she heard herself say.

Tony's mouth pursed in a frown, his jaw set, as he said, "The cop's been home for a half hour."

Katerina nodded. "What if I need to talk to you?"

"Vincent will give you a number you can call. You'll remember it?"

"I remember everything," she said.

Tony stood up. "I'll see you soon," he said and gave her shoulder a brotherly pat.

Kat nodded.

Vincent stepped forward, his hand out to help her ease out of the booth. She accepted the offered kindness. She recognized the poison of hope like a thick syrup starting to inch its way into her system, anesthetizing her; then it turned, insidious and unbearable and she pushed it down. She took the phones and buried the tiny cell phone in the false compartment in her purse.

When she looked up, she found herself alone and the door to the kitchen swinging slightly. Kat headed to the front entrance, and she heard the tinkling of the bell as she went out. No time to call her mother. Out of time.

Parked behind a copse of trees, Carter leaned back in the driver's seat of his car, the open windows allowing a cool, cross-breeze. The hiding place provided an ideal vantage point for watching traffic on the road or anyone approaching the farmhouse. The owners of the farm, two ladies, had grown accustomed to his presence. One half of the couple, a rustic, solid woman, always with a shotgun at her side, left early every morning to trek across the property to work on the construction of a tiny house. Her partner, the ethereal, delicate one, a psychologist, or shaman, or maybe both, kept to the garden or the house during the day. Late at night, he would see her venturing out alone into the nearby woods. After a time, he would see the cinders from a fire's flames rising into the night sky. But Carter watched over only one resident of the house: Linda Mills.

Katerina Mills had wanted protection for her mother and Alexander Winter had been paying for it. Carter followed Linda Mills every time she left the farm. At one particular stop, he had no choice but to keep his distance; a small cabin hidden far back from the road, nestled deep in the woods. A Russian lived there, a supposed painter by trade. Katerina referred to him as a long-time family friend, "Uncle Sergei." Uncle Sergei had young men who walked the perimeter. And Carter would bet every dime he had that Linda Mills didn't need the protection her daughter had asked for. Carter mused Katerina Mills didn't know quite a bit about her mother, or the family friend, Sergei the painter.

After Alexander Winter fled in January, the payments for the protection had stopped. Then Katerina Mills hired Keyes. The half-brothers had a discussion and decided whatever had to be done to bring Alexander Winter back would be done. Carter owed the man a life debt – and he had resolved to pay it.

Carter glanced down at the laptop, the program still running. He scrolled and clicked, peeking and poking through the cyber-world without revealing himself. The noises from the laptop told him he had found Alexander Winter's fifth bank account, and hopefully, a clue to his whereabouts.

Carter examined the information. This account, like the others, had a zero balance. The man he knew as Alexander Winter would never have drained all the accounts at once. He always left a back door. And if Alexander Winter had withdrawn all the money to flee, he would never have left without Katerina Mills. Someone had hacked the accounts and stolen the money. Carter had a choice to make: continue on and try to trace who did this or back out. The people who did this could be tracking *him* right now. Carter backed out.

From his peripheral vision, Carter detected movement. He turned his head to see Linda Mills, dressed in a flimsy, floral blouse and skirt combo, her chestnut hair flowing loose around her shoulders, striding toward the car.

When she arrived, she bent down and crooked her head. He remembered Katerina doing the same thing in January, by the downtown marketplace, in the same midday sun. Like mother like daughter, he thought.

Katerina entered the apartment and found Ryan slouched on the couch, a beer in one hand, staring at the blaring television screen. She knew at once the visit to John Reynolds' office had gone to shit. Reynolds one, cops zero. As usual.

Katerina noted the backpack on the floor, leaning against the kitchen chair, the suit jacket draped over the back of a chair, the shoulder holster strap slung over the corner of the jacket, the service weapon nestled into the holster.

"Hey," she said, as bright and cheerful as she could.

Ryan took another swig from the bottle.

Oh shit. The silent treatment.

Katerina dropped her purse on the other chair. Going to the refrigerator, she pulled out food to make dinner. At the sink, her posture stiffened.

He's up.

"What happened to my Mets cup?" he asked.

Katerina faltered at the left field question. *Not this again.* "Maybe it's in the dishwasher. I'll look."

"Not the drinking cup. I had a commemorative Mets cup, on the shelf. What'd you do with it?"

She floundered, knowing she had no good answer. "Ryan, I didn't –"

"How many times have I told you not to move my stuff, hunh?" and he bumped up against her.

She stumbled until her back was against the counter. "I – I'm so sorry – it won't happen again."

He took another swig of beer, eyeing her up and down.

"Where were you?"

"Italian class," she said.

"Are you stupid?"

Katerina stood frozen, struck dumb at the question she had just heard in Jersey, only now it was directed at her.

"Your Italian class is in the morning. Did you think I wouldn't remember? So, I'll ask you one more time, are you stupid?"

She stared at the floor, avoiding eye contact. "I was at the language lab."

"Oh," he said, drawing out the sound, "you had *language lab*." He leaned in, inches from her face, tilting his head to meet her eyes. "Who were you practicing with at the *language lab*?"

"Everyone sits at their own station with their own headphones," she said, knowing the useless exercise would end at the same place.

Ryan took another swig from the bottle.

Maybe I should have said yes to Tony Junior. Maybe I should let him –

Kat stopped, unwilling to let the thought finish.

She flinched at the clinking sound of the beer bottle on the counter, and closed her eyes as he hemmed her in against the counter.

"You know," he whispered, "if you were smarter, you would have told me you stayed in the city planning Emma's bridal shower. Except, I would have known that's bullshit, because you haven't done a damn thing about that."

Katerina turned her face away as he hovered over her, oppressing her. "I was sick."

His hands clamped around her arms with an iron grip. Kat's body curled at the pain searing through her. "Ryan –"

Shoving her into the counter, she gave a cry at the jag of pain in her lower back. With one hand he yanked her forward by a hank of her hair. Grabbing the backpack with the other hand, he slammed it on the table and maneuvered the mouth of the pack open, rooting around and grabbing a handful of photographs. He spread them out.

Katerina recoiled from the sight of Felicia Reynolds' ruined and ravaged body. His hand moved to the back of her neck, squeezing like a vise as he forced her over the table. She clamped her eyes closed.

"Open your eyes," he ordered and squeezed harder. She gasped in pain and obeyed. She stared at the dead woman, tears running down her cheeks.

"This is what happens to a girl when she sluts around. You see those marks on her wrists and her ankles, hmmm? The way we figure it, he had her tied to a bed or maybe a chair, we're not sure. Now, who is he?"

Katerina cried. "Ryan, no, please, no one. There's no one. Please, it hurts, it hurts."

"You think this is pain? She was alive when this animal started cutting her. She felt it. She felt *all* of it. She went looking for this. Is that what you want, hunh? Hunh? Now, where were you and who is he?"

"There's no one! No one! I swear!"

Ryan yanked her back, spinning her to face him. "I'll tell you what, let's take off your clothes right now, every stitch, and if I see, if I *smell*, that you've been lying to me . . ."

He tore her shirt off her shoulder.

Kat stood, her arms at her sides. "I was at school," she cried.

Kat's regular cell phone went off. Ryan made a faux look of shock. "Who could that be? I'll get it. Maybe it's the *language lab*."

Grabbing the cell phone from her purse, he connected the call and gave an exaggerated, "Hello?"

Katerina watched as Ryan's demeanor changed to serious, polite, respectful. *The cop persona.* "Hello, Mrs. Mills. Yes, she's right here. Yes, ma'am. Yes, ma'am. I'm taking good care of her. Yes, she's better. Hold on."

He held out the cell phone; Katerina tugged her shirt back on her shoulder as she took it. "Hi, Mommy," Kat said. "Yes, I'm better. Yes, I'm back to school. Easy peasy lemon squeezy," she said, their private code for Ryan's assaults. "Yes, I'm taking my vitamins. No, I haven't been taking that. Yes, I will. Yes, okay. No, I don't have that in the apartment. Yes, I'll go downstairs to the drugstore right now."

Katerina grabbed a sweatshirt off a hook. Glancing at Ryan, she caught his mild expression as she exited the apartment.

***

Entering the drugstore, Kat checked over her shoulder as she went down an aisle.

"Okay, Mommy, I'm here," Kat said.

"Katie, there is no confirmation that the professor is unable to return to school."

"Is there anything to prove he *is able* to come back?" Kat asked, clinging to her question like a lifeline.

After a moment's silence, she heard Linda Mills say, "No, there isn't. But there is *nothing* to say he *can't.*"

Even in the sliver of hope, Kat's heart still sank, weighed down by the nagging question she wouldn't dare say out loud. *Why hadn't I sensed that something had happened to him?* She had placed the sacred stone necklace around his neck in January. The stone held the promise of protection and connection, spirit to spirit. She herself had experienced a strange encounter on a snowy night; like a movie she had seen, where a person's spirit exists outside their body, walking by their side as a spirit animal.

She had encountered a fox, symbolic of a sly, cunning nature, its quick-thinking providing luck to escape in the nick of time, aided by a heightened sense of hearing and smell. *Why didn't I know?* As she turned in the aisle, she swept several bottles off the shelf and onto the floor.

"Katie," her mother's voice soothed in her ear, "you don't know if the Department Chair said that just to upset you."

Katerina, crouching down on the floor, used one hand to scoop up the bottles, dropping them again as they slipped through her fingers.

"Do you think so?"

"Yes, I do. I really do think that's possible," her mother said.

Katerina felt a slight salve of calm struggling to seep through as only her mother could provide, the one who knew better.

"Katerina," her mother said, her voice pinched with concern, "do you need something more than vitamins?"

The code. Did he hurt you?"

"No, Mommy."

"Katie, come home right now. I promise you, it'll be all right."

"Does Uncle —"

"He wants you to come home, too," Linda Mills said.

"I think he's angry with me," Kat said. "He never wants to talk to me."

"He loves you," Linda Mills said. "He's worried sick about you."

"Tell him I'm reading the book. I've been reading it every day, just like he told me to."

Katerina caught site of the familiar white T-shirt and jeans combination. Ryan had entered the drugstore.

He nodded at Katerina, and she raised the vitamin bottle for him to see.

As he reached her, she said, "Okay, Mommy, I have the vita-mins."

He took the bottle out of her hand and said, "Don't worry, baby. I'll go pay for it."

"Thank you," Kat said.

"Katie, will you call me tomorrow?" her mother asked.

"I'll try."

"Katerina, remember, if you didn't see it, you don't know."

"I'll remember, Mommy."

Kat watched Ryan accept change from the cashier and he turned, walking back to her.

"Bye, Mommy," Kat said and clicked off the call.

Ryan came to her; placing his hand on her upper back, ushering her out of the drugstore and back to the apartment.

***

Linda Mills clicked off the call. At the round, oak kitchen table, Sergei Grigorievitch Volkov sat catty-cornered to her. A solid, sturdy man, he sported a full head of hair salted with gray, and a beard to match. His eyes, dark with concern, never left Linda Mills.

Linda placed the cell phone down between them.

"We do it now," Sergei said. "What will be, will be."

"What if it makes it worse for her? Everything will be destroyed," Linda said. "She will be destroyed. And everything we've waited for. All of it, gone."

Sergei placed his hand over hers. "Every day we wait, the risk grows. One day, time will make the decision for us – and time won't decide in our favor– or hers."

Linda nodded, tears welling in her eyes. "When this is over–"

"The policeman," Sergei said, "will be taken care of."

The car pulled into the factory parking lot and idled.

"Thank you for the ride," Kat said. She went for the door, but the iron grip on her arm stopped her.

"You remember what we talked about. Home, in the apartment, by six o'clock," Ryan said. "No later, understand?"

Kat nodded. Another demand, another concession. It had to be done. *I hate you.* "Yes, home by six o'clock."

He leaned in and she reciprocated the kiss on autopilot. When they parted, he said, "Be good."

"Promise," she said with a docile smile and scrambled out of the car.

The car circled around and roared out of the lot. On her way into the plant, Katerina waved to Juan. Once inside, her eyes watered, her nose congested, and she felt the faint twinges of irritation in her chest.

Just before Kat dropped her purse on her desk, a vibration told her the secret, hidden cell phone had buzzed. Glancing around, Kat slipped the tiny cell phone from its hiding place, keeping it shrouded in her purse as she checked the message.

What's up, buttercup?
It's your fairy godmother.
I've got a job that needs a second.

Good money.

Kat read Lisa's text again. *Good money.* Last year, Kat had met the sophisticated beauty outside Joe Lessing's apartment. Lisa had come to "fix" Lessing's problem of a passed-out paramour and a wife on the way home from the airport. Kat had arrived first. Lisa had made Kat an offer: an invitation to an interview at MJM Consulting. The shadowy company served as an introduction service; for a large fee, wealthy men who enjoyed behaving badly could hire an enterprising young woman to make their problems disappear.

Desperate for cash, Kat had hired on as a "B-girl," a professional fixer who did the bitch work no one else could.

Katerina raised her head to find her boss, Conrad Wheelan, staring at her. Middle-aged with a basketball belly and a cynical expression on his doughy face, he stood with his hands on his hips.

Katerina gave Wheelan a penitent smile, shifted the tiny phone back into its hiding spot, and set to work appearing busy. She still felt his eyes on her even as he called out for Luella and disappeared back into his office. Kat slipped out the tiny phone again from under the lining of her purse and shot off a text to her mother.

Please send me a "How are you today?" text to regular phone. Now. K.

She tucked the phone back into its hiding spot. As she shoved the purse into a desk drawer, she heard the buzz of the regular phone go off.

As Kat waded into the mound of paperwork on her desk, Luella exited Wheelan's office, muttering under her breath. Kat could have sworn she heard the word "asshole" followed by an "mmm hmmm," Luella supplying her own affirmation.

She came to Kat, holding a pile of invoices. "You take care of these today for me, baby, so I don't have to hear anything I don't want to hear."

"Yes, Miss Luella," Kat said, feeling guilty she had caused the woman grief she didn't need.

"That's my girl," Luella said and moved on.

A commotion of raised voices grew louder until the connecting door to the office flew open. The voices exploded as the two men blew inside, bringing the noxious chemical smells with them.

"Jesus take the wheel," Luella said.

The two middle-aged men presented as a mismatched pair: Albert, medium height, paunch bulging over his pants, Peter, small and slight. They carried on their argument; their words tippled with the accents of their own respective countries of origin.

"I ordered forty," Peter said.

"No, you did not," Albert said.

"Your guy didn't count right. Send him back to school."

"We did not receive forty."

"So, tell them we can't make the product. I don't care. I got you forty. You don't get any more until next month."

They stopped in front of Kat's desk.

"Hey, Katerina, pull the Hollis invoice, will you."

"The invoice says forty," Katerina said, and recited each detail even as she pulled out a cabinet drawer to retrieve it.

When she held out the invoice, Peter snatched it out of her hand. "You see? You see that signature? That's one of your hombres that signed for the forty barrels, right there."

Katerina winced at the funny tickle in her chest. *It's nothing. Forget it.*

"I don't know what he did with it."

"That's bullshit."

Katerina imagined this conversation in a series of text messages written in all caps.

"Let's take a look," Peter said. "Let's go Katerina, let's see what these guys did here."

Kat wanted to say no. She wanted to say she didn't have to, but who would she complain to? And what would it cost her? *I just have to get through this. I can do this. I can do this until it's over.*

When? When will this be over?

She got up and followed them out.

As they went through the heavy doors into the large, gray, dirty space, a cacophony of noise from the jumble of machinery greeted them.

Peter put his arm around her waist as they walked. "You look tired, Kitty Cat. What's the matter? Too much fun last night?"

Katerina ignored the stale jokes and commentary. Albert, whose name was not Albert but an Americanized version of his true name, skulked on ahead, his anger clearing out a path in front of him.

They wandered over to a corner of the building and stopped in front of a closed metal door. Albert pulled open the door; using his foot, he shoved in a wedge at the bottom. The stagnant, chemical-soaked air assaulted Katerina, bringing a fresh burst of tears to her eyes as the stench attacked her nose. Entering the storage room, she sidestepped the stray, solvent-stained rags on the floor.

"Ah, I love the smell of methyl ethyls in the morning," Peter said, his signature joke.

"C'mon, knock it off," Albert said. He went to the back of the room, crouching down to check the ventilation fan. Confirming the vent was open, he flipped the fan on.

Katerina rooted around, checking labels, alternatively sniffling and trying not to breathe.

Albert, conducting his own inspection, shook his head as he grabbed a loose wire with a clip and snicked the clip onto the end of one of the barrels.

On the other side of the room, Kat counted the barrels stacked in twos. "There's fifty," she said.

Coming up next to her, Albert grabbed one of the stacked barrels, giving it a rattle. "Those are empties."

When they exited the storage room, they found the production floor deserted, the machinery idle. The workers had flocked outside for their break, sweltering in the sun instead of sweating indoors.

A side exit door hung open, the scent of cigarette smoke drifting inside, mingling with the chemical smells.

Albert went to the door, sticking his head out. "Hey, amigo!" he shouted.

After a minute, a man entered; Hispanic, medium height, wearing a blank expression.

"Hey, amigo, you put in forty, right? Cuarenta, right?"

The employee nodded, not even looking at the paper Albert held out to him. "Yeah," he said.

"Cuarenta, no menos," Albert questioned.

"Yeah," he answered.

"Who took the grounding clip off the barrel, hunh? You took if off when you unloaded?"

"No me," the employee said, shrugging and shaking his head at the same time.

Albert glanced down at the floor. Spotting a stray cigarette butt, he swiped it off the floor and held it out. "Who's smoking in here? What you doing smoking in here? You know it's no fuma in here."

"Yeah," he answered. "I no smoke, no me," and he held up his hands in the universal sign of innocence.

"Those guys shouldn't be smoking in here," Peter said, stating the obvious to annoy Albert. "Or outside the door. You mix methyl ethyls with smoke, you could make a big mess you do that, you know what I'm saying?"

A familiar recitation went off in Kat's head.

Extremely flammable liquid and vapor.

Ground/Bond container.

No Smoking.

"What you want from me?" Albert said. "I tell them. Don't smoke. Don't put empties in the room. Nobody says nothing. Nobody sees nothing and nobody knows nothing," He went to the open door and stepped outside, leaving Kat and Peter to listen to the shouting. "You don't smoke here. No smoking inside. How many times I tell you!"

Albert came back inside, slamming the door shut. "I don't know what happened," he said to Peter. "We don't have forty."

"He signed for forty."

The argument continued as Kat followed them back to the office. Once inside, she grabbed her purse and hurried off to the bathroom to wash out her eyes and cough. Locked into a stall, she slipped out the personal cell phone. Wheelan would make sure the cell phone sighting would get back to Ryan. She reviewed her mother's text. Linda Mills had done well, crafting a message of parental inquiry and concern. That might keep Ryan quiet. Maybe. She dug out the tiny cell phone and texted a message to Lisa.

Sorry, Svengali, no can do.

The phone buzzed again.

Relax, Rapunzel, I don't need you this second. I'll make it worth your while.

Kat stared at the phone. *I'll make it worth your while.* Joe Lessing had said that to her last year. *That's how this whole thing started.*

She typed out a text. *No can do.*

Katerina went back to her desk and made a mental list of the stops she had to make in the city the next day. *If I even get to the city. God knows what Ryan might do at any moment.* She felt all the loose ends of her life, dangling like deadly strings, tightening around her neck, choking the life out her. But none of it mattered. Only Winter.

***

Later, in the darkest moment of the night, as she sifted through Ryan's backpack, Katerina shifted her weight back and forth between her feet, trying to accommodate the radiating pain from the blows no one would ever see. She scanned the notebook, catching the words "re-canvas" and "Will Temple." *Shit.* One of the other cops, a Detective Morse, was returning to Will Temple's neighborhood. Last year, she had parked near the building, on a surveillance run, following Felicia Reynolds . . . *and I used Emma's car.* She cursed at the rookie mistakes she had not known better to avoid. If one of the shop owners remembered the car, remembered her. . .. Kat's heart banged in panic, but then something else caught her eye. Muting the light of her cell phone inside his bag, her eyes roamed over the printout of an employee list. Sifting through the pages, she came upon a name with a line through it and a notation. Bruce Elmont. She glanced over his date of hire – and a scribbled date in the margin – date of death.

She placed each item back in its spot. Keeping an eye on the bedroom door, she listened for the telltale snoring of Ryan's alcohol-induced sleep. She went to her purse; extracting the tiny cell phone, she sent a text message to her mother with the name and dates.

Bruce Elmont

Please give the name to Carter and tell him to pass it along

She tucked the phone back in its hiding place. Keyes would have a name. Would he have enough time?

Will I have enough time?

She glanced over at the vase on the counter; the flowers still blooming with life. The bouquets were coming closer together now. *If this keeps up, I'll need two vases.*

Katerina forced herself to focus.

Get into the city.

Get to Philip.

Get the information for Tony Junior.

Tony Junior gets the hitman.

The hitman kills Reynolds.

Investigation stalls.

I get out of here.

Winter comes home.

One move left to make.

Katerina kept her head down, scribbling notes as Professor Talbot delivered his lecture. She attended class with a sick stomach of trepidation, but viewed it as a necessary evil, an opportunity to prepare her defense. Reynolds' manipulative blackmail fantasy, his photographic evidence painting her as Will Temple's jilted, jealous lover driven to murder, was not her only worry. If the police caught on to her in any manner, how would she explain tracking, tracing, and surveilling Felicia Reynolds? And without implicating MJM Consulting? Could she be tried as an accomplice? She had been paying rapt attention, studying the cases, clocking the crimes, legal strategies, and potential punishments. With so little time left, she still had not found an answer that gave clarity – or peace.

"Now, who can give me the definition of mens rea? Katerina."

Kat's head shot up.

"Mens rea – please."

"The state of mind of the person. Did he – or she – voluntarily go out with an evil mind or intention to cause harm."

"Correct," Talbot said. "When the court examines actus reus – a criminal act – they look at mens rea. However, as we have said all semester, and I quote the text, 'under the law of complicity, the actions of each person directed to the success of the crime are imputed by the others.' Mr. Sandberg, which is the more critical to prove your case – actus reus or mens rea?"

"But what if the actions of the person, one person, was done without knowing the true mens rea of the other person, or people, in the group? What if one person's actions were not directed to the success of a crime?"

Katerina felt her cheeks burn at the sound of her own voice, as if she had spoken not of her own volition, but her body had responded to her desperation and taken matters into its own hands.

Professor Talbot considered Katerina, his eyes a touch wider at his quietest student being so forward.

"Miss Mills, I'm sure there are many guests of the state who claim to have been unaware that their actions were contributing to a crime." He held out his hands, palms up. "Alas, there is no honor among thieves. Stunning."

The class chuckled.

Katerina glanced away to hide her disappointment. When she turned back, she found Professor Talbot still considering her.

"To your question, we again look to the text. 'One person is liable for the crime of another when he or she *intentionally* aids the other person in committing it.' Miss Mills, I do believe you are crafting your defense. Well done. But, you will need to prove it. An entirely different matter." Turning away, he said, "Mr. Sandberg, we return to you, sir, picking up the thread of Miss Mills' question. So, which is more important to prove, mens rea, or actus reus?"

Katerina and a few others turned their heads. Kat knew the student. Mark. Dark hair, dark eyes, fair complexion; he had a decided "Clark Kent" quality about him. In last semester's Introduction to Ethics class, Mark had been her project partner and a possible – what? Friend? Boyfriend? They had never gotten to that point and then class ended. She hadn't given Mark another thought until the would-be environmental lawyer showed up in her class. He had made several overtures over the months. She had missed more classes than she attended, and as the semester rushed toward its end, she had caught him staring, attempting to make eye contact, a new urgency to try and connect.

"Mens rea. What someone thinks is what's most important. That's how Katerina will exonerate her client."

Katerina crooked her head down, feeling the eyes of the students on her.

"Interesting answer, Mr. Sandberg. But shouldn't this person be responsible to have known, to have had the foresight, that there would be harm?"

Katerina continued writing furiously, blinking away her tears.

"But, if this person did not *commit* the crime," Mark objected, "how could this person have known that his companions would commit a crime, or even have an idea that his actions would contribute to a crime."

"Ah, the defense becomes clearer," Professor Talbot said. "We shall call it the Red-Headed League defense. Courtesy of Mr. Conan Doyle, a gentleman, Mr. Wilson, is duped into joining the League of Red-Headed Gentlemen. He leaves his shop each day and spends four hours at the League's office, being paid handsomely to copy the *Encyclopaedia Britannica.* An odd, but by all accounts, innocent endeavor."

Katerina felt her face flush warm at the thought of her trip to Saks, under orders from John Reynolds to make contact with his wife. Even as she had hesitated, a man had bumped into her, sending her right into the young socialite's path. She could not have imagined Felicia, in a burst of spontaneous generosity, would gift her own earrings to Kat. Earrings that were now taped under a dresser drawer in her East Village apartment.

A man bumped into me . . .

"All the while, criminals are using the cellar of his shop to dig a tunnel into the bank located behind. One of Conan Doyle's most entertaining Sherlock Holmes tales. The money to copy the encyclopedia was exceptional. But wouldn't a reasonable man assume this was a ridiculous proposition? Is greed a viable defense?"

How about stupidity?

How about desperation?

"Let us return to our text. We see in *People v. Kibbe* that intention, or mens rea, is not the most important factor. Rest assured that a person who assists before the crime occurs may be charged with the same crime committed by another. Therefore, Mr. Sandberg, it does not matter what they think. It matters what they did. Miss Mills, when the time comes, you may, or may not, wish to solicit Mr. Sandberg as a member of your legal team."

The chuckles from the students sounded like canned laughter in Kat's ears.

What did you foresee, Katerina?

What did you plan?

How did you assist?

What did you do?

Where do I begin?

***

While Professor Talbot rattled off chapters to study, the class broke up with the noise of conversation, gathering books, and slinging purses on shoulders to make their exit.

Throwing her books into her bag, Kat had already flown from the classroom, her cell phone at her ear, when she heard her name called. She whirled around as Mark caught up to her.

"Hey," he said, as if he had planned to say something else but couldn't remember it now. He settled for, "How are you?"

Kat nodded at Mark as she said, "Getting there."

Mark stayed at her side as they exited the building, motioning with a hand if they could walk together. Kat nodded and slipped the cell phone back into her purse.

"Are you worried about the final?"

Kat nodded. "Uh hunh."

"I don't know if I'm going to be getting anything on the exam except a zero," Mark said. "I keep stepping in it with Talbot, making stupid statements."

"There are no stupid statements, or questions," Kat said, and a sudden stab of fear assaulted her. *What if Ryan decides to check on me today?*

Mark nodded and said, "I've hardly seen you all semester and now it's almost over."

"It's been a difficult few months . . ." and she let the sentence trail away.

"I heard you were seeing someone, a police officer."

Kat nodded. "Detective. Since January. It was a setup through a friend of mine. We were thrown together a lot, and, you know, things happen."

"Yeah, sure," Mark said with a faraway look, like he was thinking of something else entirely. "Are you happy, with him?" he asked.

Taken aback by the question, Kat said, "He has a very high-stress job."

"You shouldn't be sick all the time. You have to take care of yourself. Get some rest. I feel like you're always running away. If you need a friend, Katerina, I care. I really do."

Katerina took in Mark Sandberg, who had just gotten off the Good Ship Lollipop. Mark, who wanted to do good and rescue the world from smog and dirty water.

A nice boy who wants to rescue me.

Don't try. I'm not innocent.

"You're a good person, Mark," Kat said.

I'm not good.

"I'm your friend, Katerina," he said, stepping closer. "You can talk to me. We never did catch that movie–"

"Hey." A female voice broke into the conversation. "There you are."

A doe-eyed, sprite of a girl with a short bob of a haircut, crowded into Kat's personal space, crushing her in an embrace.

"Hi Mina," Kat said with a smile, relieved a buffer had appeared. Mina gave her a kiss, lingering a moment too long in the hug, the last to let go.

Mina had introduced herself at the beginning of the semester with a sheepish smile and a request for the favor of borrowing Kat's cell phone. She had been a kind of acquaintance ever since, eager to supply the notes and assignments throughout Kat's many illnesses.

"I'm so worried about the final, aren't you?"

"Uh, we were just talking about that," Mark stumbled.

"We should study together," Mina said.

"We were just talking about that," Mark said.

The cell phone vibrations from her purse distracted Kat and the urge to reach for it tormented her. What if it was Reynolds? What if something had happened to . . .

"We could all study together," Katerina said. "I can use all the help I can get."

"Great," Mina said. "Let's set it up. When?"

"I'm not really sure yet," Kat fumbled. "But you have my number, and I have Mark's number, so we'll do something.

Mark did nothing to hide his crestfallen look, but he said, "Yeah, sure. I'm available any time, Kat. Any time that works for you, I can be there."

"I'm sorry, I have to run," Kat said, her nerves shredding inside her. "It was good to see you both, but I have to go."

"I'll take care of everything," Mina said.

As Kat left them there, two orphans without their mutual connection, she noticed Mina smiling. A nice girl with nothing on her mind. *I wonder what that's like.*

***

Heading for the subway, Katerina dug the vibrating, tiny cell phone out of her purse. Text messages. Kat tapped and viewed the last message.

C'mon, Rapunzel. You're not really going to make me play hard to get. Two hours. Good money.

Lisa. Kat typed back.

Sorry, Charlie. Still a no-go.

As she reached the stairway, a sudden barrage of thoughts overwhelmed her like a tidal wave.

My God, Alex, what is he doing to you? How is he hurting you? Are you even alive?

Stunned by the raw force of the mental attack, Katerina stopped cold, her heart squeezing until she thought she could hear it break.

She visualized a wall in her head, a door closing, a barrier the thoughts couldn't break through, staving off the insanity welling up inside her. If the screaming started, it would never stop.

Still catching her breath, the buzz of the cell phone startled her. Seeing the word "Private" for the number, she hesitated, her thumb hovering over the green button until she tapped.

"Yes," she said.

Kat listened to the voice of MJM's iron maiden gatekeeper, Jasmine. "I have a standing assignment for all consultants. Ten Gramercy Park South. The name is Satler. The first one who says yes, gets the job."

"What is the job?" Kat asked on instinct.

"An acquisition. It's worth three hundred. You take thirty per-cent. Are you available?"

Kat thought of the cash she desperately needed. She clamped her eyes closed as she said, "Not at the moment. Acquisition? Don't you mean retrieval?"

"I meant what I said. An acquisition. If you become available, I suggest you call right away. If someone gets there before you, you're out of luck."

The call clicked off.

Feeling lightheaded, Kat sat down on the ledge of a fountain, waiting for the coolness of the water to seep into her. She coughed, feeling the familiar fog of congestion in her head. Exhaustion washed over her, but she forced herself to get up and get moving. It's nothing, she told herself. She would make a pit stop at a drugstore for something. She had no time for anything else.

She had a stop to make. She had to see someone who knew all about criminal acts, before, during, and after the fact.

Joseph Smith, dressed in his trademark suit, vest, and tie, a glacial look in his eyes, didn't bother to hide his scowl as he entered Thomas Gallagher's Upper East Side study. On the wall, two cherrywood panels had opened, revealing a mounted, flat-screen television. On the screen, the bedroom of a cookie-cutter box of an apartment in Brooklyn, and Ryan Kellan and Katerina Mills in the throes of copulation. Smith had seen it before; cheek-to-cheek, Kellan on top, always the aggressor, Katerina underneath, her eyes either clamped closed or open, vacant, wounded. Her obligatory noises of pleasure filled the study.

Thomas Gallagher leaned back in his executive, leather chair behind his expansive desk. Seated across from him, Lisa sat with legs crossed, a bored expression on her face. Smith didn't buy the act. Her eyes remained sharp, always watching, tinged with a hint of desperation.

Smith considered himself a practical man. He didn't object to blackmail, extortion, corporate espionage, even stalking a woman. Morality had no place in business, or politics for that matter. Only money mattered. As long as he got his piece, kept his employer out of prison, and covered his own ass, people like Thomas Gallagher could spend their money however they liked.

"Now is the winter of our discontent made glorious summer," Gallagher announced. "Including the sportive tricks."

Smith picked up a remote and pressed the "mute" button. "For the last five months, you've wired and bugged every area of her life. You've followed her every move and listened to her every word – and sound. Haven't you had enough?"

"Of course not. It is a truth universally acknowledged, that a single man in possession of a good fortune, must be in want of the one thing he cannot have," Lisa said.

Gallagher ignored the comment. "I must say, discounting the initial excitement of New York's finest back in January – something Miss Mills had no control over, she's been quite creative, if not a bit extreme, to avoid this."

"That should tell you something," Smith said with quiet authority.

"As I study my future life companion, every detail tells me quite a bit."

Smith folded his arms rather than call bullshit to his client's face.

Lisa had found a spot in the room to concentrate her focus on, staring with a blank look. Only her pursed lips gave her true feelings away.

Gallagher picked up the remote on his desk and unmuted the sound. "See how practiced she is, giving off that one, particular sound until she raises the volume, making him think he has done his job well, urging him on to finish. It's always the same, the same little cries, the same sound, a rote performance."

Smith took his remote and hit the "mute" button. "She knows how to fake orgasm. Congratulations, you've discovered something no other man has."

"On the contrary, you think I haven't learned that Katerina Mills is an extraordinary woman to have endured such circumstances."

"Circumstances? That's a polite way to describe the shitshow you've been watching the last five months. I wouldn't have blamed her if she said to hell with it all back in January and fled." Smith stepped up to the desk. "This girl won't give up, she won't give in, and she won't break. Some women can't be broken."

"An interesting theory," Gallagher said. "Every day she lives with the reality of how far she is from that 'happily ever after' she imagined. I don't have to break her, Mr. Smith. She's breaking herself, from the inside."

Smith shook his head. "You must be a mind reader to have come up with that."

"No, he isn't," Lisa said. "He's just spent years in study."

"This wouldn't be happening if your powers of persuasion had been stronger," Gallagher said.

A prim, proper woman, dressed in a severe, dark-colored dress, with doe-eyes, a short bob of a haircut, and a calm, vacuous look, appeared at the entrance to the study.

"Mrs. Shields, you anticipate my every need, as always," Gallagher said. "Escort the young lady to her room. She is to remain there until called for."

"Thomas—"

"You are of no use to me at the moment."

Lisa rose from her chair and walked out, her head held high, Mrs. Shields following behind.

After they left, Smith said, "That girl will kill you the first chance she gets."

Gallagher laughed. "No, she won't, but your concern is touching. Is that all that concerns you?"

"Not by a long shot. You've been attending Katerina's 'Introduction to Criminal Law' class along with her this semester. You should have compiled a list of your potential crimes: unlawful surveillance of a New York City cop, knowledge of organized crime and their illegal activities—"

"Not as much knowledge as I should have."

"Tony Desucci is twenty-first century organized crime. There's nothing I can do about a signal blocking Faraday bag. Don't forget the blackmail scheme of the highest political office in this state, and accessory after the fact to three murders. Doesn't that concern you?"

"Not in the least. I have you. I'm a bit surprised, Mr. Smith. After all, you handled the business with Simon Marcus and those two operatives. It seems a bit late for being squeamish."

Smith squared his shoulders. "It's my job to keep my clients out of trouble."

"And I have no doubt you will continue to perform your duties admirably. Now that Katerina has provided the name of the killer–"

"I have Bruce Elmont's profile. And so does that contractor Katerina sent to find her "professor." He'll build the same profile."

"Make sure your team gets there first. That is, if you have any idea where they are."

Smith smiled. "You know the funny thing about missing persons . . . and murderers? They're usually closer than you think. The professor knows the farther he goes, the harder it is to get back to the girl and make a getaway. Bruce committed three murders, that we know of, in the city. He won't deprive Reynolds of the main event of victim number four. I'd bet my last dollar the hunter and the prey are both close, in one of the boroughs."

"I defer to your expertise, but let me be clear: you and your team will find the killer, help him trap and kill the "professor," and dispose of them both after he is done."

Smith let out a breath of exaggerated patience even as he nodded. "You should know the other operative, the half-brother, has been nosing around near the professor's bank accounts. Both are on the hunt."

"How is it they're still on retainer since you have cleaned out Mr. Winter's accounts? We both know Miss Mills has no available funds. I find it hard to believe they're doing this for nothing. They're professionals, not a charity organization. Would you still be doing it?"

Smith smiled. "Of course not. I don't know how Alexander Winter crossed paths with them, but I know of these two. They have a reputation for being outliers, operating by their own code. And they're good."

Gallagher answered with a sharp look. "Then I expect you and your team to be better."

Smith nodded. "As soon as I have confirmation of the capture and the kills, I'll let you know."

"Spare no expense. 'Winter' is over. I want this situation closed out, now. That is all."

Smith nodded, and keeping his eyes off the screen, walked out of the room.

Gallagher sat back in his chair and watched Katerina, her open eyes the window to her wounded soul. A noise from nearby took his attention away. He pointed the remote at the screen and clicked a button.

"Frannie . . .?" he said in a soft voice.

A hint of black fabric peeked out from the side of the entrance.

"Come here, Francine," Gallagher said.

Francine Shields entered the room, just over the threshold, her hands folded one over the other, waiting for her next instruction. He still glimpsed the girl he had met all those years ago. Dressed in her plain, black unform, no makeup, her hair showing signs of premature gray. Only the eyes gave her away, those same wide, doe-like eyes, the eyes of a child.

There is a book . . .

"You were standing there the entire time," he said.

She nodded her head.

Gallagher stood up and came around the desk. He motioned with his outstretched hand that she should come forward. As she approached, she lowered her head in obedience.

With one finger under her chin, he tilted her head up for her to look at him.

"I know my Frannie," he said. "What is it you want to ask."

She hesitated; her eyes clouded with confusion. "The girl, the one you were going to bring to the estate."

"Yes," he said. "You met her last year. You cared for her when she was ill. You took good care of her."

"She's not good for you. She doesn't love you."

"Now, Frannie," Gallagher said, placing his hands on her shoulders. "You know the place you occupy in my heart."

"I love you," she blurted. "Not like those others. Not like this one. She's going to hurt you."

"Frannie, we will always have a special bond that cannot be broken, a bond I could not have with anyone else. What is truly on your mind?"

Francine Shields shook her head. "When she comes, she'll want to separate us. She'll want to hurt me."

Gallagher quieted her. "My dear Frannie. Haven't I always taken care of you?"

Francine Shields nodded her head as tears fell from her eyes.

"And I always will," Gallagher said. "I assure you, Katerina Mills is no threat to you. She isn't a threat to anyone. Now, be a good girl and complete your instructions for Lisa. Keep a close eye on her. I'm worried *she* might want to do me harm. And you're the only one I trust."

Francine's eyes brightened and her posture straightened as she nodded her head.

Gallagher watched her leave the room. Francine Shields represented the old life of his partners. McKittrick and Fogerty had never planned for the inevitable future; a girl who became a woman and no longer elicited desire. She had been the first and for some inexplicable reason, at that fateful meeting, he had objected to their plan to rid themselves of the doe-eyed sprite who had become an inconvenient albatross.

Under his watchful eye, she became the caretaker, guard, and warden each time a new girl had been lured to the East End mansion. Those rooms, hidden away in the basement like a catacomb, still existed but had been idle and unused for some time. He had put a stop to the practice after the partners died. He was not like those men. Through MJM Consulting, he encountered young women, beautiful and ambitious. If they wished to pursue wealth, status, and privilege at any cost, it was entirely their choice. They had to pay for that choice. No one would force them to submit. Like Lisa, every young woman who had crossed his path had come willingly and received their just rewards for their greed and avarice. He contented himself he bore no responsibility in the matter.

Katerina Mills had been the only one who had defied every expectation; she surprised him at every turn. She was different, and he would treat her that way.

Gallagher gave a sigh. Soon it would be time to clean out those basement chambers and paint them over in white, wiping away the past as if it had never existed. Francine Shields would be swept away as well. He had already decided how it would be done.

K aterina made the call just after noon. The click of the answering machine and the droning message gave her the all-clear sign. Like clockwork, Philip Castle still went out every day for lunch. Rounding the corner of the building, she slipped inside. Approaching the office door, she glanced at the "Philip Castle, Esq." lettering. A familiar pang of self-loathing nagged at her. She made short work of the lock that had been jimmied so many times that the tumbler gave up without a fight.

The low-rent office looked the same, worn guest chairs, a chipped coffee table with dog-eared magazines, cheap paintings on the wall. On the secretary's desk, a beat-up computer, printer, and an ancient Selectric typewriter for the few bills that went out every month to make everything look legal. The current secretary seemed much neater than Kat had ever been. Or maybe she didn't do as much work.

Kat had come to New York City wide-eyed, thrilled to escape a small town and be where life loomed three times the size of what she had known. This place had been everything.

Why? Why was I drawn to him? What was I thinking?

Am I my father's daughter?

She went to the desk and opened the drawers, rummaging inside. She pulled out a message logbook. Empty. Glancing down at the wastebasket, she spied a hodgepodge of discarded sticky notes. She grabbed a handful and spread them out on the desk, scanning. *Mmm, mmm, mmm. Not good, Effie. Philip doesn't like messages and phone numbers written down.* She picked out a few, stuffing them into her purse, discarding the rest.

At the panting sounds of heavy breathing, Kat's head darted up. Her eyes narrowed. Looking around, she chose the printer. Lifting it up, she let it drop to the floor, the crashing noise reverberating through the office.

The panting noises cut out. Katerina positioned herself by the desk, arms folded, facing the door to the inner office, a cockeyed smile on her face.

The inner office door flew open. Philip's head ducked out, perspiration matting his forehead, his pants hanging open, the zipper half-descending, his shirt tail hanging out.

"Hello, lover," Kat said.

The secretary peered out from behind Philip, smoothing her mass of brassy, auburn hair. Her large firm breasts and curvy backside were stuffed into a skintight dress, and she worked the hem, tugging it down toward her midthigh, a futile struggle.

"Waddya think ya doin'? You can't paaark yourself there," she said, the Boston accent cutting like a knife.

"Save it, Effie," Kat said, and directed her attention to Philip. "I have your four favorite words, Philip," and she counted them out, thumb to each finger, "we – need – to – talk."

Without waiting for an answer, Kat charged at Philip with one hand out. Pushing against his chest, she drove him back into the office, using her other hand to slam the door behind them. Kat heard, "Hey!" from the other side of the door.

***

"Zip up your pants," Kat said, twisting the lock on the door.

Philip gave an embarrassed laugh. "Yeah, the *dictation* got a little a sidetracked."

She shoved past him and crossed behind the desk. "Yeah, that happens a lot with you. I'm not interested in continuing this conversation with you and your shadow," she said, nodding at his crotch.

"You used to be," he said with a pout as he tucked in his shirt and raised the zipper.

"What a difference finding a girl in the closet makes," Kat said.

"I'm only human, Kat."

"Jury's still out," she said, perusing the papers on his desk. "What are you doing now, hanging out at the bus terminal and telling them you're a talent agent?"

"Hey, no. She came on the Amtrak," he said. "You want to tell me what's on your mind, or you want to keep trying to read all of the stuff on my desk while you distract me."

Katerina picked up a paper from his desk, scanning it. "I'm here to check in. Since we're partners and all, and I haven't heard from you, and you're concerned Abe took on another client and that client stole the negatives. How's your progress on that theory?"

"Kat, c'mon," Philip said and moved to muscle her out of the way.

"What's the matter, Philip," she said, holding her arm out, keeping the paper out of his reach, "something you don't want me to see? We're working on this together, right? You wouldn't be holding out on me?"

"Of course not," he said.

"You didn't tell Honest Abe about the package of negatives you mailed to your Boston office, did you?"

Philip laughed. "Still underestimating me, hunh?"

Katerina answered with a narrowed look.

"No," he said. "I don't have any idea how someone found out about those negatives at my office."

Kat froze. *Amtrak?*

"Oh, Philip, you really are a schmuck."

"What? What now?"

"Amtrak? Paark the caaar in the yaaard? That's the bimbo from your Boston office? You transferred her?"

Philip raised his arms in surrender. "Look, I didn't have enough work to keep both offices open, obviously. I felt bad, you know, closing up, putting her out of work. She's a good secretary – not as good as you, of course. You're the best, Kat. You weren't a secretary. You were an *assistant.* I never had an assistant like you."

Katerina made a noise of disgust. "Save your word salad. Did she tell you about the day the package disappeared?"

"I went over it with her a dozen times. She doesn't really remember ––"

Katerina rolled her eyes and went for the door, Philip on her heels.

Throwing open the door, the secretary scrambled to get away from the door.

"Did you get everything, Carla? Anything you want me to repeat?" Kat asked.

"My name is Brenda."

"Who cares?" Kat answered. "The day the package disappeared, what happened in the office?"

"Kat, I told you. Look, Brenda, she's just trying to help me."

Brenda sighed and pouted her annoyance. "Nothin' happened. It was a regular day."

"Regular day. Who came into the office?"

She rolled her eyes. "Nobody. I told him. No appointments. Nobody."

Kat nodded her head. "Okay, so you didn't have lunch delivered, the postman never rang twice, no packages for pickup."

Brenda stared at Katerina. "Oh, well, yeah. The postman came, and a courier came for an express envelope pickup."

"Who was he with? Fedex, UPS?"

"Who remembers? He wore a uniform."

Katerina shot Philip a look of annoyance. "Okay, *Brenda,* I can see you're *wicked smaht,* so, let's try to concentrate, okay? The usual guys? The usual postman? The usual package guy?"

Brenda looked to Philip. "The postman was the same. I don't remember seeing the package guy before."

"What did he look like?"

"I don't know. He was a nobody, like you forget him as soon as you see him."

"Short, tall, fat, thin," Kat pressed.

The secretary shrugged. "All of it, none of it. He was like a blob, you know?"

"What does that mean?" Kat turned to Philip. "What does that mean?"

Philip shrugged as an answer.

"There was nothin' there. It all mixed together, a head that blended into the body, you know, a blob."

"His face?"

Brenda screwed up her face as if thinking about it caused her physical pain. Kat expected smoke to billow out of her ears at any moment.

"It was kind of, smushed, you know? Like I said, everything all together. Like he didn't have a face. It was just glasses and a moustache. You couldn't see anything."

Katerina rolled her eyes and went for the door.

Philip caught up to her, jamming his foot in the door to keep it open.

"Kat —"

Katerina turned around. "Better not be holding out on me, Philip."

"I'm not, I wouldn't," he insisted. "As soon as I know anything, you're my first call."

"Uh-hunh," she said and turning on her heel, walked away down the hall.

***

Kat stopped at a drugstore, purchased a new burner phone, and dialed a number.

"Yo."

"Yo, yourself, Rebel One," Kat said. "What are you doing?"

"Chillin' like a villain."

Katerina had come across April, or as Kat knew her, Rebel One, courtesy of MJM client Lester Callahan. Lester made his living on the bottom rung of the criminal food chain and needed his identity erased on his way out of town. April, whose talents included juvenile delinquency and computer hacking, had obliged. Kat had hired April to erase her before Kat and Winter jettisoned the US for Europe and a new life together. Before April could get the job done, everything had gone wrong.

April hadn't been able to complete Kat's second assignment either, collect William Mills' laptop, hack it, find the hidden bank accounts, and drain them. A long, hard winter and one New York cop had gotten in the way.

The laptop remained hidden in a storage locker in Moose's Queens chop shop.

In Kat's mind, if she got the money, that meant she would be paying Keyes for bringing Winter home. That meant Winter would be coming home. That meant she and Winter would still make a getaway, get lost, and disappear for good.

"What's the sich?" April asked.

"The *sich* is we're back on," Kat said.

"Let's go, I'm ready."

"I need to find a way to get the thing over to you. Are you local to me?"

"No, I'm east."

Shit, Kat thought. With April back on Long Island, that complicated matters. Kat gave a few full-throated coughs she couldn't control.

"You sick?"

"No," Kat snapped. "I'll get the thing to a mailbox store. You pick up the thing and do your thing, understand?"

"You got any intel I can use? Username, password?"

"No, none of that. Is that going to be a problem?"

"Nah, I can brute force it, but . . ."

She didn't hear anything.

"But what? I paid you in advance," Kat said, chafing at the thought of another screwup or screwing over.

"No, no, I was thinking – if I'm coming there to get it, why don't I just stay there? I could stay at your –"

"No," Kat said.

"I didn't even finish."

"Because I know what you're going to say," Kat said. "No."

"Yeah, well, then that's gonna be a problem."

Kat stopped walking. "What's the problem?"

"I'm sorta between domiciles right now," April said.

"What happened to the money I gave you?" Kat demanded.

"That was *five* months ago."

Kat frowned. "The boyfriend?"

"Ass," April mumbled.

Katerina gave a sigh, considering the immediate risks. "Fine, I'll let you know where to get the thing. I'll leave a spare key. Pick it up, and you can stay at the apartment."

"I need money for the train," April said.

"Shit," Kat said. She moved over to huddle close to a building and rummaged in her purse. She pulled out the few bills she had. The cop watched every purchase, every dollar. "I'll figure it out."

"I can score a credit card –"

"No!" Kat said. "Do not do that. Give me a few hours. And I need you to do something else. Take down this number," and she recited the phone number from the sticky note. "I want you to find who it belongs to."

"Shouldn't we discuss an amended fee?" April asked.

"Sure, right after we discuss the price of the rent for staying in my apartment."

"Never mind," she heard April say.

Kat clicked off the call. The number was a five one eight area code. *Albany.* April would find out who Philip was talking to.

Kat checked her cell phone.

Shit. Out of time.

Back to Brooklyn.

Back to work tomorrow.

The detectives had been in the building for several days, arriving early in the morning, staying all day, and making a nuisance of themselves with special requests. As Detective Walter Lashiver wandered the hallways, he passed the employees in their cubes, felt the curious glances, and heard the hushed whispers; he knew they had done their job well. The constant irritation, like a pebble in a shoe, would hopefully bear fruit: John Reynolds would make a mistake.

Lashiver approached a woman hanging on a corner of a cube divider, chatting with the person sitting in the cube. Flashing his badge and a non-threatening smile, he interrupted the conversation with, "Excuse me, I'm looking for a Douglas Mathison. Could you point me in the right direction?"

"Doug? Sure, he's over in the conference room."

"Thank you," Lashiver said, and following her pointed finger like the Ghost of Christmas Yet to Come, he went off down the hallway.

***

The conference room had glass walls and contained an oblong table, executive leather chairs, and an oversized flat screen mounted on the wall. The screen displayed seven boxes, each containing a face.

While talking to the screen, Doug Mathison stood, the remote in his hand. Spotting Lashiver at the conference room door, he waved the remote to come inside. As he entered, Lashiver took in the screen, the boxes, the faces, some looking straight into the camera, other faces sharing the box with a piece of a desktop or laptop, and still others staring down at . . . something.

"Okay," Doug said, "I'll send out the invite and we'll circle back on this at the end of the week. Thanks, everyone." He pointed the remote at the screen and with a click, the faces disappeared.

"Mr. Mathison," Lashiver said, "we spoke on the phone. Detective Lashiver."

"Yeah, sure, of course, I remember," Mathison answered, showing a mouthful of snow-white teeth. He wore a white shirt, black slacks, and a red tie. He cut an unimposing figure; medium height with a full face and a thickening middle from driving a desk. "Good timing."

Mathison came around the table and pumped Lashiver's offered hand. "I remember seeing you last year, but I spoke with someone else after it happened," he said.

Mathison took a seat and leaned back in his chair as if he were sitting around with a co-worker shooting the shit and wasting time.

Lashiver took the seat next to Mathison and swiveled his chair to face him. "That was my partner," he said.

"That's right." Mathison shook his head. "Still looking, hunh? Crazy that somebody could do this."

Lashiver took out his notepad and a pen. "We're re-interviewing, switching up the interviewer, checking to see if we missed something."

Mathison nodded. "Sure, sure, go ahead."

"The day Mrs. Reynolds was killed, there was a conference call."

Mathison nodded, cutting in, "Yeah, sure."

"And you were on the call."

"Ya," Mathison nodded.

"But you didn't take the call with Mr. Reynolds in his office or in this conference room," Lashiver said, as if reading from the pad.

"No, I mean, yes, we were both on the call, but that day I was in here and he was in his office."

Lashiver looked up. "But, you usually would take a call with Mr. Reynolds, together, either in his office or in this conference room."

Mathison swiveled his chair, thinking. "Depends. We used to take all the conference calls in here. But, the boss is a busy guy. He started taking them in his office."

"When did that start? If you remember," Lashiver said.

"Last year."

"Early in the year, late in the year. . .?"

Mathison gave it some thought. "I would say after Labor Day."

"And you take all your conference calls in here."

Mathison made a face and bobbed his head, thinking. "It depends on what the schedule is, how many meetings there are."

"What about the day Mrs. Reynolds was killed?"

More nodding. "I had three calls that day, so I basically set up shop in here and just stayed."

Lashiver pointed at the screen with his pen.

"So, Mr. Reynolds was in one of those boxes? Instead of coming up and sitting with you in here. Sorry, I don't deal with a lot of tech, you know. I'm just an old school cop."

Mathison smiled and nodded. "Like I said. He's the boss. He's gotta multi-task, you know?"

Lashiver pointed at the screen. "Some of those people were multi-tasking, hunh?"

"You see the faces, the ones looking down? Don't get me wrong, they're listening, but they could be answering emails, text messages, working on something."

"A couple of them, I thought their lips were moving," Lashiver said.

"Sure, you can take calls, people do it all the time. You just mute yourself."

Lashiver nodded. "How do you know they're doing work for the company? I mean, how do you know it's not personal stuff?"

Mathison laughed. "You don't."

"Everybody does that? Mr. Reynolds does that?"

"We *all* do that," Mathison said. "You have to. These calls can last an hour, sometimes more. You take two or three of these in a day, nothing's getting done."

"Sure, sure," Lashiver said. "How can you tell if someone is on mute?"

"Oh, there's a small icon you see on the screen. You see the face in the box and then there's a little picture of a microphone and there's a line through it."

Lashiver closed his pad and gave a friendly smile. "T's are crossed, I's are dotted. My lieutenant will be satisfied." He rose from his chair. "Thanks very much for your time."

Doug Mathison stood up and extended his hand. "No problem, anytime."

They shook hands.

***

Lashiver left the conference room thinking about those little boxes, each with their own face, some looking into the camera, some staring down. Looking at what, he wondered. *Their phones.* He thought of Elizabeth, Reynolds' secretary. *Didn't she say her boss always took his conference calls in his office? Except, he didn't. He used to take his conference calls in the conference room. Until last year. Until a month before his wife was murdered.*

The life of a busy CEO required an assistant who could keep up with a man who had everywhere to be and everyone there waiting upon him. Thomas Gallagher's life required two assistants. Depending on the day's priorities, he changed his itinerary at will, leaving them scrambling to keep up, or even locate him. He could start his morning in New York and by dinnertime, he would be in Paris or the UAE.

In a career marked by exactitude, Primary Assistant Nicole Lovel had prided herself on knowing her employer's every move, domestic and international. Not so, at Eagleton Corp. She knew her employer began his day early, as most successful executives did. She could call his cell phone at four-thirty in the morning and find him already awake and working in his home office. However, Thomas Gallagher's calendar displayed a mosaic of colored boxes with one word: Busy. Early on, she had learned she would not know everything about her mercurial, secretive boss. After a while, Nicole decided it had been a blessing.

That morning, Gallagher had arrived at the office with his cell phone at his ear. After a meeting, Nicole raised her head at the snick of his office door opening.

"Mrs. Lovel, would you alert Tillman that I'm ready to leave," Gallagher said.

"He's waiting for you downstairs," she said, standing to perform the ritual of handing him his files for the next meeting and seeing him out of the executive suite.

"Mrs. Lovel, you anticipate my every need," he said with a smile as he took the files. "If anything should come up . . ."

"You'll be the first to know," Nicole said, giving her usual quip in the familiar conversation.

Nicole Lovel watched him stride out. The calendar box for today had been blank. She didn't believe it for one minute. And somehow, she felt grateful she had no idea where Thomas Gallagher was headed next.

***

Gallagher conducted his business by phone as he relaxed in the back of his limousine, its dark, tinted windows shielding him from the rest of the world. Once he had Katerina in his grasp, she would be the passenger in the vehicle as it spirited her to the Long Island estate. She would stay there for a time.

There is a book . . .

He put the thought out of his mind. That part of his past was long gone. He was not like his partners. He felt a pang of discomfort for all that Katerina had endured. All unnecessary. Last year, he had sent the two operatives to the Canadian border to retrieve her. Masquerading as FBI agents, they would have taken her into custody with quiet efficiency . . . if Alexander Winter had not interfered. If it had not been for him, Katerina could have been spared all the needless suffering. Gallagher decided the blame fell squarely on the Professor's shoulders.

While he had contented himself at the beginning that Katerina would be a rare treat he had been missing: a challenge, he had grown impatient – and annoyed, at the continuing delays. He now thought of this as an acquisition. He had to. Otherwise, he would not maintain the proper perspective to avoid foolish actions based on emotion. Yes, an acquisition – a hard-fought and hard-won acquisition that would be precious to him. And he vowed again to treat Katerina that way. After all, who knew her better than he? After all the time he had waited to take hold of her, he would treat her as a treasured possession. But he would also treat her with kindness and respect, as a wife and companion. Not as his partners had done with their wives, concealing their true nature and their peculiar activities.

Still, the acquisition had been underway for almost six months. In business, the longer it took to complete a takeover, the more doubtful it would come to pass. Gallagher rejected the possibility. He had learned long ago that life was a long game, and a man must have patience to succeed. He refused to consider any other outcome.

He felt the limousine pull over to the curb and idle in park. A smile curved at the corner of his lips as the weight of the car shifted, the driver getting out. The back passenger door opened, and he saw the young woman, the blush of excitement on her face.

"My dear," Gallagher said, as Mina climbed into the vehicle and into his arms. "I had begun to think you had no time for me, now that the semester is coming to an end."

She shook her head. "No, of course not. I mean – of course I do." And she leaned in for a kiss.

When they parted, he smiled at her, showing his teeth. "I thought perhaps you and your school friend, what was her name, the one from the law class?"

"Katerina?"

"Yes. I thought perhaps you two had conspired to run off to Europe together."

"I would never leave you," she said, holding him tighter.

"Is she helping you prepare for your final?"

"I'm helping her."

"Of course you are."

"We've had a few study sessions . . . but I think she's having problems with her boyfriend."

"Why do you say that?"

"She doesn't look well. She can't seem to focus. She's been sick a lot."

"I see. You must continue to be a good friend to her. At these study sessions, encourage her to confide in you. If she needs help, who better or kinder than you?"

Mina stared down at the floor and shrugged her shoulders. "There's a guy in the class, he comes to the study sessions, too. He likes her. I think he wants to talk to her, alone."

"I see. But she needs her friend, who will truly care about her. She needs *you*. You mustn't give up, my dear Mina. I don't believe it is an accident that you met Katerina. We are drawn into the path of people who need us. You must do all that you can to help her."

Mina's eyes clouded with anxiety. "I will, I promise. I have a lot I want to tell you. You listen to me."

"I am flattered you confide in me. I want to hear all of it, my dear. We'll have a nice, private lunch, and you'll tell me every-thing."

Gallagher lifted her chin with a gentle touch.

"I love you," he said, watching Mina's face light up like Christ-mas morning. "Do you love me?"

Mina threw her arms around him.

"I love you," she said. "I'll do anything for you."

"I know you will." He whispered in her ear. "Don't tell me, show me."

Mina maneuvered herself onto her knees between his legs.

At Thomas Gallagher's instruction in January, Joseph Smith had investigated every female student in Katerina's classes until he found the ideal candidate. Mina ticked every box: an absent or disinterested family, a tentative, shy personality, and a textbook case of low self-esteem mixed with a desperation to be loved. Smith did well, Gallagher thought as he looked down at the easy conquest. She had been quite useful. He had listened to those study sessions with careful attention. The young man, the law student, did indeed want to talk to Katerina Mills alone. An excellent idea. And this girl would help make it happen.

Later in the afternoon, Thomas Gallagher sat in a wingback armchair, considering the glass of brandy in his hand. He smiled as he listened to the familiar monologue from the man standing by the cold fireplace, one elbow perched on the mantel.

The gentleman's club hadn't changed in a hundred years. It reminded Gallagher of the library in the Hamptons mansion. He had entered that room years earlier, a lifetime ago, as a green, junior executive. A place where his partners had made decisions that affected millions, even billions of lives. Now, he was one of those men.

Gallagher listened to his drinking companion.

"The American people have had their fill of public drama and loud falls from grace. They want quiet. They want to return to peaceful prosperity."

"The American people can be quite particular about what they want," Gallagher said.

The man chuckled. "Safety, security, a little extra spending money so they can feel rich. They want good news, wrapped in an attractive package."

"And you are just the man for such a season."

Governor Richard Haley smiled.

Gallagher knew that Haley had lived a charmed life, skating by on his easygoing nature mixed with Rat Pack cool. His voice had a deep, sonorous tone, intimate, as if the conversation were taking place in a darkened bedroom. He made love to everyone he spoke to. No problem was too great, no situation was beyond his control.

He had breezed into the Governor's mansion. What appeared easy and unrehearsed had been a well-conceived, multi-year plan in the making, all leading to the bombshell announcement in January: a run for the Presidency.

"I congratulate you on your foresight," Gallagher continued. "You are the presumptive nominee, although it's still eight weeks to the convention. One must be careful there are no . . . complications."

Haley's smile came out thin-lipped, the cool image and affable nature slipping. The world knew of Haley's wayward daughter, Destiny, a party girl splashed across Page Six. Thomas Gallagher knew what lay underneath, away from the cameras: the dissipated wild child enjoyed attending invitation only secret gatherings where every sexual appetite, vice, and excess, had been indulged.

The Governor had parlayed the prodigal daughter into a public relations success when she had reappeared in January, tucked back into the mansion safe and sound. Gallagher knew the truth: Haley, having just banished his own fixer, had engaged the services of MJM Consulting for the retrieval; the hired consultant, Lisa, had brought in a partner at Gallagher's instruction: Katerina Mills.

"I predict smooth sailing," Haley pronounced, ignoring Gallagher's comment. "The convention is a formality. I'm already thinking of my cabinet. There's a place for you."

"No, thank you. I prefer to stay behind the scenes."

"In that case, I'll put you on the invite list for the fundraiser at Millicent Satler's. A small, select gathering."

Gallagher swirled the liquid in his drink. "What's the going rate for behind the scenes support these days?"

"Fifty million," Haley said without hesitation. "To the super PAC of your choice. I am nothing if not a staunch and loyal friend to business. And I always show my appreciation to my friends."

Gallagher took a last swallow of his drink. "I'll consider it, of course. As long as you have everything under control."

"Completely."

"I'm glad to hear it," Gallagher said. He thought of the Governor's optimism as amusing considering Katerina's recorded conversations. Haley should have counted himself fortunate the fool lawyer and his photographer had stuck to the old ways. If they had chosen a digital format, the situation would have blown up months ago. A thought nagged at Gallagher, the same thought that had been bothering him for some time. He wanted to take possession of Katerina as soon as possible – yet he had no doubt Katerina had the talent and ingenuity to find the incriminating negatives. If she found the negatives . . . *I will own President Richard Haley.*

"To a successful election," Gallagher said, and he raised his glass to the future President.

As he raised his glass in turn, Haley sported that same relaxed, easy smile on his lips.

***

When Governor Richard Haley returned to his office, his special assistant, Raymond George, greeted him with a revised itinerary and an anxious expression. A small, tidy, exact man with wire-rimmed glasses, George clutched a leather-bound document folder to his chest. With a nod, Haley entered his office, Raymond George following behind.

When the door closed, Haley stood behind his desk, waiting. Raymond George approached, opened the folder, and presented a sheet of paper. Haley snapped the paper out of George's hand, reading the typed message.

I KNOW WHAT YOU DID
WANNA SEE THE PICTURES?
ONE MILLION DOLLARS
LEAVE RESPONSE IN NEWSPAPER
ON BENCH IN MADISON SQUARE PARK
THURSDAY AT 10 P.M.
OR YOU CAN SEE THEM
WITH EVERYONE ELSE
ON THE FRONT PAGE

"Perhaps you should consider calling Mr. Kelly?"

Haley gave a tight smile. "He's out of the picture. Permanently. Let me think about this."

"Sir, they're demanding a response by tomorrow."

"Stall. Confirm receipt, we'll be in touch, making arrangements, we need something to show good faith, it takes time, the usual."

"Yes, sir, I will enter negotiations and prolong as long as possible."

Raymond George left the room, leaving Haley with his thoughts.

A complication.

This was the second time. It had started late last year. Then it had stopped, as if the person had dropped off the face of the earth.

Now, they're back.

Or is this someone new?

On a Saturday evening, at a sidewalk table, Kat and Ryan sat opposite Emma Flynn and her fiancé, Detective Frank Mitchell. The two men were opposite in appearance: Frank, sandy-haired and heavily muscled, Ryan, dark-haired and lean, had earned a gold shield and Medal of Valor rushing into a robbery and hostage situation together, saving lives and sustaining injuries.

After a neighbor's phone call to nine one one in March had brought uniformed officers to the Brooklyn apartment, Frank and Emma had showed up as well. Emma had taken Kat to a corner of the apartment while the boys in blue spoke to Ryan outside in the hallway. Frank had stayed behind while Kat spent the night with Emma. After that, the soon-to-be-married couple took it upon themselves to watch over their best man and maid of honor. The dinner meetups had been part of the intervention, the engaged couple modeling proper, loving behavior while guarding against another incident.

Kat watched Emma, her hand on Frank's arm, then stroking the back of his head, giving him a plaintive look with those large, brown eyes when she wanted to switch plates because she preferred what he ordered. Emma handled Frank like her favorite thing in all the world. Frank responded by draping his arm behind

Emma's back, giving her gentle caresses between accepting a forkful of his own meal as she fed him.

The tender scenes only inflamed Kat's anger. *I know how to do these things. I should be doing them now. With Winter.*

I need to talk to Rebel One about the phone number. I need to be searching for those photo negatives, not wasting time sitting here. I should be calling Carter to find out where his half-brother is. Did Keyes find Winter? Is the killer dead? Is he bringing Winter home? I'm losing time.

Katerina came back to the moment as Emma pressed her for bridal shower details. "So, when are you going to tell me?"

"All I'm going to tell you," Kat said, "is to keep your Friday nights open at the end of July. There will be more information to come."

Emma sat back. "Hon, bridal showers are held in the daytime."

"Not according to Martha Stewart," Kat countered.

Emma shook her head. "Hon, you are something. Okay. You, I'm not so sure about, but Martha, I trust."

Katerina nodded and gave Ryan an artless smile.

She's right. Don't trust me.

***

After dinner, Emma and Katerina walked arm in arm, ahead of the men. Kat had struggled to keep an ear on the cop shoptalk during dinner. *Patience, Katerina. That's what Winter always says.*

"Everything good with you, hon?" Emma asked.

Katerina tiptoed around the grenade of a question. "Fine."

Emma gave Kat's arm a squeeze. "It's the case, you know. That rich guy and his dead wife."

"I feel bad for him that he can't close it."

"It looks like things are gonna turn around now, thank God. See, you don't even know. Maybe you should tell him how you feel," Emma said. "That'll go a long way."

Katerina's lips pursed; she settled for nodding. *How is the case going to turn around? What's happened?*

"I know this is hard for you," Emma said.

"What is?" Katerina asked.

"Don't be obtuse with me, hon," Emma said. "I remember when you first came to the city. You were a magnet for all kinds of trouble, like working for Philip, remember?" she said, lowering her voice.

"Uh-hunh," Kat said, wishing Emma would let that train of thought go.

"You never had to find trouble; it would come looking for you. Now, you've got a real chance to live a normal life, with peace and quiet. It's hard to get used to, but you will. It's just been a rough patch because of the case. Ryan wants the best for you. His heart's in the right place."

Too bad his fist is usually in the wrong place. "I know," Kat said. There was nothing else to do. She couldn't disagree and she couldn't make it stop. *Just wait for this to be over. Eventually, it must end.*

What happened with the case?

At the corner, the men caught up and everyone exchanged hugs and kisses. Frank gave Kat a peck on the cheek, his eyes still sharp with suspicion and mistrust. Katerina pretended not to notice.

Katerina slipped her hand inside of Ryan's and gave him a sweet smile as they walked back toward the apartment.

***

A man and a woman return home from dinner with friends. In the tiny apartment, she sidesteps, keeping out of his way before they bump into each other. She hugs the wall; the same wall he shoved her against two days ago. Before he hit her in a place no one will see, for an offense she doesn't remember. What she remembers is the burst of pain like a firecracker exploding inside her, the snap of her head, the flashes of multi-colored stars before her eyes, the dull haze of confusion in her brain.

Katerina realized she had slipped outside of herself again, becoming a spectator. She forced herself to face the task at hand: what is the break in the case?

Did you go to Sunday School?

The sound of the low gravel of Winter's voice in her head jolted Katerina. She busied herself searching the closet for a change of clothes, stealing precious seconds to stay in the moment.

Yes, Professor.

Do you remember the story of Sampson?

Pretty concubine lulls imbecile with Vidal Sassoon hairdo and a huge ego into spilling his guts. He takes a nap and gets the buzz cut of all buzz cuts.

That wasn't the point of the story.

What is the point of the story, Professor?

Flatter a man and he likes to talk.

Flatter him more and he'll talk more.

"I like that oversized tissue you've got in your hand," Kat heard from behind.

She turned, holding the filmy, flimsy cloth in her hand. "I take requests," she said. "How about a glass of wine for a nightcap?"

"Sounds good," he says.

That's right. Sampson never says no to a drink. He talks when he drinks. Before the slamming starts, before the hitting begins, he talks.

I need you to talk.

Ryan settled on the floor, leaning against the couch behind him. Her stomach roiling, Kat set the glasses, bottle, and chocolate bar on the coffee table; she filled the glasses and then held out one glass to him. She sat down and broke off two pieces from the chocolate bar. Leaning against him, an easy smile on her face, she held out a piece. He opened his mouth, and she fed him.

He kissed her temple. "Chocolate kiss for you," he said.

She leaned against his shoulder. "I hope you enjoyed dinner. You were having a good talk with Frank. Is everything going okay with the case?"

He nodded as he took a swallow of wine. "We may have caught a break. There's another body, a woman, in Queens."

"When did this happen?"

"Yesterday. The detective who caught the case recognized some similarities and gave us a call. We're waiting for the reports."

Kat sat up, careful to keep what she knew would be a blank expression. "You think this rich guy, this Reynolds, killed someone in Queens?"

Ryan shook his head. "He didn't do it. He didn't do any of them. He knows who did, because he sent this person to do it."

"He sent someone to kill a woman in Queens?"

Ryan nodded. "I don't know how, where, when, or why, but yeah, he did."

"How do you get him to admit it?"

Ryan took another swallow of wine, snaking his arm around her shoulder. "I've been thinking about this for a while. I mean, we always knew he had someone doing this for him. *I* knew it. Where did he get this guy? Where's he been hiding him? This isn't a professional for hire – this is someone personally working for John Reynolds."

Katerina stared at him in rapt attention, stroking a lock of his hair and tucking it behind his ear. *Yes, and you won't find him because you think he's dead. He's a ghost.*

"So, how do you find this person?" she asked.

"That's just it. The question isn't why did it happen now, but what happened up until now? This is the first time this lunatic has done this? No way. There's a trail out there, somewhere. Has to be."

Okay, Sampson. Show me goddamn smart you are.

"What do you do with Reynolds in the meantime? What do you tell him?"

"There's two ways to do it. You can tell them everything you know, and it's the truth, and you overwhelm him. Or you tell him what you *want* him to think."

"You're allowed to lie to a suspect?"

Ryan nodded. "Absolutely. I can tell a suspect anything I want. And the more I pile on, the more nervous the suspect will get. The last thing a person should do is open their mouth. But they can't help it. They want to defend themselves, and that's how they get into trouble."

C'mon, flatter him. Let Sampson tell his tale. He wants to.

"So, which one will you pick?"

"I would pick door number two. Tell him whatever it takes. We found new evidence, we're about to make a major breakthrough in the case. But, I don't make the final decision."

"If everyone agrees, what do you think he'll do?"

"Panic. If we watch and wait, he'll slip up and reach out to this guy to warn him."

"Didn't you tell me you've been going to his building all the time? What's that about?"

"The employee interviews? That was just bullshit, something to annoy the shit out of him, get him off his game."

Kat sat back and took a sip of wine. "Smart cop," she said.

Ryan gave a shit-eating grin.

Kat smiled while her stomach turned. She got the information, but she still had to fulfill Reynolds' assignment, and the time had come.

"We'll make a good team when I'm on the other side," she said, parroting their first conversation. "Just like you said. You'll make the arrests, and I'll prosecute."

Ryan laughed. "That's never gonna happen," he said, and took another swallow of wine.

Katerina regarded him with a blank look even as she died inside. The opening she had been waiting for. She had no choice but to go through with it.

"C'mon Kate," he said. "Law school is a dream. You can't do that, and you know it. You're barely making it through the semester."

"Because I got sick," Kat said, and it came out with a sharp tone.

"You don't have a pot to piss in, and we're not goin' into hock for you to go to law school. You won't finish anyway. You know how hard that is? You can't do that."

Katerina felt the disconnect between her brain and the anger boiling inside her.

"It'll be good to have the summer for a break."

He laughed and said, "A break. It's gonna be more than a break."

Ryan gazed at her, his pupils turning black with desire. He took her glass out of her hand and set both glasses down on the coffee table.

"Now," he said, "how about we forget about school and talk about a real dessert."

Kat faced forward, her stomach somersaulting.

"Oh what, you're gonna sulk now? You're gonna ruin the evening over this stupidity?"

"I don't think my career is stupidity," Kat said, caught in the whirlwind. It had to play out now. It had to finish.

"You don't have a career, Kate. You never did."

Kat got to her feet. "I don't want to talk about —"

The searing pain of his grip shot through her arm. One yank and her legs went out from under her. She landed hard on her tailbone and let out a cry.

His hand squeezed like a vise. "Keep it down," he ordered.

"I don't think Frank and Emma had this in mind for dessert," Kat said through gasping breaths.

Ryan shook his head and let go. "Fine," he said. Getting up, he grabbed the wine bottle. "You want to go through with your finals, go ahead. It's a waste of time. You want to go to law school, go ahead. Enjoy yourself. Let me know when you figure out how to pay for it."

Ryan stormed off to the bedroom, muttering under his breath and slamming the door behind him.

Her body curled in pain; Katerina shifted to put her weight on one hip. She didn't know how long she sat there until she attempted to shift again and raise herself to sit on the couch.

***

In the darkness, Katerina heard the snoring sounds from the next room; Ryan passed out from the wine. She shifted off the couch, each halting step toward the table bringing fresh pain. She rifled the backpack and reviewed the notepad, committing each detail to memory for her next meeting with Reynolds. Right now, Reynolds' lunatic had – might have – Winter in his clutches. How long could he hold out? Her mind spoke the words, and her heart ached; a pain worse than she had ever felt at Ryan's hand. *Alex. Please hold on. Help is coming. I promise help is coming. Hold on.*

The meeting with Charles Penn started off unpleasant and Ryan and Lashiver couldn't blame the widower one bit. Charles Penn had not offered his hand to shake or a seat for the detectives to sit in, and his anger, once thinly veiled, was on full display.

"Mr. Penn, we just want you to know this remains an active case," Lashiver said.

"Thank you for coming by, detectives, but really, if you have nothing to share, don't feel the need to return. Since your update, that you have no update, won't be bringing my wife back from the dead, there's no point, don't you think?"

"Yes, sir, we understand," Ryan said.

"You understand?" Charles Penn said, his emotions welling over. "Do you know what I understand, detective? I understand that even if you catch this, this animal, even if he is put in prison with no chance of parole, none of it will bring back my wife. Nothing I say, nothing I do, will ever bring her back. Nothing." He stopped, forcing himself to take a breath before continuing. "I assure you, there is nothing about this you understand."

"We visited with John Reynolds, and we wanted to extend you the same courtesy," Lashiver said.

"I'm not interested in any courtesy extended to John Reynolds."

"So, you haven't spoken to Mr. Reynolds," Ryan fished.

"I have no occasion to speak with John Reynolds."

"Did you two have some kind of falling out? Business deal go wrong?" Lashiver asked.

"Detectives, I am not in business with, nor do I share any business interests with John Reynolds. I know of him, and what I know I do not care for. I have told his office to relay the message to stop contacting me. I have no interest in being involved with his foundation."

Ryan Kellan flinched at the comment, his antenna up. "John Reynolds approached you about a joint foundation?"

"Yes, he did. Let me repeat myself, I have no interest in Mr. Reynolds or his foundation. I will honor my wife in my own way. Now, please, see yourselves out."

***

Ryan and Lashiver exited the office building, leaving the frigid air conditioning behind in exchange for the blazing noonday heat. They walked in silence to the car, getting in, and slamming the doors.

"Okay," Ryan began, "you tell me. Why would John Reynolds call Charles Penn and ask him to come into a joint foundation."

Lashiver sat in the driver's seat, staring straight ahead. "Shoring up his reputation as the grieving widower. Penn provides cover, throws off suspicion."

Ryan nodded. "Yeah, but what if there's more?"

Lashiver turned to his partner. "Like what?"

"Like, you know how Reynolds gave me that story how he wants to know every detail of his wife's death so he could appeal for the death penalty as punishment? Bullshit. Total bullshit. He enjoyed hearing about his wife's suffering. Maybe he wants to watch Charles Penn suffer in his mourning."

"Penn said he had nothing to do with John Reynolds. So, what does Reynolds have against Charles Penn?"

"Good question," Ryan said. "All I'm saying is Cheryl Penn's murder started us thinking this could be a potential serial killer, nothing personal. Or maybe she was just a random target. What if she wasn't so random?"

"Reynolds and Penn don't know each other. Why would John Reynolds pick out Cheryl Penn? You said yourself, you spoke to the college friend. Cheryl and Felicia didn't know each other. They didn't run in the same circles. She wasn't helping Felicia sneak out to see her lovers. There's no connection between any of them. There's nothing there. You want to re-interview the friend?"

"She's off to Europe again."

"So, when she gets back, we'll talk to her, in person."

While Lashiver turned over the car engine and eased the car out into traffic, Ryan stewed in his thoughts. He knew now that John Reynolds had arranged the murder of Cheryl Penn.

Why?

CHAPTER

21

When Kat entered the apartment, she found April relaxing on the daybed, an open bag of chips in her lap. The girl was a cross between a goth and a punk rocker. She wore her jet-black hair chin length, accented with shocks of red and purple. Small rings jutted from her bottom lip and left nostril; a heart with a corkscrew stuck out from the fascia of her ear.

"Yo," April said. "I left breadcrumbs. Where have you been?"

"Tripping the light fantastic," Kat quipped.

April shrugged. "This is a nice place. I mean for a dump, it's a nice place. Sick threads."

Katerina's eyes flew open in panic. "Did you go in the bedroom?" she demanded.

"Where the hell am I supposed to sleep? The daybed is mid, you know?"

Katerina caught herself massaging the small of her back. "Fine, you can sleep in the bed but do not, and I mean do not, go into the dresser for any reason. Do – you – understand?"

"Yeah, I got it. I'm not peeking at your panties."

"This wasn't a good idea –"

"Oh, come on, just let me stay here," April said.

Standing in the middle of the apartment, Katerina flashed back to Winter standing with her, filling the space with his hard, fit body. A climber, that's what Emma would have said if she had ever met him. A big man, well-built, he was the kind of man you wanted to crawl into bed with and get to work, the best kind of work. But she found her memories choked away, replaced by a night in January. John Reynolds standing over her, issuing his ultimatum, his murderous maniac standing in the shadows.

Alex, I couldn't let him hurt my mother. I couldn't.

She would have had no chance.

I promised to protect you.

And I betrayed you.

Kat glanced toward the bedroom. She couldn't go in there. She couldn't open the top drawer to check underneath for the delicate, quartz, shell-shaped earrings outlined with diamonds set in yellow gold. Felicia Reynolds had pressed them into her hand that day last year in Saks. They were taped under the drawer; like a nuclear bomb, they could destroy everything if found. *And life as I know it, will end.*

"What's with the laptop?" Kat asked, forcing herself to break her train of thought.

April shoved off the daybed and sat in front of the laptop on the table.

"Working on it."

"Work faster."

"Yeah."

So, what about the number?"

"Albany," April said.

"No shit, Sherlock," Kat said.

"It belongs to a Cathy Lang. She's on the Governor's staff."

"How high up?"

"Somewhere above, 'Hey, you, whatever your name is, get me a coffee,' and a wannabe important person, twice removed. The voicemail message says Office of Administration. Whoever she is, she's a serf, but a serf who's a minor somebody."

No, she's the buffer. But to who?

"Is this her office line?"

"Cell phone."

Kat remembered the calls Philip would ask her to make. *Listen, kiddo, do it like we rehearsed. Use the code words I gave you. Understand?*

"Can you hack into the phone?"

April grinned. "Already done. She clicked on the link I sent. I own the phone now. I can see everyone she calls, everyone who calls her."

Katerina pulled out a small package from her purse, a spare burner phone she had purchased. She remembered every word of Philip's story in January about his foray into New York politics and crossing paths with Governor Haley. *So, I got an in, where I could meet him at a fundraiser. I did a few little favors for him, gained his trust. And then I got on to how he makes his arrangements.* Whoever was at the end of the cell phone had been in on the scheme to take the blackmail pictures. What had Tony Desucci said? *The lawyer. He's holding out on you.*

"Keep quiet while I make the call," she said to April.

Kat dialed the number, her heart pounding. With every ring, Kat's panic increased. What if the person on the other end wouldn't pick up because of the strange number? She held her breath and then the call clicked.

"Hello." The female voice sounded suspicious.

"I'm calling for Mr. White. He's very upset. He needs to speak to Mr. Brown immediately."

A click sounded. Katerina pulled the phone away and looked at it.

Shit. Philip changed the code names.

Kat dialed the number again.

The call connected and before Kat could say anything, she heard, "I don't know what you want, but you need to hang up now, and don't call again."

"That's not going to work. Mr. White and Mr. Brown had an agreement, and we have a situation. Mr. White obtained the product; however, he hasn't heard from Mr. Brown. Now, the product has conveniently disappeared, or should I say, stolen. Mr. Brown needs to be forthcoming and open about this situation. He needs to contact Mr. White immediately."

Katerina heard a laugh from the other end of the line. "I don't know what you're talking about. *Mr. Brown*, as you call him, isn't here anymore and has no connection to this administration. Don't call this number again and I advise you to tell *Mr. White* the same thing."

Katerina heard the call disconnect.

"Someone has seen Reservoir Dogs," April asked. "What was up with that?"

"Just the end of a beautiful friendship," Kat quipped. Whoever Cathy Lang was protecting, he or she wasn't part of the blackmail scheme. Another piece of a puzzle that didn't fit anywhere. But the photo negatives were still out there somewhere, and someone had them.

"Did she make another call?" Kat asked.

April watched the computer. "Nope. Text message."

Katerina hovered over her shoulder. "Find out who the number belongs to. Text me when you have it."

"I'm on it." April pointed to the knapsack on a chair. "You want the laptop at the same time?"

"You can't multi-task?"

April made a face. "Can you at least tell me who the laptop belonged to?"

Katerina grimaced at the thought. Out of desperation and a cancer diagnosis, William Mills had made the first of many mistakes by entrusting his laptop and the daily operation of his drug trade to the factory foreman, Richie Calico. Richie had carried on by screwing up the business, screwing over the hired transportation, and getting himself killed in the bargain. One hostile takeover and one dirty DEA agent later, and here we are, Kat thought. At least DEA agent James Sheridan had been scarce. Living with a New York cop had done that.

"My father," Kat said, still massaging her lower back.

"Why didn't you say so in the first place," April said. She grabbed a piece of paper and a pen and slapped them down on the table. "Write down his birthdate, social security number, hobbies, pet names, your birthday, if you have any siblings, their names and birthday, anything you can think of."

"Why?"

"Because most people are not creative with their passwords. They put in stuff they know they'll remember."

Kat sat down and started writing.

April considered Katerina. "You don't look so good? Did you hurt yourself?"

"I had an accident. I'm fine." Katerina put the pen down and stood up. "I'll come back again as soon as possible. Remember, don't bring anyone here."

"Who would I bring? I'm new in town, remember?"

"Don't make any friends," Kat said. "And don't open the door to anyone."

"No one comes here," April said.

Kat thought of a night last December. Agent James Sheridan at her door. . .

"Someone might," she said. "This wasn't a good idea—"

"It's fine. I'll get a baseball bat for protection, okay?" When Kat didn't answer, April said, "Do you want the laptop hacked or not?"

Katerina gave up the argument. "Just don't forget to —"

"—stay out of the bedroom dresser," April finished.

"Right."

As Kat went to leave, April called out, "Hey, this is a lot of extra work. I'm thinking we should negotiate my pay."

Katerina turned around. "I'm thinking you're getting housed and fed."

April sulked but said, "Yeah, okay, never mind."

"I'll call as soon as I can," Kat said and left the apartment, slamming the door behind her.

***

"In Casey versus State of New York, explain how the people were able to prove mens rea."

Mark held the card in his hand and waited for Mina's reply. Kat noted Mark had all but given up his, "Does she really need to be here?" attitude. A sliver of unease rippled through Katerina. *Yes, she does. She's the buffer.*

Kat struggled to pay attention as she glanced again at her phone, watching the interminable minutes creep by. One hour to the meeting with Reynolds. Fifty-seven minutes to the meeting with Reynolds. She listened to Mina give the canned answer to the question while she silently supplied her own. *In Casey versus the State of New York, the defendant was dumb enough to use his own credit card at a local gun shop and then he used his own phone on the day he committed the crime. The state was able to prove premeditation to commit the crime. If he had been smart like Alexander Winter, he would have used a pre-paid credit card and a burner phone. In conclusion, the defendant was a poor criminal and a moron.*

She came back to the conversation as Mina wound up her big finish. ". . . and the state was able to prove its case."

Mark nodded and put the card down. "Perfect," he said.

Mina downplayed her pride and focused on Katerina, reaching out and taking hold of her hand. "This has been so helpful, don't you think? I think it's been helpful."

"We're all going to be fine," Kat said. "We're all going to pass."

"I've been going to study groups all week," Mina went on. "I wish we could have studied French together, since you know it."

"I thought you were dropping that class."

"I was," Mina said. "I don't really like it, but my boyfriend might be taking me to Paris next year . . ." a flush came over Mina's complexion and her words cut off like the electricity had gone out.

"You never mentioned a boyfriend. Good for you," Kat said.

"Yeah, he's, he's amazing," Mina said. "He's—"

A cell phone buzzed. All three fumbled for their phones, but Mina came up the winner. "It's me," she said, as she brought the phone to her ear. "I'm so happy you called. Oh. yes," she said and listened. "Of course." Mina put the call on hold. "It's him," she said, her eyes bright with excitement. "I'll be back." She grabbed her purse, leaving her books behind as she fled the table.

Kat and Mark sat alone.

"She seems very happy with him," Mark said.

"I would say so. Especially since she just said, 'How high?' when he said jump." Kat caught the judgmental tone in her voice. "Maybe she's just excited."

"Sometimes, guys take advantage," Mark said. "Not every guy does that."

Katerina averted her eyes. A creeping discomfort came over her, an urgency that Mina should return as soon as possible.

"I'm going to be taking classes this summer. We could meet up, go to Starbucks, get a latte," Mark said, calling back to their time working together on a project the previous semester. "We can get a chance to talk. Really talk."

"I'm going to be in Brooklyn for the summer. Unless you're thinking of a day trip to Canarsie, we probably won't cross paths," Kat said.

"What happened to the summer session so you can graduate on time?"

Katerina couldn't hide her surprise that he had remembered an offhand comment she had made months ago.

"Sure, I remember," Mark said, reading her mind. "Why aren't you taking classes, Kat?"

"My boyfriend and I . . . we're having a bit of a disagreement over school . . ."

"He doesn't want you to go?"

Kat searched for the words but in the end, shook her head.

Mark reached out, placing his hand over hers. Her face warmed with fear, but his touch felt calm and kind. "Kat, you're one of the brightest people I've ever met. You can do anything you want. You shouldn't be with someone who doesn't appreciate you. Kat, if you need help . . . I care about you, I really do . . ."

His words hung between them as Kat tilted her head to find Detective Ryan Kellan standing in the aisle. He smiled. Kat's heart cracked as if a lightning bolt had struck. She whipped her hand away.

"Ryan," she said, hustling out of her chair to greet him with a kiss.

Ryan accepted her kiss on the cheek, while observing Mark with that same smile.

Approaching the table, he held out his hand. "How are you?" Ryan asked. "Detective Kellan. I'm the boyfriend."

"I'm the classmate," Mark said, rising and shaking hands. "We're cramming."

Ryan nodded. "I see that."

"Mina was with us," Kat said quickly, pointing to the third set of books on the table. "She had to take a call."

Ryan glanced at the empty chair and the books and then back at Mark. "So, Mark, what's your career path?" he asked.

Ryan listened to Mark's answer, nodding, engaged. Kat recognized the vacant cop look, the follow-up questions, the pumping for information. She didn't listen to the answers. *Reynolds. I won't get to Reynolds.*

"Environmental law. That's practically public service. Very nice. What are you doing in a criminal law class?"

"Just checking my motivation. Making sure it's still strong."

Ryan smirked as he nodded his head, looking toward Katerina. "I bet it is," he said. He offered Mark his hand again and they shook. "Well, thanks for helping Kate with her studies."

"I think she's helping me. She's really smart. You're lucky."

Ryan glanced at Katerina, a plastic smile on his face. "I certainly am."

***

They rode home in silence, except for Ryan's occasional snicker. A violent tremble had broken out within Katerina. It was coming. There would be no avoiding it. When she saw his usual parking spot pass by her window, her eyes closed. He turned onto a quiet, sleepy side street and eased the car into a spot, cutting the engine.

Kat released her seat belt and had her hand on the door handle when the blow struck her side. The stab of pain tore into her. She twisted away, but he held her with one hand as his other hand, balled into a fist, drove into her back again.

"You know, Kate, it's a good thing you're not a criminal. You'd be no good at it. You know why?" He leaned in close, whispering. "You're predictable. I knew you wouldn't be able to resist seeing him. Holding hands in the afterglow? Really? Did you screw him right there, in the back of the library, hunh?"

She shook her head. "We weren't alone," she gasped. "Mina was there."

He laughed. "You never get tired of lying," he said, and he delivered another blow. "You make me do these things, Kate. You bring it on yourself."

Kat made a noise, pursing her lips to stifle it. "Those were her books," she sputtered.

He looked around, checking. "Get out of the car."

"I can't," she said.

Ryan laughed. He put his hand on the back of her neck and squeezed. "Oh sure, I'll go upstairs, and you'll follow, right? You are never leaving me, you understand? There's nowhere you can go and nothing you can do. You are never getting away from me. Now get out of the car."

He got out of the car and slammed the door. Walking around, he opened the passenger door.

Katerina clung to the passenger car door. *The meeting with Reynolds. Reynolds knew the meeting wouldn't happen. He knew I would be with Mark. He knew Ryan would be coming. He knew it all. Why did Mina leave the table? The boyfriend? Reynolds. She's his new girlfriend. She has to be. He must have called her and told her to leave. Why? Because he's playing with me. He's playing with everyone.*

She sucked in a breath as he put his hand on her elbow and held her with a ginger touch, scanning from side to side for any-one who might be watching. She allowed herself to be helped from the car and closed her eyes as she forced herself to stand up straight and walk.

Alex. I'm sorry. Oh God, I'm sorry.

CHAPTER

22

Walter Lashiver shelled out the bills for the hotdogs and strolled down the sidewalk, Denis O'Connoll keeping stride with him.

"Gee, when you said you would pay for lunch, I didn't know we were going fancy again," O'Connoll said.

"I paid for the sauerkraut and the relish too, don't forget," Lashiver said. "So, what's the story?"

"Same story for six months. Good-looking kid, mediocre talent, playing around with a married woman, goes out one day, doesn't come back, and turns up dead. That's what I got. That's what I always had. A body in the rain."

Lashiver chewed on his hotdog.

"The kid's parents are calling me every day. They insist their son wouldn't kill himself. What'd you dig up?"

"Reynolds has an ex-wife. The divorce is sealed. She talks, he stops paying. She's got a lawyer who says forget it. She's got nothing to say. It was a long shot anyway. She's still alive."

"What do you hear on the vic in Queens?"

"Hooker." Lashiver said.

"Doesn't exactly match the profile of the two female victims."

"No, but the initial reports show similarities in the wound patterns. They're doing some more tests."

O'Connoll nodded. They continued walking, eating, and thinking. They both felt it; a guilty man was walking free. What they needed to prove it was out there, somewhere, and they couldn't find it. Or it was staring them in the face, and they didn't see it.

"Where's your partner?" O'Connoll asked.

"Called out today."

They stopped at the corner and threw their napkins in a garbage can.

"You called this meeting when your partner just happens to be out," O'Connoll said. "It's not good when you can't trust your partner."

"He's a good kid. He's in a tough spot right now."

O'Connoll nodded. "Tough being stuck inside a bottle. Or is it a girl?"

"A little bit of both. He'll straighten out."

O'Connoll quirked his eyebrows. "What's really on your mind?"

"I'm looking into the secretary. I got a discrepancy in the interviews. Executive says Reynolds took conference calls with him all the time, up until about a month before the wife was killed."

"So?" O'Connoll said.

"So, the secretary told us Reynolds took *all* his conference calls in his office. Plus, he keeps losing his phones. He *lost* a phone a few days before the murder."

The eyebrows quirked again. "Interesting coincidence. What do you think happened?"

"I think Reynolds had a phone the day of the murder. I think he knew exactly when his wife was killed because I think he was on the phone, talking to the murderer, getting confirmation that it was done."

"That's a lot of thinking," O'Connoll said.

"Yeah, it is."

"You think the secretary knows this?"

Lashiver shrugged. "I think the secretary knows something. I've been working her, a little at a time."

O'Connoll nodded. "What makes you think he still has that phone?"

"I don't know that he has *that* phone. But every time we talk to him, he's holding a phone, waiving it around."

"Makes sense," O'Connoll said with a nod. "He wants us to know he's getting away with it. I been doing some thinking myself."

"I figured. What are you thinking about?" Lashiver asked.

"I'm thinking the someone else he's got doing this isn't satisfied to sit around and wait for the next assignment. I think Reynolds let him off the leash and that's why there's a dead prostitute in Queens. I'm thinking there are more dead prostitutes in the five boroughs, or maybe in just one place, some spot where he's burying them."

"That's a lot of thinking."

"Yeah, it is," O'Connoll said.

"The kid will be back on the job tomorrow," Lashiver said.

"And you want to keep all this thinking between us, without telling your partner."

"For the moment," Lashiver said.

O'Connoll shook his head. "It's not good when you can't trust your partner."

Katerina came up out of the subway, taking each step with a slow, careful gait as the pain shot through her back and down into her legs. Ryan had kept her in the apartment for two days. The same routine: anger, accusations, and abuse, mixed with incessant talking, preventing her from eating or sleeping. Then the tears, protestations of love, and pleas for forgiveness. *Lather. Rinse. Repeat.* For two days. Her nerves shredded, her head in a cotton-filled haze, Kat had managed to gain permission to leave the apartment for something even Ryan could not refuse her.

Another two days lost. She checked the tiny cell phone for an answer from Reynolds with a new meeting place and time. She stared at the response.

No. I'll let you know.

Katerina didn't know what to do with the answer. Her mind spun with hideous imaginings of Alexander Winter paying for her latest mistake. She felt the strength leaching out of her body and she thought her legs would give out underneath her. Her heart sank as she spied the four, unexpected saviors waiting for her.

***

Jesus Christ, more endless babbling. Can't you shut the hell up for one minute? Any goodwill or gratitude had fled as Kat thought of one of Uncle Sergei's more polite criticisms. *Kuriatnik. Hen-house.*

Katerina never referred to the women by name. They were Emma's friends or The Bridesmaids or Them or That one, if she thought of one in particular. Jeneen, the shy, mousy one who worked in a bank and kept getting passed over. Sandra, the college friend. But from the first air kiss greeting with Michelle, the work friend from the hospital, the dislike had been mutual. Michelle's attractive features were marred by a pinched mouth of disappointment and jealousy. Kat had heard the story; before Katerina, Emma had introduced the ER trauma nurse to Ryan. Ryan hadn't given her the time of day.

The outing began with Michelle's side-eye glances of disapproval during the bridesmaid dress fitting. Katerina announced her fitting would be rescheduled. As the Maid of Honor, her dress would be different from the others. As the group made their way to their next destination, Michelle moved on to open comments.

"This girl was bent. She comes into the ER with the boyfriend, right? Third time. The guy thinks he's having a heart attack. Again. Listen to this: it was her birthday. He goes to all the trouble, the cake, the balloons, the party. First, she doesn't show up. She's hours late."

"Was she at work?"

Michelle nods. "Some kind of 'personal assistant.' Why would she be late? She has to sit around and wait to pour the coffee? No offense, Katerina."

None taken, bitch.

"She works for some executive in Midtown. I don't know what the 'personal' side of the job is. I know what she was dressed for. No offense, Kat."

At least she was getting some. More than I can say for you.

"So, anyway, she finally shows up and then complains the cake didn't have candles, the balloons weren't the right ones. She's bent. He leaves the party, goes out, runs all over town to get new balloons and another cake. When he comes back, he's gasping for air and can't breathe, and they wind up in the emergency room. For three hours, she's bitching about having to sit there, she's bitching about him and how he's not good enough. If she was good enough, the executive would have left the wife and married her. That's what they all want anyway. Sorry Kat, no offense."

"None taken," Kat said with a sweet smile. "At least she was in demand."

"So, hon, where are you taking us?" Emma cut in as she wedged in between Kat and her nemesis.

Katerina stopped in front of a building.

The gaggle, immersed in their conversation, stopped short, then craned their necks to look up at the sign.

Fitness Factory.

"Hon?" Emma said. "What are you up to?"

Katerina gave a mischievous smile. "Come inside and see," she said.

***

The instructor, slender and fit, dressed in tight, fitted clothing. Her equally thin assistant stood by the two, blood-red silks hanging from the metal contraption installed in the ceiling, shifting them between her hands.

The instructor gave her opening pep talk to the restless group. "Today you're going to have your very first class of aerial silks. You are going to use muscles you've never used before, but you will be able to pull yourself up with your own body weight."

"If I get up there, I might need a crane to get me down," Sandra said.

The ladies responded with whispered giggles.

"Katerina, where did you get this idea?" Emma asked.

The instructor piped up. "Kat used to be here every week, and I am so glad to see you're back."

The whispered giggles were replaced with mumbled comments and mistrusting glances.

"I found this place when I first moved to the city," Kat said.

"Oh, hon, you're always up to something," Emma said, and it came out as sad and disappointed.

"This isn't necessary to keep a man," Michelle said. "If you have to resort to gymnastics, something must be missing. No offense, Kat."

Drop dead, bitch.

"This looks like fun, Kat," Jeneen said, hovering at the edge of the group as if the invitation to join might have been a mistake and she could be asked to leave at any moment.

"Ladies, let's get started," the instructor said.

***

The next hour flew by in a swirl of noise, punctuated by cries of surprise and peals of laughter. The group spent the lesson hovering a few inches off the ground, learning the first baby steps of wrapping the silk around the ankle and foot to make a foot lock from which to stand.

"Katerina, why don't you give us a full demonstration?" the instructor asked.

Kat grabbed a hold of each silk and made an effortless climb until she reached halfway between the floor and the ceiling. As the sounds of the chatter below faded away, she moved each foot, one at a time, in a circular motion, wrapping a swath of material like a ballet shoe ankle wrap. She steeled herself not to grimace from the pain as she lifted herself up and stepped into the loops to a standing position.

Maneuvering the silks, she crossed one leg over the other, one silk positioned behind her, allowing her to sit back, as if leaning back into a chair. Shifting again, she slipped out of the pose. Holding on to each silk as they crossed behind her back, Katerina pressed, inverting her body, and turned upside down into a straddle. She held the pose, her hands free, floating back and forth. Her eyes closed, she searched for a sense of peace, but only found Ryan's voice droning in her head.

You're really stupid, you know that?

You think you're going to be a lawyer.

You're not smart enough.

You can't do that.

You can't do anything right.

You can't even make a piece of toast without burning it.

Katerina swayed gently back and forth.

He's right.

I can't do anything right.

I can't figure out what happened to the negatives.

A surge of emotion welled up within her when . . .

Anything you need to know, you can learn.

At the sound of Winter's low, graveled voice in her head, she inhaled a deep breath.

How can I learn to find the photo negatives, Bob? I don't know anyone connected to the Governor.

That's not true. Think.

His daughter. Destiny Haley.

I helped send her back.

Because I was working with Lisa.

Why did the Governor call MJM?

Why didn't the Governor use . . . his own fixer?

Katerina opened her eyes.

He must have one.

If he had one, how did Abe manage to take those pictures?

And where is the fixer now?

Who is the fixer?

Who would know?

"Kat, get down here," Emma's voice shouted.

Katerina curled back up and came out of the split, sitting in a chair pose. Wrapping one silk under one knee, she wrapped the other silk around the other leg and her waist several times. When she let go, Kat heard the collective gasp as she twisted out of the silk and dropped. Two feet from the ground, she jerked to a sudden stop.

Bob. I wanted to be as good as you.

Katie. You will be better than me.

***

"I could have lived without that," Michelle said, loud enough to be heard.

"That was really fun, Kat," Jeneen said. "I think this was a great idea."

As they milled around on the sidewalk, Kat witnessed the outing being re-written as it passed into history. Each woman's tale would be edited until they had climbed to great heights and swung like a Wallenda.

The group kissed and hugged goodbye, and then two friends walked, hand in hand.

"You feelin' okay hon?" Emma asked.

"I'm fine," Kat said.

"That's good," Emma said, but it came out hard and without feeling.

"Except for your friend calling me a prostitute."

"Maybe if you hadn't rubbed her nose in it by taking us here."

Kat stopped. "What's that supposed to mean? I brought you here because it's fun and different. That's what this was for."

"No, hon, it wasn't," Emma said. "It was for you to show off in front of everyone, in front of her, just to let her know that you're better than she is."

Katerina stammered, until she said, "Emma, that wasn't my intention. It wasn't."

"I told you about Michelle. I told you she was jealous because Ryan picked you."

Lucky me.

"You didn't have to be ugly about it, that's all I'm saying. Just be a little nicer to her. She'll warm to you."

Kat laughed. "No, she won't."

"No, she won't." She pulled Kat in for a squeeze. "Hon, I love you to death, but you're a handful, you really are."

They started walking again. "I'm sorry about all the fuss. If my granny wasn't doin' so poorly, but you know my momma's got this thing that the family's all got to be together at every wedding and I'm the last one. They're determined that old lady will live to see it, even if it's just the ceremony."

Katerina nodded, all the while cursing Emma's "Meemaw." The woman had been dying for fifteen years and would probably go on for another fifteen.

"It's going to be a great wedding, Emma. I will get everything done, and it will be something you will never forget."

They said goodbye and went their separate ways. Katerina checked her surroundings several times, making sure Emma hadn't changed her mind and decided to follow. By the time she noticed the car pulling up alongside her, the doors had opened, the men spilling out, surrounding her, and pulling her into the vehicle.

Too late.

Caught.

Katerina hung off the edge of a straight back chair, clutching one of the slats. She watched her tears drip onto the floor, gasping in pain from the blow that would add to the black and purple mosaic on her side. Grigory Federov sat at a table. Kat's purse lay open, the contents spilled out. A younger version of Grigory stood over her.

"So, you meet my brother, Anatoly," Federov said. "Say hello, Anatoly."

"I think he just did," Katerina said.

Grigory laughed. "You go to New Jersey, you go to Philip's office, but you don't call me. This is not good," Grigory said, picking through her wallet and tossing it aside. "I have heard of your famous memory. You look at something. You don't forget. Philip mentions this. So, you tell me, what you see in Philip's office?"

"He needs a new coffee maker."

Another blow landed in the same spot.

"Nothing, I saw nothing!" Kat blurted, her knuckles white as she gripped harder, her body twisting in pain. "I'm working on it."

"Five months, still working? This is not good. I don't think you do much work during this time."

"I was sick."

Grigory waved the comment away. "I hear all this before. No, no, it is bad winter, lot of snow. No, no, I am sick. You think I do not hear things? You think I do not hear about little Desucci Junior, hunh? You think I do not know? Here is what is to happen. You find negatives. Now. You bring me negatives. Now."

Anatoly grabbed a hank of Kat's hair and yanked it; her neck snapped and strained until she thought it would break.

"You see him?" Grigory repeated.

"Uh hunh," she said.

"He is here just for you." Grigory said. "Convenient you have boyfriend who does this thing. You, how you say, gaslight him, yes? He will look at bruises and think, 'Oh, I did not know I do this thing so hard,' hunh?" Grigory laughed. "No negatives, you get more of this. Maybe you get something else. Maybe Anatoly does whatever he want with you. Maybe he take you to one of the apartments we have. Maybe he give you to other men to do the thing they want. Until you bring me negatives."

"We both know you're not going to do that," Kat said, laboring through every word. "Because if my boyfriend the cop finds one hair on my body that isn't his, he's going to kill me, and then you'll never see those negatives."

Grigory considered this and laughed. "You see this," he said to Anatoly while pointing at Kat, "this is like real Russian girl, with that mouth."

The blow came down on the bruises and the air flew out of Kat's lungs. Anatoly released her hair, and she curled into the pain, her body shaking.

"Anatoly, be nice. We don't need annoying cop coming around."

Grigory Federov rose from his chair. "Anatoly will find you every four days, five days, six days – who knows? You won't know. You won't see him coming. But it will never stop until I get negatives. Understand?"

Anatoly hauled Kat to her feet. "We're going to be friends," he whispered. "Good friends."

"What if the cop doesn't make a space for you to work?"

"You think we do not know how to make pain without making mark?"

Fresh fear fell across Kat's face.

Grigory laughed. "Ah, no more smart mouth," he said.

Katerina took halting steps, her legs trembling.

"Anatoly, I raise you like animal?" Grigory said. "Give lady her purse."

Anatoly swept the detritus back into her purse and handed it to her.

"You can use bathroom, fix your face," Anatoly said.

"See, very good Anatoly. Very good."

Katerina hobbled to the bathroom. Anatoly held the door open for her. As she passed through, she heard Grigory Federov say, "I don't hear nothing."

"Thank you," Kat whispered.

Like a boxer the day after a twelve-round bout, Kat moved as if she were a hundred years old. The adrenalin from the day before had long since evaporated, leaving her body sore and aching. She had sleepwalked through her classes and then left the campus, wandering the city in order to check for surveillance. As the heat beat down upon her head, a headache pounded in her temples. In her exhaustion, she felt the world around her existed in slow motion and she wished she could hide somewhere, close her eyes, and sleep for a month. Convinced she was clear, Kat set out for her destination: the corner of Mulberry and Grand.

***

When Katerina arrived at the corner, she noticed the man standing across the street. Medium height with dark, slicked-back hair, he carried twenty extra pounds and looked hot and uncomfortable in the scorcher of a day. He kept pace with Katerina until he stopped. Katerina noticed he was in line with Ferrara's bakery. Another enforcer cut in front of her to reach the bakery door first. Kat noticed the "Closed" sign, but Vincent appeared at the door. She went inside, but the man stayed outside, a bellman to discourage customers.

"Mr. Tony is in the back," Vincent said.

Kat hesitated.

"It's okay, miss. You asked to see him. He's here. No one else."

Vincent motioned for Katerina to open her purse. She surrendered all her phones; Vincent tucked them away in the pouch. With halting steps, Katerina made her way across the red and white checkerboard floor; tables lined one side, the cases of pastries and sweets on the other. Vincent ushered her through the swinging doors and into the kitchen.

Katerina let out an exhale of relief seeing Tony Junior seated at a counter, alone, one cannolo siciliano and one chocolate cannolo on a plate in front of him.

Kat took the chair on the opposite side and gingerly sat down, letting her purse slide to the floor.

"Try one," Tony said, taking her in. "It's good."

Katerina, shivering now from the air conditioning, took the chocolate cannolo and dug in. The sweet ricotta cream and chocolate settled her stomach. She appreciated the kindness. Winter would have done the same.

"You were right. Philip has been holding out," she said.

Tony eyes narrowed. "How so?"

"He had someone on the inside."

"You found a partner?"

"I think I found a mark. Someone close to the Governor. Whoever it is, is out. But Philip has been trying to reach him, or her."

Tony thought about this. "It's worth knowing why. Keep after it. How did you find out?"

"You want me to tell you all my secrets? You won't need me anymore."

Tony's eyes darkened with concern as they moved over her. "I think this isn't the reason you called. What did you want to talk about?"

"Federov," she said.

"You saw him?"

"He saw me," Kat said, and she put the cannolo down. Turning, she lifted her shirt to reveal her back.

Tony cursed at the sight. "He did all that?"

Kat hesitated and said, "The cop started it. Federov finished it. Actually, his brother did."

"Anatoly," he said.

Katerina let her shirt fall. She hung her head, her emotions overwhelming her. Tears fell as she said, "He's going to keep coming back."

Chair legs scraped against the floor. As Tony stood over her, Katerina raised her head. "I can't take two beatings, please, I can't–"

Tony quieted her, his hands on her head, gently stroking her hair. "We're partners, remember? I take care of my partners."

Kat's eyes closed for a moment as he cupped his palm to her cheek with a tender, fraternal touch. "*Piccola mia.* I'll take care of the cop. Now. And bring you under my protection."

"It can't be done. He's the first domino. If he falls, everything will come down. Everyone will be destroyed. Even you. Promise me, you won't touch him."

They lapsed into a silence, Tony considering her until he said, "I got a message to that acquaintance you're looking for."

Ivan.

"And?"

"He understands that he has a commitment. He's not in New York right now, but he's making arrangements to come back."

Like a dam breaking, relief flooded over Katerina.

"When he does this thing, whatever it is, you'll be able to move out of Brooklyn?"

"The next day," she said.

Tony grimaced but nodded. "In the meantime, I'll keep the Federovs out of your way, without starting a war."

"How?" she asked.

"You want me to tell you all my secrets? You won't need me anymore," he said with a wink.

Kat smiled, but her eyes filled again with tears. He brushed the tears from her cheeks with his thumbs and kissed the top of her head.

***

Kat checked the time on her phone as she reached the subway. She would barely make it back by six. Another delay. More waiting.

The tiny cell phone buzzed again. She dug it out and checked the text message.

Last chance, Rapunzel. Offer expires in 48 hours.

She shoved the phone back into its hiding space without sending a response.

Going, going, gone.

CHAPTER

26

Fair is foul and foul is fair.
Hover through the fog and filthy air.

If it were done, when 'tis done, then 'twere well it were done quickly.

Katerina hurried out of the final exam, Shakespeare's words floating in her head.

The hit man is coming.

Finally.

She slipped into the theatre and took the stairs two at a time until she reached the bottom, her breath coming hard and fast. As she opened the door, she couldn't remember a day when she hadn't been out of breath, running, always running, but never fast enough to escape.

In the dimly lit theatre, Reynolds sat in a seat in the first row. Garett, the faithful but mute driver, a shadow standing off to the side. Katerina had already decided how she would play it. For the first time, she felt herself hold the fear in check.

"Miss Katerina, how did you *fair* on your final? I have faith that you will earn an excellent grade," Reynolds said with a chuckle, every tooth showing, the smile of the insane. "You apply yourself to every task."

Katerina watched the dead man. Soon, he wouldn't speak anymore. Soon, he wouldn't smile anymore. Soon, John Reynolds would be dead.

Aspetta, Alex.

Hold on, Alex.

Il sicario sta arrivando.

The hitman is coming.

L'aiuto sta arrivando.

Help is coming.

Aspetta, tesoro.

Hold on, my love.

"Well, Miss Katerina?" Reynolds asked.

"Fine, I did fine," Kat said.

"And did you complete the assignment I gave you?" he asked.

Katerina turned and lifted up her dark-colored blouse, revealing the purple and black blotches, like a hideous, abstract painting on her skin.

Reynolds made a noise of delight.

Kat turned back to him, already seeing him lifeless, his eyes wide open in death. "You should have seen me right after I texted you. The police are coming back," she said. "There was a killing in Queens. A prostitute. Similar to how your wife, and Cheryl Penn, died."

As if a switch had been flipped, his mood turned somber. He nodded his head, taking in every word in rapt attention. She watched his performance, trying in vain to appear as if he had prepared for this. Katerina knew what fear looked like; she saw it every day when she looked in the mirror. And she wondered if John Reynolds' killer had committed the murder without permission. Had the monster broken free of the leash?

"What else?" he asked.

"The cop wants to lie to you. If the rest of them go along with it, they're going to tell you a story and say they're close to a break-

through in the case. They want you to panic and reach out to –
him. They want you to make a mistake."

Reynolds stood up. "Excellent, Miss Katerina. You have done
well. I told you, didn't I? You would protect me and so you have . .
."

The words drifted away into silence. A thought came to Katerina in the breach. The hit man would kill John Reynolds. What
about the monster? She remembered her Shelley. To save himself,
Reynolds would have to kill his own creation. He would have no
choice.

*Would you, with a satisfied conscience, destroy your own crea-
ture?*

Can I drive you to do it?

Katerina took a step toward him. "It's getting too dangerous for
you. He's unpredictable. He could harm you."

Reynolds roused himself from his thoughts. He gave her a bemused stare. "Now? When we are so close to reaching our goal.
There is still much work to do, Miss Katerina."

What work? I have work to do. Soon, you'll be dead.

"But, I appreciate your care and concern for my person,"
Reynolds said.

A shiver went through Katerina at the familiar quote.

Reynolds held out his hand toward Garrett; the driver stepped
forward with a package wrapped in heavy gold paper, adorned
with a ribbon. He handed the package to Reynolds.

"You performed your task well," he said. "And here is your reward."

When she didn't move, Reynolds held it out further.

Katerina forced herself to take it in her hands.

"Open it. Now," Reynolds ordered, that same wide smile on his
lips.

Beneath the expensive paper, Katerina felt the softness of the
article. She pulled at the tape and unwrapped the paper, expect-

ing a silky, slinky strapless thing she would be ordered to wear for Ryan. As the wrapping fell away, she saw the fabric; a torn, filthy piece of clothing. She held it up with both hands.

A shirt.

"It had been white at one time," he offered.

Katerina brought the shirt closer and caught the scent of sweat, the scent of fear – the scent of Alexander Winter.

"Ah, I wish you could see the look on your face. That's the same look she had," Reynolds said. "That stunned expression, the shock that she should be paying the ultimate price for betraying me. I know every thought in your head. You are concerned for me? That I am in danger, at risk? Did you not study your Henry the Fifth, Katerina? Like one Richard Earl of Cambridge, Henry Lord Scroop of Masham, and Sir Thomas Grey, knight, of Northumberland, all so concerned for the young King. Alas, your too much love and care of me."

Like a predator pouncing on his prey, Reynolds grabbed her by the wrists, the shirt bunched in her hands, and drew her in close, his face inches from her own. "Did you really think I would *not* know what he does and when he does it. His need must be fed while he waits for his next banquet. Will that ever happen? Will he ever partake? We don't know yet, do we? And all the while his life is in your hands, you play these games? Is that what you do?"

In terror, Katerina shook her head, clutching the shirt to her chest.

"I had thought to show your beloved mercy. I would grant him an extra piece of bread, one night spared from his daily ritual punishment –"

"No, no, no," she repeated.

With a "tsk" sound of disappointment and disgust, he released her. "Since you are so concerned that Bruce is a danger to me, see that he is not discovered. How you do that is your problem."

Reynolds went for the exit, Garrett on his heels. By the way," Reynolds said as an afterthought, "while your beloved receives his punishment he is told again and again of *all y*our activities in Brooklyn. He knows everything."

The echo of his laugh lingered in the theater as he left.

***

Reeling, Katerina rushed out of the auditorium, clutching the shirt and crumpled wrapping. Just as the bile reached her throat, she found a secluded spot behind a building. Dropping to her knees, she retched. After, she brought the shirt close, breathing in the scent of Alexander Winter, taking in his fear and his pain, adding her tears to the fabric. With trembling hands, she grabbed her cell phone and made a call. When Rachel, one half of the owners of Rainbow Farms came on the line, Kat realized she had called the farm instead of her mother's burner.

"Katerina," Rachel's ethereal voice came through the line. "What's happened, my love?"

The words babbled out of Katerina. "I'm not a fox. I'm not clever. I can't figure out anything. I've lost the spirit animal."

"My love, you cannot lose your spirit animal. It is always close by, assisting you even when you don't feel it. It will not fail to be there when you need it."

"But my friend needs help, and I can't help him. I can't help him escape. Is this the Shaman's Death? Is this one of the other deaths you said would happen? Is he – my friend, dying away from me?"

Kat cried in the gap of Rachel's silence and said, "Please, tell my mother that the Professor needs help. Now. He must have help right now or he's lost. Tell her it's true. All of it is true."

"I will tell her. And I will light the sacred fire for you and your friend, my love, to help you both. I will call to the spirits. They will not fail you. They will come."

Katerina barely managed to say "thank you" before she clicked off the call.

She stared down at the cloth bunched in her hands.

You know what to do with this.

She jolted at the sound of Winter's voice, so clear inside her head. She cried fresh tears. *Yes, professor, I know what I have to do. But how?*

It took her a few minutes through damp eyes and halting breaths to dig out the hidden, tiny cell phone and tap out a text message.

If you still need a second, what's your address.

The phone buzzed.

Just go to 76th and Lex.

Katerina typed, a furious tapping.

No. You want a partner. We meet at your apartment. Now.

Best I can do.

She waited, her panic rising with each second.

Fine.

Katerina read the address and tucked away the cell phone. She brought the shirt close to her nose again, taking in Alexander Winter, knowing it could be the last time.

CHAPTER

27

"What's the problem?"

"I'm supposed to be asking you that," Kat said.

Lisa rolled her eyes as she opened the front door and stepped aside for Katerina to enter. "Nice try, Rapunzel. I can *see* there's a problem."

"I need to borrow your fireplace," Kat said.

The apartment resembled a set piece in a museum; it only needed the velvet ropes so people could file past and gawk at how the royal family lived centuries earlier.

"It's ninety degrees outside," Lisa said. "And how did you know I have a fireplace?"

Kat took up a spot on one side of the mantel. "You *wouldn't* have one? And if you didn't, you would know where I could find one. I need to tie up a loose end."

"Otherwise known as destroying incriminating evidence?"

"Squeamish?" Kat asked.

Lisa took out a disposable butane lighter from a drawer. "Don't be ridiculous."

Katerina watched as Lisa tore pages of a newspaper into strips and wedged them under the logs. She pressed the lighter's trigger and held the flame against the strips until they caught. The flames grew, engulfing the logs as they crackled and danced.

Katerina clutched the package to her chest.

"Let's go, Smokey," Lisa said. "Get it done so we can get going."

At war with herself, Katerina forced herself to throw the package into the fire and watched it burn.

Lisa took a poker and jabbed at the logs and cinders. "No evidence, no crime," she said. "Whatever it was, it never existed."

Katerina kept her eyes on the fire until she trusted herself to speak. "I have to be back in Brooklyn by six."

Lisa laughed. "Why? You're gonna turn into a pumpkin?"

Katerina didn't flinch.

"You're serious." Lisa shrugged. "The job shouldn't take long."

"What are we stealing now?"

"You'll find out."

Katerina tore herself away and went for the door. She stopped when she realized she was alone.

"Where do you think you're going dressed like that?" Lisa asked.

***

Katerina pursed her lips as she looked over the choice of leather and lace. "Forget it. I'm not doing any horizontal work."

"Did anyone say that?"

Katerina fingered the mesh items, some embellished with studs and chains. "No one had to."

Lisa smirked. "Relax, you won't be on your back." She looked Kat up and down and chose the most conservative of the items, a sheer mini concoction with lace on top exposing enough cleavage to excite the imagination, and a wet-look skirt on the bottom, ending just below the backside. She held it up against Katerina.

"This will do," she said.

"Where are we going?" Kat asked.

"A party."

"Don't we have to be invited?" Kat asked.

"It's not that kind of party," Lisa said.

"Who's it for?" Kat asked.

"It's not *for* anyone. It just is."

As they rode in the taxi, Lisa gave Kat a side-eye of curiosity. Kat turned her face away, staring out the window, willing herself to hold back her tears. She chided herself that she could have walked away from this. After all, the package had been destroyed. She had gotten what she wanted. *And I would burn a bridge that I might need in the future. Never a good idea.*

"You know I've been dying to ask about your back," Lisa ventured.

"I've been dying to ask about the two-way mirror in your bathroom."

"Not even a hint?"

"Why don't you just tell me what the job is."

"We need a wallet," Lisa said, and flashed her cell phone with a picture.

Kat didn't recognize the man, but she recognized the look. Two-hundred-dollar haircut, shit-eating grin of confidence. Another Wall Street wunderkind with more balls than brains, doing everything dick first while leaving the thinking for last.

"A debit card to be exact. Panama Bank."

"You don't need me for a wallet or a debit card," Kat said.

"Just in case he's a bit handsy."

"Another one?"

Lisa smirked. "Possibly. Which is why I need more than two hands."

"I don't do threesomes."

Lisa turned to her protégé. "You've got an awful lot of rules for a profession that has no use for those. I need the debit card, that's all."

"Isn't he going to miss it?"

Lisa laughed. "Trust me, he's not calling the cops. Your cut is five thousand."

"Fifteen," Kat said, "since it's so important to you."

"Ten, final offer."

Katerina managed a half-hearted fume as she nodded her head.

The taxi pulled over to the curb in front of a steel façade building in the Art Nouveau style.

"Why don't you just go back and pump the last one for more information?" Kat asked, as they piled out of the cab.

Lisa rang the bell, staring up at the building. "No longer available."

"What happened to him?"

"He slipped and fell."

"What did he break?"

"His skull – when he hit the pavement," Lisa said, as a blank-faced gentleman opened the door and stepped aside to allow them access.

Katerina followed Lisa inside the apartment building, the door closing behind her. At the empty space, she stepped back.

"What the hell is this?" Kat asked.

"You didn't think we were going to walk in the front door, did you?" Lisa motioned for Kat to follow her to the stairwell. "People who attend this soirée like their privacy. There's a connecting tunnel. The party is two doors down."

Katerina hesitated but followed.

***

After entering the apartment, the duo split off. Katerina retreated to the periphery, making a sweep of the room, all the while tormented by the scent of Alexander Winter in the air.

She watched as the scrubbed and polished beautiful people moved in a languid manner, a testament to too much money and even more time. All the while, Alexander Winter existed in the same universe, trapped, chained, starved, and tortured. A server holding a tray of hors d'oeuvres stopped in front of her. She wanted to burst out laughing. She wanted to scream.

Shaking her head, she turned away, running into a man.

"Oh, excuse me," she said.

He stepped out to block her escape. "Hello, pretty lady," he said. "What's your hurry?" He pulled back, hand to his chest in a mock mea culpa. "I'm sorry, that was too forward."

"No problem."

She moved to pass him, but he blocked the path again. "Great, then what's your hurry?"

***

Ryan took the front steps at a measured pace, the police officer performing his normal duties of investigation and inquiry.

Using the copy of the key he had made, he opened the building door and slipped inside.

Down the hall, he stood before the apartment door, listening, inhaling his anger, letting it circulate through the respiration process, passing through the organs and vessels and then out again. The anger fed his blood as he put the key in the door and twisted the tumbler, letting himself inside.

Performing his routine surveillance, he listened for sounds coming from the bedroom, inhaled through his nose for the scent of sex. Nothing. A pile of mail on a small stand. Clothes strewn on the daybed. A woman's clothes. *Not hers.* His eyes went to the kitchen table; open bags of chips and pretzels, an open can of soda, an open laptop with a black screen.

The blow caught Ryan on the arm.

***

The player had his hand on Katerina's arm. "This could be the start of a beautiful friendship."

"Thanks for the offer, Louis, but I'm taking the last plane out," Kat said, a sudden aggression spiking within her.

The player laughed. "I like that. At least let me give you my pitch."

"Sure thing, slugger," she said. "Give it your best shot."

***

Ryan pivoted, crooking up his arm to ward off the next attack. With his other hand, he grabbed at the bat and caught a look at his assailant.

A Goth with punk hair and piercings; the kid couldn't have been more than twenty.

She held fast to the bat, trying to wrench it away.

"I'm a cop," he said, seizing it and tossing it aside, the clatter reverberating as it landed.

"Bullshit," she said, kicking out her leg.

Cursing as she grazed his kneecap, Ryan pivoted. Grasping her by the wrists, Ryan pushed her back against the wall.

"I'm a police officer," he said. "And you're under arrest for assaulting an officer and trespassing."

"I'm not trespassing in my own apartment."

Ryan held fast as she struggled. "Nice try. I know who this apartment belongs to. Don't make it worse for yourself," he said, flipping her to face the wall and reaching into his pocket for handcuffs.

"I'm subletting this apartment from Katerina Mills."

Ryan stopped.

***

"Don't you know who I am?" the player asked, flashing his blinding, white teeth.

"You haven't told me yet."

"Derek Lucas, the last of the Renaissance men. I've been on the cover of Fortune, Inc. Do you know what a Renaissance man is?"

Of course, I do. You're a bullshit artist who sweet talks anything with a vagina out of her panties.

"You like jousting?"

He smirked. "Well, in a manner of speaking, yes, I do. Jousting is one of my favorite activities."

"I'll bet it is. But, are you any good at it," she said.

"Sweetheart, there's no one better than me at jousting. I'm the jousting champion."

I'm standing here, having a stupid conversation with this imbecile while Alexander Winter is screaming in pain, begging for his life.

"I'm a venture capitalist. Do you know what that is?"

"You have a shit ton of money, and you spend your days making more of it."

He laughed. "I love it. I also like to enjoy the spoils of my hard work."

"What exactly are spoils?"

"Architecture, Automobiles, Art–"

"And you're only in the A's," she said.

He leaned in, a predatory smile on his face.

"Can I tell you a secret?" Derek Lucas asked.

***

Ryan eased up, turning the girl around to face him. She flattened herself against the wall.

"I get one phone call, don't I? I'm calling her."

"Where's your lease?" he asked, ignoring her statement.

"You're kidding, right?"

Ryan took a step back, still on guard.

"When did you start renting from Katerina?"

The girl slipped away from him, going for her purse. "I'm calling her."

Ryan was at her side, swiping the purse away. "Relax. I didn't say I didn't believe you. I'm the boyfriend. I came by to check on the place and pick up her mail."

She made a swipe for her purse. "Great, I'll let you talk to her."

Ryan shifted, holding it out of reach. "What's your name?"

April didn't answer.

Ryan pulled his badge holder out of his pocket and opened it. "What's your name?"

"Melanie," April lied.

"How much rent do you pay, Melanie?"

"Why? Are you my financial planner?" she shot back.

"Where'd you two meet?" Ryan asked as he opened April's purse.

"Gee, I don't remember. I'd have to check my social calendar. You're not supposed to look through my stuff, you know. I didn't give you permission."

Ryan gave her a pointed look as he pulled out her driver's license.

"Campus, okay? I met her on campus."

He examined the license, then dropped it back in the purse and rifled the rest of the contents. "I don't see a school ID."

"I left it in my other purse."

He glanced over the living room. "I don't see any books."

"I'm a genius, I don't need to read them."

"What's your major?"

"Sociology. I'm studying the effects of oppressive social institutions on women and the loss of individual rights in an autocratic, patriarchal police state."

Ryan held out the purse. "I can see why you two hit it off," he said.

She snatched the purse away.

He wandered over toward the idle laptop, its screen black.

"Look, I'm only a month late and I told her I'd have the hundred by the end of the week. She shouldn't be pulling this shit after she said it was okay. I still have tenant rights."

Ryan wandered away from the table. "That's between you and her," he said.

April flopped onto the daybed and crossed her legs. "You thought she was here, didn't you? With someone else? Wow. That's cold. Where has all the trust gone?"

"Be good, or I'll be back," he said.

"Yes, sir, *officer.*"

Ryan picked up the pile of mail and slammed the door shut behind him.

***

"I have a penthouse in West Chelsea. It's a wonder of modern technology, totally digital, everything runs off the cloud. I speak and it's done."

I bet the women in your life wished that worked when they want you gone. Winter is gone. He's gone away from me.

"I think of it as an oasis where I keep all of my favorite things on display."

"What shelf is your wife on?"

Derek Lucas chuckled. "That shelf is going to have an open space very soon. I'd like to show it to you some time."

Kat's cell phone buzzed, insistent and intrusive. The smile on his lips thinned at the nerve of the device to interrupt him.

"Someone really wants your attention."

"Isn't it better to be with someone in demand?" she said, as she slipped the phone out of her purse and tapped.

YOU FORGET TO MENTION SOMETHING?

Katerina hoped her expression remained blank as she read the next text.

NYPD BOYFRIEND? SERIOUSLY?

Kat slipped the phone back into her purse.

Lucas leaned in, his lips inches from hers. "Have you ever seen a million dollars?"

"I have not," Kat said.

"I can arrange that. I bet you would look beautiful laying naked in the middle of it."

Desperate to answer the text messages, Kat caught a glimpse of Lisa and said, "As tempting as that is, I'm going to have to pass."

Derek turned and followed her gaze. "Hey, I'm open to a group activity."

"Sorry, slugger," Kat said, maneuvering away, "she doesn't bat for your team."

"Even better," she heard as she walked away.

***

Katerina stole away to a quiet corner and pulled out her cell phone.

She closed her eyes, her chest heaving as another wave of grief washed over her and the screaming in her head returned. *Another beating. It won't end. None of this will ever end.*

What's the story?

The cell phone buzzed.

MY NAME IS MELANIE PRUITT.
SAYS SO ON MY FAKE ID
WE MET AT THE CAMPUS.
I'M SUBLETTING.

Katerina exhaled. The kid had done good – better than good. It was still a shit show, but a quality save.

Thank you.

Kat typed another message.

What about the cell phone number? Did you get a name?

The phone buzzed seconds later.

Burner phone. Dead end.

Katerina cursed under her breath.
Another buzz of the cell phone.

Artful dodger.
Coming your way.

Katerina lifted her head. She pegged the mark heading for the stairs.
Going down.

***

Off the kitchen, a spiral staircase ran from roof to basement. Katerina opted for the elevator instead. Kat hit the button, and the carriage door opened. Stepping inside, the sound of the sliding panel caused a flashback to January. The Balboa Island home of Russian oligarch Viktor Mikhailovich. The second floor, the dead of night, cracking a safe with help from Alexander Winter. And then a figure stepping out of the elevator, the flashlight raising, the gun pointing at Winter.

The thud of the elevator broke her thoughts.

Kat stepped out of the cab into a long, dimly lit hallway with sets of doors. She glanced to her right and left. In the silence, she caught a whisper of voices, murmuring.

As one door opened, a snapping sound, and then a moan, escaped.

A woman emerged. Dressed all in black, she wore a cape with a collar, tights under panties, a leather mesh corset, and thigh-high stiletto boots on her feet. In one hand, she held a discipline crop. She closed the door, smirked at Katerina, and moved away down the hall.

Shit. Party on the first floor. S and M club in the basement.

As Kat turned away, the mark came down the stairs and into the hallway.

Well, what now? What now?

"I think you're looking for me," Katerina blurted.

He gave her a once-over. "You'll do. Let's go," he said, reaching out and grabbing her by the hand.

Kat pulled away. "No, no, baby, that's not how it works."

"Yeah. How does it work?"

She leaned in and whispered in his ear.

He gave a smirk. Taking his hand, Kat led him toward an open door at the end of the hall.

I am not taking off my clothes.

I am NOT taking off my clothes.

***

The darkened room held a king-sized bed and stands offering a variety of BDSM tools: ties, crops and paddles, chains, and handcuffs.

The mark had peeled Kat out of the mini dress, saying, "Whoa, you like it rough," when he saw her back. Left bare except for the nipple pasties, bikini panty, and stilettos on her feet, Kat's stomach lurched between terror and shame. The mark put his mouth on her, licking her skin; Katerina stood still, the bile rising in her throat. She stared at the equipment stand.

He may get handsy.

Not if he can't use his hands.

As he made his way down her belly, his fingers curled around the strings of her bikini panties. She took a hank of his hair in her hand and yanked his head to look up.

"Hey," he said.

"You're right. I do like it rough," she purred, feeling the rage bubble up inside her. "Scared?"

"I can take it."

"Stand up. Hands at your sides."

He laughed. "You're gonna order me around now?" he said. "I don't think so."

She walked away from him and went to the stand, choosing the leather punishment whip.

Feeling him come at her, she turned and brought the whip down.

He stopped short. "Whoa," he said.

"Good boys get rewarded. Now, do as you're told," she said, her voice low and cold. "If, not, you know what happens to bad boys. They get punished."

He gave a half-smile.

***

The entire procedure of undressing and settling him on the bed had taken somewhere between the blink of an eye and eternity, an equation she didn't understand. He fidgeted in the handcuffs keeping him fixed to bed while he eyed her with an open hunger, his naked body responding with arousal. Carrying a blindfold, she came to him.

"Oh, come on, you're not gonna let me see," he whined.

She kneeled on the bed. "Eventually, but I want you to *feel* everything first."

He laughed as she fixed the blindfold around his eyes. "Oh, oh boy," he managed to get out before she placed the ball gag in his mouth.

"Now, get ready," she cooed, as the smile slipped from her face.

He mumbled in response.

Shoving off the bed, she swiped his pants from the floor and pulled his wallet from a pocket. "I'm coming for you," she remembered to say as she examined the cards and pulled out the debit card.

More mumbling.

She grabbed a feather from the stand and gave him a swipe of a tickle. "Hold on now," she whispered, watching his breathing, fast and shallow with anticipation.

Did anything happen?

No, professor. I promise. I didn't do anything.

Then don't tell me.

I won't. When you come back. I won't tell you anything.

You have to come back.

Forcing down the emotion welling within her, she pulled herself back into her outfit. She remembered to keep talking at the mark, telling him what she was going to do. Taking up her purse, she gave him another tickle, then said, "Now count to twenty and get ready," and slipped out, closing the door behind her.

***

As Katerina went toward the stairs, the dominatrix came back in her direction. "You didn't enjoy yourself," the woman said. "You didn't even partake."

"No, he's all yours," Katerina said.

The woman stepped into Kat's path. Katerina stopped, then froze as the dominatrix gave a gentle stroke to Kat's cheek.

"Wounded bird. You're suffering. I can help you."

Katerina shifted her cheek away. "No thanks, I'm not a sub."

A door opened. A young man peered out. Rail thin, he had a Grecian face with mischievous eyes, and a body with baby smooth skin. He could have been the plaything of an ancient philosopher or a Roman Senator. Behind him, a young woman with long, blond hair and full bangs wore a hungry look and little else.

"*We* can help you."

"No go. Not into black sheet parties."

The woman laughed and stepped closer.

"Poor little thing. You don't know yourself. Only through bondage is there freedom," she purred, "only through pain is there pleasure."

"Listen, Count Domula, to each his own. You stick to the playroom, and I'll stick to my safe word - no."

As Kat went for the stairs, she heard behind her, "Poor little vanilla, you think whoever he is, he's the answer. He can't help you. He can't set you free."

Kat turned and said, "You want to set someone free, he's in the room at the end of the hall."

Katerina fled up the stairs, her nerves frayed. Seeing Lisa coming the other way, Kat pressed the card into her hand. Bounding onto the main floor landing, Katerina rounded the corner and crashed into Thomas Gallagher.

CHAPTER

29

Upon entering the eight-story townhome, Katerina traversed the floating limestone staircase up to the penthouse level. As she came off the stairs, Kat stopped short. Alexander Winter stood in the center of the room. He looked the same as the first day they met, dressed in black slacks and shirt, a contrast to the snow-white surroundings. Katerina blinked several times, disoriented that he should be there. A gentle smile hinted at his lips.

"I think this was a very good year."

She turned at the sound of Gallagher's voice; he came up the stairs, a bottle of wine in his hand. When Kat turned back, the vision had dissolved away.

***

She thought of Thomas Gallagher as a striking man with a face like polished stone, strong and angular. His hair was blond and his eyes a piercing ice blue. His aura still had something she couldn't describe; but it made her blood run cold with trepidation. In the kitchen, the bottle of wine stood on the counter with two glasses. Opening a drawer, he extracted a corkscrew. Pulling the cork from the bottle, he poured the wine and came to her, a glass in each hand, extending one in her direction.

***

Katerina carried her glass as she stepped through the open sliding door out onto the patio, gazing over the panoramic view of

Billionaire's Row, the site of another misadventure last year, stealing Simon Marcus' Porsche. As she looked out over Gotham City, she remembered the words of MJM's half-muscle, half-monk philosopher courier, Angel.

This ain't a love-in. This ain't even Manhattan. This is Ancient Greece. The Gods ain't dead, baby. Only they don't look down from the heavens but the penthouse. And they move the people like pieces on the chessboard.

"Do you like it?" she heard from her right.

She nodded.

"But you're not impressed," Gallagher said.

"Why did you bring me here?"

Gallagher's eyebrows quirked at the direct question. "Because I thought you could appreciate it for what it is. Beyond its dollar value."

"What is it's dollar value?"

"Somewhere north of eighty million."

Sweltering, Katerina felt as if her entire body were engulfed in flames. She wondered, if she turned around now, would she see Winter again?

"If you wouldn't mind, can we go back inside?"

"Of course," he said.

Wandering indoors, Kat found an empty room.

A small, dull, pain of a headache had come on at the party; it bloomed now, pounding and relentless. The lingering effects of the pneumonia, the fatigue, the shortness of breath, never far away, beckoned just outside the door, scratching like a cat wanting to be allowed back into the house. The room had slanted off-kilter. *Insanity. All of it. Insanity.*

Gallagher followed. "I am fascinated by renewal," he continued, "taking a blank space and seeing it reborn. Of course, that can't happen with everything. Especially in life, in relationships. Some things die. People die. Sadly, we are often the cause." At Katerina's stricken look, he added, "I'm speaking metaphorically, of course."

"I'm not an interior decorator, and you have a half-finished apartment to prove it."

"I saw the seeds of talent in what you accomplished. But, I think life has been very difficult for you since we last met. It's been six months."

It's been five months, three weeks, and two days since I've seen Alexander Winter.

"Do you go to that party often," she said, changing the subject.

"I make the rounds of several standing gatherings. Think Gertrude Stein, Paris of the nineteen twenties. It was called a salon. People of note, artists, intellectuals, politicians, writers, they all gathered in such places. It can be advantageous for business connections."

"Where do you discuss business – in the basement?" Kat asked.

Gallagher smirked. "I won't insult your intelligence by denying what we both know is true. I know all about the 'basement.' They're called playrooms."

"Gives new meaning to the phrase 'Tickle Me Elmo,'" Kat quipped, but Gallagher's words continued eating into her soul.

He gave a delighted laugh. "People use their money and their time in all sorts of ways. That has never appealed to me. I've never been to a playroom, any playroom."

Katerina took another sip of the wine that had already gone to her head while gazing at the snow-white structure. She wondered if she drank more wine and then turned around, would she see Winter again? *How can I tell you how sorry I am?* The tippling of madness was on her again, the incongruity of the desperation to undo all she had done and no possible way to make it happen.

"I wasn't intending to ask you to decorate," Gallagher said, picking up the thread of the conversation. "I was going to ask you to work for me, but I think we'll leave that for another discussion." He stepped forward. "Katerina, I meant what I said in January. I can see, clearly, that I was right to be alarmed and concerned for you. I think I'm still right that you are in need, a desperate, dire need, and I want to be of assistance."

"Why?" she asked.

"Because I am fond of you," he said, his exasperation coming through. "I'm willing to accept you don't share the same intensity of feeling for me. Tell me your most pressing need. Right now. Let me provide for it. Do that for a friend. I don't think you understand what a burden it is to want to help someone, and to be helpless to do that. And in doing nothing, I am complicit. I am responsible for what you suffer."

Katerina's breath caught in her throat. She turned away, frightened that he could see into the depths of her.

"What time is it?" she asked.

Gallagher checked his phone. "Six o'clock. May I ask why?"

Late. She needed an excuse, something to lessen the blows she knew would be coming. "I, I need to take a shower, and I left my clothes at a – friend's house. I need to get my clothes back. I'm not feeling well. I think I need to see a doctor."

"Of course. All will be done. No questions asked. I will have the driver pick up your things, and I will make a phone call. The master bathroom is through that door. I will have everything you need brought in immediately, including a doctor."

Katerina nodded, exhaustion settling on her once more. "Thank you."

***

At nine-thirty, Katerina heard the television before she opened the apartment door. She found Ryan slumped in his usual spot on the couch, an open beer bottle in his hand. She glanced into the kitchen and saw the empties on the counter.

"I'm sorry," she said. "I went to the doctor. I wasn't feeling well."

Ryan nodded. "Doctor, hunh?" he said, getting off the couch. "Is that why you skipped class today?"

Clinging to silence as an answer, Katerina scrambled to find a way out of the rat trap of a question. *Remember, a cop will either overwhelm the suspect with the truth or he'll lie outright. Either way, the suspect will feel they have to talk and defend themselves.*

Kat settled for, "What do you mean?"

Ryan took a last swig of the beer. He laughed. "I thought I made myself clear. I'm trying to help you, Kate. That's what we're all doing. Just trying to help you. But you just keep sneaking around and lying."

"I saw a doctor. I'm sick again."

"What urgent care did you go to? Hmm?"

Ryan swiped the purse strap from her shoulder.

Katerina watched him take it to the table and turn it upside down, picking through the items.

"I don't see any paperwork," he said.

"It wasn't an urgent care," she said. "It was a private doctor."

"What doctor? What's his name?"

"Doctor Tillis."

"Where did you see this doctor?"

"Uptown. The Upper East Side."

"You saw a doctor on the Upper East Side after six o'clock at night. Really? Was this in his office?"

Kat shook her head.

Ryan laughed. "No? Then, where did you see this doctor? At the apartment of your boyfriend, where you spent the whole day, instead of going to class?"

Katerina's head pounded, as if it had been stuffed with cotton. "I told you."

"You told me. Yeah, you tell me everything, don't you? How long have you had a tenant in the apartment?"

Kat looked over at the table, her mail strewn among the torn envelopes.

"Kate. How long have you had the tenant?"

"Melanie's just a student. She needed a place to stay."

"What are you doing with the money she gives you, hmmm?"

Kat clung to the wall as Ryan edged closer. "Ryan, please, I'm being good. I'm being good."

Ryan closed the gap. "No, you're not. Now, you're going to stop lying and you're gonna tell me everything. No matter how long it takes to get it out of you."

He moved to grab her arm, but the rapping on the door stopped him in his tracks. He put a finger to his lips. A second rapping, and then a third, loud, insistent.

Ryan went to the door and opened it. He stepped back at the sight of the uniformed driver.

"Yeah?" Ryan asked.

"The young lady forgot her prescription and her appointment card."

Ryan stepped aside for the driver to enter.

"Miss, you forgot these items."

"Thank you," Katerina murmured, taking the card and prescription paper.

"Excuse the intrusion." Everyone turned to see the tall, trim man standing inside the apartment. Thomas Gallagher extended his hand to Ryan. "Detective Kellan, I have heard many impressive things about you. Thomas Gallagher, owner of Eagleton Corporation."

They pumped hands.

At the suspicious look on Ryan's face, Gallagher said, "Your young lady worked for me and my company for a short time last year, in an administrative role. The late hour is entirely my fault.

My company had contacted the school. We are offering summer internships. Due to my schedule, she was at my office for an interview. I make it a point to meet with the candidates and my schedule ran late. I'm afraid I kept Miss Mills waiting for most of the day – and I noticed she was unwell."

Ryan nodded, morphing into the protective boyfriend. "Thank you for being good to my girl."

"She speaks of you all the time, most highly. And of course, you have my gratitude for your bravery and service to me and the people of this city." To Katerina, he said, "I know there are several, highly coveted internships being offered. I hope you are considering Eagleton at the top of your list. If you are chosen, it will look very good on a resume, if I say so myself."

"I'll certainly think about it," Kat said.

"Good enough."

The two men pumped hands again and the apartment descended into silence after the business mogul and his driver vacated the small space.

Ryan closed the door and considered Katerina. "Did you take your pills?"

"The doctor gave me samples, but I need to fill the prescription."

Ryan nodded. "I'll run it down for you. Get into pajamas and relax. We'll talk about everything else tomorrow."

Kat nodded.

When the front door closed, Katerina sunk onto the couch and cried.

Alex.

***

Lisa turned the debit card between her fingers. The job wasn't the trader. The job was Katerina and her trip down to the playroom. Another exercise for Thomas Gallagher to study his prey.

From the backseat of the limousine, Lisa stared out at the masses, the working stiffs, the hustlers, the homeless, the crazy. If they knew what truly went on in the world, how people were bought and sold, abused and erased, they wouldn't believe it. Sure, every once in a while some intrepid reporter caught a scoop of a scandal. Otherwise, the ultra-rich hid in plain sight. *These things don't happen. People don't do these things on a daily basis. People don't live that way.*

Fools.

Lisa remembered her last week of high school before graduation. She had a choice to make. Stay in that one traffic light, shit town, get married, get a house, get a mortgage, pop a couple of puppies, put them in daycare, go to work in an office for some middle-aged asshole who patted her ass, leered at her tits, and called her "the Girl." "Give it to the girl. She'll take care of it." The day after graduation, she left for New York.

She should have remembered her Greek literature, the danger of hubris. It had been arrogance and ego that motivated her in January to make that wager with Thomas Gallagher. She would bring Katerina Mills back from California, Gallagher's prize wrapped up with a bow. She had lost the bet, and it had cost her everything.

That first night, Gallagher had her make the requisite phone call to MJM, monitoring the conversation with Jasmine, the guardian and keeper of MJM and its secrets. It had taken less than a minute.

"I'm out," Lisa had said.

"This is irreversible. You are sure."

"Yes. I'm out."

The call had clicked off.

Every day Lisa lived the full measure of her mistake. Her bank accounts were closed. She was unregistered for law school. She handed over her passport and the remaining false documents, driver's licenses, and social security cards. The cash, the precious lifeline of cash, disappeared from all her hiding places. The apartment was wired for sight and sound, all compliments of that bastard retired spook, Joseph Smith. Her every movement was monitored.

She walked among the masses, but she was not free. She was a prisoner of Thomas Gallagher. *Fail and you forfeit everything. Everything that is yours, your work, your body, your life, becomes mine.*

As much as Lisa was a captive, she knew her captor. She knew Thomas Gallagher better than he knew himself. He could fool himself all he wanted with his notions of a love match, but he would revert to what he knew: control, possession, cruelty, and finally destruction. Katerina had no idea what was coming. When Gallagher took possession of her, it wouldn't take long until he grew tired of the broken toy he had pined for. He would want to throw the broken toy away. He would get rid of Katerina Mills.

That's not my problem.

I have to survive this.

I have to escape.

I will escape.

Lisa glanced out the window at the people.

You know nothing.

Fools.

***

"How did you find my girl?" Thomas Gallagher asked.

"A traditionalist," the dominatrix answered with a bored sigh. "What on earth can you do with her?"

Gallagher gave a thoughtful silence as an answer.

"I should warn you, if you don't know already, she's quite spirited and strong-willed. She won't sub, not willingly."

"What would it take?" he asked.

The dominatrix shrugged. "You'd need twenty-four seven protocols, no rest, no let up. She's what we call a real brat. That would have to be tamed with punishment. You'd need a combination based specifically on what she doesn't care for. I already have ideas. And she would have to be convinced she has nowhere to go. The man she loves would never accept her or take her back."

Gallagher glanced away, the glacial ice of his blue eyes flashing with anger. "Go on," he said.

"Once she believes she can never return to him, then you can begin the training. When would you like to start?"

"Never," Gallagher said. "It won't be necessary."

"Pity. My little loves think she's delicious. They would enjoy having a new prisoner to play with."

"Not this one."

"Too bad. They'll be so disappointed. I won't lose hope. If you wanted me to see her, there's still a chance."

"No, there isn't," Gallagher said.

The dominatrix smiled.

Hide, Katie. Hide.

Katerina's eyes flew open. Staring up at the ceiling, the small space at the base of her clavicle, just below her neck and above her chest, burned with warmth, as if she wore the corded necklace, the sacred stone searing into her skin.

She waited for it to pass, then sat up, swinging her legs over the side. Getting up, she went to the door. Peering out, she found the apartment empty.

Good.

***

Katerina finished dressing while the morning news droned from the television. She completed a sweep of the apartment, placing each item in its proper place, checking, and then checking again, with an obsessive attention to every detail. Anything out of place would bring punishment. She thought of the first robbery with Alexander Winter, watching him compulsively catalogue and count the tools of his trade. And she wondered what had happened in Winter's past that an expert thief should suffer from OCD. She told herself she would ask him when he returned. That meant he was coming back.

As she grabbed a sweater from the closet, the news anchor moved on to the next story.

An NYPD sting operation yielded several arrests of the reputed Russian mob. Grigory Federov and his brother, Anatoly, were arrested along with ten other men in a late-night sweep.

Katerina darted from around the open closet door.

The Federovs are suspected of having ties to the Russian mob in the United States. The charges include extortion, bribery, and running prostitution rings in New York City and Long Island.

Standing in front of the television, Kat's mouth hung open, watching the video of Grigory and Anatoly Federov being led away in handcuffs.

He had done it. Tony Junior had kept his word.

And I'll keep mine.

***

Katerina waved to Juan as she hurried to the office employee entrance door calling, "Hola, cómo está?"

He waved back. "Bien, Miss Kat. Buenos días."

Inside, Katerina dropped her purse on her desk, envisioning herself moving on to the next order of business. *Who is the Governor's fixer? And where is this person now?*

Wheelan's door opened, and Kat heard a man's laugh. Her head shot up at the sound. Ryan and Wheelan emerged, smiling and chuckling. They shook hands. Ryan turned his attention to Katerina.

"There she is, and right on time," he said.

"She's a good girl," Wheelan said. "Delia isn't coming back. The job is yours, full-time, as soon as your finals are over."

"They're almost done, right, Kate? Only one more."

Kat's heart spasmed and then it sank as if plummeting to the bottom of the ocean. *How will I . . .* She saw the two pairs of eyes staring at her and snapped to perform. "Two more, thank you," she said, and remembered to smile. "I really appreciate this."

"She's a good girl," Wheelan said, and he pointed two crooked fingers at her. "Just stay off that phone."

Katerina went to answer but Ryan cut in, "She will, don't worry. Right, Kate?"

"Yes," she said.

Ryan kissed her cheek. "I'll see you later. Be good," he said, giving her a pointed look and a squeeze of her arm. A sign of things to come.

I hate you.

"Always," she answered.

Each year, the county provided maps for the flood of tourists washing over the area. Reclusive artisans chose Vermont to practice their craft: glass blowing, cabinetry, furniture making, jewelry, photography, and painting. Visitors followed the rural routes to discover a treasure trove of hidden workshops.

One cabin, hidden far back from the main road, would never be listed on any map. For all intents and purposes, it did not exist. Picturesque and comfortable, it reminded one of a cabin in a Thomas Kinkade painting. The painter who lived in the cabin did not wish to make himself known. Sergei Gregorievitch Volkov did not exhibit his paintings. He kept a small, free-standing work-shop next to the cabin. Had anyone ever visited him, they would have found it odd that he rarely, if ever, frequented the workshop that had a secure padlock on the door.

One morning, a car tooled down the long path, emerged into the clearing, and parked. The doors opened and three men exited the vehicle. The men were neither young nor old, but well-sea-soned for their work. One stood out from the others, a specialist. He had black hair, worn straight and combed back, a cold expres-sion and a cruel mouth, with a cigarette dangling from his lips.

Inside the cabin, Linda Mills and Sergei Volkov had spent many hours discussing the situation at length. Linda Mills had been insistent on what needed to be done. In the end, her will had won the day.

The men were granted admittance into the cabin and looked to Sergei for instructions. Sergei nodded toward Linda.

"Do whatever she says," he said.

When the men had received their instructions, the one with the cold expression and cruel mouth accepted a key from Sergei. The men exited the picturesque little cabin and walked to the workshop. Inserting the key into the padlock and giving it a twist, the padlock gave up and the men disappeared inside.

Detective Tom Morse, Detective Denis O'Connoll, and Detective Ryan Kellan stood in John Reynolds' office. Off to the side, retired Detective Timothy Green, now a private investigator, leaned against the wall and stared at a spot on the carpet.

"We've made a breakthrough. We're getting closer," Detective Kellan said.

Reynolds took the news while seated at his desk, his cell phone in his hand. "A breakthrough. How did this happen?"

"We've reviewed the autopsy results from the victim in Queens. We believe the person who committed this crime is the same person who killed your wife and Mrs. Penn."

Reynolds stood up and came around his desk, waving the cell phone back and forth, as if performing a soliloquy, a man fretting his hour upon the stage. "Well, detectives, this is quite a turn. This person has moved from killing socialites to killing prostitutes."

"No one said anything about prostitutes, plural," Detective O'Connoll.

"Detectives, after your initial bungling of the case, you don't think I'm relying only upon you for updates," Reynolds said and looked to Timothy Green. "Well, Mr. Green?"

Detective Timothy Green stared at his employer for a moment and said, "I don't know anything about a Queens connection, but

I'm looking at another angle. It could be a woman, someone involved with Temple who didn't like sharing him."

"You've been back to Temple's neighborhood?" Morse asked.

"I've been looking into it," Green said. "You've got the same list I do, and I think one of those women maybe didn't like being dumped for a spoiled, rich socialite."

"You think a woman would have the physical strength to do that kind of damage?" Ryan asked.

Green shrugged. "Could be more than one woman. Could be a couple of the women got together and decided to take revenge."

Morse shook his head and Ryan gave a chuckle.

"What's so funny, hotshot?" Green said, pushing away from the wall to stand up straight.

John Reynolds tapped his phone on his knee. "Thank you, Mr. Green. Detectives, what now?"

"A task force is being assembled," Detective Morse said. "Detectives from Manhattan North and the Queens precinct have been pulled."

Reynolds nodded.

"We're confident we're going to catch who did this. Whoever it is, they keep repeating the same mistake."

"What mistake is that?" Reynolds asked.

"Leaving the body," Ryan said.

Reynolds wore a thin-lipped smile. "Why do you think the killer did that, detective?"

"Ego, a need to have the world view his handywork. A need to humiliate these women," Ryan said. "You see, whoever this is, hates women. We're building a profile."

Reynolds feigned exaggerated interest. "Really, so is Detective Green. What does your profile say?"

"This is a very sick individual. We're confident it's a man. This guy is routinely rejected by women. Actually, women are repulsed by him. He can't perform sexually. That accounts for the extreme violence of the crimes. This is a very sick individual. But he's not that clever."

Reynolds kept smiling, tapping his cell phone against his pant-leg. "That is a bold statement since no progress has been made in all this time. By the way, detectives, I apologize I kept you waiting. I was making an announcement of a reward for any information leading to the capture of my wife's killer."

"You did that already, with no results," Ryan said.

"Indeed, I did. Two million dollars. The reward has now increased to five million. The announcement will go nationwide."

Detective Morse pursed his lips and stared down at his shoes.

"That's going to waste needed man hours chasing down bogus leads," Ryan said, his voice quiet.

Reynolds smiled, as if a kindly father figure. "On the contrary, detective, I am hoping the police won't need those man hours. I have every confidence this will break the case open, and Detective Green will solve my wife's murder since you cannot seem to manage. Do you remember the first conversation we had, detective?" he said to Ryan.

"Yes," Ryan answered.

"I said, *you* are shouldering the responsibility for my wife, for justice for my wife. You want justice for my wife, don't you, detective? That is what I asked you. And do you remember what you said?"

"I said, 'I will not rest until the killer is found. I am a man of honor,'" Ryan said.

"A man of honor, but a failure as a detective. It is clear your honor, your goodness, cannot overcome this evil, as you promised. Now, you can see yourselves out, can't you?"

O'Connoll and Morse exchanged dark looks.

"Yes, sir," Detective Ryan Kellan said.

***

In the hallway, Green bumped against Ryan as he passed the detectives waiting for the elevator.

"Excuse me, hotshot."

Jostled, Ryan whirled but O'Connoll had a hand on his shoulder before he could react.

"Enjoy your new career," Ryan called out.

"Yeah, what's that?" Green said over his shoulder as he went for the stairs.

"Fiction writer. That first book of fairy tales is going to be a bestseller."

Green gave a laugh, but he had turned around. "It's better than that bullshit about a dead hooker."

"I bet you convinced him to put up the five million, didn't you? Is that your angle?" Ryan needled.

"Fucking A, I did," Green said, heading back to the elevators.

"How much of a cut do you get?" Ryan asked.

Green answered with a flip of his middle finger.

"What's the matter, can't pay for retirement by camping out in front of roach motels, taking porn videos of couples fooling around on their spouses? I bet you watch, too."

Green moved in but Morse blocked his path. "Easy, detective, let's not do something foolish."

Green and Ryan strained against the barrier, their faces inches from each other. "You think you're better than me?" Green whispered. "You think you're smarter than me? *Everybody* watches, detective. I understand my clients, just the way I understood perpetrators. Something you'll never be able to do."

"How long were you following Felicia Reynolds?" Ryan asked.

"Fuck you," Green said. "Remember what *I* told you? Do your own job. I'm not going to do it for you."

Morse moved Green back as if he were on crowd control duty; Green turned and went for stairwell door. O'Connoll patted Ryan's back and pulled him toward the elevator, its door sliding open.

***

Entering the lobby, Elizabeth stopped short at Detective Lashiver lingering by the elevators. He smiled as she approached.

"Hello, Elizabeth," he said.

"Hello, detective."

"My partner is upstairs, giving Mr. Reynolds an update."

"I see," she said, staring past him to the elevator, like a lifeline just out of her reach.

"You know, I'm glad I ran into you," Lashiver said. He nodded toward the indoor garden space off to the right; faux grass with tables and chairs, a designated public space to escape the extreme heat or cold, depending on the season. "Why don't we sit for a minute? I just have a couple of questions."

Elizabeth stared at him and then nodded.

Lashiver swept out his hand, the gentleman, allowing Elizabeth to go first. She took a seat at a table. Lashiver sat down across from her.

"I'm surprised you haven't said anything about our frequent visits," he said.

When Elizabeth swallowed, her Adam's apple bobbed up and down. "You're doing your job," she said.

Lashiver nodded. "I appreciate you saying that. We don't hear that enough, to tell you the truth. I've been thinking about these phones Mr. Reynolds has lost. Doesn't he worry that sensitive information about his business is being stolen? If they fall into the wrong hands, I mean."

Elizabeth hesitated. "The IT department has the ability to turn off access. Even if the phone is stolen, it's useless to the thief."

Lashiver nodded. "So, no one can see what's on the phone, except Mr. Reynolds."

"That's correct," she said.

"I see," he said again.

"I'd like to go upstairs now," she said.

Lashiver gave her a benevolent smile. "Of course," he said.

Elizabeth rose from her chair but stopped at hearing. "Just one more thing, please."

Elizabeth turned. Lashiver got up and came to her.

"I've been reviewing the interviews. My partner and I had asked you if Mr. Reynolds takes all his conference calls in his office. You said yes. You said he takes all of his conference calls in his office."

"Yes," Elizabeth said.

"When we interviewed the staff again, I was told Mr. Reynolds used to take all his conference calls in the large conference room . . . until late last year, when he began taking the calls in his office. Turns out it was a few weeks before Mrs. Reynolds was killed. I'm just wondering why you didn't mention that."

"Mr. Reynolds – I was right outside his door. He was in his office on the call."

Lashiver smiled. "Elizabeth," he said softly, "that wasn't my question. Here's what I don't understand, and maybe you can help me. A man routinely takes conference calls in the presence of another employee. I thought you sitting outside his office was an airtight alibi, but to be in the same room with someone, that's just – bulletproof. Why would he suddenly change that routine? Don't you think that's an odd coincidence?"

"He was in his office," she said.

"Did you go into his office at any point during the conference call?"

Elizabeth blinked and her eyes shifted for a moment, glancing away. "I'm sorry?" she asked.

"You brought him his coffee *before* the call. You brought him papers to sign *after* the call. I'm asking if you went into the office *during* the call."

"Why does it matter?" she asked.

"This is a murder investigation, Elizabeth," Lashiver said. "Everything matters. It matters that you cooperate and assist us so we can find who did this."

"I need to go upstairs now, please," she said.

"Sure," Lashiver said. "I'd appreciate it if you would think about my question, and I'll be in touch for us to talk about it."

Lashiver watched Elizabeth take quick steps to the elevator. He waited for her to look back as the elevator door slid open. She did. He smiled. She turned away again and stepped into the cab. The door slid closed, and she was gone.

Lashiver wandered back to a table and took a seat to wait for the others. She had asked permission to leave. That was good. He had her in the right mindset to be obedient, stay when told, answer questions when asked. He thought it was ironic that the kid might be right. One person to tie the case together. The secretary knew her boss was a murderer. And she was scared to death. He'd have to be careful not to push too hard or too fast. But she had the answers, and he would get it out of her. It would take a little more time.

Katerina sat in the auditorium, hunched over her desk, writing in a little blue exam book, completing her essay on the case questions. She reasoned the cases through and made her points methodically, one by one. In each one, the criminal is caught, the case prosecuted and closed. She gave a shiver as she closed the booklet and put the pencil down.

***

Outside the auditorium, Katerina struggled to extricate herself from the web of Mina's crushing embrace.

"I'm so worried about you," Mina said. "I know he's not being good to you. Don't go back to Brooklyn. It's not safe for you there. You should leave. We could leave together."

"Mina, I have to go." *Maybe you already know where I'm going.*

Mina stroked Kat's hair. Caught off guard, Kat wrenched herself away. She saw the discomfort in Mina's expression, the realization she had exposed her feelings.

Mina shook her head in vigorous objection, grasping to hang on. "No, Katerina, it would be okay."

"Mina, let me go. Let me *go,*" Katerina insisted.

"No, Katerina, don't," Mina cried, stricken. "Please don't go back. We can go away, together. Just us."

Katerina turned and fled, hearing Mina calling after her.

At the sight of Mark coming toward her, Kat turned as if she hadn't seen him and took off. She heard his voice calling her name.

I'm sorry.

***

After several unanswered texts, Katerina presented herself at Lisa's apartment. After banging on the door for five minutes, she heard the *snick* of the lock turning. Lisa opened the door, a bemused look on her face.

"We have unfinished business," Kat said.

Lisa opened the door wide for Kat to enter, eying her as she closed the apartment door.

"What's up, buttercup?"

"Where's the money?" Kat asked.

"Check is in the mail – not literally – but I can't transfer the money until you give me an account number."

Katerina didn't answer. She had been too busy chiding herself over her tactical errors. Without thinking, she had handed off the debit card to Lisa. If she had not done that, the debit card would have been a bargaining chip. Now, she had only one thing left to bargain with – and she would have to let it go.

"Did you work it out yet?" Lisa asked. "You're losing your touch, Cinderella. I can see the smoke coming out of your ears. I can see every thought in your head."

Katerina's cheeks burned at the familiar statement.

"How did you get the Destiny Haley job?" Kat asked.

"I wished upon a star," Lisa said.

Kat held fast.

Lisa rolled her eyes. "I get a call, I take the job. Same as you."

"You didn't wonder how come it was your lucky day to get a job working for the Governor."

"Where is this going, Rapunzel?"

"Where's the Governor's fixer and why was he cut out?"

"Wow, that was a multi-part question. You've got a lot on your mind. Why do you want to know? You thinking of putting in an application?"

Katerina gave Lisa a sharp look.

Lisa wandered over to the couch and took a seat. "What's in it for me?"

"I'll take a reduction in my fee. The original five thousand."

Lisa made a show of thinking it over, but Katerina knew where this would end. It's a zero-sum game. *And I'm going to come out with the zero.*

"No, you'll forfeit it all."

"The name and the reason he was cut out."

Lisa smirked. "Okay, since it's common knowledge, if you run in the right circles. Devon Kelly. Word on the street is he's out because he let someone into the inner circle he shouldn't have. I don't know the where's, why's, or reasons thereofs."

Kat nodded and went for the door.

"You're welcome," Lisa called out as the door closed.

***

As soon as she left the building, Kat pulled out the tiny cell phone and made the call.

"Yo," April said.

"Devon Kelly," Kat said. "I need everything you can find on him."

"Chillin' like a villain. You know the Moose keeps calling. He wants to talk to you."

"Soon, tell him soon."

Kat hung up the phone and dialed another number.

"Tell him I've got the name. Please ask him for a meet today."

She headed for the subway as Vincent gave her an address and a time. Before he hung up the phone he said, "He's going to be very pleased, miss. Very pleased."

Katerina clicked off the call and checked the time. Downtown, back to the apartment, and then home before six. She would make it.

In Little Italy, Katerina entered another ice cream shop and stepped back into the nineteen fifties once again. This time, with a black-and-white tiled floor and wood-carved booths lining one side from the front to the back of the store.

Kat's scan stopped at Vincent coming through the swinging door in the back, a Faraday bag in his hand. Kat dug her phones out of her purse and dumped them into the bag as she passed him by.

***

They sat on tall stools across from each other, three tubs of ice cream lined up like soldiers on the table between them. Kat and Tony Junior each had a spoon, picking at the tubs a little at a time.

"Devon Kelly," Kat announced. "He's the Governor's fixer."

"What do we know about Devon Kelly?" he asked.

"Nothing yet," Kat said. "He's still a ghost. That's being worked on now."

"You think this Devon Kelly has the negatives?"

Katerina considered the question. Was it possible? If Devon Kelly was on the other end of that burner phone, how did a seasoned operative get taken, used as a means to an end and then sacrificed, thrown out into the cold? Or did Devon Kelly let Philip and Abe Unghar do the dirty work and then steal the negatives?

She shook her head as if she had finished her investigation and it was time to announce the results.

"None of it makes sense. Devon Kelly had to know about the Governor's bad habits. That's what he's there for, to hide everything. He could have had a ton of negatives by now. There would be no reason for him to do it." She shrugged. "What I don't understand is how Philip got it in his head to go to Albany in the first place."

"He went because I sent him."

Katerina stopped, the spoon in her hand hovering halfway between the tub of ice cream and her mouth.

Tony smiled. "My family's business interests still include transportation, by truck and air. Some information came my way that the Governor regularly transports select items of delicate cargo across state lines. I looked into it; it looked promising. Philip was already doing corporate work for us, and he was good at it."

"You sent him to get photos of the Governor," she repeated.

Tony Junior nodded.

"A governor is a nice thing to own."

"A president is even better. We've been keeping an eye on Haley for a while. If my father's bookie is right – and he usually is – he's going to win the election."

"After you help him."

Tony Junior smiled.

"How long after Election Day before you lower the hammer?"

"I'll let him enjoy the inaugural balls. Come day two... new day, new rules."

"That means new business," Kat said.

"That's right," Tony Junior said. "The United States will be making new investments, domestic and international. Don't worry, we always make a profit."

"Wise Guy Incorporated," Kat said.

"Something like that," Tony Junior said.

Katerina thought of something else Philip had said. A grain of truth in the lies. *Listen, kid, you know how sometimes there's two bullies living on the same block? Well, this is kind of like that. I was hired by one bully to get the pictures and that's pissing off the other bully.*

"Philip made promises to Federov," she said.

"I know all about it. I'll have a talk with Philip when this is over."

Translation: Philip is a dead man.

"Federov is going to want revenge," Kat said.

"Federov's a mutt," Tony Junior said. "He's not in charge. He's just running wild for the moment, taking his opportunity while he can. That will come to an end soon. All the pieces will fall into place." He gave her a once-over as if seeing her for the first time. "I expected you to be looking a little better."

Katerina nodded as she licked the spoon and went in for another helping. "I am better. I have a little room to breathe, thanks to you."

"So, what's your play?"

"There was a hired courier," Kat said.

Tony Junior's eyebrows quirked. "You don't say."

"He showed up at Philip's Boston office late last year and walked off with the package of negatives. At least, that's the story. I figure, I find Devon Kelly, assess whether he's a moron or just unlucky. If he has value, motivate him that if I find the negatives, it's good for him, so he should probably work with me. Then I can keep an eye on him – just in case."

Tony viewed her with newfound admiration. "Sounds like a plan."

Kat nodded.

"Ivan will be here by the weekend," Tony Junior.

Kat's head darted up in surprise.

"Where and when does he meet you?"

"Tell him Sunday, four o'clock, the Chelsea Savoy. He knows it. I'll figure out how to get there."

Tony Junior nodded. He put the spoon down, shoved off the stool, and came around the table. Kat's eyes closed as he kissed her forehead. "You'll be out of Brooklyn by the holiday weekend," he whispered.

He went for the back door but stopped to turn back. "You're good, Katerina Mills. Don't let anybody tell you different," he said and gave her a wink. "I'll see you soon."

And he was gone.

CHAPTER

35

In Katerina's apartment, April slouched in a chair as she worked on William Mills' laptop. She stopped every few moments to eat french fries, grabbing them two at a time, then swiping her greasy fingers on her shorts before leaning down to grab the sweating soda bottle sitting on the floor next to the chair. Twisting off the cap, she took a swig. She put it back down on the floor, wiping her wet hand on her shirt, her eyes never straying from the screen.

She had cracked the username and password. The bank account password had taken some time, but a wide smile curved her lips as the circle stopped spinning, and the bank landing page loaded.

"Chillin' like a villain," she said aloud.

April put her fingers to the keyboard and typed. She hit the "Enter" key and watched the circle spin . . . and spin. She re-loaded the page and tried again. On the fifth try, the screen disappeared, replaced by a bright blue.

"Shit," she said.

She rebooted the machine, and the familiar yacht photo appeared on the desktop.

April clicked on the internet browser icon and the homepage loaded; then the screen went blue once again.

"Shit!" she said.

Rebooting the computer again, April typed in the web address for the bank, and the login page loaded. She typed in the username and password and hit the "Enter" key. The round circle in the upper left corner seemed to spin without end. The page disappeared and then a blank, white screen, a void, appeared, and then the login page loaded.

April stared at the screen, the same page, and no error message.

She tried again. The circle spun again, the page disappeared, and the login page loaded.

Sitting back in the chair, April stared at the screen in thought.

She closed the browser. Hunching over the keyboard, she typed. A dialogue box opened with a list of installed and running programs. With her hand resting on the mouse, one finger turning the mouse's wheel button, April scanned the list. She clicked an item and clicked the "End" button. Refreshing, she reviewed the list again. The program she had ended appeared at the top of the list, running. She repeated the process again. Again, the program appeared at the top of the list, running.

April scrolled through the list, then focused on the miniscule circle at the top of the laptop, in the middle, black and idle.

She stared back at the program list and then at the small, round circle.

The webcam had been turned on.

***

When Katerina entered the apartment, April jumped up from the daybed, grabbing a piece of paper perched at the edge of the dining room table.

"What did you find?" Katerina asked.

April held up the paper with words written in large, block letters.

DON'T SAY ANYTHING.

Katerina stopped short. "Knock it off. I'm not in the mood for a 'Love Actually' card scene. Just tell me what's going on."

April turned the sheet around. She tossed it away and grabbed all the sheets still on the table. She fumbled for the right one and held it up.

HACKED

Kat's eyes shifted to the laptop but came back to April as she held up a third sheet.

CAMERA IS ON

April held up another sheet.

MIC IS ON

"Why didn't you just shut it off?" Kat asked.

April rooted around for paper and scribbled an answer, then held it up.

WHY DON'T YOU CHECK YOUR TEXT MESSAGES?
HACKER CAN TURN COMPUTER ON
CAN TURN CAMERA AND MIC ON

Kat closed her eyes for a moment. She dropped her purse on the chair, walked past April, and sat down at the kitchen table. She opened the laptop, April perched behind her. Kat searched around for a piece of paper and a pencil, scribbling the question, 'What's the web address for the bank?'

April grabbed a scrap of paper and put it down next to the laptop.

Katerina typed. She entered the username and password. The page reloaded with an error message of an incorrect password.

April scribbled out on a piece of paper, "I didn't get that last time."

Katerina nodded as her stomach churned. "What's the new password?" she said out loud. "Please?"

The web page disappeared. A series of photos appeared on the desktop, a frenetic slide slow of yachts, Richie Calico, William Mills, and Katerina, first a young girl, then a teenager, and finally Kat sitting in front of the laptop, April leaning over her shoulder.

The pictures disappeared. Dollar bills, euros, pound notes, popped up on the desktop until it was covered.

Then, they all disappeared. A text box appeared and typing began.

YOU'RE LOOKING FOR THESE, YES?

Katerina didn't answer.

Screenshots of online bank accounts showing zero balances flashed and faded, followed by a typed message.

WILLIAM MILLS' ACCOUNTS ARE CLOSED

Katerina pressed her lips together.

The currencies popped across the desktop again followed by another message:

YOU STILL OWE ONE HUNDRED THOUSAND DOLLARS

"I owe fifty thousand dollars," Kat said aloud.

One word typed out onto the screen.

INTEREST

A pencil on the screen drew a man in silhouette. Typing appeared on the screen.

AND ONE DEA AGENT

One last message typed out.

YOU HAVE TWO WEEKS

The screen went black.

***

Huddled in a corner of a Pret a Manger, Katerina watched April, hunched over the table, wolfing down a sandwich, her plate crowded with a buffet of desserts waiting to be inhaled. Kat felt sorry for the kid. She didn't lie. She had skills, but she had never billed herself as an expert.

"They took me by surprise," April said through a mouthful of food.

Kat nodded. "There was no way you could have known," she reassured the girl.

April bit off another mouthful. "I thought it was sus."

"What?"

"Suspect. There was no bit locker, no two-step authentication. They had already gotten in and turned everything off. Your dad was a newb with computers?"

"He was," Kat said. *So was Richie Calico. That's why he's dead.*

"He probably had no idea."

"I'm sure he didn't. How did they do it?" Kat asked.

April inhaled a chocolate brownie cookie. "Probably sent him an email with a link, a file, a picture," she said between bites. "Once he clicked it, the trojan downloaded, and the laptop was pretty much a slave station. They watched him do everything, captured the keystrokes, and game over."

Katerina nodded, glancing at her watch. *Almost out of time.*

"So, what do you want to do now?"

Kat shook her head. "No idea."

"Does your dad have any other money?"

"No idea," Kat repeated. "I'd have to find him."

Finding William Mills had fallen to the bottom of Kat's priority list. She hadn't seen or heard from DEA Agent James Sheridan since she had moved in with Ryan. Sheridan wanted her father dead, but not before collecting ten million dollars of William Mills' drug money. Last year, Sheridan had taken Katerina by surprise in her apartment. He had pinned her against the wall . . . Kat felt the perspiration break out on her skin at the memory. *You work for me now. Find your father or you and your mother are going to prison.* But the last thing a corrupt federal officer wanted to do was hang around where a local cop could identify him. Sheridan making himself scarce had been a welcome reprieve but at such a cost...

"I went looking for my dad once," April said. "He stopped paying support for my mom, me, and my brother."

Katerina came back to the conversation. "How did you find him?"

April shrugged. "His girlfriend. I knew where she worked. I got her cell phone number and texted like I was one of her friends and told her my dad was cheating on her. She left the bar, and I followed her to the apartment they were renting. It was a nice one, too. Carpeting, air conditioning. No bugs."

"I'm sorry," Kat said.

"Does your dad have a girlfriend?"

"Yes, he does."

April went to work on the next cookie. "If you can't find your dad, maybe you can find her."

Katerina thought about "Lulu's" phone bills stuffed in the "Go Bag" hidden in a locker under the floorboards of Moose's chop shop in Queens.

"You didn't manage to get anything on Devon Kelly by any chance, did you?"

April shook her head. "I'm gonna need new equipment," she said. "I had my laptop connected to the other one, so I can't use it anymore. I need a burner laptop."

"What's a burner laptop?"

"It's like a burner phone. Configured to be anonymous, and hard to infiltrate."

"Go see Moose. Tell him I said to give you money from the bag. Use the cash and go buy a laptop."

"Sure, no one will notice me walking into a Best Buy with a wad of cash. I said anonymous. Those computers are all pre-loaded with shit you don't want. We need a small, local retailer. I can use one of my credit cards."

"I don't need you using a stolen credit card."

"I could use your card."

Katerina hesitated. Tony Junior had said she would be out of Brooklyn by the holiday weekend. Buy the laptop now, the bill won't come until next month. The cop will never know. Still . . . *Remember what happened in January, you rushed out without thinking about the consequences.* "Great, then when the cop goes through my mail and reviews my credit card bill, we can talk about why I need a new laptop since he's decided I'm not going back to school next semester," Kat said.

"Damn, that's messed up."

"What about the pawn shop? Can your ex hook you up?"

"I told you, he's a moron. All men are morons."

"No," Kat snapped. "Not all. And just because he is that doesn't mean he can't be useful. Does the pawn shop have laptops?"

April shook her head. "Things are a little hot right now in Suffolk County. They've had a couple of visits from cops with a list of serial numbers."

Katerina gave a sigh. She had another option. She didn't like it, but she had no choice. "Okay, I know where you can get a laptop. Tell Moose that I am requesting that he take you to the bank of Pablo. He will know what that means. Give Pablo the specs and he'll get you a laptop, for cash. No one will think it's unusual. Do not, under any circumstances, agree to any trade or barter of your skills for the laptop, understand? Cash only. And most important, do not mention my name. I am not involved in this. Do you understand?"

"Yeah," April said with a pout. "I got it."

Another problem, on top of the rest of her problems. Pablo was someone else Kat didn't want to see. Back in January, she had bartered with Pablo for much-needed instruction in safe cracking. And she still hadn't paid up her end of the bargain.

Katerina rushed to get ready. She had chosen a pink top with white petal pusher pants and roman sandals. She pulled the mass of her hair back into a sloppy ponytail and tried a swipe of blush to coax some color to her pale, sallow skin. In her mind, this shit show was over; she envisioned herself meeting Ivan tomorrow; he would do what needed to be done, and then she would pack up and be out of here.

Coming out of the bedroom, she found Ryan wearing a T-shirt, jeans, and an impatient expression. The scent of fresh flowers wafted through the apartment; in a vase on the kitchen counter, a riot of pink and purple flowers thrived in full bloom.

"Okay," she said, doing her best to sound bright.

"Okay, what?" he said. "You're wearing that to the party? What happened to a dress?"

"I – I thought it was casual."

Ryan made a noise of disgust. "This is my parent's party. Their friends are going to be there. This is how you're going? You're stupid, you know that? Really stupid. Put on a fuckin' dress, Kate."

"I'm sorry. I'm sorry, I'm so sorry."

"And do something with your hair. You walk around looking like a mess all the time. We're leaving in ten minutes. Do something with yourself, Jesus Christ."

"I'm sorry, I'm sorry,' Kat said as she retreated into the bedroom, careful not to slam the door; a sound that would start another problem. *Don't come in here. Please don't come in here.* She held her tears. *Don't make any noise. He'll come in here.*

As she pulled on the loose, flouncy, spaghetti-strap dress, thoughts meandered through her mind. Ryan on the job, Ryan responding to a robbery in progress. Maybe there would be a shooting, maybe the criminal would –

Katerina stopped. What if she thought it, and it happened? Terror washed over her, the fear that her thoughts had that kind of power. Like a pendulum, she forced herself to follow a new train of thought, coaching herself in conversation. *I'm fine. It's going to be fine. Get through the party. See Ivan tomorrow. Remember what Tony Junior promised. Out of Brooklyn by the holiday weekend. Reynolds will be gone. Winter will come home.*

"Hurry it up," Ryan's voice called.

***

"Hi, Ma."

Ryan Kellan and Katerina Mills stood at the front door, smiling from ear to ear as they greeted Ryan's mother, Peggy Kellan. A hard-looking woman, Peggy sported brassy, blond hair, a body still solid and shapely, and a narrowed, suspicious gaze that always seemed to settle on Katerina.

Ryan stepped into the foyer and gave his mother a kiss on the cheek.

"Hi, Mrs. Kellan," Kat said.

"How are you, Kate," Peggy answered, and they exchanged a kiss. "Don't you look nice. You didn't have to dress up. It's just a barbecue."

Katerina smiled, careful not to glance in Ryan's direction.

***

The backyard swelled with noise, talking and laughter mixed with music. Flower beds lined the house, each in their neat, strategic patches. The oblong, inground pool functioned as the centerpiece, complete with diving board at one end. The lights had been strung for a party that would go on interminably, another day into night without end.

Kat picked out the cops, an easy task. Standing tall, blank looks with no emotion, a mix of ego, arrogance, and attitude. Command confidence, that's what they called it. They were untouchables, all of them. She wondered how many of them had the same secret as Ryan: a life of less than idyllic domestic bliss.

Ryan whispered in her ear. "Go say hello to my father," he said. "Be nice to him."

Kat nodded and moved out, navigating the clusters of people.

"There she is," came the familiar call from Ryan's father, Michael Kellan. A bear of a man, an NYPD detective, member of a special, elite crime fighting unit, a King of the city. Holding a beer in one hand, he extended his other hand for her to come into his embrace.

"How's my girl, hunh?" he said, squeezing her in close.

"Good," she said, as his hand settled into the concave of her waist.

"How's school?"

"Almost over." Kat wore a plastic smile, as she made the familiar small talk, the same questions every time. Groundhog Day.

"Good girl," and he squeezed her again.

Michael Kellan's group consisted of his partner, cop friends, and his own brother, Ryan's uncle, Christopher. The uncle gave her a friendly smile as always, showing a few too many teeth. Kat interpreted the smile as either *You're a pretty girl,* or *I'd like to nail you against the washing machine in the basement,* or maybe both.

Ryan approached, beer in hand, Frank and Emma joining him.

"Here he is, the wonder boy," Michael Kellan said. "You bring your medal? Gonna take it out after dinner and show everyone?"

Everyone chuckled at the familiar ribbing.

"When's the wedding, hunh?" he said, giving Kat another squeeze around the waist. "You better put a ring on this finger," he said, holding up Kat's hand, "or I might just take her."

"Mike, leave her alone," Peggy said, even as she zeroed in on Kat.

Katerina watched as Peggy's stare spread to the others. Kat realized her dress had shifted. *The bruises are showing.*

"Oh, I take a class, aerial silks. You climb using fabrics. I got tangled and fell."

The air shifted as the tension released. The conversation resumed with a chorus of, "You gotta be more careful," and veered off on its way. Katerina and Emma exchanged glances. Kat watched her friend's stilted discomfort; Emma broke eye contact and looked away. Ryan engaged in conversation, a poor, wooden performance. When their eyes met, he viewed Kat with his usual sheepish smile of penitence.

I'm sorry.

You mean everything to me.

I love you so much.

I promise it'll never happen again.

Liar.

Of course it will.

Kat glanced around at the gathering. *Do you all know? If you do, you'll never tell.*

No one breaks the blue wall.

***

Off the patio, Katerina ducked into the kitchen, a headache pounding from the heat of the sun and the alcohol. She found a cluster of grandmothers avoiding the swelter of the late day sun. She exchanged pleasantries and received her ritual scolding.

"You have to eat."

"You're too thin."

"You'll get sick."

I'm already sick. Your grandson makes me sick.

"I'm trying," Kat said, and she excused herself to go to the bathroom. Moving down the hall, she met Emma coming out.

"Oh," Emma said. "The alcohol went right through me."

"Uh hunh," Kat said.

Emma floundered for a response. "Are you both staying over?"

"Ryan hasn't told me yet. Aren't you going to ask me?" She watched Emma squirm. *Go ahead. I want you to.*

Emma placed a hand on Kat's arm. "Frank will talk to him again."

"He's talked to him before."

"He'll talk to him again. It's the job. It's the stress."

"I don't see you having any trouble wearing a halter top," Kat said.

"Listen, he's under a lot of pressure with the case and you need to be a little more patient and understanding," Emma said. "Are you taking an interest in what he's doing?"

You have no idea how much interest I take in what he's doing.

"Did you know that he went to a funeral last week for one of the hostages he saved in that robbery?"

"No, I didn't. He didn't tell me."

"Maybe you should ask," Emma said. "That's a tough thing for him. He saved someone's life, and that person just died. You don't have any idea what it's like to have someone's life in your hands. To think you've saved them but then they're lost anyway."

You don't have any idea what I know about. You don't know me. "No," Kat said, monotone, "I guess I wouldn't."

Emma flinched in annoyance. "See, that's what you do. That's what you always do. You shut off, like you don't care. You don't think of anyone but yourself. Try doing something for someone else, Kat." Emma reached out again. "I'm sorry, doll, I am. You know I love you to death."

"I have to go to the bathroom. I'll see you outside," Kat said, and she walked away.

When Katerina came out, she crept through the house. Heading towards the den, she stopped in a blind spot as she heard the low guttural tones of the voices. She recognized Michael Kellan.

"I got some business in the Bronx tomorrow," Michael said.

Kat knew when decorated New York City Police Detective Michael Kellan mentioned he had "business in the Bronx," that was code for the latest blonde or a brunette he kept on the side.

"Do me a favor, you stop and see Sal when you're done for the day, just give him this, and tell him I'll give him a call."

Kat spied an envelope in Michael Kellan's hand.

Ryan hesitated. "I'm not part of the operation."

"Neither is this. It's nothing. Just a little favor I'm repaying. It just some business we need to settle."

When Ryan didn't answer, Michael Kellan said, "You can't do your old man a favor? You're too big for that now?"

"No, no, it's no problem," Ryan said, "I just don't know if I'm going to be in that area tomorrow."

"So, you make yourself available in that area, understand?" the elder Kellan said.

"Yeah, sure," of course," Ryan said, accepting the envelope.

This is new.

"Kate?"

Katerina turned around and saw Peggy considering her. "You all right?"

"I have a headache," Kat said. "I was looking for Ryan."

"He's talking to his father," Peggy said. "Don't bother them. Come into the kitchen. I'll give you something. You stay out of the sun now and stay with me. You can help me with lunch."

Peggy waited for Katerina to move toward the kitchen.

***

An hour later, the kitchen crowded with warm bodies and the competing scents of aftershave, testosterone, perfume, and sunscreen. They talked over each other as they hovered over trays of food, creating heaping plates.

Kat stuck close to Ryan, the dutiful girlfriend, fixing his plate for him. He caressed her back, his first-place trophy, as if to say, *Does your girlfriend do that? No? Well, mine does.*

"Oh, look at that," Michael said. "Come over here sweetheart, fix a plate for your future father-in-law."

"Mike, leave her alone," Peggy reprimanded him.

A chorus of buzzing noises interrupted, cops pulling their cell phones from their pockets.

The patio doors slid open, and two cops drifted inside, cell phones in hand.

"He's screwed now," one said.

"Kate, help me with this,' Peggy said, as she placed an open bag of Oreo cookies on the counter and then opened the refrigerator door.

"No shit," said another. "When did it happen?"

"They just got him, an hour ago."

Katerina stood by the refrigerator, half-listening to Peggy but keeping one ear on the conversation. Peggy lifted out a tray, a pudding dessert concoction, and handed it off to Kat.

Kat's mind raced as her heart pounded. *An arrest. Who was it?*

"Who is it now?" one of the wives asked.

"Junior Desucci."

The dish wobbled in Kat's hands. One of the men standing nearby grabbed it, helping her settle it on the island. "Boy, that could have been bad. You okay?"

Dumbstruck, Kat nodded as the conversation swirled around her.

Where'd they get him?

At the house, in the garage.

Look at that mess.
Capped both bodyguards, too.
Blew off half that handsome face.
Gonna be a closed casket.

"Kate?"

Katerina stared down at the pudding, the broken Oreo cookies in her shaking hands. At the sound of Peggy's voice, Kat snapped her head up. She held out her hands littered with cookie pieces. "I don't think I'm doing this right."

"It looks fine." Turning to the gathering, Peggy announced, "Take it outside, this is supposed to be a party."

The cop who broke the news apologized to Kat saying, "I'm sorry, no more bad stories, okay?"

Ryan draped his arm around Kat. "You okay?" he hovered. "Don't worry about this stuff. It doesn't mean anything."

"Everybody out of my kitchen," Peggy ordered with a wave of her arm.

As everyone piled back outside, the words grew faint.

With Junior gone, the old man is done.
The Russians will be back. They'll finish the job.
He can always go to the Feds.

The sliding door slammed shut, blunting the sound of the chuckles.

***

Once the sun went down, the drunken horseplay began. Michael Kellan fired the opening salvo, overpowering his son and tossing him into the pool. Katerina and others soon followed. After the party ended, Katerina, wearing one of Ryan's sweatshirts, her hair matted and soaked, followed Ryan as he stumbled into his childhood room. He collapsed into bed, asleep before his head hit the pillow.

The air conditioner hummed as Kat curled up under the blanket. In the darkness, Kat muffled her grief, weeping in silence for

Anthony Desucci Junior; he had shown her mercy, but there had been none for him.

She mourned for the father and the son, the living and the dead.

Philip fidgeted in his chair as he sat alone in the cold, gray, room, his briefcase on the table. He twitched as the door opened, jumping up from his seat. An officer entered, Grigory Federov in tow. The officer settled Federov in the chair and removed the handcuffs. The officer left the room, the door slamming behind him.

Federov regarded Philip with an amused smile. "So, you file papers this morning."

"Mr. Federov, this is not a simple matter, and you have an attorney–"

"I fire attorney. You are attorney now. You go to the court, you file motion for release. I know my arrest comes from Little Tony, so no problem to get charges dropped. No Little Tony, no case. Lucky for me this thing happens, unh?"

Philip flipped the lid of the briefcase and pulled out a file. He opened it, flipping the pages, and then clearing his throat. "Mr. Federov, there are still pending charges related to gambling, extortion, racketeering . . ."

Federov sat back in his chair, shaking his head. "Do not worry about this. I take care of this. I give you what you need to go to the court and do your lawyer papers to get charges dismissed. For me *and* my brother."

"Mr. Federov, Anthony Desucci, uh, Senior, is still my client and there is a conflict of interest–"

"What conflict?" Federov leaned forward. "No conflict. I don't kill Little Tony. You can work for me. Now. You do this work for me, while you still have other nine fingers," he whispered, "and rest of body parts. You work for me now. Just me."

Philip swiped his hand across his forehead, whisking the perspiration away. A knock at the door and an officer entered the room. "Time's up," he said.

Grigory Federov smiled at Philip Castle.

As Vito Massone entered the house, he heard the sounds of crying. A woman in her late twenties, her eyes still defiant in anger though red from weeping, appeared at the kitchen doorway. Vito stopped, nodding in deference to Angelica Desucci. She turned away from him and disappeared back into the kitchen. With two of his men flanking him from behind, Massone continued on and knocked at a closed door at the end of the darkened hallway.

***

Anthony Desucci ruminated in his grief. The dapper man with a full head of black hair had aged overnight; he had grown old.

Vito Massone sat in the chair next to the great oak desk. By the door, Vincent and Carlo held their posts as silent gatekeepers; Vito's men stood on the other side of the room.

Desucci heard Massone's voice, heard the words, but in the morass of his sorrow he could not comprehend. His son was not here anymore. He focused on Vito sitting in the chair, *that* chair. The chair Anthony Junior always sat in when they talked together late into the night. He had sent his son to college and then gave him a second education in the family business. He counseled him, watching him grow into his own man. The first born, wise beyond his young years, would have led the family forward after his own death. Gone.

"Sit in the other chair," Desucci said, cutting off Massone in mid-sentence.

Taken aback, Massone floundered at the request. Finally, he rose and moved to the guest chair opposite the desk. He sat down and began again. "You know I don't want to trouble you with this now. I know Jun—Anthony Junior ran this operation – and it was freakin' brilliant, no one could do this like him – but I think it's clear what's happening here. It was a double-cross. Federov played this game from the beginning. He wanted to be arrested. Him and his brother. So he could give the order from inside. It was one of our cops on the payroll; he was in on the double-cross. The word is the Federovs are gonna be released now. That two-bit lawyer is working on it."

Desucci didn't answer.

Vito Massone leaned forward. "With all due respect, we gotta get on top of the situation. These Russians. That Federov and his reptile of a brother. They're gonna come after you now. They gotta answer for Anthony Junior."

"I decide when we move, where we move, and how we move," Desucci said.

"That's what I'm trying to tell you. We can't move. We have cops breathin' all over us. We can't move."

Anthony Desucci's silence indicated an opening and Massone jumped at the opportunity. "We need leverage."

"The mayor is clean."

"Not that choir boy mayor. The honorable governor," Vito said as if he wanted to spit to get the taste of the words out of his mouth. "We need those photo negatives so Haley will come down off his high horse and put his foot on the mayor's neck. We need a clear path to the Russian." Massone lowered his voice to a reverent whisper. "Tony Junior would tell you this."

Desucci's eyes narrowed at the invocation of his son's name.

"We need to talk to the girl. The girl and the lawyer were both in on it."

Anthony Desucci looked away, his signal that he dismissed the idea.

"No matter what, she's gotta get the negatives."

"Tony Junior was working on that with her," Desucci said.

"That's right. And Tony Junior wouldn't have gone to the trouble of having Federov arrested if it hadn't been for her. I'm not saying she was in on it. I'm just saying it's possible. Let me take care of this for you. Carmela and the girls, they need you now."

Desucci narrowed his gaze.

"Federov has to pay."

The room seemed to drain of oxygen, as if everyone had taken a deep breath and held it, waiting for the decision from on high.

Desucci nodded.

Vito Massone stood up. "I'm very happy you let me take care of this. I'm gonna make things right for Tony Junior."

Desucci nodded but his eyes, forlorn and empty, stayed focused on the chair next to his desk.

As Massone went for the door, he heard, "Don't lay a hand on her. Not a finger, understand?"

"Absolutely," Vito Massone said.

Another auditorium. Another desk. Another little blue exam book. Last final. Katerina's eyes welled with tears as she answered the question, "What are you going to do this summer?"

I'm going to visit Paris with my boyfriend.

Visiterò Parigi con il mio ragazzo.

We will sit and eat at a café and watch the people go by.

Ci siederemo e mangeremo in un bar, guardando la gente che passa.

Then, we'll visit the Eiffel tower at night and kiss under the stars.

Poi visiteremo la Torre Eiffel di notte e ci baceremo sotto le stelle.

A tear fell on the page, smudging one of the words. Kat put the pencil down.

Alex.

***

Katerina entered the theater through the side door. Her throat constricted and a cough came out, the fight-or-flight response active and ready.

John Reynolds sat in his usual front row seat. Off to the side, Garrett stood silent. Kat noticed the dead, vacant eyes. *He's grooming another one.* Fear sliced through her at the thought.

"Miss Katerina," Reynolds said, ebullient as always. "This is an important day. We have much to plan and discuss."

Katerina felt the blank, vacant stare descend over her, the curtain falling. Everything was lost. Tony Junior – gone. She missed the appointment at the Chelsea Savoy. Ivan – gone.

"He beat you to it. I've already received my instructions. I have a full-time job in Brooklyn."

Reynolds nodded with a tut-tut of understanding. "Your policeman is quite the possessive one," and he said with a giggle. Kat braced as he reached into his pocket. "No matter," he said, "for I am always prepared for life's little emergencies. I don't need you to be in the city."

Reynolds pulled out a small, black cell phone and held it out to her.

Katerina took halting steps forward, snatching it out of his hand as if it would bite her.

"I suspected your beloved might want to keep you close at hand. This will be our new means of communication. This is a very special phone. You are to take this phone home to your little love nest. There it is to remain."

"Where am I supposed to put it?"

Reynolds giggled again. "That, my dear, is your problem. You will use the phone to text me your reports."

As Katerina moved to protest, he said, "Have no worries about evidence. The text messages erase themselves within seconds."

In a fit of temper, Kat said, "Is this how Bruce Elmont reaches out and touches you?"

Reynolds' smile slipped for a brief second and then recovered.

"He was on the employee list, of course," Reynolds said.

"Crossed off as deceased," Kat said. "Strange, no one ever wondered how a former Navy Seal drowned."

"It was a suicide."

"And he just happened to pick the method that's his natural skill."

"It avoids the discovery of a body. He wanted to find peace, so he returned to the only place he could find it. The sea won't tell." Reynolds stood up. "You know, Will Temple lived for weeks. He could have continued for months, but I felt it was time. And Bruce follows orders. It would be a tragedy if the police should somehow stumble on the fact that Bruce is, in fact, living. You hold the life of the one you love in the palm of your hand. Remember that, Miss Katerina. Act accordingly."

He left through the side door.

Kat lowered her head, standing in the silence.

I can't gain any leverage.

I can't do anything.

Walking toward the apartment building, Katerina fought the familiar urge to vomit as her stomach pulsed with its own heartbeat. She checked her surroundings, looking behind her. The Federovs had been released, all charges dropped. Anatoly could be anywhere, at any time.

When Kat entered the candy store, she expected the young girl behind the counter. Instead, a dour man peered at her as she picked out the pieces of Turkish Delight.

She went to the register and placed the candies on the counter. The man stared at her, then stared past her. Katerina turned her head. Two men appeared from the back of the store. She had seen them, last year, in a warehouse.

Vito Massone.

***

Katerina let out an involuntary "ooph" when her backside hit the seat, and the air flew out of her lungs. Vito Massone stood a few feet away, a cockeyed smile on his face.

Massone shot a look at one of his men. Big and solid, with a full head of hair and cold eyes, Katerina had met this enforcer last year in a warehouse; on Massone's order, he had brought the butt of a gun down on Moose's forehead three times. Now, he brought a chair forward and set it down inches from Katerina.

Vito came forward, took the seat, and sat up close to Katerina.

"You're hard to get a hold of."

Katerina didn't answer, rejecting every response as they ricocheted like stray bullets in her mind. Each one would result in her being struck. *Don't hit me. Please don't hit me. As long as I don't get hit, everything is okay.*

Katerina nodded, her eyes cast down toward the ground.

He crooked his head down, peering at her.

"Mr. Desucci is very upset."

Kat nodded. "I'm so sorry about Tony Junior. I'm so sorry."

"You should be. It's your fault he's dead."

Katerina's head darted up at the accusation.

"You think that would've happened to him if you had done what you were supposed to? You been screwing around with everybody."

Katerina shook her head. "No, I was working with Tony Junior, just him ––"

Massone stood up, towering over her. "Because of you, Junior had to deal with those Russians. You got him killed. Maybe you meant for him to get killed."

"I didn't mean for any of this to happen ––"

"No? Personally, I think you were working with Federov all along. I think you were helping him, that's what I think. You and that scumbag lawyer. He did a good job, getting the two of them released so quick, don't you think?"

Katerina shook her head as if watching a tennis match. "I don't know what Philip is doing. I was with Tony, just Tony. I just, I had to be careful. If I did too much, the cop, he'd get suspicious."

Vito smirked. The plastic bag went over Katerina's head. Her hands flew to the bag, her eyes widening in terror as the air slipped away. After interminable seconds, the bag lifted away. Katerina gasped for air, coughing and sputtering.

Vito nodded; the enforcer held the bag and waited.

"I promised Mr. Desucci I wouldn't lay a hand on you, not a finger. As you can see, I'm a man of my word."

Another nod and Kat shook her head as the plastic bag slipped back over her head. The enforcer held it closed tight and she struggled in the suffocation. Then the bag lifted away. She sucked in air as she coughed.

"You're jerking everybody around. I'm telling you. Get rid of the job. Get rid of the cop. Get back in the city."

"I can't just tell him I'm leaving. It'll cause a problem for you. Tony Junior understood that. The cop's not gonna give up. It'll make it worse."

Vito leaned in, his face inches from hers. "Do I look like I give a shit about your problems?"

Kat shook her head. When Vito lifted her head, she cried out, "No, please," on instinct.

He gave her an open, artless look. "No? Okay. Take care of this by the end of the holiday weekend. That's one week. You need to be back in the city, and you need to get those negatives. You take care of this, or I will, *capisce?*"

Vito took the chair and swung it back, setting it back in its spot.

"You know, you're a real mess. Look at you. I never could see what the big deal was. Nothing to get excited about. No one will miss you." He pointed a finger at her. "The holiday weekend, remember what I said."

Katerina clung to the chair, gasping for air.

Lashiver noted the flutter of surprise crossing Elizabeth's face as he stepped up beside her in the corporate cafeteria. He gave her a wide, friendly smile. "Hello Elizabeth," he said. "How are you?

He watched her mouth pinch as the eyes glanced away, closing off the window to her soul.

"Fine, detective," she said. "Mr. Reynolds is not in today."

"I didn't come to see Mr. Reynolds," he said, reaching out and removing the tray from her hands. "Here, let me help you with that."

"I really–" but the protest went ignored.

They stood in silence as the line to the cashier sputtered. When the transaction was done, Lashiver hung back for her to lead the way. "Please, wherever you like to sit."

Elizabeth made her way to a table in the back corner, her eyes darting back and forth. She sat down; Lashiver set the tray down and sat opposite. She made a presentation of arranging her napkin across her lap and setting her silverware just so.

"The last time we met, we talked about whether you went into the office during Mr. Reynolds' conference call. You remember we talked about that, right?"

"Yes," Elizabeth said.

"Elizabeth, do you have an answer?" Lashiver asked, his folded hands resting on the table.

"I'm still checking my notes."

Lashiver nodded. "I appreciate that, Elizabeth. I appreciate how helpful you've been. Maybe you can help me with something else? Since Mr. Reynolds had lost his phone and the IT Department had to order him a special phone –"

"How do you know that?" she blurted.

Lashiver smiled as an answer. Elizabeth flushed crimson and fell silent.

"Since the IT Department had to order him a phone, why didn't he just get another phone in the meantime?"

"Mr. Reynolds is very particular," Elizabeth said. "He knows his own mind and what he wants."

Lashiver nodded. "But he still needs a phone when he leaves the office. He's the owner of a multi-billion-dollar company. He wouldn't be walking around without a phone. No one would believe that."

"There's no point for the IT Department to download everything he needs on an emergency phone he's only going to use for a day or two," she said.

"Did he have an emergency phone?"

Elizabeth went silent.

"Elizabeth, we know, in the past, you've purchased disposable, pre-paid phones, just so he could have something. It's on your expense reports."

"I know what's on my expense reports."

"That's right, you do," Lashiver said, leaning in closer, confidential. "And we've reviewed your expense reports. You know what I don't understand? Your expense reports don't list any purchases of a pre-paid phone or any kind of phone during those days before Mrs. Reynolds was murdered. He would need to call his wife. Maybe, she would need to call him."

"Mrs. Reynolds called the office."

"Yes, I know. We looked at the records. But, Mr. Reynolds had appointments in and out of the office. He would need a phone."

Elizabeth stared at Lashiver as if he were an intruder and she hadn't figured out how to drive him out.

"Elizabeth, why didn't you buy him a phone?"

She didn't answer.

Lashiver waited, silent, patient.

"I can't recall," she said.

"You're an excellent assistant," Lashiver said. "You anticipate his every need. You never forget anything, do you?"

"No," she said.

"I wonder, if there are some things you wish you could forget."

Elizabeth stared at the tray, the fork in her hand hovering over the food.

"If you went into his office while he was on the conference call, you would have seen him there, without his phone. You would have reminded yourself that you needed to get him a phone, right?"

"Why does this matter, detective?" she asked.

"Elizabeth, you said in your interview, Mr. Reynolds had lost his phone at some point in the days before his wife's death."

"He did," Elizabeth said. "He lost his phone. He did not have it anymore. I called IT to cancel it so no one would use it. Do your reports show that?"

"Yes, they do," Lashiver said. "I just don't understand why you didn't get him a new phone. Why didn't you do that, Elizabeth?"

"I'd have to check my notes, detective."

"We can go back up to your office after lunch," he said, nodding at the tray, "and you can check your notes."

"They're archived," she said. "I need some time to go through them."

"You check your notebooks. You're a very organized person. That's good. We'll talk again. Very soon."

When she didn't answer, Lashiver said, "Have a good day, Elizabeth."

He got up from the table and left. Only after he left the cafeteria did the smile slip from his lips. Even after all these years, he could be impatient. He would have to wait a little longer.

Katerina stood at the counter. On the stove, the pan sizzled with the crackling of chicken that would come out burnt. She opened the door to the cabinet and crouched down to take out a pot for the vegetables that would come out soggy and overcooked. Removing the pot, she closed the cabinet door. Several other pots crowded the back of the cabinet. Behind them, the Reynolds phone sat dormant. Kat felt confident she had found the one place Ryan would never look.

Ryan's chatter continued behind her but in her head, she only heard his words after the incident in the university library. *You are never getting away from me.* Tilting her head to indicate her rapt attention, she noted the jacket draped across the back of the chair, the shoulder holster, with the gun tucked inside, draped over the jacket. *There's nowhere you can go and nothing you can do.*

"We caught another case, homicide. Investor's partner found dead at his desk."

"That's the third one you mentioned," she said. "What about the Reynolds case?"

"What about it?" he asked, taking another swig of his beer.

"You don't talk about it much."

"It's there. That old bastard did it." Ryan went silent for a moment. "He's trying to duck and cover with this reward bullshit."

"Reward?" she asked.

"Yeah, he's offering five million dollars for tips leading to an arrest. Now we waste all day chasing down shit leads that go nowhere. Rewards bring out all the nutjobs. Who gives a shit? It serves her right."

Katerina turned around. "What do you mean?" She hated herself for sounding stupid.

Ryan laughed. "You think she loved him? C'mon. The money – that's what she loved. She was head over heels for the money. She was asking for it."

"Felicia Reynolds was the victim of a terrible crime. Why is it her fault?"

Ryan tossed the bottle in the garbage can and went to the refrigerator. Opening the door, he pulled out another bottle, twisting off the cap and taking a long slug of the drink. "Because, she thought she was being clever, marrying a rich guy, getting everything she wanted. She was asking for trouble. Because that's what happens when girls think they're clever."

"You don't know how she felt about him when she married him," Kat said, feeling an imperative to defend the woman she had met only once and would never forget. She felt she knew Felicia Reynolds better than Detective Ryan Kellan ever would.

"I'm sure when she saw his bank account, it was love at first sight," he said.

"You don't know that she was like that. Even if she was, that doesn't mean she deserved to be killed. I thought you felt sorry for her."

Ryan stared at her, a smirk on his face. "She was where she didn't belong, like someone else I know who's always where she doesn't belong."

Katerina steeled herself.

"I got you a job to finally keep you out of trouble. Aren't you gonna thank me? Aren't you gonna be nice to me?"

"I'm always nice to you," she said, trying to sound like a teasing girlfriend, ready for play or foreplay. *And that gun, in that holster, right there, right out in the open . . .*

"I don't think so," he said, bumping up against her. "I don't think you're nice enough to me. Especially since you're going to burn that chicken, like you always do."

"That might not happen," she objected.

Ryan walked the apartment, pacing like a metronome, taking swigs from his beer bottle. She could feel him, even with her back turned to him.

"I'm trying to help you, Kate," he said. "We're all trying to help you. Keeping you out of trouble is a full-time job. Like that lawyer you were working for."

"I know, okay?" Katerina blurted in exasperation, raising her voice, "I know. Don't you think I know it wasn't good?"

At her excitement, Ryan lowered his voice, his manner suddenly calm. "Did you know he just sprung two Russian mobsters out of jail?"

"I left him," she yelled. "I stopped working for him. I don't know anything about what he does."

"Why are you raising your voice at me?" he asked, he voice soft and low.

Katerina froze as she felt her cheeks burn crimson. *It's getting too close.* "I'm sorry," she said. "I shouldn't do that."

"There's a lot of things you shouldn't do," he went on, his voice quiet and droning, the tone she despised. "You didn't leave right away, did you? No, you stayed there. I know why it took you so long to leave that job. We both know why it took you so long to leave that job."

Katerina held still, knowing there was nothing she could say to avoid the coming disaster.

Ryan laughed. "I looked into that guy. I've been following his career. He's a real crafty one. He's good, he knows the law; he knows how to bend it. That's how he got those pieces of shit Russians bailed out of jail."

Unsure she could hide her emotions, Kat turned her face away.

"What are you going to tell me Kate, he didn't have his mob clients come to the office? You didn't know about that? Of course you did. You shouldn't have stayed more than that first week, that first day. That's the problem with you. If there's a wrong door, you'll walk through it. If there's trouble, you'll find it. We're all trying to help you be good. Don't you want to be good?"

"Yes, of course I want to. Ryan, I'm trying to be everything you want me to be," she said, her voice thick with tears. *Please. I don't want to do this. I can't do this.*

Ryan came to her. "You don't want it for yourself? You don't want to live a right life for yourself, that's what you're saying?"

"Yes, I mean no, I'm not saying that – I don't know what I'm saying. I'm not saying anything."

Ryan laughed and then shook his head again. "Good thing I got you that job. You'll stay out of trouble. You need to behave yourself. Or you'll end up being taken by some lunatic and God knows what happens to you. You'll end up like Felicia Reynolds."

Kat turned back to the stove, the apartment returning to the thick, uncomfortable silence.

At the sound of rustling, she turned her head to find Ryan in her purse, pulling out her "regular" cell phone. Her anger spiked, but she held her tongue.

"Warren says you're on the phone," Ryan said. "So, let's see who you're talking to. Did you change the code?"

"No."

"Why would you do that? Why do you need to change the code?" He was walking toward her now. "What are you hiding?"

"The code is the same as it always is. Two one four six. I didn't change anything."

Using his thumb, he punched the numbers and shook his head. "Not working."

"Yes, it does," she said, the pitch in her voice rising with her panic. "It works. It's the same."

He punched the numbers again. The screen for the phone appeared. He gave her an accusatory stare as he used his thumb to swipe and then slipped her phone into his jacket pocket.

"My mother calls me."

"Don't worry, I'll talk to her, and anyone else who calls," Ryan said. He pulled out a small flip phone and held it up. "I got you a new phone. It's on my plan. This is all you need."

Kat said nothing.

"Aren't you gonna thank me for it? Or are you gonna pout?"

"It's fine, thank you," she said.

"It's fine, it's fine," he said, mimicking her. "Fine. You know, this is what I'm talkin' about, Kate."

That's not my fucking name. My name is Katerina - Katie. Like Winter calls me.

Ryan took another pull of the beer. He flipped and flicked away a lock of her hair. "And you need to cut this hair."

"Your father likes the way I look. You always want me to wear it down when we go there."

"I don't give a shit what my father likes. I've changed my mind."

"I'm not cutting my hair."

Ryan nodded as he wandered the kitchen. "Is that right? Okay, okay."

Kat's stomach roiled in the waiting.

The sudden yank made her head snap back.

"Who are you keeping it for, hunh?" he whispered in her ear. "That Perry Mason in your law class?"

"No one," she gasped.

"I bet he likes it, doesn't he? Where did you two decide to meet up this summer, hunh? Is he gonna come out here, because he's gonna have to come out here."

"Ryan," she said, every muscle in her neck straining. "I am not seeing anyone. Your mom wants to do my hair for the wedding – please, you're hurting me."

The fire alarm in the kitchen screeched as black smoke rose from the frying pan. Ryan's eyebrows quirked with mock surprise. He released her. Kat, lightheaded as the nausea rushed through her, grabbed the pan off the burner.

"Order a fucking pizza," he said. "At least I'll have a decent meal tonight."

***

Katerina slid the backpack onto the kitchen table and made fast work of sifting through the papers and notebook. She scanned the lists of tips for the Felicia Reynolds case, all crossed out, one by one. Dead ends. Closing the backpack, she turned away and crouched down by the cabinet. Reaching inside, she slipped out the cell phone. She typed the message and watched it send and disappear. She slipped the phone back into its hiding place.

A rustling. Kat froze in place, her eyes closing for a moment. Closing the cabinet door, she stood up, grabbed a glass, and flipped on the faucet. She turned to see Ryan just outside the bedroom doorway.

"What are you doing?" he asked.

She took in the scruffy face, the puffy eyes squinted with sleep and alcoholic confusion.

Did he see anything? Does he know?

"I was thirsty," she said.

He came to her and caressed her back with a light touch. "I love you so much, you know that, right?"

Kat nodded. "I know."

He took her in his arms and kissed her. "I love you. You're so beautiful. I'm sorry. It won't happen again. I promise."

She nodded and let him take her by the hand, but her mind remained preoccupied on John Reynolds and his latest maneuver to stall the case.

CHAPTER

43

Ryan eased the car into the back parking lot of the factory, shifting into neutral, letting it idle. Workers loitered near a factory entrance door, a plume of cigarette smoke surrounding them.

Ryan glanced out the front window and nodded toward Juan. "There's your friend," he said.

Katerina nodded.

"We'll leave for the Island as soon as I get in tonight."

Another nod. "Okay."

He rolled his eyes. "What's the fucking problem now?"

"I'm impatient to get to the holiday weekend."

Ryan nodded in approval. "That's better." He leaned in and took a kiss. When they parted, he said, "Be good."

"Promise," Kat said and ambled out of the car, waving to Juan as she crossed the lot and went into the building.

***

Around two in the afternoon, a buzz of heightened anticipation permeated the air. The worker bees swarmed in a frenzy to finish their tasks, primed to burst forth from captivity.

Katerina observed the metamorphosis, the restlessness and excitement for the three day get-out-of-jail-free furlough.

The weight of Massone crushed her until she felt the air forced from her lungs and she began to cough.

The shift bell blared. The sound of voices, the trooping of footsteps heralded the showers would run; in a half-hour the workers would file out, having that first cigarette of freedom for the long weekend.

In the office, the women had stepped on the mental gas pedal so they could steal a few precious minutes by leaving early.

Katerina moved at her usual snail's pace, tendrils of terror snaking through her body from tip to toe and back again. Three days to the deadline. *Get out of Brooklyn.* Unable to sit still, she grabbed the folder marked "To Be Filed" and wandered down to the Quality office. *Think of Winter. He's the one who's trapped. Think of him. You can still move. You can do something.*

Standing in front of the cabinets, she filed the Safety Data Sheet packets, staring at the symbols on the cover pages: the flame, the cylinder, the exploding bomb. Her eyes traveled down the page and lingered over the statements she knew by heart.

Extremely hazardous vapor.

Extremely flammable liquid and vapor.

No smoking.

Katerina finished filing and came back to her desk.

I love the smell of methyl ethyls in the morning.

You know it's not so good for those guys to be smoking here. Something bad could happen.

Amid the chatter, she heard Luella say, "I'll drop these at the post office."

"I can do that," Kat piped up. "I have a few last bills to type up. I'll put postage on everything and take them."

"You know how to set the alarm?"

"I've done it before. I'll use the spare key to lock up."

"Thank you, baby," Luella said, and Kat could see her manager was already mentally out the door and gone.

***

In the stillness of the empty building, Katerina finished typing the last bill. She ran the envelopes through the postage machine. Signed, sealed, delivered.

A calm had settled over her mind. She got up from her desk and went to the kitchen, grabbing a plastic bag from a drawer. Then she went to the Quality office, extracting a pair of disposable gloves from an open box.

One move left to make.

Katerina slipped her phone from her purse and went for the connecting door leading into the factory. Entering the darkness, she tapped to turn on the flashlight.

***

Reaching the chemical storage room, Katerina went to the side door that opened to the back parking lot. Pushing it open a crack, she glanced down, spying the gathering of fresh cigarette butts, the small, slender tendrils of smoke still rising. Scooping up several, she shut the door.

When Kat opened the storage room door, the noxious chemical scents assaulted her nose. Slipping further into the room, she counted at least a dozen empty drums, their vapors floating in the space. Her eyes fell on the drum with the grounding wire clamped on. She unclipped it. Moving the flashlight over the area, she found the switch for the room's ventilator fan.

Give a push. Flip a switch.

It doesn't matter.

With a gloved hand, she flipped it off.

Shining the light toward the floor, she spied the stray, chemical-soaked rags. She threw down the cigarette butts and left the room, letting the door swing shut behind her.

Making her way back through the factory and inside the office, she pulled off the gloves and shoved them in the bag, squirreling them away in the false bottom of her purse. She took the mail, set the alarm, and exited the building, locking the front door behind her.

What would Winter tell you?

Walk like you're where you're supposed to be.

Lost in her thoughts, Katerina lifted her head, and her eyes landed on Juan. She stopped short and they held each other's gaze.

What did you see?

What do you know?

You'll never tell.

Katerina, her heart pounding in her chest, turned and headed for the subway.

The Memorial Day holiday weekend heralded the official start of summer. While the locals couldn't wait to flee eastward, the tourists swarmed in, descending on the city like a flock of birds. For any visitor partaking of the city's vast cultural offerings, one item was not to be missed: a once-in-a-century exhibit at the Metropolitan Museum of Art.

The Beaux-Art style building boasted two banners mounted on its façade, both bearing one word: Leonardo.

Among the retrospective of the artist's drawings of anatomy, flying machines, and works of art, a pièce de résistance: the Met's exclusive to display the *Salvator Mundi*. The painting had disappeared for over a hundred years; when it had reappeared, it was downgraded as a minor work by a member of the artist's studio. Finally, it was discovered as a Leonardo, confirmed, argued over again, and confirmed again.

Over the years, it had been badly damaged by age and decay; at one point the wood canvas had split into pieces. Restoration had taken years of work. The painting had changed hands several times until it had been sold at auction to an unknown buyer for over four hundred million dollars. Not unknown to everyone. Governor Richard Haley, a staunch defender of New York's place as the world capital of all things cultural, had personally appealed to the owner. The anonymous owner had graciously agreed to lend the canvas for the exhibit. The governor was only too happy to claim the feather for his cap.

Upon entering the museum, the throng passed through the Great Hall, then traversed the staircase and joined the line to wait. As the visitors entered the exhibit, they passed the giant wall mural with a self-portrait of the genius and the title underneath, "The World of Leonardo DaVinci." *The Salvator Mundi* waited at the end of the exhibit, flanked by Met guards, reminiscent of the protection afforded decades earlier to a different Leonardo masterpiece, the *Mona Lisa.* However, the *Salvator Mundi's* owner insisted on having his own, undercover security, watching everyone and everything. These private guardians would not disappoint their employer; failure to safeguard the painting was not an option.

On Saturday morning, the museum had been open for three hours when the first whispered rumblings traveled through the crowd. Then, the restlessness, the heads turning, craning to see behind them. Once the smoke snaked into the exhibit rooms, panic broke out. At the blare of the fire alarms, gasps of excitement went up as people pushed toward the exits.

Following the emergency protocol, the museum guards ushered everyone out of the area while the owner's private security flew into action. As per the plan that had been practiced countless times, they lifted the *Salvator Mundi* from the wall, rushing it to the nearest stairwell. Flying down the stairs, they communicated by radio to the transportation van, always at the ready on Fifth Avenue. The van would pull into the North garage, receive the treasure, and whisk it away to a safe location.

Like a tornado unleashed, the plainclothes security burst onto the loading dock as the van jerked to a halt at the entrance and backed into the empty bay, hauling up and slamming to a stop. One man opened the back doors of the van, the other putting the painting inside the waiting, open case. He slammed the case shut, then slammed the doors shut, and with a fist, banged on the closed doors twice. The van shot out of the North garage and sped off.

That was the last anyone saw of the *Salvator Mundi.*

Including the owner.

The same lights strung around the backyard. Balloons bobbed on the surface of the pool's water. The Kellan Memorial Day barbecue bash had started at one in the afternoon and gone full speed all day. Even the bridal party hen house had been invited. Kat had exchanged hugs and kisses with Jeneen, the poor girl talking too loud, smiling too much, hoping to be noticed even as she was ignored. Michelle looked like she had been sucking on a grapefruit all day; she didn't bother to hide her annoyance that Katerina was still alive. Instead, the rival took her revenge by finding every opportunity to be in the vicinity of Ryan, a hand on his shoulder, a word or two of exchange.

Kat gave Michelle her sweetest smile as she chatted with everyone. All weekend, her mind had been elsewhere, looking for opportunities to check the news or read a paper. Had she done the right things in the right combination? Would there be a fire? Would everything burn? What if it didn't?

"All right everyone, settle down," Michael Kellan boomed. "We're very happy you're all here with us to celebrate the holiday. Especially you, Frankie. Wasn't sure our hero was gonna make it, since you were busy with that cat in that tree."

"Did you do the CPR on the old lady first and then get the cat out of the tree?" someone called out.

"He did the CPR on the cat first and then got the old lady out of the tree," another said as laughter filled the backyard.

"Nah, he did 'em both, same time," yet another said.

"Shoulda left the cat for the rookies, Frankie," Michael Kellan said.

Everyone laughed.

"Just kidding. We're proud of our boy, here," Michael Kellan said.

Frank Mitchell raised his beer, his arm around Emma.

Katerina turned to Ryan as he glanced down at his feet, the smile slipping away as the disappointment in his eyes bloomed. Ryan and Frank had made their careers together, rushing into a hostage rescue. But the rescuer became the rescued when a gunman had Ryan trapped. Frank had pulled the trigger; the elder Kellan had never let his son forget who had been the greater hero that day.

"But I think we may have something else to celebrate today," the elder Kellan said and turned toward his son. Ryan took Katerina by the hand. A collective "oooh" sound rose as he led her into the center of the backyard.

Katerina kept her head crooked downward, playing shy, while the panic rose.

Balloons on the water.

A celebration.

Of what?

Oh God. Not this.

It can't be.

He wouldn't.

"Let's see in about a minute," Ryan said, and everyone laughed.

Katerina imagined her smile looked like Jeneen's. She raised her head to Ryan, remembering to gaze up at him in innocent adoration, playing the girl in love with the man in front of her.

Ryan began with a halting voice, and he cleared his throat. "Kate, I never thought I would meet anyone like you. And you turned everything right side up instead of upside down. I want you in my life . . . until death do us part."

Katerina kept the smile pasted in place and her eyes widened as if on command, that delicate mix of stunned delight.

"Make me happy by saying yes," he said as he got down on one knee. "Will you marry me?"

Tears ran down her cheeks.

Alex.

Bob.

Professor, what do I do now? What do I do?

Michael Kellan's voice broke the silence. "Is that a yes?"

Everyone laughed.

Katerina nodded. "Yes," she said, crying.

Ryan slid the ring on her finger; Kat stared down at the square stone. In her mind, she saw the delicate, curved ring containing the elegant sakura diamond shaped like a cherry blossom. Winter had placed the ring on her finger back in January.

Gone. All gone.

Katerina, her eyes wet with tears, the false smile still on her lips, threw her arms around Ryan to the sound of clapping. She caught sight of Peggy Kellan's unsmiling face, the eyes narrowed with suspicion at her prospective daughter-in-law.

Family and friends descended, crowding them with congratulations and kisses. Michelle wheedled her way next to Ryan. "Hey, you, congratulations," she said.

"Yeah, thanks," he said, with a quick kiss.

Michelle moved on to Katerina.

"Well, congratulations," Michelle said.

"Thank you," Kat said. "I guess *I* do know what's necessary to keep a man."

Michelle's eyes blazed and her face flushed. "You little bitch—"

"Welcome to the family," Michael Kellan boomed as he stepped between them with a chuckle and enveloped Katerina in a bear hug.

Christopher caught Michelle by the arm and whispered in her ear as he shifted her toward Emma.

"I got the best guy in the whole world," Kat heard herself say.

The conversation crossed over the speed bump of the awkward scene and picked up again.

Emma, her face a thundercloud, spirited Michelle away; Jeneen followed on their heels, talking at them both in a low voice.

Kat met Frank's gaze, his expression dark and disturbed. Kat glanced away, sucked back into the torrent of babbling discussion of how a maid of honor would be an expert on wedding planning.

"When's the wedding?" someone asked.

"Christmas," Ryan answered, firm and final.

Noises of approval went up again. Katerina took it all in like a poison. Using her thumb, she fiddled with the engagement ring on her finger, the ring she despised and wanted to rip off and have out of her sight.

What now? What now?

The elder Kellan bellowed that she and Ryan should pose on the patio for a picture and wouldn't that make a beautiful shot with the lighting. Ryan slipped behind her and wrapped his arms around her waist, her arms pinned underneath.

The guests raised a glass, and the elder Kellan called out, "To the happy couple."

***

Later in the evening, when the lights in the backyard had been extinguished, Katerina stood in the darkness, listening to the pool water lapping softly from the warm breeze, inhaling the strong scent of the chlorine. She felt him come up behind her; her eyes closed for a moment in dread.

Ryan maneuvered Kat, turning her around. He crooked his head down and gave her a kiss. "We're forever now," he said.

She glanced up, the vague outline of his features in the darkness. "Forever," she repeated.

Alex.

The insistent buzzing of the phone pulled Katerina from sleep. Through filmy eyes, she watched Ryan rifle through her purse and pull out the cell phone.

He said a few words, eyeing her as he spoke. "Yes, she's right here. Is everything okay?"

He held out the phone.

Rousing herself from her stupor, she grabbed it.

"Hello," she mumbled.

"Katerina, thank God, baby," she heard Luella say.

"Are you okay?" Kat said, as she raised herself to sit up.

"Turn on the news, baby. The whole place is gone."

"What whole place?" she asked.

"Work. The whole place went up."

Ryan left the bedroom. Katerina heard him padding down the hallway, his heavy footsteps on the stairs. Scrambling out of bed, the phone still at her ear, she followed him.

"We all knew it was just a matter of time, baby. Thank God no one was hurt. I was worried about you, because you know, you just never know, you were the last person to leave, and your mind starts to wander . . ."

As Katerina approached the den, she heard the noise of the television.

Remember. Act surprised.

Katerina stared at the screen, fire ravaging the building.

Residents as far as four blocks away heard a loud bang at two o'clock in the morning. Rushing out of their homes, they were greeted to the spectacle of the plume of smoke from the explosion.

Katerina said a few parting words to Luella and clicked off the call.

Her mouth hung open, watching the obligatory "man-on-the-street" interview; he had been walking his dog and saw the fireball. *People v. Deitsch. A warehouse fire broke out. One person was trapped, killed in the fire – the defendants created unsafe conditions which led to a death. People v. Warner-Lambert. There was evidence of a foreseeable and indeed foreseen risk of explosion. "We subscribe to the requirements that the defendants' actions must be a sufficiently direct cause of the ensuing death before there can be any imposition of criminal liability."*

Kat's heart skipped in trepidation until she heard, "No firefighters have been injured." But her insides jolted again as the reporter ended with, "the cause of the explosion is currently under investigation."

Peggy Ryan came in carrying a cup of coffee and held it out to Ryan. He took it as Kat sat down on the couch.

"Guess you're not going to work anymore," he said.

"Guess not," Kat said.

"You'll stay here. You can start planning the wedding," Ryan said with a note of finality.

Katerina sat very still. "I need to finish planning Emma's shower," she said. "I need to be in the city to do that."

"I'll bring you into the city one day next week," Ryan said. "Then I'll bring you back here. It's okay with you if Kate stays here, right, Ma?"

"Sure, of course," Peggy Kellan said without enthusiasm.

"Shouldn't I look for another job?" Kat said, daring the comment because of Peggy.

"Don't worry about that. My dad and I will find you something. Maybe Eileen needs help at the floral shop a couple of days a week, Ma."

"I'll ask her," Peggy said.

Staring at the destruction on the screen, Kat could only wonder. . . If it had been two hours later, someone could have been . . . Katerina forced the sickening thought from her mind. And now, after all the risk . . . *I just moved from one trap to another.* She wanted to open her mouth. She wanted to yell.

She wanted to scream.

The problem is your temper, Katie. It's always your temper.

Katerina felt the comforting rush of Winter's voice in her head.

Yes, professor. But I'm stuck.

Did you go to Sunday School?

Yes, professor.

Do you remember the story of Moses striking the rock?

Head counselor has worst camping trip ever, loses temper with automatic beverage system, misses out on best timeshare ever – permanently.

That wasn't the point of the story, Katie.

Alex, what is the point of the story?

Lose your temper, you could lose everything. What motivates him? What does he want?

To keep me trapped here.

And how do you get out of that?

Katerina caught the unsmiling glance from her future mother-in-law.

Make her want to get rid of me.

"Thank you very much, Mrs. Kellan," Kat said with a docile smile. "I appreciate it."

***

Katerina began waging her campaign by doing as little as possible. Under Peggy Kellan's disapproving eye, Kat began her day by the pool, slathering herself with sunscreen and lazing about. She interrupted her taxing activities by taking sips of water, going for a swim, or reading a magazine. Only when she disappeared into the house to take a shower to cool off, could she muffle the sounds of her infuriated screams of frustration into a towel.

It didn't take forty-eight hours for her future mother-in-law to get annoyed with the lazy girl lounging about in a skimpy bikini, and her husband making a beeline to sit poolside when he came home from work. Katerina made a point to laugh out loud at everything Michael Kellan said, and as his invincibility complex rose, so did his wife's anger.

To pour salt on the wound, Kat made sure to enter the house at just the strategic moment when husband and wife were in a heated discussion, the octaves of their voices taking a sudden dip at her entrance.

"You having a good day, sweetheart," Michael Kellan said.

"Easy peasy lemon squeezy," she said with a smile, noting that Peggy's granite face hardened further.

Katerina's easygoing manner belied the cyclone raging within her. Cut off and captive in her sunny, gilded cage, her thoughts ran wild and unchecked; each new song blaring into her ear buds evoked fresh horrors of Winter's captivity, and Tony Junior's death, until the sorrow threatened to overwhelm her. She found herself re-living her encounters with each man, one a lover denied, the other a man who had shown more fraternal care and affection than her own brother had ever done. The sorrow soon turned to desperation.

I have to get out of here . . .

Every day I don't report to Reynolds . . .

And Federov will be coming back . . .

And the drug dealer's hitman . . .

Katerina remembered meeting the hitman on that cold day in January. As she had made her escape from Richie Calico's house, her father's laptop hidden under her heavy winter coat, he came up from the basement . . . the basement where he had just murdered Richie.

Time is almost up. He'll be coming now.

And he'll be coming to . . . shit. The apartment.

Katerina realized she needed to send text messages. She found it ironic that the firestorm she set off during the barbecue would come in handy. Swinging her legs over the side of the lounge chair, she got up and sashayed through the patio door and into the kitchen.

"Mrs. Kellan, can I please use the phone to make a call?" At the older woman's look of confusion Kat added, "Ryan has my phone."

Peggy Kellan nodded toward the phone on the counter. "You don't need to ask permission."

"Thank you," Kat said, casting her eyes down in embarrassment. "I need to call Emma."

Peggy nodded. "I'll bet you do."

***

Hiding out in the bathroom, Kat used the Kellan household phone to call Emma. "I'm sorry I didn't call sooner. I'm still out on the Island."

Emma wasted no time. "Why did you have to say that to her? Didn't we talk about this? I mean, I'm happy for you, hon, I'm happy for you both. I didn't want to say anything at the party, after all Ryan had just made the announcement. But, why, why would you say a thing like that to her?"

"I'm sorry, I didn't mean it." *Liar. You certainly did.*

"I didn't ask you to be close with any of them, but they are my friends and my bridesmaids, and the least you could do is get along with them. It's two months until the wedding and all my bridesmaids don't want to talk to the maid of honor."

Kat heard Emma's voice like white noise in the background as she held the phone between her ear and her shoulder. She held the tiny burner cell phone in her hand, and she sent off the first text message to April.

Leave the apartment ASAP.
No, you didn't do anything wrong.
Expecting unwanted visitor.
Don't ask questions.
Tell Moose I'm asking if you can stay with Gigi.

Katerina tapped the phone on her knee in impatience until it buzzed.

Got it.
When are you coming back?
There's a problem purchasing the thing.

Katerina cursed under her breath. *What now?*

Emma's voice continued to drone in her ear.

"Michelle doesn't want to be in the bridal party anymore."

No great loss. "Emma, I'm so sorry. I'm so sorry. I'll call her. I'll apologize."

"No, don't you call her yet. I have to work on her some more. She is plum infuriated with you. That was a thoughtless thing to do, Katerina, really. To embarrass her like that."

"I'm sorry." *You should have known better. You should have known I'm not good.*

"Listen, hon, you and Ryan are the maid of honor and best man for our wedding. I'd put you out of your misery since you obviously don't want to do this—"

"Emma, that's not true."

"Oh, hon, I've just about given up on you, I really have. But, I can't have Michelle take over as maid of honor, that wouldn't work with Ryan."

Kat typed back a message to April.

Back as soon as possible. Hold tight.

Kat sat on the lid of the toilet, stewing in her situation, still listening to Emma.

"When are you gonna finish the bridal shower? Are you even close to being done?"

"Emma, Ryan wants me to stay out here. I *can't* tell him no."

She listened to Emma flounder for an answer until she said, "Well, I'm gonna talk to Frank about this, and he's gonna talk to Ryan."

"Emma, no, please," Kat said, knowing it would have the opposite effect. "You can't tell him that. He'll be *upset* with me."

"Frank will tell him that *I* need you to finish these arrangements."

Kat knew it was a start. But it could take another week for Emma's complaining and Peggy Kellan's bitching to force the Kellan men to move.

I need to get the hell out of here.

I need a job.

I know where to get one of those.

"Hon, are you even listening to me?"

"Yes, of course I'm listening," Kat said. "I don't know what else to say."

"Don't say anything," Emma said. "You let me work on this and after I do, I expect you to fix this before I don't have a bridal party. I need you to mend these fences."

"I will, Emma, I promise."

They ended the call.

Katerina stared at the miniscule phone, hesitating, her finger poised over the tiny keypad. She inserted Thomas Gallagher's phone number from memory and typed out a message.

> Mr. Gallagher. I hope you're doing well.
> Thank you for the opportunity to apply for the summer
> internship. I am writing to inquire if I have been
> fortunate enough to be selected as I am most
> anxious for this opportunity as soon as possible.
> Thank you for your time and consideration.
> Katerina Mills

She waited a few minutes, staring at the tiny screen. She left the bathroom and stowed it away in its hiding spot.

More waiting.

"I advised you against this," Joseph Smith said. "You've had Human Resources calling for three days. She's not calling back."

"Of course not. She doesn't have control of her phone," Thomas Gallagher said, leaning back in his chair. Lisa sat in a chair off to the right. "A clear sign that Miss Mills is in desperate need of assistance."

Smith approached the desk, his knuckles resting on the edge. "She needs assistance? She just blew up a building to get *out* of a job. I told you this girl is different."

"And I agree with you," Gallagher said and glanced over at Lisa. "What I had hoped for with you. And what a disappointment you turned out to be."

"I brought her back to you," Lisa said. "You should have let me go after those photo negatives. I would have brought them to you by now."

"Worse than a disappointment," Gallagher continued, as if he hadn't heard. "A liability."

"Have you considered this could cost her another beating," Smith interrupted.

"I will take the risk." Gallagher said, wrapping his knuckles on the desk. "Moving on."

Joseph Smith went quiet at his employer's uncharacteristic display of annoyance.

Gallagher rose from his chair and addressed Lisa without looking at her. "The limousine is waiting for you downstairs. The driver knows where to take you. Mrs. Shields has what you need. You will go and do what you're told," Gallagher said and strode out of the room.

"Thomas–" Lisa appealed.

Gallagher kept walking.

***

Thomas Gallagher congratulated himself on his good fortune. He expected the policeman would become more intractable and controlling. The delay had worked in his favor. Now, to finish this. Gallagher had observed his partners spiriting young women away and cutting them off from the rest of the world. In those last days before accomplishing their goal, the gravest threat to their plan came from one person, and one person only. The one person Gallagher needed right now to bring Katerina Mills back to New York City.

Walter Lashiver, Ryan Kellan, Denis O'Connoll, and Tom Morse sat around the desks, eating out of takeout cartons. A chalkboard stood off the side, scribbled with notes.

"You know they got whiteboards now," Ryan said.

"Sometimes the way the dinosaurs do it is best," O'Connoll said.

Ryan laughed but shrugged, giving up the argument.

"Let's go over it one more time," Lashiver said. "Felicia Reynolds."

"No hairs, no fibers, no murder weapon," Ryan said.

"Cheryl Penn autopsy reports."

"Nothing," Ryan said. "It's like the killer was wearing a plastic suit. The only hair and fibers belong to the victim and the husband. No murder weapon."

"Will Temple autopsy reports?" Lashiver said.

"Nothing," O'Connoll said. "A body in the rain. No hairs, no fibers."

"What about Random Girl Films?" Ryan asked. "Anything new?"

Morse shook his head. "I tried variations of the name. No such company. Nothing."

"What about the film, Love's Fury?"

"No such film. Couple of people said he had an audition. The kid didn't give any specifics, just said some guy called and he was supposed to see some woman. Office in the East Village. He said he met a pretty girl. No name. No description. There's nothing there."

"Love's Fury. It's him," Ryan said. "It's Reynolds. It's gotta be him."

"John Reynolds doesn't own any film or television production companies or any minor or major controlling interests in any film or television production companies," Lashiver said.

"That name means something," Ryan said. "Especially since we got a dead hooker."

"Right now, a dead hooker doesn't have anything to do with two dead socialites and one dead actor," Morse said. He wandered up to the board and looked over the names, the tacked photographs. "Maybe the two aren't related," he said.

"What do you mean?" Ryan asked.

"Reynolds doesn't have an interest in killing a prostitute."

"Reynolds didn't kill a prostitute."

"You're thinking copycat," O'Connoll said.

Morse shrugged. "Not necessarily. Another diversion, to muddy up the investigation."

"We're back to that. Like you think Cheryl Penn was just to muddy the investigation," Lashiver said to Ryan.

"Anything more on that?' O'Connoll asked.

"Cheryl's college friend is out of town again," Lashiver said. "First interview led nowhere. She's still on the list to talk to again."

"What about the friend of Felicia's, the one who kicked in the line?" Morse asked.

Ryan shook his head. "Felicia dumped her shortly after the marriage. Felicia's stock went up. The friend's didn't."

"Or maybe John Reynolds didn't want his new wife associating with old friends," O'Connoll said.

Ryan shrugged, conceding the point. "It's been six months since Will Temple died. Now, we got a dead prostitute. Whoever is doing this for Reynolds, has a need to do it. No way he's been waiting six months."

"So, the prostitute is different from Cheryl Penn. The prostitute is just to feed the need?" Morse asked.

"Right," Ryan said.

"Okay, suppose that's true," O'Connoll said. "Suppose all the cases are connected, somehow, for whatever reason, to John Reynolds. We're back to how does Reynolds come across this person, doing these things, and convince this person to kill his wife for him? What circles do they run in together? How do they even meet? We talked to all the employees. Where's the connection?"

The room fell into silence.

O'Connoll turned to Morse. "What happened with the recanvas near Temple's apartment?"

"Nothing. No one saw anyone out of the ordinary or someone who shouldn't be there. Nobody saw retired Detective Timothy Green, either. Since he's the only picture I had to show, I don't know who else they should be looking for."

"What about the businesses on the line opposite the apartment building?" Ryan asked. "Anybody remember anything new?"

Morse flipped through his notebook and shook his head. "That little old lady is still wandering back and forth, clutching her purse. Nobody knows anything."

"Tenants?"

"Yes, Temple had a lady friend. He'd had several lady friends, but Felicia seemed to be the flavor of the month. Yes, the walls are thin. Felicia was coming over once or twice a week, they made some noise, and then she left. No one doubts that. Nobody suspicious lurking in or around the building. No angry or jealous girlfriends, no angry or jealous boyfriends or husbands. No one identified Reynolds or his driver. There's nothing there." Morse put down his food carton in disgust. "If the same guy is the doer for this prostitute and the two socialites and Will Temple, well, like you said, what the hell has he been doing since January? It's June. Where's he been?"

They ate in silence for a moment.

"It's the same doer," Ryan said.

"Go prove that," O'Connoll said.

A cell phone buzzed. Ryan reached around in his pockets, digging out the buzzing cell phone. Katerina's phone. He looked at the number and put the phone away.

"Look, we're not gonna be the schmucks that are still sitting around after ten or twenty years and we can't get this guy," Ryan said.

"Hey, you need to stop listening to that shit Reynolds is feeding you," O'Connoll said. "Who's irritating who? You need to get straight in your head that you're not the only one carrying this. And I don't consider myself a schmuck, hotshot, and I think you should get yourself in line and remember to watch how you talk to your elders."

As Ryan got up, O'Connoll followed. Lashiver shot up and stood between them. "No one's saying that. We're all a little wound up and we're all a little impatient."

"Some of us more than others," Morse said.

"What is that supposed to mean?" Ryan asked.

"It means, maybe it's more than what Reynolds said. Maybe, if it's not a press conference where everyone's kissing your ass and handing you a medal, and you have to dig, that's just too much of a bother for you."

"Maybe if you hadn't blown off the disappearance and done your job–"

"Everybody take it down," Lashiver said, stepping between the two men. He looked to O'Connoll for back up.

Everyone settled back in their corners as the scent of male anger floated in the room.

"What about his garbage?" Ryan asked.

"What about it?" Lashiver asked.

"Why don't we dumpster dive again?"

"What are we looking for?" O'Connoll asked.

Ryan shook his head. "Nothing. But it's gonna piss him off and right now, that's enough for me."

The detectives exchanged glances until Lashiver said, "Okay, let's do that."

"Since you're the forward thinker here, you can go first," Morse said.

"No problem," Ryan said.

The phone buzzed again. Ryan ignored it, but with the eyes of the detectives on him, he pulled out the phone. When he saw the number, he rushed to answer.

"Hi, Mrs. Mills. Is everything okay?"

"I should ask you that. Why isn't my daughter answering her phone? Where is my daughter?"

"Oh, she's fine, Mrs. Mills. She's staying at my parent's house. It was an accident that I have her phone with me." Ryan glanced at the cops around the table, quiet, listening. "Are you okay?"

"I'm getting phone calls from someone in Human Resources at an Eagleton Incorporated. They have an internship for Katerina. They'd like to offer her the job, but they're not able to speak to her. They've been calling for days."

"Mrs. Mills, uh," Ryan said, and he got up from the table and exited the room, closing the door behind him. "I'm sorry, I've been so busy with cases, I guess I didn't see the calls come in today. I don't know why she hasn't called them back or what happened with that. But Katerina will call you tonight, from her phone, as soon as I get home. And I will make sure that she calls back about the internship."

"Katerina will call me, now, and I will explain the internship to her. I'm sure your mother has a cell phone that Katerina can use."

"Of course. Absolutely."

"If I don't speak to my daughter in ten minutes, I am going to call the authorities for a wellness check, while I'm on my way to New York."

"We'd love to see you, of course. We were just talking about making a trip to Vermont to visit. She'll be on the phone with you in two minutes."

The phone clicked.

Ryan turned around to see the detectives staring at him through the window.

In the back of the limousine, Lisa shifted in discomfort. That bitch housekeeper gave her the dress, but nothing to wear underneath.

The limousine pulled over to the curb. Lisa waited while the driver got out of the car, came around, and opened the door for her.

She exited the vehicle and walked with her head held high, with as much dignity as she could muster.

Just as she raised her finger to ring the doorbell, the front door opened.

She followed the houseman's instructions and went to a second floor sitting room. A man entered, mid-fifties, strapping, with salt and pepper hair. Dressed in slacks and a shirt, he was in the process of fastening the buttons of the cuffs on his shirt. He looked her up and down.

"How can I help you?" Lisa asked, as if she had just reported for assignment.

"Take off the dress," he said.

Lisa smarted at the comment. "I think you have me confused with someone else," she said. "If you no longer have an assignment—"

"You are the assignment," he said and went to a small table in the corner where a coffee waited for him. He picked up the cup and took a sip. "You've been given to me until I say otherwise. Now, take off the dress. Or I will."

Lisa undid the tie on her dress and let it slip to the floor, leaving her bare before him.

"Go over to the desk," he ordered.

Lisa obeyed the instruction. He came to her and turning her around, he pushed her forward to bend over. Lisa heard the sound of the zipper and stared at the wall. When it was over, she heard the sound of the zipper again. When she turned around, he had gone back to the table and was sipping his coffee. She retrieved her dress and slipped it back on.

"Get out," he said. "Go back to your apartment and wait until I call for you again. If I call and you don't answer, I call Gallagher. He can take you back and send you to whoever is next. When I get tired of you, I call Gallagher. He can take you back and send you to whoever is next. Understand?"

Lisa nodded and walked out with her held high, with as much dignity as she could muster.

***

Francine Shields stared at the security camera, watching the young woman rushing up the steps to the building. She stopped short at the door, her face flushed with anxiety, her hands going to her hair to smooth it down. Her finger went to the buzzer, halted an inch from the button, hesitated, and then pressed.

Francine took her time walking to the door and then delayed a few seconds longer before opening it. The girl, her eyes wide with uncertainty, her cheeks pink with the heat of the day and embarrassment, stared as if she had forgotten what she had planned to say.

"Yes," Francine Shields said.

"I – uh – is Mr. Gallagher in? He, he knows me. My name is Mina Roberts."

"Mr. Gallagher is not in," Francine answered.

"I've called and he doesn't call me back. I was – worried about him."

"If Mr. Gallagher has not returned your call, he has no reason to speak with you."

The girl glanced around, unsure of what to do.

Mrs. Shields took a slight step forward and the girl stepped back.

"Maybe, maybe, I could leave a message?" Mina asked, her voice meek and small.

"If Mr. Gallagher has not returned your call, a message would seem redundant. I will mention that you came to the door."

Francine stepped back to close the door when Mina said, "But why isn't he calling me back?"

Francine opened the door an inch. "I assume he no longer wishes to speak with you."

"Why?"

"I'm sure I don't know. You'll have to figure out yourself what you did to displease him."

Francine closed the door and heard the quick patter of the girl's footsteps mixed with crying as she fled. Francine Shields walked back to the kitchen.

It would not be the last conversation with this one. No, this girl would be back. Francine had already begun preparing for the training. It didn't concern her. He saw what this one was, what they all were. Worthless. Except the one he had been after since last year. Katerina Mills. Francine had taken care of Katerina Mills last year after she became ill at a restaurant. She had undressed the girl, seen her young, smooth, toned and tight naked body while putting her to bed.

Francine Shields stopped before a mirror, examining herself with dissatisfaction. The lines on her face, the body slack and soft. She didn't have a body like Katerina Mills anymore. She didn't have a face like Katerina Mills anymore.

She turned away from the mirror. Katerina Mills was a danger to Thomas Gallagher; he didn't see that yet. Francine Shields resolved to protect him from Katerina Mills, even if he didn't know he needed it. He would remember she was the only one who truly loved him.

The quartet ate at the table on the patio, the barbecue still smoking. Ryan looked stunned, like a puppy whose treat had been taken away.

Michael Kellan gave Katerina a squeeze of congratulations. "That's my smart girl, good for you."

Kat nodded. "I hope it's okay with you that I took the internship," she said to Ryan.

"Of course, it's okay with him," Peggy Kellan interrupted. "Why wouldn't it be?"

"You got a smart girl there," Michael Kellan added. "That's important."

Ryan nodded. "I think it's great. We'll leave after dinner. You'll be there first thing in the morning. Nine o'clock."

They ate in silence until Ryan said, "You liked spending time with my mother."

"She's been like my own mom," Kat gushed.

"It's been nice having a girl in the house," Peggy said.

"Your mom's going to throw the bridal shower."

"Lot of work to do," Peggy Kellan said. "We'll get it done, don't worry."

"You need to see the landlord about giving up the apartment," Ryan said. "I don't know what's in the lease and how much notice he needs. That college student is gonna have to go."

Katerina nodded as if she were a doll, wound up, moving automatically. "I'll take care of all that tomorrow. I'm sure I get a lunch time," she said.

As they finished the dinner, Kat joined the conversation, docile and calm. A woman at peace with her situation.

She watched Ryan interact with his father, the son quiet and deferential to the father's overwhelming personality. *No, he's afraid.*

What does it matter?

I'm still stuck in Brooklyn.

Did you go to Sunday School?

Yes. Professor.

Before Moses ever wandered in the desert, before he struck the rock in anger, there's another part to that story, what came before. Do you remember the story of the Israelites leaving Egypt?

Suffering captives seek new digs. Longest going away party ever, including free plagues for everyone. Don't drink the water on the way out of town.

That wasn't the point of the story, Katie.

What is the point, professor?

Make your plans. Be ready for your exit. One last move to make.

I will, professor. You, too.

CHAPTER

51

Like a prisoner being processed for release, Katerina waited the interminable minutes from the moment she opened her eyes, through showering and dressing. She emerged from the bedroom wearing a conservative silk blouse and skirt combination. Her fiancé, Detective Ryan Kellan, stood at the table, the backpack on the table, the mouth open. He had both hands in the backpack, rooting around.

Katerina pretended to check her makeup in the mirror, keeping an eye on his reflection. *What the hell is he doing?* Would he notice something was off in the backpack, papers moved or out of order? She reviewed each step of her nocturnal examination. No, she had done everything right. But, if he began questioning her. . .

He withdrew his hands out of the backpack. *Surgical gloves.* He grasped a torn envelope. An envelope like the one Michael Kellan had handed to his son at a weekend barbecue and asked him to do him "a little favor." *Another delivery. He switched out the envelopes. Why?* Katerina answered her own question. *The same reason he's wearing gloves. Fingerprints.* She watched Ryan look around. *For what? A place to hide it. He doesn't want to throw it in the garbage. He's afraid someone will go through the garbage.*

She watched him turn toward the kitchen, scanning the cabinets, upper and lower. If he opened the cabinet under the counter and rooted around in the back… Katerina saw the next few moments exploding as Ryan discovered the hidden cell phone. He folded the envelope and tucked it into his inside jacket pocket.

Katerina turned away from the mirror and checked her purse, cataloguing makeup, tissues. She heard the zipper of the backpack and turned to her fiancé. He stood at the table, clasping his watch around his wrist, slipping the holster containing his service weapon off the back of the chair, shrugging into it, and snugging it over his shoulders.

"All set?" he asked as he slipped his jacket off the chair.

"Yes," she said with a shy smile. Her fiancé nodded, averting his eyes.

***

They left the apartment, taking the stairs down to the street. As they exited the building and headed down the block to the car, Katerina watched Ryan check the area, taking in the parked cars, the pedestrians. She knew the habit. Cops called it situational awareness, checking their surroundings, anticipating what could come next. When they reached the car, he didn't look at her as he opened the driver's side door and slid behind the wheel. He didn't need to look at her. Katerina knew Detective Ryan Kellan was terrified.

What are you looking for? Perpetrators? Cops? Both?

Katerina settled into the passenger seat. Detective Ryan Kellan was in shit. *And if I stay here much longer, I'm going to be in the middle of it.*

***

Ryan's fingers tapped the steering wheel in rhythmic impatience at the stop and go traffic. Kat knew him well enough that traffic snarls never bothered him. He pulled the car over to the curb in front of the behemoth building of Eagleton Incorporated.

"Ryan," Kat said, soft and tentative, "is everything okay? With you?"

Staring at the radio console, he gave a vigorous nod of his head. "Sure, everything's fine. No problems."

"It's just," she started, placing her hand on his arm, "you've seemed, upset, since the barbecue a few weeks ago, after you talked to your dad. Is he okay?"

"Yeah, he's fine. It's just, work, and he needs some help with a few things, and I'm the only one he trusts, that's all."

Ryan took her hand and squeezed it. He leaned in for a kiss. When he pulled back, the cop mask had slipped back on, the eyes blank.

Kat reached for the door when she heard, "Oh, wait, take these." He held out a few bills. "Can't go without eating, Kate."

"Thank you," she said, slipping the money into her purse.

He held out her regular cell phone, the "Ryan" cell phone. She figured he had already made sure the GPS options had been turned on. "Thank you," she said.

"Hey, good luck today," he said. "I'm proud of you."

Katerina gave him a smile. "Maybe if I do well, I can get a permanent job."

"We'll see. Maybe you should go back to school."

Katerina's eyes brightened. "Really?"

"Yeah, maybe. We'll talk about it. You go on now," he said. "Be good."

"I promise," Katerina said and ambled out of the car.

***

Before Katerina could pull out her driver's license to show the security guard, he said, "Welcome back, Miss Mills. Just a moment, please," and picked up the phone. Katerina shifted from one foot to the other, agitated and restless. The conversation in the car had annoyed her in a way she could not describe. She needed to know more, and Ryan had stonewalled her. Maybe it was all legit undercover work, and he was simply out of his depth?

Maybe. Maybe not. The monologue went on in her head until she heard, "Katerina?"

Katerina recognized the woman in a severe, dark dress with peep-toe shoes. They had met last year. "How nice to see you again," Nicole Lovel said. "Please, follow me."

***

When Nicole opened the door to the Executive suite, Thomas Gallagher rose to his feet. Three other executives, late thirties or perhaps early forties, also stood. Katerina recognized them from her first assignment. Gallagher had required her to attend meetings and take note of what each executive said. He had taken Katerina to dinner and asked about these three executives. He announced he suspected one would betray him and the company's secrets. Gallagher had asked Katerina to name the traitor. She had refused; she would not destroy a man's career on such a reckless pronouncement. She watched them view her with vague recognition, and then calculate a rapid re-evaluation of her importance.

"Gentlemen," Gallagher said, "this project will be off the ground by the fourth quarter. It's going to be a tight deadline with no room for error. Remember the giants of this industry. Remember their words of wisdom. Sometimes you can't get from Point A to Point B in a vertical line. Sometimes to get a desired result, you have to be creative," he said and paused for effect, "you have to drill horizontally."

The executives chuckled.

"You all remember Miss Mills. She was here on special assignment last year, as my project assistant."

With bland smiles, they nodded, and each offered their hand. Katerina gave each hand a pump in turn, and they took care to give her a warm smile on their way out.

Mrs. Lovel, still hovering in the background, asked, "Will there be anything else, Mr. Gallagher?"

Gallagher recited a list of items and tasks that needed to be taken care of, finishing with "and please make the lunch reservation and then have my suits picked up and brought to the office instead of the apartment. I have a dinner engagement this evening. Thank you, Mrs. Lovel."

"Yes, of course," Mrs. Lovel said and left the office.

Kat watched the exchange, the calm, quiet, slow way Gallagher spoke, something Katerina couldn't put her finger on, and let the thought go.

Gallagher took Kat's hand and held it for an extra moment before releasing her. He guided her to come to the small conference table and be seated.

"I see they survived," Katerina said, nodding towards the door.

"Thanks to your levelheaded and fair assessment," Gallagher said. "Otherwise, I might have done something foolish. That's what I admire about you. You are methodical and careful."

Katerina didn't answer.

"Did Mrs. Lovel show you to your desk?"

"Yes, and she gave me a tour."

"And what do you think?"

"I think I appreciate that you are willing to help me."

"And you think you need to flatter me."

"You didn't ask me the question because you wanted to be flattered?"

Gallagher gave a delighted laugh. "That's what I've been missing. That razor sharp wit, wise beyond your years. You look somewhat better, but not back to yourself."

"I'm fine, thank you," Kat said.

"I'm glad to hear it. I have been considering your program here, the projects I would like you to work on. A large component will be spreadsheets you will need to create and quite a bit of data entry . . ." Gallagher noted Katerina staring at the floor.

"Is something wrong, Katerina? You're not pleased with the program?"

"You've been very kind to me," Kat said.

"And now you are flattering me, and I didn't ask you to. I have told you before that I'm your friend. And I hope you are mine. A good friend will always tell you the truth."

"It is best if it appears that I'm working here."

"Ahh," Gallagher said. "I see."

"If you could let me stay on a week, maybe two. It will give me a little time. Make it an unpaid internship. You shouldn't be paying for nothing."

Gallagher pressed the pads of his fingertips together, forming a steeple. "Perhaps we can come to an arrangement where you allow me to assist you without offending your sense of fair play. I should be familiar with that. I propose that you are on the books here, working five days a week, eight hours a day. However, you don't need to be at your desk."

Katerina's brows knit together in confusion.

"I believe the term is 'ghost employee.'"

"Why would you make such a deal when you get nothing out of it?"

"Not nothing."

Katerina's heart sank. Of course, there would be a price. She only knew one man who never asked for anything in return. "What did you have in mind?"

"Have lunch with me."

"When?"

"Let's stipulate a minimum of twice per week. I will have my assistant assign you one or two benign projects, paperwork shuffling, since I know your conscience will insist that you perform some work in exchange for the money."

"What else do you want?"

Gallagher's mouth pinched. "To be of service, where I can. I am hoping, quite honestly, that our lunches together might convince you to take me into your confidence. But we shall see. Now, will you be staying in the building the rest of the day?"

After a moment's hesitation, Katerina shook her head. "Mr. Gallagher, I am grateful—"

"Miss Mills, I am convinced, now that you are under my wing, you will find your footing, and a way forward. I think we have pushed on enough for today."

He stood up, her signal that she should follow. He took her hand his. "I am glad you called on me. And I hope you realize that I am worthy of your trust. Until tomorrow."

***

Katerina had her picture taken and received her badge. Nicole Lovel handed her a fob and a cell phone. "What are these for?"

"This building operates twenty-four hours a day. If you need to enter, you will be able to. Also, you are being issued a company cell phone. Mr. Gallagher's instructions," Nicole said.

Katerina found herself back on the twentieth floor, with a cubicle of her own. Sitting at her desk, Katerina dug her "normal phone" out of her purse and tucked it into her desk drawer. She had the badge and key fob to be able to return for it. Slipping her purse on her shoulder, she got up and left the building, without asking anyone.

Free.

Stepping outside, Katerina glanced around, scanning the area. In a city of eight million people, what could be the odds of running in Ryan? *Better than I think.*

Pushing the company cell phone off to the side, she dug the tiny burner phone out of its hiding place and dialed.

"My girl," she heard her mother say. "Where are you now?"

"Out – in the city," Kat said. "I went to the internship this morning. Mom, how did you even know about this?"

"That company, some woman in Human Resources, kept calling me."

Katerina knew by instinct that made no sense, but even as the questions swirled, she couldn't deal with it.

"Katie, you're still in that apartment with him?"

"Yes, for now. How are you?"

"How do you think? My girl is in trouble."

"Where are the half-brothers?"

"Searching, still searching."

"Is Uncle Sergei there? Can he talk to me?" Kat asked.

"Not at the moment."

Kat stopped. "Is he angry with me?"

"No, my girl. Why would he be angry?"

"I don't know. He never wants to talk to me."

"It's hard for him, Katie. He feels helpless. You'll call me every day now?"

"Yes, Mommy. If I can."

"Katie, how are you ever going to get away from that cop?"

Katerina didn't want to say out loud the thoughts floating in the back of her mind, still opaque and unclear. "I'm working on it, Mommy."

***

When Katerina entered the Pret a Manger, she found April huddled at a table in the back.

"So, what's the sich? Where you been?"

"Somewhere over the rainbow," Katerina shot back, her cheeks warming. It was the same, smart retort she had said to Winter at their first meeting. "What's the problem?"

"I went to the place to get the laptop, but the guy said you have to come personally."

Kat leaned in; her voice low. "What was the one thing I told you *not* to do."

"I didn't mention your name," April protested. "I'm not exactly his customer demographic. He took one look at me and said to tell you, you have to come yourself. I told him I didn't know what he was talking about. He didn't believe me."

Katerina closed her eyes. A visit to the "Bank of Pablo" was the last thing she needed right now.

"Look, I'll use your school laptop and reconfigure it to a burner. It'll take time."

"That's something I don't have," Kat said. "And how am I supposed to explain that I don't have my laptop?"

"You said the cop wasn't letting you go back to school."

Kat bristled at the statement. "He might change his mind."

"Say it was stolen?"

"He's a cop."

"You're letting me borrow it."

"I'm supposed to be telling you to leave so I can get rid of the apartment."

April made a face. "That's messed up. Tell him I need time to find a place."

"Great. He can come by and see I didn't make you move out, and you're using my laptop that you didn't pay for, *and you're still not paying me any rent.* None of this is going to work and you can't go back to the apartment."

"C'mon, why not?"

Katerina inhaled for patience. "You remember the message on the laptop? Two weeks. It's been two weeks. I don't need you in the apartment when shit starts happening."

April slouched in her seat. "I'm a civilian. They're not gonna do anything that brings cops. Especially since you've already got one, and they probably know that."

Katerina chided herself for this new shit storm. She had gambled and lost. Of course, Pablo wanted her to come personally. He wanted his job done. *And I owe him.* Another marker she was not to prepared to make good on.

"So, what do you want to do?" April asked.

Katerina considered her available move to make and decided she hated it. But there was nothing else to be done. With a sigh, she got up from the table. "What's the address of the branch office?"

***

"Imelda," Pablo's voice boomed, calling Kat by his chosen nickname, an inside reference to their first meeting.

Katerina sidestepped the bustling activity of Pablo's latest residential warehouse. People streamed in and out of the apartment carrying a variety of goods and electronics: televisions, DVD players, cell phones, designer shoes, and gift cards purchased with stolen credit cards. Pablo also provided personal instruction in select methods of theft, such as safe cracking. Through Moose, Katerina had crossed Pablo's path in January. She had purchased pre-paid gift cards and bartered for lessons: How to Drill a Safe for Beginners. She had not completed her end of the bargain.

"New branch location," Kat said.

"I'm like any other growing commerce site, chica." In his late forties, Pablo had a round face and playful eyes. He still wore the goatee consisting of a small, razor-thin line of facial hair. He wore a ready smile on his face and kept a loaded firearm by his side.

"Your own private Amazon. Does Bezos know?"

"My profit margins are better," Pablo said.

"What do you call them?" Kat nodded at the crew. "Sales associates?"

Pablo laughed. "You can call yourself anything you want. You the same as them."

"The girl brought cash. You don't like cash? You don't like to make a sale?"

"Not as much as I like getting my jobs done. I still got a job for you."

"This is not a good time," Kat said.

"You said that twice before," Pablo said, leaning back in his chair, the glint of the gun in his hand. "No more 'no,' chica. I got a job. You need to do it."

"Sure," Kat said. "If you want, I can bring my cop boyfriend with me. You can get two for the price of one."

Pablo smiled. The smile had a shade of what Katerina could only term as *unfriendliness.* He leaned forward. "That shit don't wash, chica. Not anymore. I got lots of *sales associates* with cops in the family. But, I like the little niña you sent here. She's asking for a special laptop, that means she's got special skills. You want to pay off the marker by having her work for me—"

"That's off the table."

Katerina realized the apartment had gone quiet, broken only by the gentle hum of the fan completing its rotation back and forth.

Pablo gave a nod. Kat didn't bother to turn around. She heard the rustling of the room clearing, except for the bodyguards who would remain.

"Don't worry, chica. I got a nice easy job for you. *Muy facil.*"

Pablo handed her a slip of stationary paper with a midtown address at the top and a name, *Gold Star Imports.*

"You want me to break into a warehouse?" she asked.

He shook his head. "That's an office. You gotta get into that office and get into the safe. Inside the safe, there's a small briefcase. Bring me the case."

"What kind of safe?"

"*No se.*"

"What's in the case?"

"You don't need to know."

"I don't *need* to know, or I don't want to know?"

"*Es lo mismo.*"

"What if there's more than one case?" she asked.

Pablo held up a forefinger. "*Uno.*"

Kat stared at the paper. "I need to crack a safe to pick up a briefcase, but I don't know what's in the case? Marcellus Wallace, I'd love to help you out, but why not just send your own lockman? He can crack it faster that I can."

Pablo gave a chuckle. "There's been a little problem in the building."

"What kind of problem?"

"Break-ins."

"In this office?"

"The office next door."

"How many times have you tried this?"

Pablo held up three fingers in a w-formation.

"Shit," Kat muttered. Maybe the fourth time is the charm, she thought.

"It's gonna work this time, chica. Hundred percent. You got the right——" and he wiggled his fingers as he searched for the word, "qualities, to avoid attention."

Katerina put her hands on her hips. "Qualities?"

"They see you walking in the hallway, no one gonna think twice."

"You mean I have the right skin color. Now you figure it's a good idea to send in the white girl?"

"Chica, in los Estados Unidos, this is *la igualdad de oportunidades*."

"Forgive me," Kat said. "It's my first time being the token."

Pable broke out into a laugh. "I wanted to send you in months ago." He stood up, the gun in his hand, loose and relaxed at his side. "No more delays, chica. You got two weeks. Get me the case."

It was on the tip of her tongue to say, "I'm not good enough and you know it." She didn't dare.

Pablo came around the desk and stood before her. "Remember, chica," he said in a low, soft voice, "you made the deal. It's you and me. The Moose is out of it, like you wanted."

"I'll do a different job," she said.

"Ain't no other job. I need this job. You don't do this, you gotta pay up some other way."

Kat nodded. "I'll take care of it."

"You pick up the laptop when you make delivery."

When she turned around, the bodyguards moved to either side of the door to allow her to leave.

***

Katerina exited the building and walked to the end of the block. Turning the corner, she felt someone come up behind her. She let him come alongside.

"Mami," Moose said.

Katerina inhaled a ragged breath at the sound of the friendly voice, reminding her of a time she wasn't out there alone, a time when things were almost good.

She caught a glance at him. He had a face of sharp angles, and he wore his hair cut short. A teardrop tattoo sat below hie left eye. He had on jeans, work boots, and a short-sleeved T-shirt, revealing a tattoo on the inside of his left arm, stretching across the bicep.

FEAR NO MAN

"You got a job?" Moose asked.

Kat nodded. "It's my job, I'll get it done."

"You understand what happens if you don't. It's ain't like the sign on a restaurant menu."

"No substitutions. He explained that. I'll figure it out."

The subway stop loomed closer.

"Luther wants to talk to you," Moose offered.

Katerina had met Moose through Luther; and she had met Luther through Philip. Luther had his own limousine and a stable of clients that appreciated Luther's business model. He took cash, asked no questions, and never said a word during the drive. He saw nothing, heard nothing, and remembered nothing. Luther was very popular.

Alexander Winter had used Luther's services as well. Luther had picked up Katerina at the airport in January. She had given him strict instructions not to call Winter and tell him she had veered off the plan and returned to New York. Luther had done it anyway and Katerina could not forgive him for it.

"There's nothing to say," she answered.

"You got it wrong, mami, you got it wrong."

"No, I don't."

"That's between you and him. I'm just telling you, I think you should hear him out."

"I'm going to need a car one day this week. I'll pay you."

"No es necesario. I'm here, mami, I got you."

Kat stopped and turned to him. "Why?"

"'Cause someday you gonna get a job and you gonna let the Moose loose and get in on the action. I know you gonna have something on. I know it."

They started walking again. Kat leaned into him and he wrapped his arm around her shoulder and kissed her forehead. "Why don't you stop in with Gigi for the night," he offered.

"Can't. But please tell Gigi I appreciate her taking the hacker in, and I'll make it right with her for it."

"It ain't no problem, chica. Never a problem. If you change your mind, any time, day or night, the Moose has got a lot of that goodwill for the right person."

Katerina forced herself to walk away, her heart heavy leaving Moose behind.

***

"So?"

Katerina had the phone at her ear as she came up out of the subway. "I need you to get all the details on a Gold Star Imports. They have an office in Midtown. I need to know everything about the building. Entrances, exits, service elevators, sprinkler systems, cameras, and alarms. You keep staying with Gigi. If you need help, you can ask Moose. Got it?"

"Chillin' like a villain," April said.

The buzz of the Eagleton company cell phone ended the conversation. Kat connected the call. "Yes?"

"Mr. Gallagher needs you to return to the office. Immediately."

***

Katerina listened to Ryan's voicemail messages asking how she was doing, what she was doing, and she should call him back immediately. Then she scrolled through the list of text messages, *Call me. Where are you? What are you doing? Why aren't you calling me back? I want you to call me back. Now.*

"It was fortunate that my assistant happened to pass by your desk. She heard the constant buzzing of your phone and alerted me to the situation."

As the phone buzzed yet again, Katerina averted her eyes, the heat of embarrassment adding a rose blush to her cheeks.

"Katerina, you have nothing to be ashamed of," Gallagher said. "I'm sorry to say this is not the first time I have seen a talented, intelligent young woman find herself in these unhappy circumstances. Maybe that's why . . . that's why I can't stand to see another young woman destroyed."

Katerina tucked the cell phone back in her purse. "Thank you for letting me know. I appreciate it."

She rose to leave but his hand on her arm surprised her. He let his hand rest there with a light touch. "Leave everything. Now. I will make your way of escape."

"Mr. Gallagher, I can't–"

"Katerina, listen to me now. You can leave the building through a private exit that leads into an underground garage. I'll have a driver take you out in a car with blacked out windows. You'll go to my estate on the East End of Long Island. No one will find you there. The official story will be that you left the building to attend a conference across town. You never arrived. In a day or so, there will be whispers that you wanted to escape an abusive relationship. You can call family members, of course, to establish that you're doing well, and no harm has come to you."

"You don't know the – situations going on now, the things I've done."

"Katerina, I'm in a business that is in the thick of world governments and power brokers. Trust me, nothing you tell me will shock me. I promise you, whatever the issue is, I will make it go away."

Katerina felt the exhaustion overwhelming her, down to the bones.

"Katerina, it's time," he pressed. "You need to trust me. Leave it all behind."

I'm coming, Katie. Wait for me.

I'm coming.

"I can't do that," Katerina said, bolting toward the door. "I won't do that."

Gallagher, taken aback at the force of her response, said, "Katerina. Just a moment."

Katerina stopped.

"Is this about your friend?"

Katerina's cheeks burned fresh. "I can't – I can't leave him behind."

"Don't you think he would want you to take care of yourself? Is he worth your health, your survival, your life?"

"He's worth more than my life. He's worth everything."

Gallagher went still, as if weighing every word before one slipped out beyond his control. "Everything," he said. "A special person, indeed." He placed his hands on her arms. "I understand. For the moment, we'll go to the conference room where you can call your fiancé. It will be better for you there, with people around, so he can hear the background noise of the meeting. And I will have my assistant type up itineraries for you each day, with talking points you can use."

"Mr. Gallagher ––"

"Thomas, it is always Thomas," he said with a smile. "You are an extraordinary woman, Katerina Mills. I hope your friend understands that and appreciates you."

***

The meeting broke up after seven p.m. Thomas Gallagher checked his watch. He had several hours to go. A dinner at eight and then emails and reports to read. By that time, it would be one in the morning, time for a quick call to Brussels and then he would sleep for a few hours.

When he went back upstairs, he found Nicole still at her post, as he knew he would. "Go home," he said with a smile, though he expected nothing of the kind. He insisted and waited while she collected her things. When he heard the elevator slide shut, he waited for Joseph Smith to come down.

While he waited, he wrestled with himself, something he had not done for many years. He didn't deal in uncertainty, second-guessing, wondering. Not until now. He remained determined, now more than ever, to complete this acquisition. She had wavered; but for the *professor.* It would have been over by now if he was truly gone. The snick of his office door opening broke his thoughts.

"How long does it take to kill someone?" Gallagher asked with a sigh.

"Until it's done."

"I assume you will erase the recording of my conversations with Miss Mills, as you have already erased the tape of my visit to the Brooklyn apartment."

"Of course, I work for you."

Gallagher smiled. Another problem he would have to deal with. He already had a new operator lined up. One spook spying on another. Everything would be swept clean and destroyed, after he had Katerina Mills in hand.

He turned away and stared out the window, lost in his thoughts.

She had to yield.

***

By the time Katerina climbed the last set of stairs, the clinging oppressive humidity had left her nauseous and light-headed. Her sinuses had that strange feeling again and she vaguely remembered she needed to drink more water.

When they had spoken on the phone, Ryan had sounded suspicious at first, then pleased. She answered his questions with an unrehearsed ease; where she went, who she saw, what happened in the meetings. Now, as she reached the apartment, she heard male voices from the other side of the door. The nausea threatened to overwhelm her as she listened to the muted sound of Ryan's voice and the deep male voice responding. *Who the hell is this?*

She opened the door, being sure to keep her expression a cross between artless innocence and timid confusion. She found Ryan sitting at the table with a man. In his late forties, he had dark hair with shades of silver coming in, and a round, full face. When he stood, she could see he was a six-footer with a solid build. He looked like he'd been lean and mean in his younger years, but he had started to fill out. Command confidence. *Cop.*

"Hello Katerina," the man said, offering a meaty hand. "I'm Detective Horman."

Katerina reciprocated, his warm, strong hand pumping hers once, twice, then letting go. She gave a shy smile.

"I'm here about the manufacturing plant where you worked," he said. "Just need to ask you a few questions for the report, okay?"

Kat nodded her head.

You play your part, before, during, and after.

Yes, Professor. I remember.

She coughed a few times, the tickle in her throat coming in and out.

"You have a cold?" he asked.

"Always," Ryan answered for her. "Pneumonia twice this winter."

Horner nodded. "Yeah, that was a brutal one. Now, everyone's getting summer colds. You need to take care of yourself."

"I'm trying," she said with a nod. She took note of the empty table. "Would you like something to drink?"

Horner shook his head. "I'm fine, thanks."

Ryan sat next to Kat on the couch, his arm around her shoulder.

Horner pulled over a chair, facing them. He took out his notepad.

The fucking notepad.

"I understood you were supposed to lock up the building the Friday before the holiday, is that correct?"

"Yes, I did," she said.

"Why were you there after everyone left?" he asked, looking up from the pad.

You already know the answer to that, prick.

"Finishing invoices."

Don't say any more or any less. Answer the question, that's it. If you lie, keep the lie as close to the truth as possible.

Horner nodded and bent his head, scribbling. "Did you see or hear anything out of the ordinary?"

"No," she said. *Just me.*

Another nod, more writing. Katerina turned her head to glance at Ryan, knowing her face appeared angelic in its innocence. But, in his eyes, she saw . . . something. What?

"Nobody lurking around?" Horner asked.

It could be a trick question. What do you know about Juan? What if Juan already outed me?

"No," she said.

Horner nodded.

She coughed a few times and Ryan stroked her head, saying, "You need a glass of water, baby?"

Kat shook her head.

"Just a few more questions," Horner said. "You ever hear of any problems at the plant, unhappy employees, ex-employees, like that?"

"No. Sometimes the Production Manager or a Supervisor complained the workers didn't follow directions."

Horner looked up. "Didn't follow directions. What kind of directions?"

Katerina shrugged. "They didn't put stuff where it belonged."

"Like what?"

Kat hesitated.

"Katerina," Horner soothed. "You're not doing anything wrong by telling me. Like what?"

"Like product. Sometimes the Purchasing Agent had to go out and find stuff. I would help him because I pay the bills, and they had to match what we received."

"What was being received?"

"Raw materials."

"Like chemicals?"

"Yes."

Horner nodded. "So, they weren't stored in the right place?"

"Sometimes."

"You ever notice the employees stealing the product?"

Kat shook her head. "No, the stuff was always there, it was just in the wrong place."

"Any smokers at the plant?"

Katerina bit her lip and avoided Horner's stare.

"C'mon Kat," Ryan prodded.

"If you know something," Horner said, adjusting to sit forward on the edge of his seat, "you need to tell me."

"I don't want to get anyone in trouble," Kat said.

Horner gave her a pointed stare.

Kat nodded. "When I come in, I see people smoking by the back door. They keep the door open."

"I took her to work sometimes," Ryan said, with a nod, as if his agreement made the statement true. "I've seen them out there."

Horner nodded. "What about inside, hunh?"

Katerina hesitated just a moment, "Sometimes, there might be a cigarette butt inside. The Production Manager would get angry."

"Anything else?"

Just a pair of exam gloves I wore to start the fire. They're balled up and hidden in the basement of an NYPD detective's house out on Long Island. I hid them there over the holiday weekend.

Katerina shook her head. "No."

"Okay kiddo, thanks." He closed his notepad and with a wink, he stood up.

Katerina moved to stand up, but Horner motioned for her to stay seated. "Feel better, hunh?"

Ryan gave Kat's shoulder a squeeze and got off the couch. The two men stepped out into the hall.

Katerina listened to the sound of the voices.

You get anything from the staff?

The production guy, the purchasing guy, they said the same things. It all matches up. You got cigarette butts, flamm liquids, soaked rags, poor procedures, and that's a wrap. EPA is there. OSHA's gonna give it to them on this, right up the ass. Listen, take good care of that girl of yours.

You bet.

Ryan came inside and then Katerina saw the relief in his eyes. *You're afraid. You thought he was coming to talk to you. Why?*

Kat got off the couch and went to the kitchen counter to start dinner.

I have to get out of here. As soon as possible.

***

At two o'clock in the morning, Katerina crept out of the bedroom. She did a thorough review of the backpack. More dead-end tips.

Fishing the phone out of the back of the closet, she sent a text.

Case is stalled. Nothing happening.

She stared at the screen, watching the letters disintegrate and disappear.

Katerina stored the phone away. She sat on the cold floor.

You are never leaving me.

You are never getting away from me.

There's nowhere you can go.

There's nothing you can do.

Staring out into the darkness, her eyes adjusted and fell on the service weapon snug in its holster, draped over the jacket, draped over corner of the chair.

She stared at the gun for a long while before she returned to the bedroom.

"No eating while on duty. You get a thirty-minute meal break at ten o'clock. You can listen to headphones. If I find you talking on the phone while you're supposed to be working, you're going to be fired. If I find you texting on the phone while you're supposed to be working, you're going to be fired. If I find you taking anything from the desks or the drawers, you're going to be fired. Understand?"

"Yeah."

The shift supervisor, a woman in her fifties with short, tight curls all over her head, her skin slick with sweat, handed a clipboard to the new hire. A small, slight girl with a big attitude, she had jet black hair with shocks of red and purple, and piercings in her lip, nose, and ears. The supervisor had already decided she was another useless one. But with three employees disappearing to avoid *La migra,* she needed another body.

"You're assigned to three buildings. You start in the Midtown building at Forty-fifth Street. If you're later than seven o'clock, like seven-o-one, don't bother showing up, you're fired. Understand?"

"Chillin' like a villain," the girl answered.

She gave the girl two days before she was gone.

CHAPTER

54

Katerina drove across the upper level of the GW bridge in a Lexus, a car from Moose's fleet of vehicles. After she finished with it, it would wind up a different color, with different plates, on a slow boat for Afghanistan. Her mind swirled like a vortex as she prepared for her second visit to the Widow Unghar. She thought of the counsel Winter had given her last year. *Remember Katie, it's what the other person wants, what motivates them, what frightens them, that's what matters. Once you understand that, you can think like they do, and then you can maneuver the situation for what you need to accomplish.*

She had to keep her head together now and do this right. In the back of her mind, the threads of her long game dangled, not yet coming together. It would come. It had to.

***

Katerina listened to Bunny Unghar's show and tell of her craft projects, a repetition of the cases filled with large spools of wide ribbon material. After a while, Kat wasn't sure if Bunny was obtuse or skilled at playing obtuse.

"Bunny, you know what your husband did for a living, right?" Kat interrupted, deciding to get to the point.

Bunny, still holding her latest cross-stitch project, adopted the familiar faraway look in her eyes as she said, "What do you mean?"

"Bunny, you know what your husband was doing for a living while he worked for Philip. You know that he took pictures of couples having illicit affairs."

"Oh," Bunny said, and she stared off into the living room. "He never really talked about his work."

"He talked about retiring. You said that he started talking about retiring late last year. You knew photographing married people cheating on their spouses wouldn't give him enough money to retire and travel. You knew he was into something big for Philip."

"But Philip is a lawyer, so he's always doing the right thing."

Katerina sighed. "Being a lawyer and doing the right thing aren't the same and they don't always go together. You knew that your husband was working for Philip, taking pictures, and they were *not* on a case. You know this because a lot of people are looking for the photo negatives your husband took. These people are becoming desperate. They're not going to believe you when you say you don't know anything about it, so you should stop saying that."

"I don't know who's in the negatives. He wouldn't tell me."

Katerina calculated her next move. "When did Devon Kelly come to see you? Was it before or after your husband died?"

Bunny stared at Katerina. "It was after."

Bingo. "And he told you that your husband was working on a case for *him,* right, not Philip. He said he was the actual client?"

Bunny nodded. "He said it was a very important case. He said Abe had been chosen because he had such a good reputation, and they needed the best. He said it was part of a special corruption investigation and Abe had signed a confidentiality agreement. He needed all of the material that Abe had collected, and he said that it was okay to give it to him."

"You never told Philip that Devon Kelly had come around?"

"No, Mr. Kelly said Philip would say the negatives were his, but I shouldn't tell him anything or give him anything or even say that I know about anything. He said he was from Albany, that he worked in the government."

Katerina nodded. "Bunny, was this house really broken into?"

Bunny's eyes lit up. "Yes, several times. My brother told you that?"

Kat nodded. "Was it before or after Devon Kelly came for his visit?"

Bunny had to think about it. "It was after. The police said there had been a rash of break-ins. They thought it was some neighborhood kids."

"You gave the negatives to Devon Kelly?"

Bunny shook her head. "I didn't have anything to give him. I just have a few boxes of the fine art photographs Abe took. I wanted to keep those."

"Can I see them, please?" Kat asked.

Kat followed Bunny upstairs, Bunny chattering all the way. "Abe told me he wanted me to have them. He spent time looking at them – before he died. After, I thought he had been doing that because he was suffering from the depression, over how his life turned out, you know?"

Katerina felt a pang of guilt that the widow would never know, it wasn't Abe's life, his house, or his spouse that had driven him to take his own life, because he had not been driven to take his own life; he had been murdered.

Kat followed Bunny into an overcrowded, cluttered craft room. In the center of the room, a large table held fabrics and fillings, a sewing machine, sewing boxes, and more plastic boxes filled with ribbon rolls.

Bunny rummaged in a closet and brought out a small box and set it on the craft table. Katerina made short work of the box, rifling through the photo prints. She stopped. Sandwiched between two prints, a thin, small envelope. Blink and she would have missed it. Peeking inside, she saw the strips. It couldn't be this easy. Could it?

She took them out and held them up to the light. One by one, her disappointment grew. No bodies in the throes of copulation. Just an empty room. Katerina picked up one of the strips again and held it up.

An empty room.

Whose room? Where?

Katerina put the strip back in the envelope and put the envelope in her purse. "Bunny, I'm going to take these with me."

"Did Mr. Kelly lie to me?"

"Yes, he did."

"If I ask you, why you want those negatives, are you going to lie to me?"

Katerina searched for a simple answer to the complicated question. The interrogated had become the interrogator and Katerina had lost the room. "I need the negatives to save myself."

"Was my Abe in trouble?"

"Yes, he was."

"Are you in trouble?"

"Yes, I am," Kat said. "Bunny, did Mr. Kelly leave a number where you could reach him?"

Bunny nodded.

They went downstairs in silence. Katerina tried to temper her anticipation as Bunny Unghar brought her a plain business card with a name on one side and a phone number on the other. Kat looked at the number and handed back the card.

"Don't you want to take it?"

"I won't forget," Kat said. "Bunny, you didn't show Mr. Kelly the craft room and the box, did you?"

"No, he wasn't interested in the crafts, or Abe's photography. You seemed interested."

By the front door Kat said, "I really am sorry about Abe. He was a nice man. When I saw him, he was always nice to me. It shouldn't have—I'm sorry."

Bunny reached out and gave her a hug. "You're a sweet girl. Good luck."

When Kat exited the house, she found Bunny's brother leaning against the parked Lexus.

"More condolences, hunh?" he said with a sneer, and he took the cigar from his mouth. "Imagine that."

Katerina didn't answer. She stopped short when he shifted to block her path.

"What'd I tell you. I don't like youse up to no good with my sister."

"And you're just a Boy Scout," Kat said.

He leaned in, the pungent stench of his aftershave assaulting her nose. "This could get uncomfortable for you, ya know? Real uncomfortable. I got friends. You don't want a visit from my friends. *Capisce*?"

Katerina nodded. A visit from the local mob was not what she needed right now. "*Capisco.*"

His eyes quirked at her correct use of the verb. He glanced past her, and Kat turned her head to see Bunny standing at the front door. He backed away just enough for Kat to squeeze past him and get into the car.

***

When Katerina arrived back in the city, she parked the car and sent a text message to Moose. Bringing the envelope home to Brooklyn was out of the question. She found a UPS store with twenty-four-hour luggage rental lockers and stowed the envelope. Pictures of a room. What room? Where? Who would know? Devon Kelly? Destiny Haley? Another needle, another haystack. She needed to call that number. To do what? Arrange a meeting?

Where? When? For what purpose? Did she need Devon Kelly? She had no idea how to play this.

Wandering uptown on Fifth Avenue, she entered Central Park. Making her way down the path, she spied couples with their children by the pond up ahead. On her left, she came upon King Jagiello on his horse, his sword raised, ready to do battle. She stepped into the grassy area behind the statue. Will Temple, a young, handsome, second-string theater player with big dreams of his name at the top of the marquee, had been found dead there almost six months ago. His body had been wasted from starvation, marked and scarred by abuse, with a gunshot in the side of his head. She knew the report by heart; she had seen it countless times in the dead of night. She felt the surge of emotion, the sting of tears in her eyes. There were no flowers, no makeshift memorial. No one remembered a young man had died there.

In a cemetery somewhere, another man had been laid to rest, Anthony Desucci, Junior. She had never paid her respects to him, either.

Coming back out onto the path, Katerina found it empty. At a noise, Kat turned her head. A puff of white, the tip of a tail. Her eyes widened as the fox appeared. It wore a scar that ran from its crown down along the eye, ending at the nose. The soulful eyes staring back at her were full of pain. It had been in battle; it had been wounded. In a split second, the orange-brown coat with white tufts disappeared behind a tree.

Katerina rushed forward. Rounding the tree, she found an empty space.

Gone.

Hide, Katie. Please hide.

The sound of Winter's voice jolted her.

Hide where, Bob? Where can I go?

She noticed passersby were eyeing her with curiosity.

Embarrassed, she lurched back onto the path in the opposite direction, running smack into the man she had been waiting for.

"*Myshka,*" Ivan said.

The hit man had come.

He wore his hair a little longer; the small spectacles had disappeared.

"Come, I have car," Ivan said as his eyes searched her. "We take ride now."

***

In the passenger seat of the car, Katerina stared out the window, noticing the slight tickle in the back of her throat. She realized her right cheek vibrated, and she coughed. *Not possible.*

"You are sick?" Ivan asked.

"You are late?" Kat answered, mimicking his Russian accent.

"No, not late. I have been here," he said.

"Congratulations. What have you been doing?" she demanded.

"I work. You are not only client."

"Do you *not* take care of the business of your other clients or is it only my job you can't do," Katerina said.

Ivan made a snicker of a noise. "Business, this is very polite. I always do job."

Kat turned to look at him. "If you always *do job*, why isn't John Reynolds dead? It's almost six months. That's not enough time?"

Ivan shook his head. "You don't tell me the job is – how you say – complicated. This Reynolds. He is smart man. Lot of television cameras, special dinners. You sure he does not know you are after him?"

"He knows the NYPD is after him."

Ivan shrugged. "*Da, da*, but you forget to mention this. This is - how you say - critical information."

"What's the matter? You don't kill people who have public profiles?"

"This is not nice talk for nice girl."

Katerina shifted back to look out the window. "I think you should cut the bullshit and do the job."

"*Myshka*, if this man dies, lot of publicity, lot of attention. This is not good. This man, he knows this. This is smart man. He hides *in public.*"

"So, you're going to welch, is that what you're saying?"

Ivan wrinkled his brows. "What is this . . . welch?"

"It means to go back on your word, crap out, give up. Anthony Junior told you to do the job," she said.

"Anthony Junior is not here anymore. His father says different now."

"Take me to him," Kat said.

"*Myshka,* you do not want this. Now is time to wait."

"You still work for me. Take me to see Anthony Desucci."

Ivan sighed. "I know you would say this thing. You want to see him? Okay, *myshka.* We go."

Katerina stewed in her own thoughts. When she first met Ivan, it had been snowing. She had been the driver, trying to navigate Midtown traffic, with Anthony Desucci on the phone, and Ivan in the back seat, directly behind her, the cold metal of the gun against her neck.

"You're working for Desucci again," she said. "How is it a Russian is working for an Italian?"

"I enjoy to talk about employers. This is favorite thing to do. If I talk of you to other people, this is okay?"

"You were chatty last year," Kat said, the familiar, hot anger welling inside her, and the cathartic anticipation that she would be able to let it out. "We talked about books and national origin."

"You were not employer. I don't do the chit-chat with employer. It is, how you say, outside my wheelhouse."

"But you chatted with Anthony Desucci, your employer, on my cell phone, last year. After the chit-chat, nothing happened to me."

Ivan didn't answer, the silence in the vehicle marred by the blaring of horns, the rumbling of buses, the sounds of the city.

"*Boris*, last year, were you here looking for something or someone?"

Ivan laughed. "Sometimes that is same thing."

"You were here in December," Kat said, almost to herself.

"I know when I was here," Ivan said. "You want to stop asking questions. Is not good, little mouse."

Katerina's anger burned hotter.

What had Anthony Junior said about his father? *I intend to protect him. Times have changed. I have my own way of doing things. It's not my father's way.*

The truth settled on her.

"The photographer, the one who took the pictures, the photo negatives *Anthony Desucci* sent you to find while Tony Junior was out of town. The photographer didn't commit suicide, did he, *Boris*?"

Ivan didn't answer.

"You had to kill him?" Kat asked without expecting an answer.

"I don't know what you're talking about," Ivan said.

"Don't patronize me," she said.

"I don't know any photographer."

"You didn't have to kill him," she repeated.

Ivan turned off Mulberry Street and two men, built like tanks, wearing slacks and fitted silk shirts, stood at their posts and waived Ivan forward.

Ivan pulled into a spot and killed the engine. He turned to Katerina.

"If a photographer wants to spend time with bad people, doing bad things, bad things happen. I am not killer. I am cleaner. What should I do? Chit-chat? He promises me, no, do not worry. I tell no one. Everyone tells me this. I believe them, of course. You are nice girl. Maybe you are *too* nice girl. Maybe this, all this, is not for you. Maybe you want to sit home, wait for husband or boyfriend. But now, you ask to see boss. I take you to see boss."

Katerina pulled the handle on the door to get out.

The soldiers cleared a path to allow them entry. Inside, more soldiers camped out on the stairwells. Ivan led the way. Katerina smelled the scent of rich food before they entered the apartment, an open, airy space, and saw a gathering of men, one standing at a stove. Ivan turned to the right and Kat followed into a smaller, private apartment. An apartment reserved just for the boss.

The studio was sparse but livable with a good bed, a table, and a separate kitchen area in the corner. A single glass of wine stood on the table, set before Anthony Desucci.

Vincent and Carlo stood nearby. Kat struggled to hold her emotions in check. The reports had said the two bodyguards with Anthony Junior had been killed as well. She had assumed it had been them.

Vincent nodded at her in recognition as he stepped forward. She handed over her purse without being asked.

Ivan went to Desucci's side and handed him the envelope of photo negatives. Katerina shot Ivan a look; he remained stoic and unreadable. He had been with her all the way to Jersey and back, and she had never spotted the tail. *After all Bob taught me.*

"Please, can we talk privately," she said to Desucci.

He nodded; Vincent, Carlo, and Ivan stepped away.

She took the seat across from him, a man engulfed in the rage of mourning. He had aged ten years in the six months since they had last seen each other. Sorrow did that; it drained life right out of the body. She didn't care what the police said about Anthony Desucci. He had lost a beloved son. It should never have happened. *And it was my fault.*

Desucci lifted the negative strips and examined them each in turn. He tucked them back into the envelope and tossed it on the table in her direction, with a wave of his hand that she should take it away.

"So, here we are again, Katerina," he said. "But it's different now."

She wanted to tell him how sorry she was, but the words sounded so trivial in her head.

"I'm making progress."

"It's an empty room."

"I'm making progress. I have to be careful. If I make a mistake, someone, someone else will get hurt – or worse."

"Is that what you told my son?"

Kat nodded.

Desucci sat back, considering her. "What else did you and my son talk about?"

"The negatives were stolen from the lawyer. I know who the inside man is. I'm searching for him."

"Or maybe you're working with the lawyer. He's working for the Russians. He got the charges dropped against the Federovs. Maybe you're working for the Russians. Maybe you sold out my son."

"Tony Junior and I were working on this *together*. He was willing to keep Federov out of my way, so I didn't get beaten to a pulp twice. He even offered to take care of the cop so I could get out from under. I didn't want to bring him into that."

"Ivan will clean up the mess with the cop now," Desucci said. "That'll free up your time."

"No," Kat said, and Desucci's eyebrows went up at the force of her comment. "If you take out the cop, the whole NYPD will come down on me. They'll dig into everything – and everyone connected to me." Katerina said. "All he wanted was to protect you. I know you blame me for his death."

Desucci glanced away, his eyes glassy.

"So, what now – you'll tell Vito Massone to wrap another plastic bag around my head? You think another fun with asphyxiation session is going to get you that set of negatives any faster?"

Desucci stared at the wine glass, his jaw set, his eyes ablaze.

"Tony Junior was kind to me. He was the only one. Let me finish this."

"You don't have a choice. The lawyer and the cop are going."

Katerina's anger flared. "No, no more of this. Your son wanted this done with brains, not blood. We do it his way."

Desucci banged his fist on the table. "You don't tell me about my son, about his intelligence, his talent. He was worth ten of this cop. You think I give a damn what happens to him? I know all about him. He's a piece of garbage, like his father's a piece of garbage. His old man has had his hand out for the last twenty years. You name it, he's getting a piece of it. Drugs, prostitution, gambling, extortion. Let him hear the bagpipes play. I don't give a shit."

Kat quaked in fear at Desucci's rage; he wanted, needed, someone else to suffer. "I will take care of this," she said. "I will see it through, the way Tony Junior would have wanted it done."

Desucci's mouth twitched in his anger, but the blackness in his eyes ebbed just a touch. "You don't want me to touch the cop, fine, but that big mouth lawyer is going."

Katerina's mouth opened to speak, but Desucci had already nodded at someone behind her. Ivan appeared at Kat's side, his hand on her shoulder and then her arm. The meeting had ended.

Anthony Desucci would have blood.

***

They drove in silence until Ivan said, "Myshka, I think Reynolds problem is causing Brooklyn problem, yes?"

"I think you are genius," she mimicked, "yes?"

"I will clean Reynolds problem. I have never missed job," he said.

The words stabbed at her heart, reminding her of Winter. *I've never missed a delivery.*

"Don't do this, with the lawyer," Kat said.

"Little mouse, I have job. I am paid. Lawyer is not on television. Not in papers. No problem to do job."

"Take a left and then I'll tell you where to stop," she said.

Kat gave directions. Ivan followed until she instructed him to pull over.

Ivan pulled the car in at the curb and cut the engine.

Katerina grabbed the handle to get out, shifting away from his reach before Ivan could take hold.

"Little mouse, what you think you're doing?" he asked as she slammed the door shut.

Kat leaned over, her head crooked down to peer into the car. "You want to kill the lawyer, let's do it right now." And she took off into the building.

"And now mouse has become bear," Ivan said with a sigh and got out of the car.

***

Katerina threw open the door to Philip's office and sauntered inside. She found Philip sitting at his desk on his cell phone. He pulled the phone from his ear, saying "Not now, Kat."

| 311 |

As Ivan came in, Philip shot up straight in his chair, said, "I'll call you back," and killed the call.

"Who's this guy?"

"He's here to kill you," Kat said.

"Funny, Kat," Philip said, but his laugh came out short and uneasy. "Seriously, who are you?"

"I am Ivan, the cleaner," Ivan said.

Philip bolted from his chair and backed away against the wall.

"Not going to help you, Philip."

"Are you the guy who did Abe?" Philip asked Ivan.

"I thought Abe killed himself," Kat said.

"I think I'll go to lunch now."

Everyone turned to see Brenda.

"Get in the bathroom," Kat said.

"Hey!" Brenda protested.

Ivan sauntered toward Brenda; stepping backward, she tripped over her own stiletto heels. He caught her by the elbows with both hands, moving her across the threshold into Philip's private restroom.

"That is good girl," Ivan said, and he closed and locked the door.

Kat turned back to Philip. "You got the Federov's released. Not a good look for you, Philip."

"Like I had a choice."

"Let's cut the crap. Since you've been lying to me from the beginning, why don't we try something different, like, the truth."

"You first. I know you better than you'll ever admit, Kitty Kat. You went back to see the widow, right?"

Kat didn't bother to hide her annoyance.

"Uh hunh. When were you gonna tell *me* what you two talked about?"

"As soon you tell me all about your connection to Devon Kelly, the Governor's former fixer, since you've been calling and getting his voicemail. Tell me, did you screw him, or did he screw you?"

"There is no connection, anymore." Philip shook his head. "He was an in, that's all. I sold him on the idea of the offshore accounts for Haley. I told him that I had discovered a workaround no one else had, and I promised him his boss was never gonna end up in a Panama Papers scandal."

"How much of that spiel was crap?"

"None of it," Philip said, petulant now. "You may not want to admit it, but I'm a very good lawyer, Katerina. I've always been a good lawyer. And I've done very well by my clients. Anyway, I get in, and I get a whiff of what's really going on."

"I thought you were hired by one bully to get the negatives and that was pissing off the other bully."

Philip laughed. "I should have *remembered* that you remember everything. No, it was me, it was all me. I nosed around, I got on to how the Governor gets his companionship delivered to him, across state lines, under the cover of darkness. I send Abe on the hunt. He figured out the rest."

Philip's bullshit and bravado, cutting Anthony Desucci Junior out of the narrative as if he had never existed, rankled Katerina.

"Where's the love nest?"

"That's the one thing Abe never told me."

Kat turned to Ivan. "You can go ahead."

As Ivan maneuvered behind the desk, Philip hugged the corner. "Hey, Kat, I told you I don't know. Abe was doing the surveillance. The place got switched at the last minute, that's all he would tell me. I wasn't there. He took that with him to his grave."

Katerina went for the door.

"It's not like I had a choice, Kat. When a Russian comes around and says he wants in on the action, you're gonna give him a piece of the action. I still had everything under control, except for Abe."

Katerina turned around.

"You want to call off the dog?" he said, nodding at Ivan.

Katerina nodded at Ivan, and he stepped back.

Philip sank into his chair and gave a heavy sigh. "The deal was, Unghar takes the shots and gives me the negatives. One set, that's it. He clears out, takes the wife, they go on the road, and he waits while I make the deal. He gives me a PO Box number and he gets his cut regularly. But no, he doesn't want to wait. He decided to go straight to the source."

Katerina approached the desk. "Are you telling me that little Abe Unghar, Abe who always did the job exactly the way you asked him to, no more, and no less, tried to blackmail the Governor himself?"

Philip nodded. "I get wind there was a ransom demand and before anybody knew it, Devon Kelly's out in the cold, and anybody connected to him was cut off. Before Abe gets a chance to collect," he said, looking at Ivan, "he turns up dead."

"He delivered your set of negatives to you, the set I was holding for you, before you mailed it off to Boston, and then went and made a ransom demand on his own?" she said.

Philip nodded his head.

Katerina hesitated in disbelief. With both hands resting on the edge of the desk, she leaned over and spoke slow and clear. "There are *two* sets of negatives missing? Abe had one set, which has vanished, and your set that was stolen from your Boston office. This is the truth?"

Philip lowered his head and nodded.

"You little shit, holding out on me all this time," she said. "That's why you're calling Devon Kelly. You think he's behind the theft in Boston?"

"Well, at least you believe me now." Philip shook his head. "I thought, maybe, maybe, he took the negatives from my office and he's just laying low somewhere. Maybe he's got Abe's set of negatives, too."

Katerina didn't know why, but she didn't believe it, any of it.

"Hey, the Governor doesn't exactly look worried. He's about to accept the nomination at the convention next month." Philip stared over at Ivan. "So, what now?"

Kat looked to Ivan. "Well? What now?"

Ivan shrugged. "I can't do now. There is no – how you say – element of surprise."

"I'll tell you what," Kat said. "I'll give you a head start before he changes his mind."

Philip laughed. When Katerina didn't, Philip grabbed his briefcase and his phone and scooted around the desk and dashed for the door. He stopped short when Katerina called out, "Aren't you leaving something behind?"

Philip turned and Katerina nodded toward the bathroom door.

"Oh, well, she's a smart cookie. She'll be able to handle herself. Tell her, I'll call her as soon as possible."

Kat shook her head in disgust. "Unbelievable," she said as she sank into Philip's executive chair.

When the outer office door slammed shut, Ivan said, "I let secretary out now."

"Do me a favor, wait another ten minutes," Kat said.

"Little bear," Ivan said.

"Can I have the strips, please."

Ivan handed over the envelope. Kat took out the strips, holding them up to the light. In her head, she heard Winter's voice, that low gravel, like the rumble of a storm that quickened her heartbeat. *You know what to do with this.*

She reached for the garbage can and pulled it over. Rummaging in Philip's desk drawer, she pulled out the lighter he kept for clients who smoked. She lit each negative strip one at a time, watching it burn down until it licked at her fingertips, and she let it drop into the garbage can.

"What are you going to tell Anthony Desucci?" Katerina asked.

"I tell him not to worry. The little bear has everything, how you say, under control."

She let the last burning strip drop.

"And I tell him now you find two sets of negatives, not one."

Katerina nodded.

Shit.

In the darkest moment of the night, she lit the kindling and watched the flames grow as the firewood caught and burned.

Rachel, an apparition in her white gown, hair flowing wild, began the chant, calling for the spirits to come and help the girl; she needed help.

Struck by a sudden intense pain, she fell to her knees, her body weaving from side to side, tears streaming down her cheeks.

The Shaman's Death, the dismemberment, the tearing down of the body, the heart, and the soul.

She had told Katerina of The Shaman's Death. She had told Katerina not to be afraid. The girl had to come apart to be made new; to become what she was meant to be.

Rachel realized she had been wrong.

Katerina should be afraid.

Something was coming for her.

Rachel didn't know what it would be.

But it would be a living death.

Raymond George didn't like to wait. He spent his days in constant motion, seeing to a thousand details. He had tended to every detail of this drop. He had stalled as long as possible, but the blackmailer wouldn't hear of another delay. George had negotiated the payment down to ten thousand dollars in exchange for an item of proof; a negative that showed this *creature* had something to trade for. The blackmailer had insisted George come alone; if he didn't, the blackmailer would know. And the negatives, all of them, would become photographs. And the photographs would be on the front page of every major newspaper before the end of the week. And wouldn't that be a boost for the Governor's presidential campaign?

So, Raymond George stood in the dark of the night, at Seventy-fourth street, at one end of the Bow Bridge, its cast-iron, smooth, elegant curves, the hallmark of its namesake. He squinted, searching for a figure, a messenger, to come toward him. He would then walk across the bridge and upon meeting in the middle, would make the wordless exchange and continue on their separate ways across the sixty-foot expanse of the bridge, surrounded by the lake on each side, the city in the distance.

No man, no envelope.

Raymond George's cell phone buzzed, and he checked the text message.

Leave the bag. Walk to the other side.

Raymond George grimaced and cursed under his breath.

What about the item?

He waited. The phone buzzed.

You pick it up at the other end of the bridge.
You got one minute.

The ransom payment would be lost if the blackmailer left nothing on the other side. Raymond George scanned around. The blackmailer was here, somewhere close. He had no choice. He dropped the bag and took off for the other side of the bridge.

When he arrived at the other end, he spied the flashlight from a cell phone. Following it, he found a man holding an open envelope with an eight by eleven photograph in his hand, examining it under the light. Average height, rail thin, easy smile, careless hair, with a few strands that fell over his forehead.

The man looked up. "Hey, Georgie Porgie, what do you say? You stepped right into this one, you know that, right?"

Raymond George stepped forward and snatched the envelope and photograph out of Devon Kelly's hands. Kelly held up his hands as if to say, "no harm, no foul." Raymond George flipped on the flashlight of his phone and looked at the photograph. His heart leapt into his throat. A green room. Green carpeting, green couch. He knew that room.

My God. It's real.

As he crossed back over the bridge, Devon Kelly, attorney by education, fixer by trade, kept stride with him.

"You're not getting another dime," Raymond George said.

Kelly laughed. "You're not serious. Georgie. What reason would I have to do this? I've known about the old man's . . . *habits* ... for quite a while. I set up the system for him. It was foolproof."

"Apparently not every fool thought so. It would seem the only fool was you."

Devon Kelly smarted at the dig. "By the way," Kelly said, changing the subject, "I bet you thought the blackmailer was around somewhere, watching you."

At Raymond George's silence, Devon Kelly laughed. "You really don't know anything about how to do this. He was *never* here. I spied a courier on a bike making the drop. *Two hours ago.* When we get to the other side, you're gonna find the bag is gone, because another courier was hired to pick it up. You're not cut out to be a bagman, Georgie. How come the old man has you doing this?"

"Since you couldn't do your job properly and a bagman is required."

"I'm telling you, I got shafted, same as you."

"That's your concern, Mr. Kelly, not mine, and not the Governor's."

Kelly took Raymond George by the arm and pulled him to a stop. "Whoever this guy is, eventually, he's gonna start sending you the goods. Georgie, we both know I'm the best man for this job. Haley doesn't need to know. I'll be deep in the background. You keep me up to date, I find the negatives, and you take all the credit, for now. What do you say?"

"I say, goodnight, Mr. Kelly, and goodbye. I don't expect to see you again, and please don't give out my number to any future employer for a reference."

Raymond George strode on ahead, leaving Devon Kelly standing with his hands in his pockets.

"You know, I bet the old man hasn't been getting that itch scratched," Kelly said.

Raymond George stopped, his back to Devon Kelly.

"How long do you think he's gonna put up with that? He's gonna want to scratch that itch. Who's gonna set that up for him, Georgie? You?"

Raymond George started walking again. He walked past the empty space where the bag containing ten thousand dollars had been. He was not a man prone to maudlin pessimism. He would not allow it. He was a practical man. He would make sure to keep his boss out of any further trouble while he took care of this matter. This person would need to be found, eliminated, and the negatives and any resulting photographs recovered. It was that simple.

***

What a mess this is, Devon Kelly thought. The widow of the photographer didn't know shit. And now, who is this idiot and how did they get a picture of the love nest? Did they have the negatives, *all* the negatives? How the hell did they get them?

If it wouldn't have caused more trouble, he would have liked to put that two-bit hustler lawyer in the ground. He started the whole problem. And that phone call Lang had taken. Thank God, he'd kept her on the payroll. What was that call about? Did that girl really work for Philip Castle? Kelly wasn't convinced. She would have known he hadn't been in this with the lawyer. What the hell was going on? Whoever that girl was, she was damn right that lawyer didn't have the negatives, and damn right they'd been stolen. *But I don't have them either.* Devon Kelly considered his situation, and he didn't like it. He'd been boxed out, cut off from everyone and everything. Nothing but trouble, that's all he had now. He would have to find a way out.

Katerina called April's cell phone three times. Each time it went to voicemail, her anger spiked higher. She called Moose's cousin, Gigi.

"No, blanca nieves, she ain't been here in days. She's a *loca* that one. Wonder where she gets it from. When you coming by?"

"Soon, Gigi. As soon as I can. I promise. I miss seeing you. I miss everyone."

"*Cuidate, blanca nieves.*"

Katerina clicked off the call.

She wouldn't.

Her anger leading the charge, Katerina hustled back to her apartment building, leaving the daylight behind when she entered the gloom of the building. Entering her apartment, she found it dark and silent. She tossed her purse on the table amid several days' worth of newspapers.

Kat went into the nook of a kitchen. Opening the refrigerator, she cursed at finding it stocked. She slammed the door closed. Coming back into the living room, a rustling sound from the bedroom caught her ear. Katerina rushed for the door and threw it open, finding April in her bed, sound asleep.

***

"What the hell?" the younger girl shouted.

She sat upright in the bed, while Kat stood over her, grasping the lightweight cotton blanket in both hands.

"I told you not to come back here. And I'm not paying you to sleep the damn day away!" Katerina exploded.

"You're not paying me at all!" April shot back.

"This isn't a game. You don't want to do the job, do what I ask, then get out and go back to the Island!" Kat said.

"What do you think I've been doing?" April yelled. "I just came off the night shift!"

"You're not supposed to be out hustling! You're supposed to be finding out about that building!"

"I'm working in the building!" April shouted.

Both women stopped and caught their breath.

When Katerina computed the words, she said, "What do you mean you're working there?"

April maneuvered out of bed. "Just what I said," she said, padding past Kat. "I'm with the cleaning crew. Don't get all happy at once."

Katerina followed April into the living room. "I am happy. I'm overjoyed. The earth is moving. Did you find out anything?"

April held up her phone. "I got everything."

***

They sat on the couch side by side, watching the footage again and again. Kat pointed to the screen. "So, that's the back-alley that runs behind the building?"

"Yeah, and there's the service entrance door. When you go in the door, you walk down the hall and then off to the right are the electrical boxes and around the corner is the main utility closet where all the cleaning supplies are kept and from there, you go to the service elevators."

"But what about going the other way? If you go down the back-alley the other way and try to re-enter the building, where do you come in?"

"There's a couple of fire escape doors that will put you in the back hallways near the stairwells."

Katerina considered the possibilities but without seeing the layout of the building for herself, she felt that she was working blind. "And if you come up through here?"

"You'll wind up in the front lobby, so you don't want that."

"What's off to the right there?" she said, pointing.

"When you come in the front of the building, if you go off to the left, there's a staircase that takes you down to the basement level."

"And what's down there?"

"Restaurant."

Katerina looked up from the phone. "Restaurant? What kind of restaurant?"

"Sushi, Asian fusion, something like that. I heard the food is good, good reputation. Nobody died from eating there."

"They should put that in the ad," Kat said drily. "Where's the exit from the restaurant if you don't want to come back up and go out through the lobby."

"There's a door off the alley. If you go in, you're in the restaurant kitchen."

Katerina nodded, her antenna up. Using her finger, she swiped the screen, separating her fingers to zoom in. The seed of an idea that had been struggling in the soil of her brain took root, weak, but there. She felt her mind alive and focused, working, as if kneading dough with her knuckles and the heel of her hand, massaging the idea, testing options, discarding, then picking up the threads once again.

"You have the information on where all the cameras are located?"

"Yeah, and the guard rotations."

"What guard rotations?"

"Ever since the robberies, the building hired more security. They have guard rotations. They cover each floor at designated intervals, so you have to avoid them or look like you belong there."

Kat grimaced. "How exactly does it work?"

"Each guard takes two floors, and they perform their inspection the same way on each floor, working from the front to the back and then up again. Then they take the stairs up or down. Basically, the guard is always rotating back around within about two minutes, unless he's not in a hurry. A couple of them like to talk to the cleaning crew, try to get something going."

"Sounds dreamy," Kat said.

April laughed. "I was in the office. I saw it," she said, reaching to take back the phone.

Kat hung over April's shoulder while the girl swiped through the phone's gallery. She stopped and held out the phone. "Here you go."

Kat stared at the photo of the safe, swiping to zoom in.

A keypad panel.

It's a digital lock.

Shit.

"What's the problem?"

Katerina paced the tiny living room. "The problem is, I don't know jackshit about electronic safes. I have no idea how to crack them."

April shrugged. "I would suggest a computer, but a program like that needs time to run."

"And we don't have a laptop," Kat said. She wanted to ask if the boyfriend knew anything. It was on the tip of her tongue, but she just couldn't do it. April didn't want to see him, and she wouldn't force the issue.

What would Winter say about this?

Anything you need to know, you can learn. If that's what you want.

She stared at the phone again.

"Is there anything on the Web that could tell me how to break into a digital safe?"

"Yeah, sure. There are a couple of websites, message boards, you can get any info you need on the Dark Web. I can try to rig up a burner phone."

Katerina made a face. "I have a place where I can access a computer."

***

"Hi, mommy," Kat said, closing the door to the bathroom.

"My girl, how are you?" her mother asked.

"I'm okay, mommy," Kat said, her heart lighter at hearing her mother's voice. "I'm just a little tired. How are you?"

"Better now that I hear you. Tell me, what can we do?"

"Nothing right now," Kat said. "What do you hear?"

"Now, I don't want you to get your hopes up," Linda Mills said.

Kat's eyes flew open. "Did they find–"

"No, not yet. But, they are making progress. They have a lead. They're following it. And they feel there's a good chance, a solid chance, that they are getting close. Just, don't try to reach out to them now. Let them do their job."

For a brief moment, Katerina felt the weight of her sorrow lift even as her panic increased. "I know. I know. I just don't know how much time he has left for them to do their job," Kat said.

"Are you on a throw away phone?" her mother asked.

"Yes."

"For once, Katerina, after all this time, please, what is this all about? Don't be like your father and hide everything. Can't you tell me something, please."

Katerina, holding the phone to her ear, went to war with herself, until she said, "The cop's been working on a case. Three cases, really. Two murders and a suicide. To solve them, he needs to find the connection."

"I see," her mother said. "And you are –"

"Yeah," Kat said.

"I see," her mother said. "And your professor –"

"Is in the mix, because of me."

"Can you tell me more?"

"Not even on a burner phone. And it's best you don't know."

"I see," her mother said again. "Katerina, your uncle wants to know if you need money."

"No, mommy, I'm okay," she said. "Don't tell him any of this, please. I don't want him to think that I'm bad."

"Katerina, he loves you. He would never think that."

"Mommy, I have to go now."

"All right, my girl. Call me tomorrow, please?"

Kat clicked off. When she came out of the bathroom, she found April sprawled on the couch, eating out of a bag of pretzels, one of the newspapers spread across her lap.

"Didn't I buy anything better to eat?"

"What? It's bread." April unfolded the newspaper and held it up for Kat to see the two-page spread on the missing Leonardo. "Is this wild? They walked off with a four hundred-million-dollar painting. Vanished."

Kat shrugged. "A real pro would have done it at night, so it wouldn't be discovered until the museum opened the next day."

April lowered the paper, spreading it out on her lap, her head tilted down. "They say it's out of towners. Like that professional group in Europe, you know the Pink Panthers."

"They steal jewelry, not paintings."

"Another group, but like them," April said. "There's been like four or five robberies of stolen artwork in the last few months. Belgium, Italy, London. Real pros. No one can find out who it is."

I bet I know who it is. Katerina imagined that Daniel Clay and his band of thieves had crossed the pond and decided to ply their trade overseas. Daniel had no problem with museum jobs. Kat and Winter had crossed paths with Daniel Clay and his group in California back in January. Daniel had been instrumental in getting Katerina out of the clutches of oligarch Viktor Mikhailovich; it had cost one of Daniel's men a beating he wouldn't forget. It had also cost Winter something he wouldn't admit to Katerina.

"Maybe it's your ghost," April offered. When Kat shook her head, April asked, "Why not?"

Because Alexander Winter doesn't like museum jobs. "Because not," Kat said. "I'll be in touch as soon as I know more. And I want you out of here."

April rolled her eyes. "Nobody's been here. I'm telling you, I come home late and I'm here all day. No one comes here."

"Get over to Gigi's. And if the cop comes around before you're gone, you heard that I'm trying to get a hold of the landlord and break the lease and you'll be out of here any day now."

"Got it," April said.

"I'll call you tomorrow when I'm at the computer so you can get access."

"This is gonna be lit," April said.

When Katerina left the apartment, she looked to her left and right. *Situational awareness.* Seeing nothing out of the ordinary, she hustled up to the corner.

She felt certain that this was going to be many things. "Lit" was not one of them.

Katerina sat in her cubicle, a tiny earpiece in one ear as she leaned forward, studiously searching the internet.

Scanning the headlines on the homepage, she pored over the story of an ambush; three of Federov's men, dead. Federov and his brother, Anatoly, had escaped. The war had started. Desucci would have blood.

"Did you send the email?" Kat whispered, as if speaking to herself.

"Chillin' like a villain," she heard in her ear.

Kat clicked to open the email, then clicked on the link. A screen popped up in the lower right corner and she clicked the "yes" box to the question, "Do you want to allow access?"

She watched the mouse move on its own. Dialogue boxes opened and closed in rapid patterns and formations.

"These people have crap cybersecurity," April said. "Seriously."

A few more clicks and a purple web browsing box opened. Kat leaned forward.

"Welcome to Tor, baby," she heard April say. A few more clicks and a forum page opened.

"I'll be in touch as soon as I have the information."

"Chillin' like a villain," and the call disconnected.

As Katerina hunched over the computer, she imagined sitting next to Winter, their bodies turned toward each other, as they did in the warehouse in January. He had schooled her in the rudimentary skills of cracking a manual lock by touch. As she read the material now, she heard him reciting the words, teaching her, as if he were there by her side. She researched the make and model of the digital safe, then did a search on electronic safes and how to open them. After several false starts, she found the video with a clear explanation and steps.

Keep it simple.

She took a mental inventory. What did she have? The layout of the building, the camera locations, the guard's inspection schedule, and now a way to get into the safe, if it worked. The thread of the plan snaked its way through her mind, but her plans hit a brick wall when a sudden thought sprang forth, strong and clear.

He's gone. I've lost him.

Startled, she sat up, shaken to her core that the thought should come to her like an irreversible truth. Her eyes welled with tears. *It's not true. It's my mind playing tricks. It's nerves because the half-brothers are getting closer.* Still, she tormented herself: when was the last time she had heard the true call of his voice within her?

Out of the corner of her eye, she spotted Gallagher's assistant approaching. Kat swiped her cheek with the back of her hand and hurried to click and minimize the open web pages.

Katerina had company paperwork laid out on her desk to look studious, and Nicole Lovel smiled as if she didn't believe any of it.

"Mr. Gallagher is ready for your lunch meeting," Nicole said.

"Yes, of course, thank you," Katerina answered.

***

Katerina Mills had observed Thomas Gallagher over several lunches. She noted his unhurried manner, the soft voice, the slow, methodical cadence. His communication style never wavered. From the servers to the secretaries, everyone existed and functioned for his benefit. Everyone revolved around his bright, blazing sun in his private solar system, as small, inconsequential, replaceable minor planets and stars. After the server left the table, Gallagher sat back, considering her.

"You've been quite attentive during our meetings," Gallagher said, reading her mind again. "Have I passed inspection?"

Kat blushed at being caught. "Yes."

"And how do you find me?"

"Do you eat here every day?" she asked, glancing around the elegant, private dining room with its small number of tables sporting linen tablecloths and fine silverware.

"Not every day, but often enough, I suppose. May I ask what this has to do with my question, because I know it does."

She looked at him head on.

"What's the server's name?" she asked.

Gallagher smirked. "I don't know."

"That's because he doesn't have a name. He's just a blank space where the next server will be. Everyone is."

"That's not a character flaw, Katerina. That's simply reality."

The server returned, a plate of steaming food in each hand. He set each plate down.

"Thank you, Louis," she said.

Gallagher took the dig in silence.

"You're very welcome, miss. Will there be anything else?"

Katerina looked at Thomas Gallagher. He kept his eyes on her as he answered, "Not at this time, Louis, thank you."

"Very good, sir," Louis said and left.

Katerina spread her napkin on her lap. Gallagher picked up his fork to eat and she followed suit, picking at the salmon on her plate.

"Would your friend have known the server's name?" Gallagher asked.

Katerina faltered at the unexpected question. "I – I can't answer that question."

Gallagher nodded. "That's fair. Is it possible he isn't the saint you think he is? And if it is possible, then is it possible you might have to admit your friend is no more a saint than I am a villain."

"You're not a villain," Kat said. "I just can't figure out why *I* have a name."

"You're not like any of the people who work in this building. You want more. If you didn't, you wouldn't be working for MJM."

"I work for MJM because I need cash."

"Yes, but you don't leave. You stay. Why?"

Lisa's words came back to her. *I think you want to be a success. I think you want the power that a successful life brings.*

"You are remarkable," Gallagher continued. "You put on no false airs, you don't censor yourself to pander or play to my generosity. Extraordinary. This is exactly what I had hoped for. An open and honest conversation."

"Maybe a little too honest?"

"Not at all. I assume your friend encouraged you to speak your mind?"

"Yes, always," she said without hesitation. "He wanted me to be my best. I was at my best when I was with him."

"You are perfect, just as you are right now," Gallagher said. "So, if you don't object, let us talk frankly, truthfully, as you would with him. What project are you working on right now?"

"I'm planning a theft," she said.

Gallagher choked on his food and coughed several times to clear his throat. "You don't say," he said.

Kat nodded.

"How's it coming?"

"Swimmingly. I've been using your computer to do my research."

Gallagher chuckled as he wiped his mouth with a napkin.

"You probably want to have your IT department wipe the computer when I leave."

"Leave? Why would you be leaving?"

"All things must come to an end," she said.

"Good or bad?"

"What?"

"Good things or bad things? Good end or bad end?" he asked.

"Jury's still out."

"I don't suppose I could assist you with anything?" he asked.

"You're not going to ask to come with me, are you?"

Gallagher laughed. "Would you mind? I think I would enjoy that."

"I would love to fulfill your Thomas Crown fantasy, but I work alone," she said, and a twinge of pain snicked at her heart.

"Isn't there anything I can assist you with?" he repeated.

"Sure, you can be a character witness at my sentencing hearing. I'm sure they'll knock a few years off."

"I hope you're not intending to steal something from a museum like the *Salvator Mundi*."

"I don't like museum jobs," and her face warmed at the sound of the words.

"You lead a very exciting life, Katerina. I take it your friend also leads an exciting life."

Kat quirked her eyebrows but said nothing.

"Loyal to a fault. Of course," Gallagher said.

They ate in silence until Gallagher said, "Thomas Crown. Are we talking about the original version or the remake?"

"The original, of course. Steve McQueen all the way. Classic American cinema."

"I was hoping you would choose the remake. After all Pierce Brosnan is British, like myself. I should mention, we still have to finish negotiations for the apartment."

"Please tell me you're not waiting for me."

"No, I was going to suggest that you move into the apartment. Even though it's not finished, it would be more comfortable for you. I assume you are in the thick of planning to leave the detective."

Katerina didn't answer.

"Katerina, your secret is safe with me."

"Yes, I'm going to make a change."

"Excellent, I'm relieved to hear it. I am curious, why didn't you ever press charges, request a restraining order?"

"It would damage his career."

Gallagher nodded. "Of course. I should have suspected as much."

***

Katerina left the building, the burner phone already at her ear. The time for mulling over how to get the job done, how to get out from under Ryan, had passed. She gave a shiver as she passed from the frigid air conditioning into the oppressive heat. She knew the weather was not making her shiver, but rather the plan that had formulated in her head.

When the call connected, she heard, "Yo."

"What are you doing?"

"Chillin' like a villain," she heard. "You need more Cocoa Puffs."

"No, I don't, and you're supposed to be eating chicharrónes, not Cocoa Puffs."

"It's dead over here. What is it with you and throwing me out?"

Kat stopped walking. "Go to Gigi's. I've got something for you to do there."

"Can I ask, 'you know who' to get me a car?"

"No, you cannot ask, 'you know who,' for a car, because I have something else you need to ask, 'you know who' for."

"Chillin' like a villain. What am I getting?"

"You're not *getting* anything. You're picking something up. Ask 'you know who' to get a four by one-and-a-half neodymium magnet. A rare earth magnet. Tell him to get it in a disk shape, like a hockey puck. He'll figure it out. Tell him to take money from the go bag."

"So, he gets this thing, and you can get into the thing."

"I hope so."

"All right. Listen, if I'm picking this thing up, why don't you just tell me what to do—"

"This is something I have to do. I have my reasons."

"Yeah," April sulked.

"This is not the only reason I'm going to the place. Something else needs to get done and I'm the only one who can do it."

"Whatever," April said.

"It's not because I don't trust you!"

"Then what is it?"

"If you get caught, you're going to have to 'break under questioning.' They won't give you any choice. I won't put you in that position."

"And what if you get caught?"

Kat swallowed hard. "If I get caught, you get the hell out of that building, clean out every trace of yourself in the apartment, and get back to 'you know who.' Tell him to give you the money in the go bag as payment. And then you erase yourself and disappear. Hide where no one will find you, and I mean no one. And you forget you ever knew me."

Kat listened to the dead air on the line, until April said, "You got it. Anything else I should be doing?"

"Yes, two things. If I give you a phone number, can you send text messages to my regular phone and make it look like it came from that number?"

"Spoofing, got it," April said. "Is that all?"

"No, If I give you a second phone number, can you hack into the phone and take control of it? I have the phone."

"You want me to hack the phone? On purpose?"

"I do. And then when I tell you, I'm going to want you to send text messages at specific times on specific days exactly as I tell you. Can you do it?"

"I told you I got skills. I'll get it done."

Katerina gave her the numbers. "All right. Go see 'you know who,' get the thing, and come right back. I'm almost set. Then we'll take care of the phones."

"Chillin' like a villain," April said, and hung up.

Katerina clicked off the call, tossing the burner into a trash can. Heading toward Midtown, she spotted a white van on her left. She glanced and saw the light at the corner turning yellow.

Hide, Katie. Hide.

Katerina quickened her step and ducked around the corner. As she flew down the block, a side door of a black van slid open.

Shit. Plan B.

She pivoted to double back.

They were out of the van.

Too late.

Then she was gone.

A painter's plastic drop cloth covered the van floor. Two enforcers worked as a tag team: one held Katerina's arms behind her back until she thought they would break while the other fastened the zip ties around her wrists. Anatoly plastered tape over her mouth. Grigory appeared bored, a mild expression on his face.

Anatoly took out a gun and held it up to her. "You have one chance in five." Without ceremony, he spun the cylinder, placed the gun to Kat's temple, and pulled the trigger. Katerina's body gave a violent jerk at the click, the tape muffling her screams.

The van careened as it made a sharp turn, accelerating down a side street.

"We go to Philip's office," Grigory said. "We don't see Philip. We see burned bits of negatives in trash can."

Kat shook her head as Anatoly put the gun to her head. At the click, Kat screamed again.

"Why you burn negatives?" Grigory asked.

Katerina's whole body shook as tears streamed down her face. Grigory ripped the tape away from her mouth.

"There was no one in the negatives. Just an empty room!"

Grigory nodded and the tape was pressed back over her mouth.

Katerina's scream strained against the muzzle of the tape.

The van swerved and Anatoly yelled at the driver in Russian. The van adjusted to a slow, steady pace.

"You have something to say to me?" Grigory asked.

Katerina nodded her head.

"Is it location of photo negatives showing Governor doing nasty things?"

Katerina cried.

Grigory made a *tsk tsk* sound.

The driver and the enforcer in the passenger seat spoke to each other and the van weaved again, making sharp turns. Grigory cursed at them in Russian. When they answered, Grigory eyed Katerina. He gave the driver instructions and mumbled to his brother.

Anatoly held the gun against Kat's temple, hesitated, and then pulled the trigger. Katerina's breathing came fast and heavy through her nose; her eyelids fluttered as consciousness slipped away.

"Keep her up," Grigory said in his own language, "smack the cheeks, keep her awake."

Anatoly smacked Kat's face several times, shaking her until she recovered.

"There is war now," Grigory said. "I did not kill Little Tony, but it does not matter."

Anatoly handed the weapon to Grigory; Grigory put the gun to Katerina's forehead. He hesitated; Katerina's eyes flew open, wild with terror. He pulled the trigger. As if a switch had been flipped, Katerina stared out, her body still, her eyes blank and empty.

"I find out you lie to me and Desucci has negatives, I finish you."

The van pulled into a tunnel. Grigory handed the gun back to Anatoly. He opened the chamber of the gun and with a flick of his wrist, he tipped the gun over. Kat stared as if she had fallen in a stupor, watching as a single bullet fell out and hit the plastic. The zip ties fell away, the sliding panel door opened, and Anatoly pushed Katerina. She tumbled out of the van and onto the ground. She heard laughter as the sliding panel door shot closed. The tires screeched as the van took off.

Katerina, on her hands and knees, retched. It took several tries for her to stand, her legs wobbling like jelly. She glanced around, seeing the postal trucks idling in the dock. With halting steps, she made her way through the tunnel and back out to the street.

CHAPTER

63

Katerina banged around the pots and pans without enthusiasm, her legs threatening to give out at any moment. She struggled to answer the evening's interrogation, as the waves of disoriented fatigue kept rolling over her.

Did you leave the office today?

Where did you go?

Did you eat lunch with anyone?

Who did you eat with?

What did you work on?

Katerina knew the rules of this game.

Don't act happy.

Don't act sad.

Don't act impatient.

Don't act annoyed.

Ryan gave up and moved on to one of his usual monologues; she turned her head every few seconds to show she hung on his every word.

Kat went to the cabinet and crouched down to rummage through the pans. The phone lay dormant, silent, hidden in the back. Kat made a note that she would send her report tonight, like clockwork. Nothing. Always nothing. She pulled out the soup pot; as she straightened up, she glanced at the jacket draped over the chair, the service weapon jutting from the holster draped over the jacket.

She turned toward the sink.

Oh shit.

He was behind her. She heard the sloshing of the beer in its bottle as he took a swig.

"Finally learning to cook," he said.

"I'm trying."

"Yeah, well, there's more to a relationship than cooking dinner, burned or not. You gonna do something tonight or are you gonna give me shit that your nose is stuffed."

"It's not exactly romantic," she said.

"Take a pill like everyone else," he snapped.

The conversation fell to a lull, and she could feel his eyes on her as he hovered.

"You still need to take care of that goddamn bridal shower, so Frank doesn't have to listen to Emma bitching all the time."

"I'm almost done," she said, fighting the urge to double over and dry heave as her stomach muscles contracted again.

He brushed her as he passed behind her. "You better. What about that bullshit you caused with Michelle. What'd you mouth off at her for? Can you tell me?"

"She'd been saying mean things to me. I got angry. She's jealous because I have you and she doesn't."

"Yeah, well since you're so lucky, you should show me how special I am."

Kat stumbled for a response. He muscled her aside from the counter, backing her out of the kitchen counter and toward the bedroom.

Tears sprang to her eyes. "Ryan, please."

"Oh, what? Another excuse?"

"I don't feel well . . . please . . ."

"Yeah, you'll sweat it out. It'll make you feel better," he said, and he pushed her again.

On instinct, Katerina put both hands up and pushed back on his chest.

Ryan gave a laugh with an expression of mock surprise. "Oh, you're pushing me around now? Is that what you're doing? Hunh?"

She stumbled. "No."

"You want to fight, hunh?" he asked as he tormented her with little shoves.

She pushed back. "No."

"C'mon, let me have it. You want to fight, okay, let's fight," he said, and he laughed as he grabbed at her wrists.

"Ryan, please, I can't . . ." and she wrenched her wrists away.

The open-handed slap across her face stopped her cold.

"You want to fight, let's fight," he said.

Reeling, Katerina said, "I'm sorry."

He tilted his head, as if hard of hearing. "What was that?" and then slapped her again.

Kat's hand went to her cheek. She shook her head as she backed away saying, "I'm sorry."

He smacked her hand away from her cheek. "You want to fight, hunh? Let's fight."

"Ryan, no, I'm sorry, I'm sorry. Don't. I'm sorry."

He drove her backwards, slapping her again and again. "Yeah, you will be now," he said and pushed her into the bedroom, the sound of her crying muffled by the slamming of the door behind him.

***

After he had finished with her, he wept in her arms.

"I'm so sorry," he cried, "I'm so sorry. I'd never hurt you. Never. I love you. It'll never happen again. I'm sorry. I love you. You know I love you so much."

In that moment, Katerina made promises to herself. When Winter returned, she would never speak of what had happened in the apartment. Nothing happened. That would be the story. Winter would never know. Instead, she kept a vision of him in her mind. She saw Winter looking at her with kindness in his eyes. She saw Winter taking her in his arms and making love to her with tenderness. The vision gave her strength.

Katerina held Ryan close. "I know, it's okay. I know," she soothed, as the pain pulsed in her cheeks and her lower belly.

"I don't know what's happening to me. I don't know how it all went wrong. How did I get into this?"

"Ryan, tell me what's happened. Please. I love you. Is it the job?"

Ryan shook his head.

"Is it your father?"

After hesitating, he nodded.

"It's those envelopes he's giving you, isn't it?" she said. "Please, tell me. What is he doing? What is he doing to you?"

"He's a good cop. He's always been a good cop. It's just – the stories he would tell. The things that people would do. They're skels. They're animals. And he has to be in there with them – and you gotta survive."

"But why is he asking you to help? You don't work in that unit."

"He trusts me," Ryan said.

Kat wondered how long Ryan had repeated that lie until he believed it.

"He can't trust anyone else to do this. That's what I thought. It's deep undercover and he can't trust anyone else. It was just a couple of times. Just deliver the envelope for him. I thought, you know, I can say no whenever I want."

"Ryan, it's not undercover work, is it. Where did the money come from? What's he doing?"

In between a lull of crying, Ryan said, "There was a bust a few months ago, an apartment in Brooklyn. Heroin, cocaine. The bag checked into evidence was light. The money is from a sale . . . he's got another guy, Smitty from the Eight Three . . . He gives me the envelope; I drop it wherever he says. What am I gonna do? I couldn't say no. I couldn't say no."

"It'll be okay," she soothed.

Ryan shook his head. "Every day, every fucking day, I think I'm gonna run into someone from Internal Affairs. Or they're gonna show up at the door. Like that cop who showed up with questions about the fire."

"You thought he was here for you," Kat said.

"Even if someone shows up, what am I gonna do? Turn on my own father? I can't do that. I can never do that."

As Ryan cried in her arms, Kat found herself annoyed. *You want sympathy. The man I love is suffering every second, and you want sympathy because your father turned you into a bagman. You're trapped? Good. Now you know what it feels like.*

"Shhh," she whispered. "No one will find out. No one will know."

Kat held him until he fell asleep, but she stared up at the ceiling, wide awake, her mind swirling like a vortex. Ryan couldn't know he had just confirmed a critical piece of the plan.

She had lied to Ryan, telling him she was almost done preparing the bridal shower. There would be a bridal shower, eventually, but she would not be part of it. She had put her own plan in place and made all her phone calls. She needed the bridesmaids to make this work. The most important member of the party, the last outstanding RSVP, had come through. The plan couldn't go forward without her.

It was time to mend fences. And then get out.

As Anthony Desucci entered the room, Vito Massone and his men stood in respect. Vincent and Carlo followed behind their boss. As Massone came to him and took his hand to kiss the top, his head and body bowed in reverence, Desucci's face appeared like a thundercloud.

"We hit another one of Federov's hideouts last night?" Desucci asked.

"No, Boss, I swear," Massone said.

"What about Federov? His brother?"

Massone shook his head. "They weren't there."

"They're blaming us. They hit us?"

"We're watching. Not yet."

Like a cat, Desucci struck without warning, smacking Massone across the face.

Vito faltered, in shock at the blow. Desucci followed with another smack and Vito stepped backward. "Boss," he said.

"I told you not to lay a hand on her," Desucci said.

"She's holding out on us, she's holding out on you," Vito said. "She's going to double-cross you. I had to put the pressure on."

Desucci answered with another smack. "When I give you an order, you follow it. Who gave the order to hit that safe house before I said we were ready?"

"Boss, I would never do that. I don't know what game Federov is playing. He killed his own men to blame it on you. These crazy Russians, they'll do anything. They'll kill their mothers if they can use them."

Desucci stared at Vito like he hadn't decided what should be done next.

"With all due respect, why does this girl deserve such consideration?"

"Because I said so," Desucci said. "From now on, I deal with her."

"Boss, she can't be trusted."

Desucci glared at his capo.

"Yes, Boss."

"Do nothing until I tell you, understand?"

"Understood," Massone said.

Desucci turned away from Massone, his signal the meeting was over.

The men filed out, leaving only Vincent and Carlo. Vincent nodded at Carlo to step out. After the door closed, Vincent stepped up to the desk, waiting for his boss to acknowledge him.

"What can I do, Boss," he said.

"Make the call," Desucci said.

"What do I say? Is a conversation being demanded?"

Desucci considered this. "Make a request, not a demand. Say it's important or I wouldn't ask."

Vincent nodded his head and left.

The women sat next to each other on the colorful couch, holding their oversized clip boards with one hand. They chattered in excited, breathless whispers, punctuated with nervous giggles. If they wanted to take a sip of wine, they had to lean the board on their lap, one-handing it so they could grab their glass with the other.

The sterile, medicinal white space did nothing to tamp down the eroticism of the nude, chiseled, male model posing in front of them.

"Do you think he's—you know—average?" Jeneen whispered in a voice loud enough for the model to hear. He responded with a barely concealed smirk as he held his pose.

"Uh-oh," Michelle, broke in, "Jeneen's got penis envy."

"I do not," she protested.

"She doesn't want to have a penis," Sandra interjected. "She wants to have someone else's penis other than Chris'."

This brought a fresh round of laughter.

The Bitches of Eastwick, Kat's latest name for the hens, had all accepted the invitation, no doubt at Emma's urging. They had come dressed in light, cotton dresses, while Kat had favored a sleek and simple dancer-style look, black bodysuit with a wraparound skirt and black ballet slippers. The awkward greetings and kisses had subsided when Katerina offered the first olive branch, giving Michelle a hug and admitting with teary eyes that all had been her fault and her fault alone.

After a glass of wine on empty stomachs, the alcohol began to do its work, exactly what Kat needed. Kat had remembered to sip from the glass.

"Chris is plenty big," Jeneen jumped in, to the snickering laughter of the other two.

Kat never had to decide who would be the best canary for this caper; it had always been Jeneen. The weakest link of the group, Jeneen lacked in every area: looks, figure, career, and relationship status. It was a trifecta plus a cherry on top. The other two mean girls had already piled on; Jeneen would be ripe for the picking.

Kat knew that guilt should have been consuming her; the force of her dislike of these women consoled her.

"How does Ryan compare to him?" Michelle whispered, eyeing the model.

Katerina had calculated this opening. She gave an embarrassed eye raise with her hand palm down, tipping it left to right to signify "so-so." The "oohs" that went up from the women told her she had done her job well. Another nail in her coffin that would get back to Ryan in short order.

For Kat, the sight of the model's nudity caused a warmth to bloom in her lower abdomen, and she felt the ache of emptiness for Winter. The desire to see him bare, to touch him, rose so strong in her, she thought for a moment she could feel him close, brushing her skin.

The art teacher hovered beside them, giving them tips as they attempted the assignment.

"You should have booked this for the shower," Sandra said.

"I thought about it."

"Emma's gonna be so mad she missed this," Jeneen said, but no one paid attention.

"Does he ever do it while he wears his uniform," Michelle pressed.

"I bet he just wears his holster," Sandra said, and the giggles broke out again.

"No, boxers!" Jeneen said.

"Un-unh," Michelle said, "I'll bet he wears briefs."

Katerina leaned in, speaking in a low confidential voice. "Tighty whities," she said to peals of laughter. "And," she said, "he likes to wear his uniform hat and say "assume the position."

Fresh squeals of laughter broke out as a flash of nausea swept over Kat.

"All right, ladies," the instructor said. "Let's see your works of art."

Katerina checked the clock. It was almost nine. They had a late reservation at the restaurant. Time to go.

***

They got off the subway at Grand Central and Katerina ushered the trio on the short walk until they reached the glass building with its address on a simple plate over the entrance. A small white LED sign next to the door, like a Lite Brite with no covering, held a series of Japanese symbols. If they had blinked, they would have passed it by. Katerina ushered them into the building's pristine, white marble lobby and gave the bored guard at the desk a girlish smile as she said, "Restaurant?"

He dismissed the group with a gesture of his hand toward the stairs.

They trundled down the slim stairwell hemmed in by concrete block walls. With the chatter and giggling grating in her ears, Katerina's muscles had tensed while her stomach knitted itself into knots. When they arrived at the basement, they passed through the short, black curtains adorned with symbols. They were ushered through the long, shotgun "L" portion of the restaurant until they made a sharp turn to a set of tables hidden in the back.

Katerina made sure she snagged the seat next to Jeneen. Once the sake started flowing, Kat watched the women's eyes glazing over. Next, small, delicate dishes of sashimi, tuna, and shitake mushrooms littered the table. Kat's nerves stretched and frayed with each passing moment.

They talked about everything and nothing, hometowns, growing up, first boyfriends, first kisses. Katerina lied with ease and leaned in as she spoke, exhibiting a conscious confidentiality as if taking each woman into the most secret places in her heart. Seated next to Jeneen, Kat directed most of her comments to her, intimating that she liked the picked-on bridesmaid better than the others.

Slipping out her cell phone, Katerina swiped it awake, having already removed any security to unlock it. Glancing at it, she tapped out a quick text.

After the third time, Kat said to Jeneen, "You know I heard the bathrooms here are wild. They're shaped like a sake barrel. You want to see it?"

Jeneen gave an enthusiastic nod, and they slipped out of their chairs. "Ladies room," Kat said to Michelle and Sandra. "We'll be back."

Michelle and Sandra gave Kat a smile.

Bitches, Kat thought.

Kat slipped the spaghetti strap of the purse over her shoulder, took Jeneen with one hand, while holding her cell phone in the other. They wended their way and found the two life-sized sake barrels near the kitchen.

"You know, you were really good about all that earlier," Kat said. "I'm sorry they did that to you."

Jeneen feigned ignorance. "What?"

"Talking about your boyfriend like that," Kat said. "I mean I can say something about my boyfriend if I want to, but I don't want anyone else saying something about him."

"Oh," she said. "They're just, you know, you know how they are."

"Yeah, I know how *they* are." She gave Jeneen a hug. "I'm so glad *you* came."

"Me, too," Jeneen said. "I mean, I don't know why they say stuff about you. Michelle always says mean stuff about you. She's been saying it from the beginning. But you're really nice. You're a good person."

"Can I tell you something? You won't tell anyone else?" Kat whispered.

"Of course not. I would never."

Kat held up her phone. "I need to make a phone call. He's just a friend. *Just* a friend. From school. Really. Nothing ever happened. But he keeps texting me. And I need to go outside and make a call and talk to him."

"Oh my God, you're not leaving Ryan, are you?" Jeneen said, her voice hushed.

"No, of course not! No, I would never! I just need to talk to him. I just need to try and cut this off, I mean not that there's anything going on that needs to be cut off, but I just feel bad, you know? You know, telling him 'don't ever call me again.' It's not like he's doing anything wrong. I'm not doing anything wrong. Can you cover for me at the table for a few minutes?" She nodded behind Jeneen in the direction of their table. "Don't tell them, please. Promise me."

"Oh, I wouldn't, never. Sure. What do you want me to tell them?"

"Tell them I'm talking to my mom."

Jeneen nodded vigorously. "Absolutely," she said.

Kat gave her a sweet smile. "Thanks, I knew I could trust you. Do me a favor, when you go back, just hold on to my purse for me, will you? I know *you* wouldn't go through it."

Jeneen took the purse. "I've got your back. Not a word."

***

Katerina hustled through the back of the kitchen, the staff staring at the girl wandering where she didn't belong. Walking with purpose, Kat strode to the back door, slipped out, and moved down the alley.

She saw April walking toward her.

Katerina and April stopped when they reached each other.

"Are we good?" Kat asked.

April gave a wide smile. "Chillin' like a villain."

***

"So, she's calling him right now?"

Jeneen nodded her head like a bobblehead doll, having dutifully reported every word Katerina had said, with a few added embellishments. She reveled in the rapt attention of the two women, relishing her one, brief moment of having the upper hand; a piece of information they did not possess.

"She said he's just a friend," Jeneen said.

"Bullshit. She's sleeping with this guy, while she's sleeping with Ryan. I told you she was a skank," Michelle fumed. "I knew it."

"So, how long has she been sleeping with this other guy?" Sandra said.

"All she said was, 'It's been going on all semester,'" Jeneen said.

The other two girls leaned in. "No," they said unison.

Jeneen nodded her head while taking another sip of sake.

***

In the restroom, April slopped the mop around in a lazy figure eight, the pail next to her, a tall garbage pail in the corner. A woman stood before the mirror, painstakingly applying her lipstick. April hoped the woman felt her eyes drilling into her, but the woman ignored the pointed stare. April inched closer, sloshing the wet liquid.

"Do you mind," the woman said, turning her head. "Can't you come back?"

"I'm on the clock," April asked, averting her eyes.

The woman huffed and snorted but held her ground, making an elaborate motion of finishing her eye makeup, taking the mascara out of her purse, pumping the wand, and lingering over every lash. With a final shove of the wand back into the bottle, she threw the item into her bag and huffed over having to lift her outfit bag, so it didn't drag on the floor. Muttering under her breath, the woman slammed out of the bathroom.

April went to the garbage pail and lifted off the supply tray and the large garbage bags piled onto the top. Katerina popped up out of the can as if she had come out of a cake. She extracted herself with her hair now pinned up and piled on her head. She turned and dove back in, bringing out a miniature backpack. She unsnapped her skirt, slipped out of the ballet slippers and folded them into the backpack. She perched on the sink and pushed out a ceiling tile. Motioning for April to pass up the backpack, she hoisted it over one shoulder. She placed her hands on the insides of each respective tile and hauled up her body weight, disappearing into the ceiling. Her head stuck down through the opening.

"When I'm done, I'll text you."

"Got it. I'll come back down after I finish the next floor."

"Don't be late."

"Chillin' like a villain," April said. Katerina disappeared and the ceiling tile slipped back into place.

April hauled the rolling garbage pail, the mop, and the rolling pail out of the restroom, making noise all the way.

***

"Should we call him?" Michelle asked.

"No! No!" Jeneen objected. "No, we can't do that. I promised her I wouldn't say a word."

"How long has she been gone?" Sandra asked.

"Five minutes," Michelle said. "You know, this isn't fair to Ryan. They're gonna get married?"

"Maybe she's breaking it off with the other guy, that's why she's calling him," Jeneen said.

"How do you know she's on the phone with him?" Michelle said. "Really, Jeneen, don't be naïve. She probably went off to meet him and it's close by and she left us here. She's using us as cover while she goes and meets this guy."

"She gave me her purse to hold," Jeneen said.

"Well, let's see it," Michelle said, snatching the bag away. Overturning the purse, a lipstick, tissue, and condom pouch fell out.

"Uh-hunh," Sandra piled on. "You were right."

"She's playing us," Michelle said. "She's playing Ryan. She's not done tonight. She's gonna dump us and go see him and sleep with him. She's totally bent this girl. Seriously, she's ill."

"Yeah," Jeneen said and poured out more sake.

***

Katerina, on hands and knees, crawled with a ginger hand, knee, hand, knee combination until she had counted out the distance April had measured for her. She stopped, tugging at the tiling until it jarred loose. Taking her phone out of the small, heavy pack, she flipped on the flashlight and peered down into the darkened space. She scanned, looking for the landmarks. Jackpot. Tucking the phone back into the pack, she grasped the tile on either side of the open space, contracted her stomach muscles and hung suspended as if on the parallel bars, and then dropped onto a desk, finishing in a crouch. She breathed out and held still, remembering Winter's words.

There will be a moment, and you will say to yourself, this is insane. I am doing this, and it is insane. You must put that thought out of your mind —or you will fail.

Kat looked at her watch and calculated the security guard's next rotation. Five minutes. *Or life as I know it, will end.*

***

"She's entered the office," Joseph Smith whispered into the headset.

Thomas Gallagher sat behind the executive desk in his study, Smith's voice coming through the speaker, soft but clear.

"Abort it now," Gallagher said.

"Negative," Smith said. "Not possible."

Gallagher sat up. "Why not?"

"We're not the only players in the field."

"Who?" Gallagher demanded and grimaced when he heard the name.

***

"Whoops, whoops, hold the phone, we've got movement on the twenty-third floor." Burnett was medium height and sported a full head of hair and an easy smile. He had a roll of pudge hanging over his pants as he sat hunched over the scope, one eye resting against it as he peered into a glass window of the building across the street. The darkened office would illuminate from the occasional snatch of a cell phone flashlight before going dark again.

"What's she doing?" Daniel Clay called out with a mouth full of food, standing by a table with a sloppy array of sandwiches and salads. He was in his late thirties, wiry, with a runner's body. He had a smooth complexion with an aquiline nose, and his features came together to make an attractive face complemented by a full head of short, thick, coal-black curly hair.

Nicholas, wiry, with a serious expression on a face of sharp angles and planes, chuckled and shook his head. "She's committing a robbery," he said.

"You know, this girl is crazy. You know that, right? She was crazy in California and she's crazy here," said Halliday, the worrier of the group.

"Relax," Daniel Clay said. "If she's in there committing a robbery, that means Alexander Winter is in there, committing a robbery with her. I've been waiting six months for this."

Prescott, always even and steady, talked softly into a cell phone. "Hey, you see anyone matching a description, male, six feet, muscular, hair cut close?"

A bit of static and then, "Negative. It's only been the girl on the cleaning crew."

Burnett turned and gave Daniel a pointed stare. "She's on her own, man. I told you."

"He missed something."

"That's *our* guy," Prescott said. "He's been tracking the little one, the girl with the purple hair and the piercings. It's just the two of them."

Nicholas made a noise of disgust. "More time wasted. For nothing."

Clay threw down the sandwich and went to Burnett, tapping his shoulder to move out of the way. He situated himself in front of the spyglass and peered at the young woman, the outline of the black, skintight outfit pronounced when the flashlight popped on and then off.

"What kind of business is this again?"

"Import export," Halliday said.

"Of what?" Clay pressed.

"Stuff," Nicholas said. "Food, manufactured goods, nothing that stands out. There's no reason for her to be in there."

"This an American company?"

"Peruvian," Burnsey said.

Clay continued to watch Katerina as she made her way into the back office. He shook his head as he mumbled his thoughts out loud. "What the hell is she doing?"

***

"That's it," Michelle said. "We should leave right now, and I'm calling Emma. I've heard of some extreme maid of honor bullshit, but this takes the cake."

"No, no," Sandra said. "We should totally wait."

"Why? She's a skank. She's a user. She doesn't love Ryan, and she doesn't care about Emma. She's bent."

"No, we can't leave, or she'll know I told you," Jeneen said.

"We have to wait," Sandra said. "We have to wait until she comes back. Act like nothing happened and see what she looks like. Maybe she's meeting him right now to do the deed. Did she take a condom out of her purse before she gave it to you?"

"I didn't see her do that," Jeneen said.

"She probably took it out and stuffed it in her bra. They're probably in the alley somewhere," Michelle said. "Skank. Poor Ryan. I feel really bad for him. She's gonna ruin him."

"Let's just wait," Sandra said.

***

Katerina flipped on the flashlight and zeroed in on the safe tucked underneath the return of the desk. Her shoulder ached from the weight of the pack. She knelt down in front of the safe, placing the backpack on the floor, and stared at the electronic keypad.

Keep it simple. That's what Winter taught you. Simple is best.

Reaching into the pack, she brought out a pair of heavy gloves. Slipping them on, she pulled out the cylindrical disk, like a hockey puck, but heavy in her hand. She put it down and then brought out a man's sock. Wrangling the disk into the sock, she lifted it, the perspiration gathering on her forehead as she maneuvered it to the door of the safe. She grunted with exertion as she moved the disk in incremental inches over the area. A trickle of sweat ran down her neck and she began to panic the whole thing would be a bust.

Patience, Katie. Patience. Breathe.

Closing her eyes, Kat heard Winter's voice in her head, coaching her, and for a split second the air changed, as if his lips were close to her ear.

Your sense of touch is your best friend.

The digital mechanism is fitted with an actuator.

The magnet has a draw of over five hundred pounds.

When you hold the magnet against the door in the correct spot, the metal actuator responds to the force of the magnet. This magnetic force is strong enough to pull the actuator and unlock the safe.

Kat inched the magnet again and felt a shift.

Did it happen? Or was it only wishful thinking?

With one hand, she grasped the handle and pulled, the door giving way under the force.

Katerina flopped back on her backside and put on the burner phone's flashlight. The light illuminated a small briefcase.

Holy shit. I did it.

***

Daniel Clay hovered as Burnett hunched over the scope, his eye glued to the lens.

"So? What's she doing?"

"Well, the light just went on. She's doing something by the desk, but not on the desk, underneath it. My guess is, she just got into something. One of the desk drawers, maybe, a lock box–" he pulled back and turned to look at Clay, "or a safe."

Clay nudged Burnett to get up and out of the way. He planted himself in the seat and looked through the lens. "She's on the move in the office. That light keeps going on and off . . . she's got something. She's carrying something. And he's nowhere in sight."

"He's not here. I'm telling you," Nicholas said behind them. "And if he's not here, she can't tell us shit about what we're looking for."

Clay waved his arm at Nicholas.

"She's going out the way she came. She's up on the desk . . . she shoved something up into the ceiling, a briefcase. Then something else, probably a backpack. Shit, this girl is smokin' hot. She must have killer abs. She pulled herself up like it was nothing."

"Great, next time she goes to that aerial class or whatever the hell it is, maybe she can get you a Groupon," Nicholas said.

Halliday grabbed the headset. "She's going back the way she came."

"Wherever that is, there's no windows."

The group looked at each other and spoke in unison. "Bathroom."

"That means the kid's gonna be coming back with the garbage pail."

Static noise and then a voice. "No, she isn't. She's got a problem."

***

"Why isn't this office cleaned? What have you been doing?"

April kept her head down in penitence, while the supervisor tore into her for sloppy work and overall laziness.

"I'm cleaning," she mumbled.

"No, no you don't. You just walk around and empty the garbage, but you don't clean. I've gotten complaints. Well, you stay here now. You clean this, and I'm going to watch you. You think I'm going to lose my job because of you? No. Do it. Now."

April bit her tongue, hung her head, and went to work with a spray bottle and a rag. She glanced up at the clock. She should be on the elevator in five minutes. She wouldn't make it.

***

Kat made her way back. Using a small bungee cord, she had the backpack, and the briefcase, rigged up and slung over her shoulder. Removing the tile, she surveyed the empty bathroom. Maneuvering herself, she dropped to land in a crouch. She checked her watch. *Where is she?*

***

Kat made short work of smoothing out her skirt as she snapped it back on and snugging back into her ballet slippers. She took a minute to grab a few tri-fold towels to whisk the sweat away. *Don't take away all of it. You need it.* Glancing in the mirror, she noted the flush in her face. That would do nicely. *But I can't keep waiting in this bathroom. What the hell happened?* She hesitated. Once she walked out the door, there would be no avoiding the security cameras. What had April told her? The cameras are in each corner and in the stairwell, situated right inside the stairwell door. She would have to stick to the blind spots and hope April could hack the system and erase the footage later.

Facing the mirror, she took the pins out of her hair and let it tumble down her back.

Deciding she could wait no longer, Katerina pulled open the door to the restroom and stepped out into the hallway. *Walk like you're where you're supposed to be.*

She heard the faint whistle. The security guard. She glanced at her phone. He was off schedule. He was early.

Katerina threw open the door to the stairwell, ducked inside, and grabbed the handle before it slammed shut. The whistle grew louder just as she went through the door and she wondered if he had caught sight of her, the girl with the small briefcase and backpack.

The surge of panic welled within her. *Running out of time.*

She coached herself with his words. *If there's even one move left to make, it's not over. What's your move, Katerina?*

She took the stairs with a slow, measured gait, tilting her head toward the right, knowing the camera had captured her from the back. She lowered her head as she opened the door at the next landing and stepped out onto the floor.

Hearing the noise of a vacuum cleaner, Kat followed it toward an open office door. As she passed, she noticed a woman with a clipboard standing watch as April pushed the vacuum back and forth. *Shit.* Without missing a beat, Kat kept walking. There was a service elevator on the floor, but it needed a key fob. *That's sitting on April's key chain.*

Kat heard the opening of the stairwell door. *The guard.* She lurched forward as if pushed from behind.

Kat arrived at the general elevator and pressed the button. It was too late now. She was on the security camera in at least three locations. When the elevator stopped and the doors slid open, she entered the elevator and hit the button to close the door. She hit the "B" button for the basement. What had seemed an eternity had taken barely fifteen minutes. But it didn't matter.

Everything is screwed.

***

Something wasn't right.

He was sure he'd seen that girl before.

What was she doing sneaking around in the hallways?

He glanced up at the elevator panel.

The elevator was headed toward the basement.

Why would she be going down to the basement?

The guard went for the stairs.

***

"What's he saying?" Clay demanded.

Halliday turned to Clay. "He says the kid is stuck in the office on the twenty-second floor and he thinks Kat's on the same floor. But the main elevator is running down to the basement. Danny, you know she's been caught on the security camera."

Clay shook his head. "We'll take care of that."

"The guard on his rounds is headed down there now. She's not gonna get out of there."

"Tell our guy to do his job or the boss isn't gonna be happy."

"Where are you going?" Prescott said.

Everyone turned to see Nicholas grabbing his jacket. "She needs an out, right? Or you just want to write her off and forget the whole thing?"

Clay considered the ultimatum. "Go," he said.

***

Katerina rubbed her palms together to whisk away the sweat as the elevator door opened. Emerging into the basement, she glanced both ways and looked for the supply closet. Coming around the corner, she saw the open door but heard voices. People in the supply closet, the guard coming up from behind. Kat receded into a space that had a mesh gate, and on the other side, the main electrical panels. She heard footsteps coming in her direction.

"Hey."

A man's voice.

"What are you doing down here? What? I'm gonna wait forever? I did my floors. You're supposed to come and relieve me."

"I'm checking on something."

"On what? I already checked this area. C'mon. My dinner break started five minutes ago."

"I saw someone."

"Who?"

"I thought I saw someone on twenty-three coming down here."

"So? There's nobody down here. You gonna give me shit or what? I wanna eat."

Silence.

"I told you, I already checked down here. What do you think I've been doing?"

"Okay, but–"

"No buts man, this place is clean."

The voices moved away. Chattering from the supply closet moved out into the hall and then off to the right toward the service elevator. Kat waited until she heard the service elevator door beep and close. Coming out of the recessed darkness, she rounded the corner, breathing a sigh of relief to find the supply closet door still open. *Bet this is a no-no.* She ducked inside and found a space between the wall and the stocked shelving units. She took her cell phone out of the pack and then slid the brief-case and the backpack behind the unit and sent off a text to April in code.

I placed an order for bridal shower gifts.
Lower Level.
There are two separate gifts.
Please advise when order received. Thank you.

With a knot in her stomach, Kat ducked out of the supply closet.

Katerina retraced her steps, coming up out of the basement to the back alley, back to the stairs leading down to the kitchen, until she found her way back to the table with her cell phone in hand, making sure to look and sound out of breath.

"There she is," Michelle said, all smiles. "We were beginning to worry about you."

"Sorry, sorry, sorry," Kat said, waving the phone. "Long distance call from my mom. I had to take it," and she looked at Jeneen as she said it.

The girls nodded, talking over each other, lavishing Kat with understanding and support. She caught their sly looks at her wild, loose hair and then the shared looks between them. She had ex-pected it, planned for it. It had to be done.

***

April cursed under her breath as she came off the elevator into the basement. She checked the phone and hurried to the supply closet, acknowledging that finally the universe had decided to cut her a freaking break by having no one in there. She gave another silent note of thanks that this was the last night she'd be working this shit job.

April went to the shelving units and crouched down, reaching her hand behind. She laid her hand on something, tugging at it until she maneuvered it out.

The backpack.

She reached in again and then sat back.

She leaned in and tried again.

April took out her cell phone and switched on the flashlight, pointing it into the darkened space. She needed to be sure before she sent the text message.

She sat back on her heels.

No briefcase.

***

A group of giggling women came up the stairs from the restaurant. Michelle and Sandra clustered close together, whispering among themselves with glances in Kat's direction. Jeneen stayed close to Kat, clinging to her new best friend.

As they traversed the snow-white marble lobby, Kat heard, "Just a minute, miss." Her heart pounded within her. She ignored the call, even as the other three swiveled to see who was speaking.

"Miss! Stop!"

The trio stopped, forcing Kat to halt as well. She turned. A security guard approached, zeroing in on her.

"Were you looking for something in the basement?"

"I'm sorry?" she answered and then heard from behind, "Ladies, did you call for a ride?"

Katerina turned her head to see Nicholas, clean shaven, dressed in jeans and a dress shirt, playing an Uber driver.

"Party of four for the Two-Thirty Fifth Rooftop Bar?"

"Yes," Kat said, without missing a beat. "That's us!" She turned to the trio. "Surprise! One last stop before the night is over."

Nicholas ushered them away toward the exit, giving the guard a wide smile. The guard stepped forward just as his partner came up alongside, waved at Nicholas and said, "Go ahead."

Nicholas shepherded them out of the building and down the street toward a car. When he turned to hold open the door, he saw the guard standing out in front of the building, his eyes locked on Katerina as she slid into the car. After they all piled in, Nicholas slammed the doors, gave the guard a nod and crossed in front of the vehicle, watching for oncoming traffic until he could open the driver's side door and slide in behind the wheel.

***

Inside the vehicle, adrenalin coursed through Kat's body, while the girls chattered over each other. She slid out her phone to check for the coded text message that would tell her April had the case. She tapped on the phone.

MESSAGE RECEIVED.
SMALLER OVAL-SIZED KEEPSAKE AVAILABLE.
LARGER SQUARE MEMENTO GIFT BOX - NO.
NONE IN STOCK.

Katerina stared at the words as if she hadn't read them right. *What the hell happened to the briefcase?* Keeping a neutral expression, she glanced up and found Michelle staring at her, a hard smile on her lips. Kat shifted her gaze to the rearview mirror — and found Nicholas staring back at her.

***

At Two-Thirty Fifth, Nicholas held open the rear passenger door as the women exited the car like clowns at the circus. "Ladies, enjoy yourselves. Send a message when you're ready to leave. I'm in the area, so I'll be back."

Katerina shot a hard look at Nicholas but soldiered on as they trooped down the rope line in the lobby to the elevators. Kat had lost interest for the charade but had no choice but to follow through.

Coming off the elevator, they found themselves under a blackened sky punctuated by the brilliant city lights; the specter of the Empire State Building illuminated before them, a lightshow just for them.

Over drinks, Michelle said, "We were worried about you when you disappeared for so long. I hope your mother is all right."

"Yes, she's just upset that she can't help plan the wedding, so she wants to talk at all hours about gowns and arrangements."

Michelle and Sandra gave plastic smiles and nods.

***

After a while, Kat and Jeneen stepped away to a quiet corner.

"Everything okay?" Jeneen whispered.

"Yes, it just took longer than I expected. He just wanted to keep me on the phone. He was upset, and I didn't want to hurt his feelings. You didn't say anything . . ." Kat led.

"Oh no, nothing," Jeneen said. "I just said that you were a little tipsy from the sake and had to use the ladies' room and then they kept asking and all I said was maybe you had to call your mom . . ."

Kat gave Jeneen's hand a squeeze of solidarity and gratitude. Jeneen wore the lies like a see-through jacket, but Kat's mind was on her immediate problem: the case.

The bartender announced the last call. Time to go home.

***

"Stop the car," Kat said.

"I'm taking you home," Nicholas said.

"Great, my boyfriend the cop would love to meet you. Stop here. Where's the case?"

Nicholas put the car in at the curb and twisted around. "Why are you living with a cop? Where's your guy?"

"Cut the crap. Where's the case? Why are you following me?"

"Following is an ugly way to put it. Where's your guy?"

"You didn't answer my question."

"And you didn't answer mine." In the standoff, Nicholas said, "We are not *following* you. We check in when we can. Danny's concerned about you."

"Wow, that is bullshit," Kat answered. "Daniel's feelings are hurt because he got bested."

"So, where's the champion?"

Kat took a breath before answering. "Out of town."

"When's he back?"

"No idea," she said.

"What about Viktor Mikhailovich?"

"What about him?" Kat asked.

"You seen any Russians lately?"

Oh boy, have I seen Russians. And if you had been following me all the time, maybe I wouldn't have been in a van with a gun to my head.

"No, should I have?"

"You busted into Mikhailovich's safe. I'm sure he noticed. He's probably looking for you."

"What you mean is, you're afraid he's looking for *you*. And you're afraid I'm going to throw you over." Kat shook her head. "I was a shiny toy Mikhailovich wanted to play with. I'm not on the radar as a safecracker."

"You hope."

"I know. Are you gonna give me the case?"

Nicholas pulled something up by a handle. Kat's gaze narrowed in anger at the small briefcase.

"For the record, this is not your case," he said.

"Possession is nine-tenths of the law."

"Right now, I possess it."

"You don't want it."

"Speaking of which, you shouldn't be pulling jobs by yourself," Nicholas said. "You have friends, you know."

Not in this car. "Price is too high," Kat said.

Nicholas frowned. "Hey, I took a beating for you."

Katerina had no wisecrack response. "I know. If you hadn't been there that night, it would have been bad for me. Really bad."

Nicholas nodded at the offered olive branch and passed the case over into the backseat. "You did a good job tonight, but if we hadn't been around, that other guard could have been a problem for you. You're welcome."

Katerina took the case by the handle. "Are you gonna let me out of the car?"

Nicholas smiled. "The door isn't locked."

Katerina pulled on the handle and pushed the door open.

"Wait."

Katerina stopped. Nicholas pulled a small card out of his pocket and held it out. Kat took it and read the phone number.

"You still have friends," he said.

Kat moved to get out of the car.

"Hey, no tip for the service?"

Kat stopped. "Yeah, I've got a tip for you," she said as she tossed the card onto the front seat. "Stay away from me. I'm not good for you. I'm not good for anyone."

***

"Imelda!" Pablo greeted Kat with open arms as she placed the small case on the table. He sat forward and put both hands on the case, pulling it toward himself, taking possession. Using his thumbs, he scrolled the two combination chains until he stopped and then used his thumbs to press the levers. The case locks popped, and he raised the lid.

"We clear?"

"We clear, niña," he said. "You want the laptop now?"

"No, she'll come by to pay and pick up."

He regarded her with that bemused expression when someone exceeds expectations. "Chica, you ever want to do business again, we can do that."

"I'll keep it in mind. Right now, all I'd like to do is buy a burner phone."

Pablo pulled a small box out of a carton. "On the house," he said.

Katerina handed over a twenty-dollar bill and took the box. "I'll catch you on the way back," Kat said. *Not.*

On the ride home, the rhythmic noise of the subway train droned in Kat's ears as it crossed the Manhattan Bridge. Staring out at the water, Katerina reviewed the night; everything that had gone wrong, what she should have done better. That's what Winter would've done; he would have helped her to be better. Duplicate key fobs for the service elevator and duplicate keys to the supply closets. A Plan B for the supervisor showing up unannounced. The safe cracking had worked; she couldn't quite get over that it had. She found herself curious about the contents of the case, but the adrenalin of the night had already begun to fade, and she began to look ahead.

You are never getting away from me.

There's nowhere you can go.

There's nothing you can do.

She had set something in motion tonight and it wouldn't take forty-eight hours before it came home to roost. Kat dreaded what would come next. There was no other way. It had to be done. But Ryan had been mistaken. There was something she could do; something that would make it possible to get out and the change would be permanent.

She pulled out the burner phone and typed out a text to April.

I HAVE THE BRIDAL GIFT BOX
DETAILS LATER

GO BACK TO THE BANK
PICKUP IS WAITING FOR YOU
BACK IN BUSINESS

When Kat got off the subway, she dumped the burner. She walked in the pitch black of the night. Glancing around and up at the cloudless sky, she found herself alone. No spirit animal, no friends, no Winter. A shiver ran through her as she reached the building.

Inside, Kat reached the door of the apartment and stood there, head bowed. It could be over right now, tonight. She had prepared for this. She had already clicked the link April sent to the Reynolds phone and let April infiltrate and take over the phone. It lay dormant now, hidden away behind the pots and pans. Once Kat sent April the text with instructions, she would follow the message schedule.

Katerina twisted the key in the lock and turned.

Entering the apartment, she stepped into the darkness. She hesitated. Would the light suddenly turn on? Would he be sitting in the chair, waiting for her?

Her eyes adjusted to the darkness. Stepping closer to the coffee table, she saw the faint glint from the empty beer bottles. Listening, she heard the sound of snoring coming from the bedroom.

A small reprieve for one night.

The storm was coming.

CHAPTER

66

"So?" Daniel Clay asked.

Nicholas glanced up from his phone, giving Daniel a blank stare.

"Since your phone went conveniently dark, what did she say?"

Nicholas shrugged. "According to her, he's out of town. No idea when he'll be back."

Prescott entered the room, a sandwich in one hand. "He dumped her?"

Nicholas gave it thought. "No, she didn't look like a girl who'd been dumped. She'd be angry. She was upset, worried. I think he's in shit."

Clay took in the information. "Sure, he took the painting, and now he doesn't know what to do with it."

"Danny, are you forgetting the note? He doesn't do museum jobs," Burnsey said.

"Have you forgotten your training? Details. Everything is in the details. What did the note say Mr. Halliday," Clay called out.

"It said, 'I don't *like* museum jobs,'" Halliday said.

Clay turned back to Burnett. "That's right. He may not like museum jobs, but he'll do them. With the right circumstances and motivation, he'll do them," Clay said. "I think he's our guy."

"That's not our concern anymore," Burnett said.

Nicholas' head darted up in surprise. "Why not?"

"The boss sent new instructions," Prescott said. "If Winter is nowhere to be found, then following Kat, even intermittently, is a risk. The boss' order is to back off and discontinue any surveillance. She just walked off with something and we don't need to be anywhere near that."

"We are already near that," Nicholas pointed out.

"We don't need to be anywhere near that *more than we already are.*"

Nicholas shrugged and went back to his phone.

"Hey," Clay said. "Next time, if there is a next time, make sure we can eavesdrop through the phone."

"Yes, sir," Nicholas said, without looking up.

For the next two days, Kat left the apartment early and made several stops, a Pret a Manger, a residential building, places where she had no business; once the dominoes started to fall, they would be useful for her purpose. At Gallagher's office, Katerina figured nine o'clock would bring a visit from Assistant Nicole asking if she would "kindly join Mr. Gallagher for 'a brief meeting,' or the inevitable lunch invitation. Kat ducked into the office for a few minutes and headed right back out again, taking her normal "Ryan" cell phone with her.

***

Lashiver could tell his partner had become preoccupied. No, that wasn't the right word. Obsessed. The lack of focus, lack of attention. It had been better after the engagement announcement, but like Groundhog Day, here they were again. It was the girl. It had to be.

They sat opposite each other at their desks, sifting through boxes of files.

Ryan's eyes shifted from the paperwork to his cell phone, a constant back and forth.

"Hey, tomorrow's another day," Lashiver said. "You'll start fresh in the morning."

Ryan nodded, closing the folder and picking up his phone. He got up and shrugged into his jacket. "We might have another vic to put on the map. Out in the Rockaways."

Lashiver nodded. "Tomorrow."

"Are you heading out?" Ryan asked.

"I'm gonna grab some dinner and go through a few more files."

"Hey, I can stay, no problem."

"Call it a night, okay? Tomorrow's another day."

Ryan's cell phone buzzed, interrupting their discussion. "Hello?" He listened and then made a face. "Shouldn't you talk to Emma about this?"

Ryan listened again and knit his brow in confusion. "Uh, okay, sure. I'm on my way home. I'll swing by for a couple of minutes, okay?"

He clicked off the phone and tapped on the icon for a GPS tracking program. He scrolled.

Lashiver watched him. "Is there a problem?"

Ryan snapped back to attention. "Bridesmaid problems, wedding problems," he said with a smile. "These girls, man. It's always a crisis with these girls."

"It's their day," Lashiver said. "Keep a good thought. Maybe they'll elope."

Ryan laughed. As he left the squad room and went for the stairs, the smile melted away as fast as it had appeared, leaving an expression of stone in its wake.

***

Lashiver stayed at the desk for another ten minutes and then grabbed his jacket and left.

Elizabeth gathered up the grocery bag, chucking it under one arm.

One block from her apartment building, she stopped short at a car door opening; Walter Lashiver got out.

"I'm glad I caught you, Elizabeth," he said as he approached. "I called the office, and they told me you'd left for the day."

Elizabeth stood dumb for a moment, staring at Lashiver, his arms outstretched, like a pleading lover. She watched like a spectator as he removed the bag from her hands.

"You have plans for tonight?" Lashiver asked.

"No," she said.

"Just dinner for one, hunh?" he said, sounding surprised.

"Yes," she said.

"In that case, I'm sure you won't mind if I impose a bit. I need help, Elizabeth. We're at a dead end and I need help. I need *your* help."

"I – I – can't. . ." Elizabeth said.

Lashiver, already at her side, his free hand at Elizabeth's elbow.

"Why don't we go to the station? It won't take long, and it'll be more comfortable there to talk."

In the space of her hesitation, he prodded her. "Just a few minutes," and he had the car door open. "It's just an interview, Elizabeth," he said.

When faced with a police officer, most people obey; it's what they've been taught to do. Lashiver settled Elizabeth in the car.

***

In an office, Lashiver set a steaming cup of tea before Elizabeth; she sat with her hands folded in her lap.

"I can see why Mr. Reynolds asked you to transfer to New York," he said as he took the opposite seat. "It's hard to find someone who's really good, professional, loyal."

Lashiver watched the muscles in Elizabeth's jaw working, clenching.

"Didn't you find it strange he wanted to move to New York? I mean, there's a lot of big businesses in Illinois. You got John Deere, Caterpillar . . ."

"General Mills," she said.

"Right," Lashiver said, affable as ever. "I don't eat cereal in the morning myself. I prefer coffee – and a doughnut, of course."

Lashiver waited in the silence, waited for Elizabeth to budge, or blink.

"Mr. Reynolds wanted to see the company grow and that required expansion."

"What kind of expansion?" Lashiver asked.

"You know very well Mr. Reynolds' company has a controlling interest or shares in different industries."

Lashiver nodded. "Oh sure," he said. "Manufacturing, electronics, telecommunications. I'm just surprised he came East. Why not Chicago or–"

"You'd have to ask him," she said.

"And your husband didn't want to come with you, hunh?"

Elizabeth's eyes widened.

"We know you were married," Lashiver said. "Your husband didn't want to come to the big city."

"No," Elizabeth said. "Our marriage, any marriage, is never what you think it will be. We were no different than any other couple."

"Preaching to the choir," Lashiver said with a chuckle. "What about Mr. Reynolds – his wife – or girlfriend – or both. You're the secretary, you'd know," he said.

"If you have a question about Mr. Reynolds' personal life, you'll have to ask him."

"John Reynolds' wife didn't make the trip," he said. "Because . . .?"

"Mr. Reynolds was not married at the time of the move. He was already divorced," she said.

"See, I knew that's why we needed to talk again. The secretary knows everything."

"Mr. Reynolds never spoke to me about his personal issues, and I didn't ask. It was not my place to do so."

"Elizabeth," he said softly, "we're almost done clearing John Reynolds as a suspect."

"He never – never should have been a suspect," she said, but her voice wavered, and the sentence died out.

"I know," Lashiver said. "I've been thinking how we should've gotten to this sooner. That's why I needed to speak to you. All we had to do was ask you."

"Ask me what? You've interviewed me countless times."

"Yes, but we didn't put it together. Some detectives. You said he was in his office on a conference call."

"Yes," she said, exasperated now. "We all know that."

"And you went into his office while he was on the call."

Elizabeth went silent.

"You can do that – because he trusts you."

Her mouth parted but no words came out.

Lashiver leaned closer. "Did you go into his office while he was on the call?"

"I –," and their eyes met.

Lashiver held fast.

"Yes," she said.

Lashiver nodded. "That's very good, Elizabeth. But, I think something has been bothering you since that day, hasn't it? Something you've been trying to forget."

Elizabeth stood up. "I – I need to leave now. I have work to do this evening for Mr. Reynolds. If it's not completed, he's going to ask me why not."

Lashiver, on his feet now, stood between Elizabeth and the door. "You can't tell him why not? You're not doing anything wrong. You're helping us. You're helping Mr. Reynolds."

"I have a lot of work to do, detective."

"Just five more minutes," Lashiver said, gesturing to the chair. "Just a few more minutes. I promise."

Elizabeth wavered before allowing herself to be settled back into her seat.

Lashiver pulled up a chair next to her. "I understand. I do. You think you're being disloyal. But you're not. Right now, the only person you're being disloyal to is yourself. Because it's been eating at you, from the inside. You have to get it out. You have to speak, because it's hurting you, inside, not to tell the truth."

Elizabeth stared straight ahead, her eyes clouding, her lips pressed together, guarding the gate lest anything escape.

"Elizabeth, why did you go into John Reynolds' office?"

She bowed her head and then said, "I heard . . . something."

Lashiver nodded. "What did you hear?"

"I thought, something had happened to someone on the call. I don't know . . . someone got hurt, or fell or . . . I don't know."

"What did you hear?" he pressed.

"It sounded . . ." she lifted her head. "It was low, but it sounded like a cry."

Lashiver hesitated a moment. "A cry. A woman's cry?"

Tears fell as Elizabeth nodded her head. "I, I thought someone was hurt. Then, I heard the scream."

Lashiver set his jaw before he continued. "So, you took action, to help, didn't you, Elizabeth?"

She nodded her head. "I rushed into the office. I didn't think about knocking."

"And what did you see?" Lashiver pressed. "What was John Reynolds doing?"

"He was sitting at his desk, watching something."

"Watching. On the computer?"

Elizabeth hung her head.

"Where was he watching something, Elizabeth?" Lashiver prodded again.

Elizabeth lifted her head and turned to Lashiver. "A cell phone. He was watching something on a cell phone. The noise was coming from the phone. A woman, crying, screaming. She screamed his name."

"Elizabeth, did you recognize the voice?"

Tears ran down Elizabeth's cheeks. "It was Mrs. Reynolds. It was Felicia."

Lashiver swallowed hard as he nodded and patted her shoulder. "Thank you, Elizabeth. Thank you."

S he knew. If someone had asked, Kat would not have been able to explain how, but she knew. Any number of things told her tonight would be the night; the sound of the slam of the door, the tension that infected the air, the anger that had its own scent. Standing at the sink, she didn't have to turn around; she knew. The inside of her body, the organs and muscles, began their familiar, violent shaking. The nausea rose from her belly into her throat. She waited for the next step of the ritual. First, the jacket came off. Draped over the chair. Then, the shoulder holster came off. Draped over the jacket. That's what she needed. She needed the gun. If she didn't get to the gun first . . .

She had rehearsed it in her head countless times. Now, the panic sent her mind scattering in every direction. *Just survive this. Then you're out.*

The fridge door opened, then slammed shut. The twist and pop of the cap.

"What happened at work?" His voice sounded soft. *Dangerous.*

"Not much, same old," she said. She knew the plaintive sound in her voice would make it worse. She turned her head and gave him a smile full of innocence. "How's the case?"

Ryan took a swig of his beer and swallowed. "Which case?"

"Felicia Reynolds."

"The dead wife who slutted around on her husband. Coming along."

This is it.

It's happening today, right now.

He hovered behind her. She knew the classic blocking maneuver to box her in where she couldn't escape.

You knew this would happen. You knew you'd have to take it.

The panic, the doubt, the fear, exploded like blinding fireworks within her. She felt unsteady on her feet, a blaring white noise in her head. *Steady.* She reminded herself how she would move. The gun rested in the same spot. She had arranged the chair just so. There was every chance to reach it.

You know what to do. Do it. Survive this.

But the trembling sickened her . . . *Was I insane to think I could do this?*

"I was going to make a late dinner, unless you wanted to eat out, or order in . . ." she babbled.

She felt his body heat as he hovered over her. She heard his breathing. She felt his eyes on her until he tipped his head back and took another swig from the bottle. Another swallow.

"I ate a late snack," he said.

"Okay," she said.

"Aren't you gonna ask me about it?"

Kat didn't look at him as she said, "Sure. What about the snack?"

Ryan gave a short, bitter laugh. "I met someone for a quick bite and a chat. Actually, it was an urgent call. Someone was worried about me."

Kat turned to him. "Worried about you? Why? What's wrong?"

Ryan gave her a cockeyed smile, lopsided, cruel.

Any second now. Just get to the gun.

"Didn't you hear?" he asked, the smile on his face wide, the voice dripping with sarcasm. "My fiancée is fucking someone else."

Kat dropped the plate and darted, turning her face away as the bottle shattered against the cabinet, sending shards of glass flying and liquid spraying everywhere. He grabbed her arm, squeezing, yanking her off her feet. She cried out.

"Shut up," he seethed, one hand squeezing her cheeks. "Shut the fuck up before somebody hears you."

He drove her back with his other hand, slamming her against the refrigerator door, the handle driving into the center of her back. The terror exploded that she had got it all wrong.

What made you think you could do this?

"You like being a whore, hunh? You like making a fool out of me in front of my friends while you flash your pussy at anybody who smiles at you."

Kat's words came out as muddled sounds. Ryan squeezed harder.

"You want to tell me something, hunh? You want to tell me everyone's lying. Hunh? Hunh? It's not true. Your phone's been on the move for the past couple of days. Where you been doing it, hunh? The bathroom in the coffee shop? Is that where you're doing it? You're disgusting. That's where you would do it."

Katerina gripped the refrigerator door handle, but Ryan ripped her away, the door flying open. Kat balled up her fist and struck out, catching him near the chin.

Running for the holster, Katerina shoved the kitchen chair at him. Ryan swiped it aside with one hand. He caught Katerina from behind; she toppled to the floor. She scrambled toward the other chair, the gun dangling in the holster. Ryan grasped her ankle. Twisting, she shoved her other foot at him, kicking to escape. Lurching on top of her, Ryan gave an open-handed slap to her face, once then twice. She tasted blood. With both hands, he flipped her over onto her belly.

"You don't learn, do you," he said, digging his knee into her back, "you just don't learn. Now, you will."

As her arms flailed, he grabbed a hank of her hair and slammed her forehead against the floor. Katerina's head swam in blurred confusion as the room went off-kilter.

Ryan ripped off his tie, looping it over her head and around her mouth. She tried to catch his hand in her teeth. He smacked the back of her head and gagged her mouth, yanking the ends and pulling them tight. "Trying to bite me, hunh? Does he like that?"

Katerina gasped for air, coughing. As she reached to pull at the tie, Ryan grabbed her hair and shoved her forehead against the floor again.

"You want to be a whore, you'll get treated like one," Ryan said as he unhooked his belt. "Now you'll tell me who it is."

He doubled the belt in one hand and grabbed the ends of the tie in his other hand, yanking on them like reins.

Kat sobbed and her garbled words dissolved into blunted screams as the belt came down on her.

"You make me do this," he said as the blows rained down. "Why do you make me do this?"

Katerina threw out her arms; one hand found the leg of the other chair. She reached for the holster. Ryan shifted, knocking the chair away. It fell over, the holster and gun tumbling to the floor. As Kat laid her fingertips on the gun, Ryan let go of the tie and swatted the gun from her hand. It slid away, out of reach.

Kat twisted, bringing her knee up into his groin.

"Bitch," he grunted as he curled in pain.

Clawing out of from under, she wrenched the tie from her mouth and screamed.

"Fucking bitch," he said, rising and lunging for her.

Kat dove for the gun.

They tumbled to the floor.

"Shut up," he said, clamping a hand over her mouth; she sank her teeth into his fingers.

Ryan jerked back. Katerina heaved herself forward, grasping the gun. Scrambling to her feet, she spun around, pointing the weapon at him.

Everything stopped.

Ryan sat on the floor, breathing heavy, blood dripping from his fingers, considering her.

"You gonna shoot me, Kate," he said. "That's what you're gonna do? I got three bridesmaids that say you've been fucking around on me."

"I don't give a shit what they told you, it's not true."

"Who you been talking to?"

"My mother."

"You're such a liar, you really are. Why don't you put the gun down. You're not going anywhere."

Katerina scanned and found her purse on the floor, open, her belongings scattered. She grabbed the regular phone.

"Go ahead, call Emma, ruin another night for her," Ryan said as Kat pressed a button. "Sleep on her couch, inconvenience every-one before you come right back here."

"Mr. Kellan, help me, please."

Ryan's eyes flew open as he scrambled to his feet. "Kate, hang up that phone–"

"I have your gun! Come near me and you'll see what happens! Everyone will know what you did! They'll know everything!"

The sound of Michael Kellan's voice bellowing through the phone stopped Ryan cold.

Kat listened and then said, "Your father is gonna call you on your cell. You need to answer the phone."

Ryan chuckled without smiling. "Very nice, Kate. Very nice." Ryan's cell phone buzzed. He swept his jacket off the floor and pulled the phone out. "Listen–" and he stopped. His father's voice came through the phone, loud, with authority.

"Go into the bedroom and lock the door," Ryan repeated, his voice dull and monotone. "He said you should do it now."

Katerina backed into the bedroom and slammed the door, twisting the lock.

Flopping down on the edge of the bed, her back and legs on fire, her head exploding in pain, the gun shaking in her hand, she cried.

Every minute passed like its own eternity until she heard the opening of the front door and the noise of other voices. Frank's voice. Strange voices. *Cops.* Then the low, deep voice of Michael Kellan, chuckling, exchanging greetings. *His people. His cops.* Cops who would keep Ryan Kellan's domestic violence squabbles hidden, as a favor to the father. If the son came under scrutiny, who knows what could come out? *Detective Kellan, why were you delivering envelopes stuffed with cash? Who gave you those envelopes?*

"C'mon, sweetheart, open the door," she heard Michael Kellan say.

Katerina summoned her last ounce of courage to cross the finish line. "I want Emma," she said, her voice hoarse. "I want Emma to come. I won't come out unless she's here."

She heard whispered voices from the other side of the door and then Michael Kellan said, "Okay, sweetheart, Frank's gonna call now."

Another phone call. More waiting. More talking on the other side of the door. She heard one of them tell a neighbor to go back inside. Everything is fine. *Command confidence.*

She heard the shuffling of feet, furniture scraping the floor. She heard Michael Kellan's voice, giving orders, explaining how it was going to be. "You're gonna take her in for now, okay, sweetheart? she'll stay with you."

She heard Emma's voice. "Okay." No one said 'no' to Michael Kellan.

Kat heard footsteps approaching the door and the soft southern twang of Emma's voice. "Hon, it's me. Open the door."

Katerina stifled a cry as she rose from the bed, slow and painful. She had packed, leaving the cell phones on the night table. She put her hand on the knob and twisted it.

She kept her head down as Emma ushered her out, her arm around Kat's shoulder. Michael Kellan tried to move in for a hug, but Kat clung to Emma. His heavy hand patted her shoulder as he said, "Okay, sweetheart, don't worry about it. You'll stay with Emma now."

"Yeah, of course," Emma said. "As long as she wants."

As Kat left the apartment, she heard Michael Kellan tell his son, "Let it ride. Just let it ride."

It's over.

I survived it.

I survived the Shaman's Death.

I'm out.

You're getting out too, Alex.

They're coming.

Please hold on.

They're coming.

KATERINA MILLS WILL RETURN

I^N THE FIXER: THE GOOD CRIMINAL
PART TWO

SNEAK PEEK

Dressed in a short, blond bob wig and black Chanel, Katerina listened to the metronome ticking from the walnut clock as she took in the room at nine o'clock, twelve o'clock, and three o'clock. The way Winter taught me, she thought. She surveyed the Italian furniture, the Persian rugs, the Chippendale claw foot side tables. A room to receive; a room to show off.

A woman entered. She had voluminous hair, heavy makeup, couture that made her look like she was trying too hard, and a bored, annoyed expression on her face.

Katerina didn't rise at the woman's appearance.

"Can I help you," the woman said.

"No," Kat said. "My appointment is with Frederick Satler."

Most people would be thrown by the rebuke. Rebecca Satler suffered from no such problem.

"I'm Mrs. Satler, his wife."

"Congratulations, but I only speak with the client."

Rebecca huffed in exaggerated insult and injury. "This nonsense with this agency. My husband and I share everything."

"I'm thrilled to hear it. I only speak with the client."

"The last consultant didn't have a problem."

"And look how things turned out for her."

"You girls have nothing to be arrogant about. Three of you and nothing – not a thing. We pay for services and all you give is excuses."

A man entered the room, late fifties, tall, thick, wearing a tailored gray suit, the clean skin and neat haircut a testament to the frequent, personal grooming for the wealthy and privileged.

Another one with the chin up, Kat thought.

He glanced from Katerina to Rebecca and back again. "What is this? I'm not expecting anyone from the agency."

"Who are you?" Rebecca Satler demanded.

"My name is not important. What's important is I'm the person who can accomplish what you need done."

"I'm calling building security. They shouldn't have let you in."

"I was notified in May you had a problem."

Frederick stopped, the phone in his hand lifted halfway to his ear. "That was weeks ago."

"I was stuck in traffic," Kat said. "We should talk alone, Mr. Satler. Perhaps we could take a walk in the park."

Satler floundered, his eyes flitting toward his wife. "I – I don't have the key handy. I don't know where my mother keeps it. The other girls couldn't deal with our – issue."

"I'm not like other girls," Kat said.

"I should call the agency," Frederick said, but the words had no bite.

"Why don't you explain to me how I can help you," Katerina said, soft and low, soothing. "Alone."

Upon closer inspection, Frederick Satler had a roundish face, but his nose and mouth had a sharpish quality, and the eyes shifted, not quite looking at you. Kat pegged this milquetoast as a mark; Rebecca Satler was the client. But he had the right anatomical parts so that made him the winner.

He gave his wife a pleading look. With a pout, Rebecca Satler stormed out of the room. When the door shut, Frederick turned back to Katerina.

"Have you heard of Millicent Satler?"

Katerina shook her head. "Should I have?" she lied.

Frederick Satler shook his head in disbelief. "My mother is one of the greatest philanthropists this city has ever had. Her name is synonymous with New York society, Slim Keith, Babe Paley, C.Z. Guest, Nan Kempner. . ."

Katerina shook her head at the list, even though April's research had been full and complete. "And Millicent Satler."

"Magnificent Millie," Frederick said. "That's what they called her. My mother is in need of looking after."

"Is she ill?"

"She had a fall," Frederick said. "We are concerned that she has failed to thrive since the incident. She just had another incident. She became erratic and wandered out of the apartment. She wouldn't see reason to come back inside. She became belligerent. *Unstable.* This is background you need to have."

"I understand. But, I'm not a licensed nurse. And I don't think you're looking for a nurse, are you."

We – I think her social secretary is taking advantage of her."

Kat nodded. "How long has the secretary been with her?"

"Bethany has been there for over twenty-five years. She's taken care of everything. She knows every inch of my mother's life. But we think Bethany is taking funds, gifts from mother."

And you're the one who wants the gifts. And your wife wants it all.

"Why don't you move her to a facility," Katerina said, as a statement rather than a question. It was a bullshit play, but her instinct told her she needed to see how he would react. *The job is never the job.* Frederick Satler excelled in beating around the bush and she needed him to say it. Kat wondered if she smacked his back, it might be forced to come out.

"No, no," he said. "We – we couldn't possibly. We feel it's important to keep her in her own apartment."

Maybe you couldn't, but I'll bet your wife could – in a heartbeat.

"What we need is someone to look after her. Someone we can trust."

Katerina made a calculated decision to push. "Mr. Satler, after I fire the secretary, you would like me to be the replacement, correct? To what purpose? What is it you would like to see happen here?" *C'mon Frederick. Say it. You know you want to.*

As soon as Frederick glanced toward the double glass doors, Rebecca breezed back inside and took a confrontational stance that meant she wouldn't be leaving. She had been on a call and the cell phone was still in her hand. Husband and wife shared a private glance between them.

Frederick turned to Katerina. "We need to make an adjustment to certain legal documents, to ensure I can best protect the family fortune. It can be difficult to get mother's agreement–"

"You mean signature," Katerina said. "That can be arranged. Mr. Satler. I understand that you've been dissatisfied with the agency. If, however, you contact the agency and cancel the assignment, you can hire me direct for the bargain price of two hundred thousand dollars, and your wife can talk to me all she wants while I make the necessary arrangements."

"You need to be there twenty-four seven, to make sure this gets done," Rebecca Satler said.

Katerina continued staring at Frederick Satler as if they were the only two people in the room.

"We agree," he said.

"I'll wait while you call the agency," Kat said, "and I'll dial the number for you."

Frederick, his Adam's apple bobbing up and down, took out his phone, holding it as if he didn't know quite what to do with it. Kat took the phone and punched in the number and then handed it back to him.

Frederick held the phone like it carried a disease, even starting a little when the connection clicked. "This is Frederick Satler. I'm calling to let you know we are no longer in need of your services. I expect the funds, minus the penalty, to be wired back immediately. No, this is our final decision. We—"

Kat's eyebrows arched.

"We no longer need your services," he repeated.

He clicked off the phone while Kat could still hear Jasmine's voice speaking.

"Now, we have a deal. Two hundred thousand dollars. Half now—"

"Absolutely not," Rebecca said. "We've already paid money for those no-good girls who did nothing. It's pay or play. Do the job, get paid."

Katerina calculated. She had come this far. "The money is to be held in an escrow account."

After getting the approval from his wife, Frederick said, "I agree."

"Fine. Now, feel free to tell me everything about Millicent Satler you feel I need to know."

"She got rid of the first one within a week," Rebecca said. "The second one woke up with a gun to her head and packed up and fled. What makes you think you can do better?"

"I told you," Kat said. "I'm not them. Now, what's on Magnificent Millie's schedule for tomorrow?"

Jill Amy Rosenblatt is the author of *Project Jennifer* and *For Better or Worse*, published by Kensington Press. The Fixer (Katerina Mills) crime suspense series is Jill's first adventure in self-publishing. She has a master's degree in creative writing and literature from Burlington College.

She lives on Long Island and is currently at work completing the fourth book in The Fixer series, *The Good Criminal, Part Two*.

You can visit her at her website, http://www.jillamyrosenblattbooks.com